All That Is Common To Man

Hiram Foster

Copyright © 2022 by Hiram Foster

All rights reserved.

No part of this book may be reproduced in any form or by any electronic or mechanical means, including information storage and retrieval systems, without written permission from the author, except for the use of brief quotations in a book review.

For my Family...

"No temptation has seized you except what is common to man."

— 1 Corinthians 10:13a

Chapter One

Hancock would wish he'd never gotten out of bed. His truck jostled along the dirt road, vibrating his body and making his bones ache. Visibility was piss poor, a thick soup of fog and mist, which caused his eyes to narrow into thin slits as he strained to see through the cracked windshield. He rubbed his fist across the hazy glass, and for a fleeting moment, a clear streak appeared. Soon, it fogged over again. The truck's defroster was at full blast, but it was of no assistance; somehow the air it pushed was colder than the temperature outside.

Sleet had come in waves and taps that morning, lulling him back to sleep in his cocoon of wool blankets. Even his bladder, for all its urging and protesting, couldn't convince him to emerge, but when push came to shove, he caved. The happy delay in bed had caused him a rush later, and he hadn't bothered to warm the truck before leaving. Not that it mattered much. On a normal day, he could make the short drive to the barn twice before his truck had worked its way up to temp. Exchanging a chilly drive for the extra few minutes in his warm bed was a worthwhile trade.

Muscle memory told him to veer left of center, and

aside from the squeaky suspension, the truck moved past a dip in the road without incident. He'd driven this dirt road so many times he could have done it blind, making the windshield haze almost irrelevant. But he was a cautious fellow, so he took it slower than normal. The wipers flicked and flung drizzle off either side. His breath came out like a cloud and clung to the glass like murky fog.

Miserable weather for outdoor work, he thought as he rubbed the windshield clear again. Hancock found himself especially grateful for the coat he wore. It had been a Christmas gift to himself last year, and an early gift at that. He had found it tucked toward the back of a clearance rack during a Black Friday sale, but it met all his criteria for a work coat: warm, durable, and on sale. He hadn't used it much this year, as it was still early in the season, but last year it had seen its fair share of work; the coat had lived up to his every expectation. He passed the dead pine on his left and instinct told him to avoid the pothole coming on his right. He cleared it and let the truck come back to center.

Life didn't seem to become any easier. Despite the lies he told himself about still being young (and only a little slower than he used to be), old age was winning the war, wearing him down, season by season, year by year. As he recalled, in his younger days, it was nothing for him to work sunrise to sunset, and still find energy to hit the local tavern. Now, he was giving serious thought to a sick day. A subtle grin spread across his grey stubbled face as he recalled he had some grunt labor coming today. In the rush to get out the door, he'd forgotten all about it. What time were they due? Not for a few hours, at least. Maybe he'd save a few stalls for the hired hands. Maybe he'd save all of them. Let the young pups handle the heavy lifting and muck work.

In times past, Hancock had an experienced team at his disposal. But as always, things changed, and the help dwindled, which somehow meant he got more and more chores added to his plate. As a result, the stable management had grown more difficult, and that's not including the other random odd jobs and projects that seemed to fall in his lap. So, he welcomed any day he had assistance with the stall cleaning. He'd put in more than his fair share of time, and he'd earned his keep with each shovel full. It didn't take long for him to convince himself it would be a crime to deny an eager up and comer the same opportunity for advancement.

His fist squeaked on the windshield again, and he dodged a well-worn rut on his left. Blue smoke puffed from the exhaust as the truck bounced on the dirt road and neared its destination. Hancock saw the trees clear into pasture on his left, and he allowed the truck to coast. The entrance tended to creep up, and in this weather, he might slide right past, or worse, straight into the gate. As expected, he timed it just right.

The truck rolled to a stop and Hancock climbed out to untie the framed metal gate blocking the entrance to the barn. The hinges squealed as he swung it to one side. A thick chain clanged like a bell as he secured it in place. He climbed back into his truck and noted that the defroster had worked its way to warm, and the glass was clearing.

Figures it would work now. I'mma sell this to the scrap yard one of these days.

Rolling his eyes, he put the truck into drive, and it lurched forward with a growl toward the barn. Reaching his destination, he shifted to park and pulled the keys out. Over the quiet ticks of the cooling engine, Hancock could hear agitated whinnying inside the stables. Without warning, a crack shot through the air, and he jumped. He saw the outside stable wall flex from impact. It was as if a contained explosion had detonated, but he knew a horse's kick when he saw one. He'd witnessed that power more than once over the years, and it scared him every time. Most people didn't understand, but there was enough force in an equine kick to kill a man. Even two, if the beast had a mind to do so.

He wondered what would have caused the horses distress so early in the day, but it wasn't shocking. In all his years working the stables at Thurman Manor, he'd become accustomed to the frequent agitation of the horses. The first few years on the job were baffling. Multiple veterinarian consultations revealed nothing. There was even a stint when they attempted experimental drugs, but of course, nothing worked. The opinions around town were abundant, most involving mysterious rumors and speculation of a supernatural type, all of which sounded absurd to his rational mind. With time, he grew to assume it was just the way of the world, some sort of cosmic balancing act at play, at the moment misunderstood but capable of being explained. In the meantime, he figured there was nothing much to do about it. Just the way things were. As further proof, he reminded himself that dogs always seemed to look like their owners, (or maybe the other way around, depending on your perspective). It stood to reason the horses shared the same agitated state that the Thurmans seemed to emanate (not that Hancock ever said that out loud). No, saying something like that would more than likely cost him his job, a foolish thing to do this close to retirement. And Hancock was anything but a fool. Still, it was curious, and this, as well as other odd occurrences on and around the grounds of the Thurman Manor, would cause nagging questions in the back of his mind until he drew his last breaths.

Sleet stung his face as he stepped out of the truck and pulled his coat tighter around his shoulders. The waterlogged barn door sagged; another reminder of the repairs that needed to be made. Hancock gripped the cold metal handles, and with protesting creaks and groans (from both him and the door), forced it open. His blood ran cold.

The horses stomped and kicked and bared their teeth, but his attention was fixated on what he saw in the middle of the barn. She hung suspended in mid-air from a massive wooden beam, like a grotesque abandoned marionette. A thick rope, rough to the touch, was fastened around her neck, and a short three-legged stool lay nearby on its side in a pile of stale hay. Her face had turned a deep shade of blue, although appeared black to him in the early morning light. She stared at him, without a single sign of movement, and he knew deep in his bones she was dead.

Chapter Two

Nathan Stevens' house sat at the end of a quiet dead-end street, sealed off from any annoying traffic looking for shortcuts. On the rare occasion a stray car happened down the road, the driver would have found themselves in front of a quaint yellow house, with white shutters and an inviting front porch. Tall, well-aged trees decorated the entire neighborhood, but there were extra at this end of the street. During summer, when the trees reached their peak capacity of green, they provided increased privacy to those who hid underneath. The covering provided a sense of security, a shield from the outside world, which had attracted him to the house in the first place.

This time of the year, however, only a few of the more stubborn leaves remained, clinging fast to their high position. Their fallen peers covered the ground in a blanket of red, yellow, and orange. When the wind darted through, it would blow the leaves in a playful swirl, and then die down and lower them to the ground with care. The days were shorter now, and while temperatures weren't at the low point for the year, they were a far cry from the warm summer months recently passed. In fact, this winter would become the coldest of Nathan's life.

He and Rachel had married in July, one year prior, and what followed was nothing short of newly wedded bliss. They spent the majority of their first summer on the front porch, a simple thing, neither large nor fancy, but warm and inviting in the way people like to imagine a front porch should be. White spindle columns lined the front, and the floorboards had a thick coat of paint to match. Two rocking chairs occupied a corner, and a small table off to one side. Nathan remembered back to that initial summer, when Rachel had first discovered their local farmers market.

"What are these?" he'd asked, pointing to a pile of fresh strawberries beside her. She had quartered them, and was rinsing the last of the bunch.

"A little surprise," she said. "I thought we could have the good ones this time, instead of the tasteless ones from the grocery, you know? Just for fun."

Nathan kissed her cheek. "I love that idea. How can I help?" He rolled his sleeves up, ready to pitch in.

Rachel blew a stray hair out of her eyes. "I'm about done here, but you could get some ice cream from the freezer. I thought we could put these on top and then enjoy the night."

And that's how it was for them. They found happiness in each other, and in sharing simple things. A cup of tea and a sunrise, the changing leaves when fall came. Wrapping up in blankets with hot chocolate and navigating corn mazes in the crisp fall air. Now, Nathan sat alone at his kitchen table, looking at his vacant porch and the echo of happy memories.

He looked down into his untouched coffee. Light wisps of steam rolled over the edge of his mug. The dark reflection was a stranger to him; his once vibrant blue eyes were bloodshot and surrounded by dark circles, reminding him of black holes. His stubble had grown out into something unruly. Before, one might have described him as "handsome in a rugged sort of way", but no one would use that phrase now.

I don't recognize this person.

Nathan pushed the palms of his hands hard against his eyes until the blackness sparkled. The lights danced and grew until it transformed into TV static. When he pulled his hands away, and the stars faded, the stranger in the black liquid remained. He could only think *It actually happened. I became the type of man Rachel was warned to steer clear of. Guess it turns out her mom was right. I wasn't good enough for her... Not good enough to stick around for, anyway.*

Their dating stage had been short-lived, and despite the disapproval of Rachel's parents, they opted for a small courthouse wedding that July, observed by only a few close friends. Rachel's parents refused to attend. While Nathan never received specifics of what was said, the sideways glances and cold shoulders confirmed his suspicions regarding their feelings toward him.

"Are you sure this is what you want? I always thought girls dreamed about their wedding day?" Nathan asked.

"I'm not like most girls," Rachel said, "And I'm getting exactly what I want."

Nathan couldn't mask his skepticism. "Listen, I want to make sure you aren't giving up something you feel strong about for my sake. What if we waited? With time, it's possible your parents will warm up to me. Then we can have a real wedding, and your whole family could come and celebrate with us."

She scoffed, "My parents are many things, but warm isn't one of them. They will never change their minds."

"How can you be sure? Once they get to know me better..."

She held up a hand to stop him. "No, there is no getting to know you better." She paused, gathering up her thoughts before she spoke again. "Nathan, I need you to do me one thing, to make one promise to me before we say our vows."

Nathan looked at her, concerned and confused, but nodded in agreement. "Yeah, I'd do anything for you. You know that. I love you."

She smiled at him, but there was a sadness deep in her eyes Nathan couldn't quite understand.

"I love you too," she said. "If you love me, then promise me this - please let this be our fresh start. Just you and me. Not my family, not my past. There's nothing for me back there. My future is with you. Can you do that? Can you let the past stay where it is and start something brand new with me?"

Nathan leaned forward, nuzzling his head into her shoulder. "I want nothing more than to start a new life with you. The only thing I want is for you to be happy. I didn't want you to feel like you settled or something by getting married in a courthouse."

She grabbed his hand and led him up the worn marble steps, taking two at a time, almost as if to demonstrate she had no reservations about eloping.

He remained skeptical, ready to change plans and have a big wedding with all the bells and whistles, but that never came. She had seemed content to proceed exactly as things were. After the judge declared them husband and wife, Nathan cupped his hands around his wife's face and kissed her, committing that moment to memory. He'd never been happier in his life.

. . .

Now, he found himself questioning how happy Rachel had been in reality. All this time he'd been blind, missing symptoms, overlooking things. If he'd been paying more attention, he might have been able to save her...

His hands found their way to his forehead. His head was pounding, almost nauseating in its intensity. Maybe it was from a lack of sleep, or maybe it was the stress. Maybe it was from the fact that he wasn't eating well. Maybe he needed that cup of coffee, or maybe he'd had too many cups of the stuff over the years. Nathan decided the answer was coffee, for both reasons. He brought the hot drink to his lips, and taking the first sip too fast, burnt his mouth. He cursed under his breath. A slow second attempt yielded better results.

Nathan set the cup down and peered across the dining room table toward Rachel's place. Her half-eaten plate sat there, untouched, like a shrine to their last meal together. It was a simple thing, crafted with white ceramic, square in its essence, but rounded at each corner. Rachel's food had crusted and had taken on a brownish hue, reminding Nathan of dried blood. Grief, always consistent with its odd timing, caused a fresh wave of pain to wash over him.

They had both been in such a rush to get to their separate destinations that they left their dirty plates for another time. There were expectations that needed to be met. People to please and careers to advance. That night, it had seemed so important to not be late, and now, looking back, he barely remembered where they were going. Time and destination, now so terribly meaningless. In that moment, Nathan decided he would never clean this plate; to do so would somehow wash away her memory.

. . .

The meal had been a celebration of sorts. While neither voiced any complaints, money had been tight for the couple. Nathan worked as often as it was available to him, but the checking account often ran thin. So, when a big job offer came through, they decided to treat themselves to a nice meal, at least by their standards. They'd set the table with candles, and over low light and Sinatra in the background, enjoyed their food and a cheap bottle of red wine. Now Nathan was wondering if things would have turned out differently if he'd refused the job.

"You have to accept the offer. It's an incredible opportunity! And it'll make Christmas a little easier too," she said.

"I hate being away from you, though. There will be other opportunities. Ones that don't take me so far," Nathan replied.

Rachel shrugged and looped a strand of brown hair behind her ear. "That's not necessarily true. You know how the photography business is. You have to take advantage of these things when you can, strike when the iron's hot and all that."

Nathan took her hand in his and pulled her closer to him. "Then come with me. We can go together."

Rachel scrunched her nose up. "You'll be working and focused on the shoot. Which means we aren't really together, even if we are in the same room. You remember the last time we tried that?" Nathan started to apologize, but she stopped him. "You were focused on work, and your head was right where it should have been. I'm only saying there's nothing for me to do. I sat bored while you figured out clear balance for way too long."

"White balance."

Rachel looked puzzled.

"It's called white balance. I have to make sure it's right

or the shots don't come out right. I can't fix everything in post."

Rachel smirked at him. "Fine. But there's also the issue of the models. Do you remember that self-obsessed girl at the last shoot I came to? When she wasn't looking at herself in the mirror, she was glaring at me. I still don't understand what I did to her."

Nathan rested his head on top of hers. "Generally speaking, models are used to being the most attractive person in the room, but that wasn't the case that day. She was intimidated by you. She was probably worried about job security."

Rachel bit her lip and smiled at the compliment.

Nathan continued. "It didn't help that I think she overheard me tell her agent I could fix her complexion in post. The makeup artist was new. I think he had messed up the coloring. I can only imagine what sort of a complex she gave herself after that."

They laughed together, and Rachel took a step back to look Nathan in the eye again. "My point is, you'll be focused on work. That's a good thing. It's just not for me."

Nathan looked at her with uncertainty. "I don't know. These types of shoots aren't even my thing. I realize they pay the bills, but it's not fulfilling. It's not *real* art." Nathan sighed in frustration. "I want my photos to be exciting. Something meaningful. I always wanted to capture the wonder of nature; that's where my heart's at." Nathan's eyes went to the ceiling as he searched for the words. "I need a shot that National Geographic would buy. Leaving you to take pictures of wannabe models selling cheap acne cream is soul crushing. If I have to be away from you, it should count."

She came in close to him. "It'll count. Someday you'll get your shot. I know it. And don't worry about me. I'll be fine - I'll go see my parents. I've been meaning to see Dad, anyway. It's been a while."

This unexpected statement set Nathan back. He'd been making subtle suggestions that it might be time to reconcile with her parents, but until this moment, Rachel had resisted. Contact with her parents had been minimal; in fact, almost nothing at all. Nathan, wanting to keep his promise from their wedding day, had left his concerns unsaid. Mostly. But as time went on, his worry grew and he feared Rachel would end up with deep regrets. So, if she wanted to make an attempt to reconnect with her parents before it was too late, he was all for it.

He examined her, trying to discover where this was coming from. "Are you sure? Maybe I should be there too, for support."

Rachel shook her head. "No, I think I need to do this alone. Just this time. I don't want to, but I think I should."

"You're positive? I know this isn't easy for you."

She paused, but only briefly. "Yes, I'm sure. I know you'd come if I asked. You always want to be my knight in shining armor. But I'm not really a princess that needs saving."

"Can I still be a knight?"

She smiled and ran her fingers up his arms, feigning impression with his muscles before leaning in and squeezing him around his middle. He pulled her slender form close to his and inhaled, savoring the sweet scent in her thick brown hair. It reminded him of melons.

"Honestly," she said as she rested her head on his shoulder. "Take the job. I'll be fine for a few days. When the photo shoot is done, you can come up to the house with me. I'll have some time to sort things with my parents, and then you and I can be up there together."

Nathan booked the flight, and Rachel drove to her childhood home.

The police called him while he was still on site at the shoot. He didn't remember the conversation in full, only bits and pieces. After the initial punch to his gut, Nathan simply couldn't process the information. He recalled an officer saying, "Mr. Stevens, I'm sorry to have to tell you this, but..." The remainder of the call was like a cell signal breaking up. *Rachel, ------ it, -----, can you --- now?* He'd thrown up, but he didn't remember that either. The entire flight home was a mystery to him; getting back was purely mechanical, like driving yourself home and not remembering how you got there.

Chapter Three

As Nathan continued his dark descent, a car rolled down the single lane drive toward his house, crunching dried leaves under its tires. The vehicle was driven by a man dressed in pressed, slate grey pants and a crisp button down. He wore the sleeves rolled precise and tight on his ebony forearms and filled the shirt to capacity with his broad shoulders. There was an air around him that communicated this was not a man to be trifled with. As if to highlight this point, the right side of his face bore violent, jagged scarring, which inevitably drew the silent curiosity of everyone he encountered.

He parked his car at Nathan's house (which, to his great dismay, was no longer a home), and took long strides to the front door. He knocked out "shave-and-a-haircut, pop-pop" and listened to the boomy echoes within. After a short silence, he heard a chair screech as it moved across a floor, and the sound of shuffling feet headed his way.

"Hey, Lewis," Nathan grunted out. His voice had a gravelly quality that made him sound older than he was.

"Good morning," Lewis replied. His voice, a stark contrast to Nathan's, was deep and commanding, as if he were instructing the morning to be good, and fully expected it to comply. Nathan stepped to one side to allow Lewis to enter. Lewis took a step inside, careful to duck his head as he crossed the threshold. At that moment, the pair couldn't have appeared more different. Lewis, dressed in clothes tailor fit for his frame, was a polar opposite to Nathan's baggy hoodie, fit only for yard work, and coffee-stained jeans.

"Get your boots. We're going to get some breakfast," Lewis said.

"I've already got coffee."

"Coffee ain't breakfast."

"It could be. And I'm not hungry, anyway."

After Nathan told him about Rachel's death, Lewis had been checking in daily, attempting to draw Nathan out of the shadows. To this point, his attempts had failed, and he was not a man accustomed to failure.

Lewis kept his voice even but didn't provide an alternative. "Well, I am hungry. I already know you don't have any food here, so if I wanna eat, we gotta go someplace. So, get your boots on. You can drink your coffee at a restaurant."

Nathan sighed in surrender. He grabbed his boots, laced them up, and they were out the door.

Lewis drove. They already had an unspoken agreement on where to eat. Just a few miles down the road was a small, family-owned diner that was frequented by locals. It wasn't a fancy place, but they cooked good food and served generous portions. The restaurant sat out by itself in a small plaza. A neon sign filled a window facing the street, spelling out the name *Chuck's* in curvy script. The only other businesses nearby were a Rite Aid and takeout Chinese place. The pair had eaten at Chuck's many times before, and it had become their chosen spot for long conversations.

Their waitress greeted them by name and allowed them to pick their seats. They walked to a back corner, away from the door, for some additional privacy. They sat in a booth with high backs and faded blue benches, the imitation leather cracked and creased from years of use. A light hung over the table, but not so low as to hit anyone's head. Soon, the regulars would fill the remaining tables for the morning breakfast rush. Lewis ordered scrambled eggs, hash browns, and a side of bacon. They ordered a pot of coffee to split between the two of them, which came strong and hot, Lewis's only real preference when it came to a cup of joe.

"When was the last time you ate?" Lewis asked.

Nathan shrugged. "I had some toast yesterday. An apple last night. I just haven't been very hungry."

"You need to eat. You gotta take care of yourself," Lewis said with concern.

"I do eat. But I'm not hungry right now."

Lewis took a bite of potatoes, swallowed, and aimed his fork at Nathan. "You're not eating, at least not enough from what I can see."

Nathan shrugged as if it were of no concern. "I'll eat when I get hungry."

"All I've seen you eat the last few days is coffee. You need real, healthy things. Actual food." Lewis drew his lower lip into his mouth, as he often did when he was thinking. "Listen, why don't you come over? I'll make dinner for you."

"You mean Rita will make dinner," Nathan said with a hint of a smile.

"Ok, fine. Rita will make dinner, but I promise I'll help." For all his qualities, Lewis's cooking experience was limited to the MREs he made while serving his country.

The reality was he couldn't cook to save his life - and being married to a woman like Rita made it unfair to even try. He had once made an attempt, which was rewarded with a proverbial pat on his head and a *"nice try, honey"* for his efforts. Rita was possibly the only person on the planet that would be afforded such a gesture.

"If you're helping, I'm definitely not coming," Nathan joked.

"Very funny," Lewis said as he mimicked being hurt. He grinned back toward Nathan as he put another bite of potatoes into his mouth.

"Just think it over. I won't force you, but a good home cooked meal would be good for you, not to mention the company. I'm worried about you. I can't imagine what you're going through. Hard enough losing someone, and the way this all happened... Just a hell of a thing." Lewis shook his head in disbelief. "Don't do it alone."

Nearby, their waitress was seating a small family. A boy, no more than five years old, stared wide eyed at Lewis, his innocent blue eyes tracing the scars that crisscrossed Lewis's face. Whether due to addiction or design, the kid's parents had their noses buried in their phones, oblivious to whatever mischief the kid would find himself in.

Lewis rubbed at his face and mouthed, "Shaving accident." The boy's mouth hung slack as he nodded like that made all the sense in the world, as if he'd received a grand word of cautionary wisdom from someone of experience. Lewis gave him a wink and a sideways grin and returned to his plate.

The scars never bothered him. Rather, they served as a reminder of how close he'd come to death, had it not been for the seemingly chance encounter with the man sitting across from him.

. . .

Lewis had been leading a team of soldiers overseas, spending the majority of his time doing intelligence work for various three letter organizations residing stateside. As expected, the work was often sensitive, and always dangerous, so when some top tier brass in DC assigned a photojournalist to his division, Lewis was predictably infuriated.

Their first conversation had been less than cordial.

"I don't have time for this, and I certainly don't have the patience, so I'm only going to say it once. Do you understand?"

Nathan had only smiled politely in return, and while devoid of sarcasm, it had only served to annoy.

Lewis continued to set the ground rules. "If it were up to me, you wouldn't be here. I've got men perfectly capable of snapping a few photos for the powers that be back home. But somewhere up my chain of command, somebody decided to bring you in. Said it was better for PR, something about recruitment. In my opinion, it was a stupid decision, but here you are just the same. So, let's set things straight. I'm in charge. You do what I say when I say it. Is that clear?"

"Very," Nathan said. "I don't want to be in the way."

"I'm not done. Today, we're going on a patrol. You'll be in the front car with me. I can't do anything about you being here, but I can make sure you aren't a nuisance to my men. You keep your mouth closed while we drive. You take your pictures, and you'll be on your way, understood?"

Nathan shrugged. "Ok, you're the boss."

"Get your gear. We leave in ten."

The Humvee flew down a dirt path. Lewis was shotgun and Nathan was in the backseat behind the driver, the main reason being so Lewis could keep an eye on him. Nathan had honored his given instructions; he took pictures as they'd prepared, and after, from his seat inside the truck. But he remained silent, as Lewis had commanded. Everything was going fine, up until it wasn't.

A concussive blast rocked the side of the Humvee, lifting it off its wheels and spraying Lewis's face with shrapnel. The world spun, and then came to a crashing stop, albeit upside down. Lewis's head was in pain. All he could hear was high pitched ringing, coming from all around him. His arms didn't seem to want to move. If Lewis would have had his hearing, he would have heard the crackle of fire, which had started to spread in the vehicle.

Lewis felt hands tugging at his seatbelt, followed by a sudden release. Hands gripped his arms and dragged him just shy of fifty feet before the truck ignited. Smoke and flame engulfed the vehicle in a near instant, along with the bodies inside. This would be something that would stick in Lewis's mind for the rest of his life; death wasn't like what it's made out to be at a funeral. At a funeral, the bodies were tuned down in a sense, as if reducing the volume of death. They were made to be more presentable; you could almost believe they were still alive. Maybe they really were just sleeping? But there was no mistaking death here. War wouldn't permit death to be sanitized.

After that, the war was over for Lewis, and seeing as how the military had been his only real family, he was ultimately left with no place to return home to. Moving to the hometown of the man who saved his life seemed as good a place as any.

"Shaving accident?" Nathan said from across the table. "Is that what you're going with now?"

"You're welcome to tell them the real story, if you like."

Nathan sipped his coffee. "I think I'll pass."

"Still don't like to talk about that, huh?"

"Do you?"

"That's not what I mean. I'm able to talk about it. You keep it all buried deep. I've seen guys blow up from the pressure that causes."

Nathan shook his head. "Nothing to discuss. Just did what needed done, that's all."

"You and all the other guys over there. But the ones that make it back bring demons with them. Most of em' anyway. It helps to talk it through."

Nathan paused for a moment, looking like a man that had drifted into a dark place, lost to himself and the world, alone and unsure how to come back.

"Where you at, man?" Lewis asked. Seeing Nathan like this only caused his concern to grow. Nathan had bottled up everything he'd seen that day. Lewis was watching him do the same with Rachel, and this time it would probably do him in.

Nathan gave him a grim smile. "It's different this time. After the bomb, when I got home, I was *glad*. Glad to be home, glad to be done with all that. I realize I was lucky - the other guys weren't. And I felt guilty for it. Not so much now, I guess. Only sometimes. But this is different. I'm not a survivor this time. I'm just... left behind."

Lewis held his tongue, fearing that if he opened his mouth, Nathan would clam up and retreat again to his dark corner. And if he did that, Lewis wasn't sure he'd ever come back out. He only allowed himself to lean forward, a subtle invitation that allowed his friend to continue.

Nathan laughed nervously. "Uh, sorry. It's kind of hard to focus, you know? It all feels so hard to explain. None of this feels real. In my head, I know it is, but I don't feel it. I wake up each day and expect her to be there. I'll go to say something to her, and suddenly realize she's not there. It's like I forget she's gone, or like my mind is playing tricks on me. I actually dialed her phone the other day. Honest to God, I called her phone. It just went to voicemail, but I..." Nathan's voice trailed off, and Lewis saw the tears forming at the corners of his eyes.

"I get that," Lewis said in a calm, measured tone. "Everyone deals with this stuff in their own way, and in their own time. Listen, I'm not trying to add to your stress. God knows I don't want to make anything worse than it already is. I just want to help you, if I can. You were there for me when anyone else would have bailed. But you didn't, even though you probably should have. I haven't forgotten that, and I won't bail on you. I got you."

"Yeah. I know."

"I've got a counselor. A good one, none of that psychobabble crap or anything like that. I could get you their number, put you in contact. If that's something you want."

Nathan frowned. "Can we talk about that some other time? I don't think I can do that right now."

"Yeah. Sure, we can talk about it another time. Just... when you're ready. You let me know, ok?"

Nathan swirled the remains of his coffee, watching the black grit twirl in circles at the bottom of his mug.

Nathan didn't look up as he said, "Her parents called me back. Finally. Did I tell you that?"

"No. When was this?"

"A couple days ago. Her Mom called. They want me to head to their house. She said they want to talk to me about Rachel's funeral, and it would be easier in person."

"What exactly does that mean?"

"Honestly, I have no idea. I'm sure they want to play a part, but I don't know to what extent. It's weird to say, but I barely know them. Rachel wanted things that way. So, we didn't visit, and there was hardly any contact at all. There was obviously some tension there, but she never went much into it."

"Are you ok with this? What about them coming here? Seems like a lot to ask of you."

"The same is true the other way around. And, after I thought about it, it's sort of a way for me to help finish what Rachel was trying to do. Rachel went back to mend things. This can be a way to honor that."

Lewis looked thoughtful. "Maybe they are trying to right some wrongs too. Is it possible all this is making them reconsider some of the choices made in the past?"

"Could be. I don't really know."

"Do you want me to come with you?"

"What? Up to Silas Ridge? No... I think it's best if I do this on my own."

"Are you sure? I can come at any point. I'm just a phone call away. Just a few hours and I can be there."

"I'm sure. You'll be at the funeral though, right?"

"Of course I will. You name the time and place and I'll be there."

"Would you swing by the house while I'm gone? Maybe take the trash out for me?"

"Anything you need."

They sat again in silence, like old friends do. The waitress came by to check on them and she refilled Nathan's coffee. Lewis was still working on his plate. They turned their heads toward the front door as it chimed, welcoming the brunch crowd. Nathan picked his phone out of his pocket.

"Do me a favor? Will you read this for me? I've been going blind reading over it. I'm still not sure if it sounds right."

Nathan tapped the screen, navigated to his document, and flipped it around to Lewis. He read the obituary with care and reverence, allowing the weight of it to press upon him. All the standard details you'd expect to be there were included: her name, birthdate, a vague description of her passing. But Lewis focused on one line in particular.

She is survived by her husband, Nathan Stevens.

Until this point, that phrase had meant something like *the one left behind*. But looking across the table at his friend, seeing the physical toll it had taken, it became something more. It described someone who had gone through a traumatic experience and had come out the worse for wear. They may have survived, but not without their fair share of scarring and damage.

He finished and let his summary be simple and concise. "It's beautiful." He handed the phone back to Nathan.

"Would you change anything? I realize it needs work. And once I have the funeral details figured out, I'll add those in too."

"No, it's great. You should keep it exactly like it is."

"Thanks. I've been thinking about it constantly. All this funeral stuff. It's stressing me out." Nathan let out a tense breath of air. "I really don't see how I'm going to afford it."

Lewis leaned in and made sure to maintain eye contact with Nathan. "Hey, don't worry about that right now. I can loan you some cash."

"I appreciate it. But no, I'll find a way. It'll slow down, and then I can get my head around everything."

Lewis spoke in a low tone, one containing every quality that made you want to believe his words. "Listen to me. You're going to be alright. You're going to make it through this."

A puff of disbelief escaped Nathan's lips, masquerading like a laugh.

"Seriously. You're tougher than you know. I won't promise it's all rainbows and butterflies on the other side;

but there is another side. There is a life for you beyond this."

"I know you're right. At least in my head."

"I sense a *but*..." Lewis waited for the reply.

A moment passed. And then Nathan completed his thought. "But I'm not sure the other side has anything I want anymore."

Chapter Four

Nathan arrived home from the diner shortly after noon. Lewis dropped him off, and after reiterating he was a phone call away, left Nathan to his thoughts. Nathan stood on his porch and watched Lewis drive down his tree-lined street, swirling crunchy leaves up in the wake of his truck. They skirted across the road and gathered up in the curbs and gutters. Across the street, his neighbor raised a hand, fitted with a canvas work glove, in friendly greeting. He was older than Nathan and wore a wide-brimmed hat. A pile of leaves was scooped high on a blue tarp, soon to be hauled to the street for pickup. Nathan waved in return, but they exchanged no words.

What was his name again? I've been here a year; I still don't know his name.

The neighbor resumed tending to his chores. In a stark contrast, Nathan's lawn was barely visible under the decaying blanket. But his leaves weren't going anywhere; he'd figure that out later. Maybe. He walked inside, determined to wrap up some loose ends before heading up to Silas Ridge, where his in-laws were waiting.

His phone vibrated inside his jacket pocket. Nathan

pulled it out, and on the screen was a message, sent from a well-meaning, but long forgotten friend.

Just heard the news. So sorry for your loss. Let me know if you need anything!

Since Rachel's death, it seemed like everyone was coming out of the woodwork. Calls, texts, and social media messages had bombarded Nathan, each expressing a heartfelt condolence for his loss. While innocent in intent, Nathan couldn't help but feel it was all a bit superficial; a good deed done for the day, checked off and soon to be forgotten. Still, all things considered, he appreciated the sentiments, and preferred the acknowledgement of Rachel's passing rather than pretending it didn't happen.

At fourteen, his own father passed away. Life had been filled with those well-wishers then too; people who cried with him and gave awkwardly long embraces. They made casseroles by the dozens, more than he and his mom could eat. It wasn't long before it got to the point where they had to choose which meals to give away and which to throw out.

People said *take time to grieve. Let yourself go through the process*. It seemed like people understood. For a while, anyway. When their recommended steps didn't work as fast as prescribed, well... Nathan learned then shared grief only went so far. In reality, what people expected was for the kid to *get over it*. Move on. Being around the kid whose dad died was just a bummer for them.

Nathan knew the condolences received today would be under the same expectation. Although they never said it out loud, at some point they would look for him to re-join the dating scene, find some girl, and settle down all over again. At the core, it all boiled down to *get over it*. But for Nathan, *getting over it* was for people who had never suffered a loss before. He wouldn't say he'd gotten over his dad all these years later. Nor his mom when she'd passed five years later. At best, it got different. But without fail, there would be something each and every day to remind him. Unexpected things, like a smell, or seeing a deodorant brand his father favored while grocery shopping. A song on the radio would bring back memories of his mom. Pretty soon, Rachel's death would be the same. Other people would move on, content to let it be just another thing that happened. For some, maybe it already was. But he'd never get over Rachel. He promised himself he never would.

Time to focus. Gotta get through this. Just focus on what you can do.

He took a deep, cleansing breath and let out a long, steady stream of air. He walked to his desk and began to clear off a small working space. The surface was covered in photographs, highlights from the last year of their life together, each a candidate to consider for the photo remembrance he was crafting.

Nathan tapped the spacebar on his computer and the screen flickered to life. The new silence in his house seemed to amplify the soft buzzing from deep in the machine, as if insects were inside, vibrating and fighting to escape. Rachel's obituary was still up from his last round of edits. The cursor was blinking at the end of the document, like a taunt, reminding him that there wasn't anything left to write, and there never would be. Nathan snapped his computer closed, but this action felt more harsh than the hateful cursor.

Get over it.

After another deep breath, he reopened the screen. As

difficult as this was, a funeral was coming, and he could stop it about as well as he could the setting of the sun. And regardless of everything else, Nathan was determined to give Rachel his very best. He owed her at least that much. Maybe he'd failed her in life; he wouldn't fail in this.

Nathan tapped a few keys and a cascade of photos displayed before his eyes, all arranged in a neat grid. He'd been working on converting all his physical photos to digital for days. The sheer volume of pictures guaranteed a lengthy production time, and he didn't want things to get away from him. This, among other things, had led to a lack of sleep. The obsession with photos wasn't the sole cause of his insomnia; nothing felt right with Rachel gone. It was like trying to fall asleep with the crippling thought you've forgotten something critical, and you need to remember.

He zoomed in on the earliest photos and started clicking through them in chronological order. Nathan had captured every moment. It was the nature of being a photographer. He saw the world through a lens. Some moments were captured with specific, deliberate effort, shooting with professional camera and lighting, and (to Rachel's frustration) too much fuss over his white balance. He'd experimented with various lenses and distances, testing multiple angles to ensure the perfect composition. And at the same time, there were countless others that were taken with his phone; quick candid shots that captured her real smile the moment it happened. Honest, organic, and exactly the way he remembered. Despite the higher quality of his more detailed photos, the raw and genuine ones were his favorites. Those were the snapshots of real life, honest and unplanned. Those were the smiles that showed life had been happy; at least when the shutter snapped. Nathan wondered how happy Rachel had actually been.

The only sound in the room was the crisp click of his

mouse as he advanced the photos, shot by shot, until one caught Nathan's attention; one that had burned into his memory. The light was something special, but it was nothing compared to the girl. Nathan had known he would have to capture this moment, or at least try to.

"Like this?" she asked.

She smiled back at him, letting her dress flow around her. They had been walking down a skinny path worn by years of use, with white birch trees on one side and a field of tall grass on the other. She swayed back and forth, her red sundress swinging like a bell. The sun had reached its "golden hour", which in reality meant Nathan had only a few minutes to get the photo he wanted. The light was behind her. Her back-lit hair glowed like flame in the sun. She was spectacular.

"Yes, just like that. That's perfect."

He twisted a ring around the lens and the path behind Rachel dissolved as she came into focus. He'd clicked only once. The golden hour had evaporated.

He closed his eyes, imagining himself there again, allowing himself to get lost in that moment. In his fantasy, she was still there, in the next room, waiting for him. He could almost smell her perfume...

A sudden, loud crack broke the spell. Startled, Nathan shoved his chair back with a screech and rose from the desk.

"Is someone there?" There was no response. He padded his way toward the sound, navigating around corners at wide angles, half expecting to see a hooded figure on the other side crouched and ready to pounce. When he discovered the last corner was empty of threat, he found not relief, but confusion. Rachel's plate lay shattered across the floor, no longer a memory, but seven jagged shards.

Plates don't just break... Someone knocked this over... And they're still here.

Nathan spun around, searching for the mysterious figure his mind had conjured.

He didn't dare breathe. He put all his focus on listening for the slightest hint of movement from within the house, but aside from the blood ringing in his ears, it was silent. After double checking the locks on his doors and windows and finding everything in order, Nathan accepted no one was in his house. He crept toward the plate, fearful of it, as if it was a dangerous object, its sharp edges dipped in poison. But that was ridiculous; after all, it was just a plate he'd eaten off, many times before. But at this moment, it felt different; it felt *alive*. Kneeling, he reached for the broken pieces, his mind searching for logic that escaped him.

How did this happen?

He looked around the room, trying to assign blame, but found none. The plate had rested as he (and Rachel) left it. It was impossible that it had been too close to the edge. And as the windows were closed, it was equally impossible for a gust of wind to knock it to the floor.

Soon, his mind accepted the impossibility of it all, and instead began to remind him that he'd lost this last remaining relic. The last thread of evidence that he'd shared a meal with Rachel gone, shattered and broken on the floor. And like his deceased wife, this too was irreparable.

The stiff bristles of the broom swished against the floor as he gathered the remains of their last shared meal. He knelt down to grab the larger pieces, careful to not slice his hands on the sharp edges. Tears filled his eyes. Guilt and anger were welling up in him; regret was on its way. With each section of the plate, his anger grew until, in a fit of rage, he flung the remaining shards against the wall. They smacked the other side in unison and clattered to the floor in a heap, now silent. Small, dried flecks of meat stuck to the paint, and scattered gouges dented the wall like pockmarks.

Nathan focused his breathing, and his heart rate began to slow. After he calmed, he wet a paper towel with warm water and wiped down the wall. Nathan looked around his kitchen, the last dirty dish now cleaned up. Emptiness and stunning finality struck him. Rachel wasn't coming back.

"When was the last time you saw your wife?" the officer had asked.

"We had dinner together. Here, at our house," Nathan answered.

The officers had arrived on his doorstep just a day after he had gotten word about his wife. A man and a woman, dressed in their official navy-blue uniforms, badges shiny in the sun. Nathan had thought the sun shouldn't be shining today. The sun had no right to be so bright on such a dark day.

"Hello, Mr. Stevens," the man said, "I'm Officer John Schmidt." He moved an open hand toward the woman beside him. "This is my partner, officer Lisa Sudgkin. Can we come inside? We need to ask you a few questions."

Nathan had expected their arrival. He'd received a call that morning, confirming he would be home. Nodding to the officers, he turned to the side and gestured for them to enter. The officers stepped through the entry, removing their hats as they crossed the threshold. Officer Schmidt was of average height and above-average weight. His large belly flopped over his thick duty belt. He wore his hair cropped short, maybe because of regulation, but it was just as likely because of his thinning hair. Officer Sudgkin was younger, thinner, and maybe in her mid-thirties. She had dark hair and dark, kind eyes. Her fingers were slender, especially compared to the sausage-like fingers of her counterpart. Her wedding ring sparkled in the light, and Nathan wondered how long she had been married. *Does she have kids? She looks like she would have kids.* Her eyes reflected a type of patience that only comes from motherhood. Schmidt had no such ring, and no air of patience about him.

Sudgkin spoke first, breaking Nathan from his thoughts. "Mr. Stevens, first, let us state we are sorry for your loss. These things are never easy, and it's one of the worst parts of our job."

Nathan replied, "No, no. I understand. Thank you for coming."

She began, "We need to ask you a few questions. I assure you, it's all routine stuff. Please just answer to the best of your knowledge."

"I can do that."

Officer Schmidt pulled out a paper notepad and pen. The pen looked skinny and out of place between his bloated fingers. Nathan couldn't help but notice his fingernails were chewed down to nubs. In a monotone and procedural voice, he began his list of questions.

"When was the last time you saw your wife?"

Nathan answered, "We ate dinner together, here at the house." He pointed to the table as an explanation.

"And what day was that?"

"Sunday night."

"What happened after dinner?"

"I had a photography job out of town. I was kind of rushed. The shoot started early Monday morning, and I had to hurry after dinner to make a red eye flight."

"Where was the photo shoot?"

"Columbus. In Ohio."

He glanced narrowly at Nathan. "You have receipts for this flight?"

"Of course."

"And your wife? Why wasn't she going with you?"

"She was heading to her parents' house."

Sudgkin jumped in. "Was there any specific reason for her going to her parents?"

Nathan thought about why Rachel was there, and about how she'd been hesitant to go. He thought about the years of unspoken tension she carried around, and how long it had been since she'd spoken with her family. What he said was, "Basically just to visit. She hadn't seen her family in a while."

Schmidt eyed his partner from the corner of his eye. Nathan thought he detected some annoyance that his line of questioning had been interrupted.

Schmidt took a deep breath and resumed control. "Prior to your wife's death, had she shown any signs of depression, or made any mention about wanting to end her life?"

Nathan racked his brain. There had been no signs, at least that he had seen. They had shared a pleasant meal the night before she went to her parents. They laughed together, shared hopes for the future. Rachel had even been making hints toward children. Not the sort of things one would expect from a suicidal person.

"No, everything seemed fine. She seemed happy to me."

How happy was she? How could you possibly think she was happy after what happened?

Schmidt asked again, "At the scene, no note was recovered. Was anything left here at the house? Anything to indicate she'd intended to harm herself?"

The scene. It sounds like a sick, twisted play.

Nathan responded, "No, there was nothing."

"To the best of your knowledge, had there been anything to indicate she may try to take her own life?"

Nathan searched his mind.

I should have seen this coming. There must have been signs. I didn't see... Why didn't I see anything? I could have stopped it. Was it my fault? What did I do wrong?

He kept his reply simple. "I can't think of anything. She seemed happy to me." He looked down at his feet, feeling shame he hadn't seen it coming.

Sudgkin spoke again. Schmidt physically turned his head this time, his cheeks flushed red. She gave it no attention. "Was it just your wife going to her parents? Anyone else go with her? A friend? Family member?"

"She went by herself. She drove our other car, alone."

"Aside from her parents, are you aware of anyone else that would have been present at their house?"

"I don't know. I wasn't there. I guess they probably had some other people there. Her siblings. And they have workers there, like house staff."

With undertones of accusation, Schmidt said, "Why weren't you there? If my wife's family had a get-together, no way I could've gotten out of it."

Something hot started to rise in Nathan. He resented the question and the implication. His voice reflected some of the heat. "I said already, I was working. I was out of town, doing a photoshoot. Rachel went first, and I planned on heading there as soon as the shoot was done. Check my flight records, and you'll see."

Officer Schmidt made a note on his pad, and Nathan felt a twitch of paranoia. He got the feeling he was under more scrutiny than would be standard, and he wasn't liking the feeling. Officer Sudgkin noticed the visible discomfort on his face.

"We can wrap this up soon, Mr. Stevens. Just a few more questions and then we can go."

"Am I under some sort of suspicion? I wasn't even there. Like I said before, I was working. I can show you."

"Mr. Stevens, we are just following protocol," she replied. "Everything will be verified. There's a process. At this point in time, we are treating this as a suicide. It's standard procedure while the coroner's report is pending."

Nathan didn't feel any better with this news. He hated the thought of the coroner doing his work on his wife. Thoughts of a sterile room and cold metal beds filled his mind. Sharp objects designed for nasty work under bright lights. He saw dark, undetermined fluids running toward a rusty drain in a tiled floor. He saw something resembling his wife (but not his wife) cold and lifeless on a metal table.

Schmidt continued, "Now, tell me more about this photo shoot..."

In total, the cops questioned Nathan for about twenty minutes. They were looking for anything that might suggest foul play, asking variations of the same question at different points, trying to see if he would stray from his original story. But Nathan told them the truth, and his story didn't waiver. He had been out of town on a photo shoot. She had been with her parents. He knew the cops would verify his story with receipts, maybe even check with his client for an alibi. Once they did that, they would see, given the physical state of our world, it was impossible for him to have had anything to do with his wife's death.

He escorted them to the front door. Officer Sudgkin handed Nathan a business card and encouraged him to call if anything came up. Nathan turned it over in his hands, looked at the thick ink on the front, and thanked her.

. . .

Nathan's mind snapped back to the present. He moved back to his desk, knowing he needed to continue his funeral preparations. Photo by photo, one by one, he made his selections. By evening, he reached the last picture. He backed the file up to a thumb drive as his eyelids began to droop.

Nathan climbed the wooden staircase toward his bed, each step dragging more than the last. Since Rachel's death, he hadn't slept soundly, and exhaustion was catching up with him. He reached the top of the stairs, turned, and moved toward the bedroom. He stopped at the threshold and looked into the dark room. His feet felt frozen in place, and something inside him felt sick and empty. Without stepping foot inside, he closed the door. He turned around, walked back down the creaky staircase, and ended up on the couch, just like he had the night before, and the night before that. In fact, without ever having intended it, he'd slept on the couch every night since Rachel's death.

Nathan tossed and turned. He was on the very edge of sleep; his dreams were dark and tortured. He was back at the morgue, what had been his first stop after receiving that impossible call. In his waking hours, that experience seemed a blur, but in his dreams it felt as real as anything he'd ever experienced. He was moving toward a metal table in the middle of a bright, sterile room. There were no shadows, not even his own. Rachel was on the table, covered in a semi-translucent sheet, her body muted and blurry through the sheer plastic.

He was standing beside her, looking down. Her features were indistinct, but Nathan imagined she was still beautiful under the plastic. Her dark hair was still shiny, and her brown eyes were entrancing. Rachel's eyes had always drawn him in, and he had been more than happy to follow. He remembered her contagious smile and perfect teeth. And then the sheet was pulled back, revealing the truth.

Rachel was no longer beautiful. Her face was pale and lifeless. The skin around her once perfect neck was ripped and torn, rubbed raw from her own body weight. And most upsetting of all, she bore a hideous smile, surgically wide, stretched from ear to ear. Suddenly, her eyes popped open, black and oily as ink. She looked directly at Nathan, and that's when he woke up in a cold sweat.

Chapter Five

Morning finally came. Gentle sunlight rolled over the neighborhood rooftops, melting the overnight frost and erasing Nathan's nightmares. Night was the worst time for him. Only his thoughts were there to keep him company, and they often betrayed him. Exhaustion had become his normal state; each day was like he was recovering from an enduring sickness.

Prior to Rachel's death, Nathan had enjoyed outdoor activities, hiking in the mountains being his favorite. Now, he had serious concerns he may have a heart attack at any moment. Stress and lack of sleep had taken its toll on his body, even leading to hallucinations. His nightmares followed him, in that small space between dreams and reality. In that tiny moment, just as he'd crossed the line, he would smell her shampoo. But just as quickly as he could register the scent, it vanished, like a trick he played on himself, leaving him with just the memory.

Nathan groaned as he sat up. As he worked up the will to stand, he massaged his aching neck. Off to the side, on top of his coffee table, was the stack of funeral home quotes he'd been compiling. He chewed on the inside of his cheek, a bad habit he developed as a kid when he got nervous. No matter how many times he'd worked the numbers, it always came out the wrong way for him. There was just no way to cover the cost. He looked again at the stack of funeral expenses and wondered what options might be available to provide a fitting funeral. Not many that he could see. And what would Rachel's parents be expecting? A trip to Silas Ridge to discuss the funeral would certainly come with some expectations, and Nathan grew concerned he wouldn't be able to live up to them. But right now, there was nothing to do about that. He'd have plenty of time to worry himself sick on the drive up to Thurman Manor.

As a slight reprieve, packing was a breeze; he hadn't even unloaded from his work trip yet. All that was needed was to exchange the dirty clothing for fresh, which was simple enough. He spent a couple minutes grabbing clean underwear and socks and threw them into his suitcase. He also packed his computer into a backpack; there were some finishing touches needed for the photo remembrance.

After starting a pot of coffee, Nathan headed to take a quick shower. He lingered in the warm stream longer than necessary, allowing the hot water to sluice off his chin and fingers. The steam cleared his head; the heat relaxed his muscles. He towel-dried his hair but skipped his back, letting his shirt finish the job. As he headed to the kitchen, the aroma of fresh coffee invited him to partake.

Silas Ridge was an easy three-hour drive; a long enough trip to end up with numb legs, but not a long enough distance to justify air travel. Not that Silas Ridge had an airport anyway, unless you counted the makeshift airstrips in open fields. Nathan was anxious to get on the road; a late arrival would reflect poorly on him. He choked down a piece of dry toast and swigged down the last drops of his coffee. With his luggage in tow, he headed to his Civic.

His car was far from ideal for his trip; four-wheel-drive trucks were the choice mode of transportation. In the city where Nathan lived, it wasn't as noticeable. But once he reached the outskirts, the majority of vehicles would be heavy-duty trucks with loud engines, outfitted for hard work. Bonus points if they blew smoke. But he'd scored a deal on the Honda, and generally it worked well for him. As long as heavy snow was kept at bay, he'd be fine. And it was early in the year. His chances were fair. Even the bright sunshine over his head seemed to say, *this is going to be easy. Clear skies, easy ride.* He'd make it in plenty of time before dinner.

He didn't encounter much traffic on his way out of town. Before long, he was humming along the highway, watching white stripes fly by his left side as he moved north. Nathan kept the radio off, opting to use the quiet to rehearse conversations with Rachel's parents. It reminded him of preparing for a big job interview. Unfortunately, Nathan's problems would soon be far beyond how his car handled in a heavy snow.

Nathan had very little relationship with his in-laws. In fact, nearly none at all. He'd only been to their home once before, around Christmas, and Rachel had rushed them out at the first opportunity. The Thurmans had a massive estate, having been passed down from generation to generation, and with each passing the money seemed to grow. Nathan was speechless when she fessed up to the amount of money she came from. But she seemed embarrassed by it. Never once did Rachel play up the fact that she had been born into "old money", the kind that's difficult to get rid of. She wouldn't even consider taking advantage of her fortune, instead opting to live paycheck to paycheck, something Nathan was all too familiar with. His upbringing had been very middle class in every way. It's not that he'd had no experience with wealthy individuals, but his exposure was limited almost exclusively to photo-shoots, and the camera provided a comforting barrier. He'd never met anyone with the kind of wealth his in-laws commanded.

Rachel had been hesitant to go back, even for the holiday, but Nathan had pushed her.

"I just don't understand why you won't even try. Don't you think there's at least a chance things could change and be better?"

Rachel scoffed at even the idea. "My family? Changing? It's impossible."

"It's not impossible. People change. I've seen it happen."

Rachel shook her head. "Not my family. You don't get it." Rachel paced their living room, struggling to find the words, stuttering, and stopping in frustration. "It's like... Like the dysfunction is built in. Like tradition or something. You wouldn't understand."

"You're right, I don't understand. How can I when you won't talk to me about it?"

"I already told you. I just want to move on from that part of my life. Why can't I just forget it and live my life from here on out with you?"

Nathan shook his head. "I don't think life works like that. You don't get to just ignore your past. Sure, you can move on, but it's still a part of you. If you don't ever deal with that, it's just baggage you have to carry."

Rachel jammed her hands deeper into her hoodie and said, "Why won't you let this go? Why do you constantly feel the need to fix this?"

Nathan sighed. "I'm not trying to fix anything. I'm just worried you are going to end up with regrets."

Rachel smiled like she'd caught him in a trap. "See! That's you trying to fix things!"

He held up his hands in frustration. "Ok. Fine. I'm trying to fix an issue that, apparently, only I can see. Rachel, it's a problem that you don't speak to your parents. And I'm telling you, as a guy whose parents are both gone, you're going to wish you had that time back. Don't let this go so far that it can't be undone. You have time. You should use it."

She went silent for a beat, and then said, "If this situation were reversed, they'd never tell me to reconcile with you. They'd count their lucky stars this whole thing was over."

Nathan thought it over. "You're probably right. But we aren't them. We can live better."

Though she resisted, Rachel conceded, but only on the condition that they only spend the day with her family; the evenings would be theirs. She even insisted on getting a motel reservation, despite the excessive number of rooms Thurman Manor had to offer. She claimed she wanted the privacy, but Nathan had suspected something else. Being Christmas, he didn't want to push the issue and risk ruining their holiday, so he let it slide, promising himself to revisit the issue another time. He never did.

"Are you sure you'd rather stay here than your parents?"

Nathan pulled into the motel parking lot. The accommodations he'd seen advertised online were slightly exaggerated. Actually, it was almost criminal how much liberty the motel had taken in its marketing. It boasted a pool, which was technically true, but as they say, the devil's in the details. Nathan looked over at the area in question, wondering how the swimmers would fare in the summer months. There was a hole in the ground, but that's about all he could swear to seeing. One corner had a severe tear, and if there was any water in it, it was bound to be on par with sewage. Rusty fencing surrounded the pool, and a padlock secured the gate.

There were few cars in the lot; theirs, an old Cadillac straddling a faded parking line, and a Toyota pulled close to the office, which Nathan took to be the property of the sole employee on duty.

Nathan looked over at Rachel, secretly loving how she somehow managed to bite her lower lip and smile at the same time, unable to hide her delight with the accommodations. How a girl with her upbringing and privilege could find happiness in a place like this baffled him. There was probably some sort of lesson to be learned, however, it was lost on him.

"You're serious? You really want to stay here?"

She nodded her head. "Yeah, I really do." She opened up her door and headed toward the office to claim their room. She was halfway across the lot before Nathan got out, and she waved at him to hurry up.

He caught up with her at the office door. The inside reeked of decades of cigarettes and cat piss. Behind the desk, Nathan could see Dr. Phil on the TV, scolding some young couple about the responsibilities of adulthood. A man, apparently styling his hair after Dr. Phil, turned his head around as they entered.

"Be right there," he called. He lowered the volume on the TV and met them at the desk.

"You checking in?"

Nathan nodded. "Yes. We had a reservation."

"A reservation?" The man looked puzzled.

"Yes. I called a few days ago. I even put a deposit down. It should be listed under Stevens."

The man looked over a binder, turning his pages back

and forth as he searched for the name. He leaned in close and then, in a near shout, said, "A-Ha! I found it. What room you want?"

Nathan shrugged. "I didn't realize we got to pick."

"I'm mostly empty. No sense in setting rooms aside with business the way it's been. Haven't had a full house in quite a while."

"Well, what would you recommend?" Rachel asked.

The man looked thoughtful for a beat and picked at something stuck in his teeth as he considered the question.

"Well, I guess I'd stay away from the ice machine. It gets kinda loud. And maybe I'd stick away from the south side of the building. It's right by the road and you can really hear the trucks. So, I suppose I'd get the far room on the north side. Room 203.

"Sounds great," said Nathan, not knowing which side was north. In a place like this, he didn't figure it would make that much difference.

The bald guy grabbed a key, complete with a rabbit's foot, and handed it over. He wished them a good evening and then went back to his regularly scheduled programming. By now, Dr. Phil was giving his mind to a husband who had sworn off work for good.

They got to their room and Nathan opened the door for Rachel, the way his "momma" taught him as a boy.

"You be a gentleman, young man. That means opening doors for ladies, and if you're walking a girl home, you stay on the street side. You let her be closer to the grass. And walking home means walking home, nothing more, you hear? You be respectful. You treat her right, you hear?"

"Yes, Momma," he'd said.

Momma's voice was still reverberating in his head as Rachel walked past him, her perfume sweet and wonderful and perfect.

Rachel looked around, her face glowing. She appeared she might skip through the room.

Nathan shook his head in wonder.

"What?" she asked.

"Nothing... It's just, I don't get it. I mean, you've got this perfect house - no, a *mansion* - and you seem to be happier here."

"What's wrong with here?" she asked, twirling a lock of her hair.

"It's a dump! Anyone can see that."

She raised her eyebrows, a sure sign she was about to tease him. "You too good for this place, Mr. Fancy-pants?"

Nathan laughed. "No, not at all. I'm just surprised that you seem to prefer this."

Rachel's face grew more serious. "You wouldn't understand," she said. "Not really. Growing up in a place like that - it's not what you'd expect. It's complicated. I like this because it's simple. I'm comfortable here. It feels safe. You... You feel safe."

Nathan smiled and wrapped his arms around her. She hugged him back, and there was that wonderful, sweet, perfect smell again. He could live in this.

Near 11pm, as they lay in bed, Nathan felt Rachel stir. In a half-asleep state, he watched as she got up from bed and walked over to the coat closet. She stood still, staring at the open door for a couple of seconds, and then closed it.

As she crawled back into bed, Nathan asked, "You ok? Can't sleep?"

She snuggled in tight next to him and simply said, "I just don't like the dark."

The highway was coming to an end. Nathan retrieved his mind from the past and focused on navigating. Once he exited the highway, he'd be on back roads for the final stretch, often without cell service, and by extension, his GPS. He'd need to pay attention, or risk getting lost.

Gravel kicked up and smacked the bottom of his car as he turned off the highway. Nathan found himself hoping his car would survive these neglected roads. Something like a punctured gas line was the last thing he needed at the moment. Nathan made a mental note to look at a truck when it was time to upgrade his car. Maybe there was something to a more rugged vehicle.

Dusk was setting in, turning the sky red and purple: the sun just a sliver off to his left. He was in the middle of no-where, alone on a road that seemed to evaporate in the distance. A line of mountains was on his side, snow-capped and cold. Years ago, he had hiked there, trying to capture a photo of a grizzly, but without so much as a sighting, his dreams of selling to National Geographic were dashed. At the time, Nathan had been incredulous; naïve tourists came from all over the world, their sites getting ransacked by the bears, and he hadn't been able to track a single one. Before long, towering pines hid the mountains from view, and the road deviated from its straight path into a winding one.

The drive was nearing an end. He checked his phone to make sure it still had a good signal. The GPS reported just under fifteen minutes, which was good news because his legs were achy and stiff. A high-pitched chirp sounded as Nathan's phone rang.

When he looked at the screen, he saw the impossible. His heart skipped, and he was unable to look away. While unimaginable, the caller ID's large white type proved otherwise. Only one name was there, the one he most wished he could hear from.

Rachel.

Somehow, beyond reason and hope, Rachel was calling him.

Impossible, Nathan thought. *This is a trick, or a wrong number.* His mind told him to ignore it, to come back to reality.

This isn't real.

Nathan answered the call. His thumb shook as he tried to slide the virtual button across the screen. He tried and missed, then got it on the second try.

"Rachel?" His breathing was shallow and quick. His heart pounded like a mallet inside his chest. He was desperate for a reply, but there was only silence on the other end. No, not quite silence. There was a faint static hissing in the background, as if far away.

"Hello?" Nathan said, half wondering if the call had dropped, but that faint static remained, confirming the connection. He pulled the phone away from his ear and glanced at the screen for further proof the call was real. The call timer ticked away. Twelve seconds had passed.

Thirteen.

Fourteen.

"Answer me, please." He was hoping for the impossible, and as a response, the hiss grew louder, somehow *closer*, gaining momentum and volume, until it had revved itself into a squeal, piercing his ear and causing him to wince.

It was at that exact moment that his car took a wild turn to the right. Although he'd been moving fast, time seemed to slow, and the world became molasses, a sluggish crawl toward his inevitable conclusion. Nathan struggled with the steering wheel in a desperate attempt to keep his car in a straight line but couldn't seem to get control. He stomped on the brake, but the wheels were skidding in the gravel, unable to find their grip. In vain, he pressed his foot harder, but soon saw the road transition into grass, and then time resumed its natural pace as the car careened into its final spin. The vehicle rolled like a crocodile had it in a death spiral. Nathan's head jerked to the left, and he felt a sudden blunt impact as he smashed his window. All the light left his eyes, and the world went dark.

Chapter Six

Silas Ridge was a small community and had been that way since its inception. The area the town now occupied was once dense forest, but an enterprising man by the name of Silas Thurman changed all that in the late 1800s. Felling trees was a dangerous business, and more than a few men lost their lives in the course of their work. Rounds of new hires replaced the old, and the work continued as if nothing out of the ordinary had happened. There was nothing odd about this, at least in theory; most men those days would find a fair bit of danger regardless of their chosen profession. But under whiskey-soaked breath, rumors spread of a witch roaming the woods. Even with their daytime bravado, they always worked in pairs, and under no circumstances would anyone enter the woods after nightfall.

Silas Thurman continued his logging, and as the forest thinned, his wealth grew. He expanded his operations and used his own product to erect a small town, which his workers soon occupied. Whether due to marriage, or people looking for a new start, the small little logging community continued to expand, until eventually, it earned its official recognition as Silas Ridge.

Wanting to place roots himself, Silas began construction of a grand estate for his family. Unfortunately for Silas, he never lived to see the final result. The construction crew found him early one morning on the frozen earth, having thrown himself from the incomplete roof. Official documentation noted his suicide to be the result of intense stress; unofficially, people said he was driven mad by the witch. His oldest son inherited the lot and saw the Manor through to completion. And on it went, expanding the town, passing the Manor down generation after generation, and spreading rumors of the supernatural, until the present time.

Thurman Manor stood alone, just as it always had, on the outskirts of Silas Ridge. A lake divided the Manor from the small town, either side being just visible to the naked eye. As it happened, Elisabeth Thurman, the current matriarch and newly grieving mother, was standing in a window of the Manor (her Manor) looking out over the lake and nursing a glass of wine as she waited on Nathan Stevens' arrival. The light was all but gone, the last remnants shimmering off the water's surface like dancing crystal. Elisabeth took another sip from her glass and looked at her wristwatch. Nearly 8pm, an hour since her son-in-law was due to arrive. She clicked her tongue and called his cell, only to have it go to voicemail. Elisabeth hung up without leaving a message.

Elisabeth was the first to receive word about her daughter, Rachel, the morning they found her. Her groundskeeper, Hancock, had discovered the body during his morning chores. He called the house first thing, and through gasps and panting, told her to come right away. When she got there, it was clear there was nothing to be done. Rachel was beyond saving. The sheriff was called, but it was strictly a formality, and a necessary legal step. Soon, word started to trickle through the town, reigniting ancient fears. A few days later, the local press ran a story about Rachel, which Elisabeth deemed inflammatory. In response, she threatened anyone connected to the piece with a defamation lawsuit, shutting down any further speculation regarding her family, at least in terms of print.

Elisabeth married Edward Thurman in 1988, a decision motivated by her expanding belly, but one that worked well for her. There had been one pregnancy scare prior, but it ended in miscarriage. As Edward had put it, "they had dodged a bullet". Elisabeth hadn't felt the same. They kept the news of it quiet, and Elisabeth mourned alone in her own humble home. As she sat in her grief, she became pregnant again. Fearing another miscarriage, and the prospect of enduring it alone, she pushed Edward toward marriage, and he'd agreed. However, she insisted on staying in her own place until the wedding, citing the need to keep up proper appearances. Edward had chuckled, pointing out the rather obvious fact that her increasing size might be a dead giveaway.

"Better make that wedding happen quick then," Elisabeth told him.

On a particularly hot summer day, she and Edward had gone into town hoping to find the finishing touches for their nursery. Elisabeth had been fawning over a decorative bassinet, complete with white spindles and a curved rail, which she said would be the "perfect thing for our perfect baby". Edward, a self-described born "saver", wasn't as certain. He flipped the tag over in his fingers, revealing the price in black magic marker, and a number that caused him to drop the sticker like it had bitten him.

"Uh, Liz... Let's look at some others, huh?"

Elisabeth was humming to herself, inspecting the finer details of the crib, oblivious to Edward. "Eddy! It's adjustable! And it even converts to a toddler bed later. Not that we necessarily need it to do that, but it's nice to know it could, don't you think?"

"Uh-huh. What about this one over here?" He went to another model nearby in a mark-down section.

Elisabeth frowned. "That one's gross. Look at it. It's probably defective."

"It's not defective. Maybe a scratch and dent, but not defective."

Elisabeth's face was serious and resolved. "I don't want my baby in a scratch and dent crib. Don't you want the best for your baby?"

Edward shrugged and walked away, leaving the topic alone for the time being. Elisabeth couldn't understand it. Why wouldn't he want the best for his child? There was no lack of cash; in fact, it seemed to be the complete opposite. They could have lavish dinners, top of the line cars and entertainment, but whenever the topic of child expenses came up, the couple was bound to fight. Edward would argue the virtues of being frugal and thrifty. Elisabeth could only think of him as "cheap".

From behind and several rows over, Elisabeth overheard whispers, pulling her out of her thoughts. Three young boys, pre-teens based on their greasy, pimple faced appearance, were staring at her and whispering back and forth. One kid elbowed the other, an obvious nudge to accept a proposed dare. Elisabeth turned away, hoping they would disappear if she paid them no attention. For a moment, she thought the trick had worked, but then she heard a voice behind her.

"Are you one of them?"

She turned around and saw it was the red-haired kid in the trio. His hair looked matted and oily, and his nose had one big blackhead front and center, like a soldier called to attention.

"Um... I'm Mrs. Thurman." She wasn't. Not yet. But she would be soon enough, and she didn't see any harm in a white lie so long as it maintained proper appearances.

The kid's eyes lit up. "Hey, Mikey, come 'ere. It's really them!" By this point, Edward had noticed them and worked his way back over.

"Listen, we're just trying to get some shopping done," Edward said. "Give us some space, huh?"

The kid ignored it and urged the one named Mikey closer. He was mousy looking and needed a haircut. He stared a long time, well past it being awkward, until Edward broke and reiterated his plea. "Guys, I already asked once. Just give us space, ok?"

The red-haired kid started again. "Is the house really haunted? My uncle Joe says he saw a ghost there once, but my dad says he's full of you know what. Mom says I can't use words like that, but that's how my dad says it anyhow."

"I don't have a clue what you're talking about," Edward said as he turned his attention back to the baby section.

"Sure you do, man! Don't pretend like you don't know." Red turned his attention to Elisabeth. "My uncle Joe also says you and your family are a bunch of liars. Guess he was right about that."

The insult caught Elisabeth by surprise. "Excuse me?"

Red folded his arms across his chest, letting his accusation stand.

Elisabeth felt a tug at her hand as Edward stormed off.

"We're getting out of here. We don't have time for this." Heads turned toward them, and she could feel hot stares on the back of her neck. She could hear light murmurs behind her.

Once in the car, she asked, "What was that all about?"

"Nothing. Just stupid rednecks, that's all. Forget them." But Edward didn't appear to be ready to forget anything. "If I find out their father's work for me, I'll have them fired. Greasy little runts... People who have kids like that shouldn't breed."

Elisabeth turned back and could see peering eyes gawking as they sped away. This would mark the first time Elisabeth experienced the reality of what living in Thurman Manor would entail. It would not be her last. She went back to her own home, confused by her own feelings. She would sort through her emotions for years to come, until she grew tired of enduring the rumors and gossip, and she'd come to despise the residents of Silas Ridge with a passion of her own.

Elisabeth downed the last of her wine and set the crystal glass on the windowsill. A rapid knock drew her attention to the doorway. In it, a short little man, with a long, crooked nose and glasses, gave her a courteous half bow.

"Dinner is ready, Mrs. Thurman."

"Very good, Upham. I'll be down momentarily."

"I assume no sign of Mr. Stevens yet?"

She looked back out the window, and down the long drive leading away from The Manor and into the woods. She shook her head as she told him no.

"Has Lily returned home yet?" she asked.

"Unfortunately, no. Not that I've seen."

"Let me know the moment she returns."

"Yes, Ma'am, I will." He lingered a moment, as if unsure he should ask an uncomfortable yet necessary question.

Noticing, Elisabeth said, "Out with it, Upham. Say what's on your mind."

"Well, if I may, I was wondering if you'd had a chance to speak with the family yet? About what to tell Mr. Stevens, should he ask about any, let's say, oddities?"

Elisabeth's smile turned grim. "Oddities, you say. Why not just call it what it is, Upham?"

"With your permission, I'd rather not. It's not my place. I just wondered if there was any direction you'd decided on that I should be aware of prior to his arrival?"

"Edward and I spoke this afternoon."

The direction Upham was referring to had been in constant discussion by Elisabeth and Edward for the last few days. There was some back and forth, but in the end, they decided it would be best to make things as simple as possible, if only to keep the story straight. That afternoon, Elisabeth had called a family meeting in order to relay orders. They met in the den, a room they hadn't stepped foot in for years, but was suitable for their needs. In the center was a couch, with a coffee table placed in front, although its current function was for dangerous varieties of dark liquid rather than books. Sitting on the couch were her twins, Tommy and Lucas. Tommy was the older (only by minutes) of the two, and they had been inseparable from birth. He smacked his chewing gum as he stared off in a daydream. His left knee bounced unchecked, something of a nervous habit he'd picked up. All in all, he appeared like an inexperienced poker player projecting his tells.

Lucas, on the other hand, was sitting in solitude, his arms wrapped around his midsection as if expecting an imminent attack. He wore a hoodie, which was pulled down to hide his bloodshot eyes. His skin had a pale quality to it, like he'd avoided the sun for too long. Lucas appeared to be about halfway through his glass of whiskey, which was a fairly constant place for him to be.

Tommy's mouth was open before Elisabeth had even entered the room. "What are we doing, Mom? This isn't a good idea. Why are we even bringing him here in the first place?"

She ignored his question for the time being, delaying her response to her own time. Tommy's impatience wouldn't pressure her into an answer before she was ready. She scanned the attendees and noticed her daughter was missing.

"Where's your sister?"

Tommy and Lucas looked at one another, and Tommy shrugged. "No idea. Who cares? We have more important things to worry about than where Lily is right now. She can take care of herself. We need to figure what to tell Nathan. Or better yet, let's find him a different place to stay."

That much Elisabeth knew to be true. It was all but certain Nathan would notice those "oddities" as Upham had so vaguely described, but that was what she and Edward had planned for, wasn't it? She needed him to feel like part of the family, at least for a time. As long as everyone followed her direction, it would play out according to plan.

Elisabeth turned her attention to Tommy. "I'll decide what's important. You're here to listen. Do you understand?" Tommy opened his mouth to protest, and Elisabeth held up a hand to stop him. "A simple yes or no will do."

"Yes," Tommy said, and he slumped down in his seat.

"Nathan is coming here because we need to work together for the funeral. If we want to keep with our traditions, he's going to have to be on board. As much as I don't like it, he has some say in the matter - legally. As for what we tell him, it's important we are all on the same page. I need each of you to be on your best behavior. Lily, too. Make him feel welcome. We need him on our side for the time being."

In the back corner, a towering figure was occupying himself with something curious on top of a bookcase. He blew a puff of air and there was an eruption of dust, evidence of years gone by, now falling like snow toward the floor.

"Jonathan, have you seen Lily?"

"No, not since this morning," he replied. "Do you want me to go look for her?"

Elisabeth imagined the room vibrating as Jonathan spoke, his voice thick and booming. She admired his arms, thicker than an average man's legs, but looked away before the boys noticed her stolen glances. But based on the sly grin on Jonathan's face, he had noticed. He positioned his hand on the bookcase to show off his frame, an obvious tell, and one that Elisabeth would have to discuss with him later. Some things were better off kept secret.

"No, I don't think so. She'll return, I'm sure of it."

Tommy was growing impatient, and all at once started blurting out, "I can be friendly, that's easy enough. Nothing to it. But what happens when he sees something? What are we going to tell him? Being his pal isn't going to explain anything."

Elisabeth shot him a stern look. "Quiet. The grownups are talking." He shrunk back down like a dog with its tail tucked between its legs.

Elisabeth looked back at Jonathan, signaling for him to weigh in.

"Tommy's right. Nathan will ask questions. Maybe not

the first day, but for sure by the third." Feeling validated, Tommy sat up straighter, but Elisabeth's glare put his tail right back in place.

Lucas downed the last of his drink before speaking. "Screw it. Maybe we just tell him. Get it over with."

Elisabeth was quick to respond. "No. There's already quite enough gossip in this town. The last thing we need is to give any validation to the local rumor mill. Your father and I spoke. We will tell him it's an ongoing electrical problem. Something about having an electrician on the way. Nothing complicated, but we all should have the same story," she said. "It's best to stay quiet. If you can be silent on the subject, do that. There's a chance he doesn't notice anything."

No one in the room, Elisabeth included, believed that. And no one had the courage to acknowledge the plan only addressed the lights. There were worse things to consider, but those things were better left unsaid. They sat in silence, each considering what the next few days would bring.

"Can I ask a question?" Lucas said. "What if Rachel told him, before she died? What if he already knows?"

Again, there was silence as each considered this question, one so obvious that it went unnoticed. And now that it was known, so devastating that it wanted to be ignored.

"There's no way," said Tommy. "Rachel wanted out of here more than any of us. All she wanted was to leave and forget this place."

"You don't know that for sure," Lucas said.

But Elisabeth did.

Looking back, what happened should have been predictable, but at the time, Elisabeth just couldn't comprehend it. She'd been blindsided, never having dreamed things could have escalated the way they did.

It happened after Rachel brought Nathan home to meet the family. Dinner had been pleasant enough, filled with niceties and the usual conversations one has when first meeting someone. But Elisabeth had known from the moment she met him that Nathan wasn't what her daughter deserved, let alone what she needed. She'd known that from the second he'd driven up in his dirty used car and worried over his appearance in a way a legitimate man, one of proper stature, would never have done.

Rachel looked giddy with excitement, a bright smile plastered on her face, an obvious victim of infatuation. Her dress was something simple. It looked like cotton, maybe the sort of thing someone from the nearby town might wear. But even in the simple, cheap dress, Elisabeth thought Rachel was trying too hard. But trying for whom? Nathan? The thought was impossible; under no circumstance could her daughter need to try for a man like this. To be sure, he was handsome, in a rough and tumble sort of way, the kind of man you might spend an exciting weekend with, but only the weekend, because you knew that to be anyone of importance required surrounding yourself with other people of importance. Nathan was not that sort, that much was clear.

What happened was brief but had long-lasting effects. Nathan, in an effort to bond, as he had put it, was off with Lucas and Tommy playing video games, or some such nonsense. Elisabeth and Rachel found themselves alone in the den, the same one that Elisabeth wouldn't set foot in again until her family meeting was called.

"What do you think of him, Mom?" Rachel asked. Elisabeth saw her daughter's face was full of anticipation, but she knew that deep down, perhaps unknown even to Rachel herself, the relationship was childish and destined to be short-lived. Ultimately, it was foolishness, innocent enough, but foolish all the same.

Elisabeth chuckled, the laugh coming out more demeaning than she intended, but perhaps not.

"Why are you laughing?" Rachel asked, her eyes narrowing into a warning gaze.

"Oh, honey," Elisabeth said through a cover girl white smile, "it's just that, this... this relationship?" She shook her head, as if sorrowful for her daughter, as if she were a thing to be pitied. "Let's just say you should cut this off before it goes any further."

Rachel's eyes widened. "Cut it off? Why on earth would I do that? I love him."

"Love him?" Elisabeth was incredulous. "No, dear. No. You do not love him."

"How would you know? How do you know how I feel?"

"Do you really not see it? Well, I suppose you are blind with infatuation, Rachel. It's clear to everyone but you that this - whatever it is - isn't a lasting thing. Nathan isn't... our stock, if you know what I mean."

Rachel laughed, sounding mocking and sarcastic. "Our stock? Are you serious? Do you hear yourself?"

Elisabeth slammed her glass down, sloshing red liquid over the brim.

"Oh, I hear just fine, dear. I've heard plenty. And I'm telling you, it's time to break it off. Take him home, explain that you realized you don't see a future with him or something." Elisabeth batted her hand as if at a buzzing insect. "It doesn't really matter, so long as you end this."

"No. I won't do it." Rachel shook her head; her eyes had welled with tears. "I love him. I need you to understand that. For you to take this seriously. Please."

Elisabeth looked her daughter in the eye, straight and without a hint of empathy.

"I'll do that when you do something worth taking seriously."

Rachel's mouth dropped, and when the tears came, they flowed freely. The silence hung in the air between them, until Rachel broke it with the three words so many parents have heard, in various ways, often not taken in earnest but always to be weighed.

"I hate you."

If the words had hurt Elisabeth, her face didn't show it. She looked back at her daughter, unwavering, face set as stone, and then uttered what should never be spoken by a parent.

"Well, I hate you too."

Elisabeth let that sink into Rachel like a slap, and as if to drive the magnitude of her indifference home, sipped her wine like those words were of no cost to her.

Rachel and Nathan left the Manor without another word. Elisabeth watched, just as she had at their arrival, hidden behind her invisible glass barrier.

Her mind now present again, Elisabeth looked at Lucas, who a moment before had suspected Rachel confided Thurman secrets to an outsider.

Elisabeth's tone was serious and measured. "No. I don't think Rachel said anything to him at all."

Chapter Seven

Nathan woke up to a clicking sound, repeating over and over like a metronome. Dazed, he looked around, struggling to find his bearings in a world that had somehow turned on its side. The road had vanished, lost in murky darkness. He lifted his head off the driver's side window and winced as he touched his head. His fingers came away slick with blood. He could taste copper in his mouth.

Click... Click... Click...

What is that? The turn signal. His turn signal was on. Without conscious thought, he moved it back to a neutral position. Likewise, the car was still running, so he turned the key and placed it in his jacket pocket, out of pure habit. Gentle ticks sounded from the engine as it cooled down.

Nathan looked around. He was in a channel of dirt and water, cold and slime. An earthy smell filled his nostrils. As his mind cleared, he realized he was in a ditch and the car was overturned on its left side. He patted around his body, and despite some soreness on his head, everything appeared to be intact. In the coming days, Nathan's body would come to realize the full impact of what he'd just survived.

He reached down, pressed the buckle release, and the

belt retracted back to its starting point. It was difficult to move, but he shifted himself into a better position. The car being sideways meant putting his feet on the window of the driver's side door. He heard it crunch underneath his weight. Dirty water flooded his shoes and soaked his feet. He reached above his head and pulled at the door handle, and pushed up with his legs. The door budged, but even with his arms extended all the way, he couldn't quite open it. He let go, and the door slammed closed above him.

He reached back for his keys, hoping the car would at least have power. With a half-turn, the dash lit up. He fumbled in the murky water and found the switch that controlled the power windows and clicked it down. Nothing. He tried again, flipping it back and forth, but nothing engaged. Nothing moved. He reached above his head to try the switch on the passenger's side, and the window retracted above him. The cool air flooding in was a welcome relief.

He reached into the backseat for his backpack and tossed it out the passenger window. It landed on the car with a thump. He searched around for his phone and found it in a puddle of dirty water, the screen now a spiderweb of cracks. Out of pure muscle memory, he tapped it twice, expecting it to light up. When nothing happened, he stared at it dumbly, the reality of his situation sinking in. Nathan's grip tightened around the phone until his knuckles turned white. He hurled it back into the sludge. He climbed out, using the headrests like ladder rungs. After wiggling his torso through the passenger side window, he sat on the top, and then pulled his feet up.

His new vantage point showed just how steep either side of the ditch was. No way the car could get out without a tow truck and winch. The front tire was all shredded into strips, and the rim exposed. A catastrophic flat. The civic had massive damage on all sides. Crumpled doors. Caved in hood. The front bumper was hanging on by a thread. In all likelihood, the car was totaled. Again, he assessed his body for any physical damage. And again, found everything intact. Just the nasty bump on the side of his head, and the beginnings of a deep bruise across his chest from the seatbelt. He put his hand up to his head wound, and it came away covered in blood.

He screamed in frustration. No phone to make contact, and very little chance of running into a single soul out here. There had only been minutes left in his drive, and now he would endure hours of walking. He looked at his car, and then down the road leading to the Manor.

He started walking.

Soon, night set in, and even with the chill, a light bead of perspiration had formed on Nathan's forehead. His back, bearing the weight of his pack, felt saturated with sweat. If he stopped moving, he'd be in serious trouble. The combination of chilly air and damp clothing would be a death sentence. His backpack was cumbersome; it was built for computers and cables, not hiking. Under different circumstances, Nathan might have enjoyed this. Hiking was a favorite activity of his. He loved being outdoors, enjoying fresh air, and getting exercise. But with the right equipment, and at his choosing. Instead, he found himself in a situation forced upon him, and this wasn't a recreational stroll.

Before the wreck, he seemed to recall about ten to fifteen miles to go. So, he calculated the mean and assumed about twelve miles. Not a significant time for a car; fifteen minutes maximum. But that was at sixty miles per hour. Walking speed put him significantly behind schedule, turning minutes into hours. In his prime, he would have hiked it two and half hours, but he was anything but prime right now.

He reached his hand up to his head. He could feel where his head hit the window. The skin seemed tight. Like it might burst. Nathan pushed the lump and flinched at the pain. He couldn't see it, but he knew blood had dried on his face. It was caked and sticky on his cheek. At least it seemed the bleeding had stopped.

The straps of his backpack had rolled to the edge of his shoulders. Nathan repositioned them to sit better and kept walking. His feet ached. They were wet too, not so much from sweat as the ditch water he'd stood in. He put his head down and forced himself to move forward. To his knowledge, The Manor was the closest thing around. Yes, Silas Ridge was close too, but that lay on the other side of the lake, which put it even further out of reach. There was nothing out here. Nothing except for The Manor.

Nathan glanced at his watch, and the illuminated hands informed him he was nearly three hours beyond his expected arrival time. Although he reasoned the family would understand, somewhere inside, he felt the panic that comes from being late, as if already failing a scheduled evaluation. From the first time he'd met Rachel's family, he'd sensed the judging eyes, and the silent assessment he'd somehow failed.

While the inevitable call that came after Rachel's death shouldn't have been surprising, nevertheless, he was. To date, it was the longest Elisabeth had ever spoken to him. Nathan thought she had sounded thin through the phone. They exchanged the standard conversation points that one does when losing a loved one:

It's hard to process right now.
I'm trying to wrap my head around it.
I think I just need time.

After the initial formalities, Elisabeth said, "What were you thinking for the funeral?"

"Uh, I'm actually still sorting that out. I have an obituary written, and I'm putting together a video of her. Photos and memories kind of thing."

"A video would be nice. What sorts of other things are you planning?"

Nathan looked at the growing stack of papers on his desk, a visual representation of the expenses to be incurred. Expenses he couldn't possibly afford.

He kept his financial situation to himself. "I'm considering my options."

"Well, listen. I want you to come up to our house for a few days. There's a lot to consider, and we have some things we'd like to discuss with you."

"What sorts of things?"

"Mainly service arrangements. Specifics would best be left for when we're face to face. When can you be here?"

No request had been made; a point not lost on Nathan. While there was a part of him that didn't want to go, what Elisabeth was saying made sense. Of course Rachel's family would play a role in her funeral. And it would simplify things to all be in one place, where all the family could make a focused effort.

Don't forget, it was your brilliant idea she go there in the first place to repair things. What right do you have to say no now?

"I guess I could do that. When were you thinking?"

They agreed on the time, and the wheels were set in motion.

Nathan's walk toward The Manor continued until he came to a small offshoot in the road. There was no sign marking its existence, making it easy to miss if you didn't know where it was. It wasn't much more than a single lane drive, coming out of nowhere and leading into a thick line of trees. If you were speeding past, you would have gone by and been none the wiser to its whereabouts. But Nathan was walking, and that made it easy to see.

Two stone lions stood guard on either side of the entrance like ancient sentries. The mouths on both were closed, and their heads held high and regal. They looked like they once had thick majestic manes, carved and polished, but they were now weathered with age. A black iron gate spanned between them, spindles of thin twisted iron that ended in a decorative top. Trees surrounded everything and got thicker yet just beyond the entrance. Nathan avoided the barrier with ease by walking behind one of the lions. As it happened, the gate was strictly ornamental; no security fence ran the perimeter. The remote location provided sufficient privacy for Thurman Manor.

The mansion sat back approximately a half mile from the entrance, which was the only way in, provided you were coming by land. In theory, one could use a boat and cross the lake that divided The Manor from Silas Ridge. Nathan had only ever arrived by car, although now he could claim by foot as well. Old trees made a canopy over the road, their branches spread like boney fingers trying to block out the moonlight.

Although long forgotten, echoes of the rumors surrounding the witch in Silas Ridge still haunted these woods. The quiet was oppressive; even his soft footsteps seemed like a violation, like he was disturbing something that would be better off left alone. Primitive instinct urged Nathan to be cautious; all his senses were on high alert.

He grew more aware of the darkness the deeper he

went in. A sense of unease settled around him; something about being in the woods alone and exposed.

And watched.

He felt like a child, fearing the dark and the nasty creatures that lurked in shadows. Over and over, he told himself it was silly, foolish even, to have such an irrational fear, but it did little in the way of shaking the dread. He pushed it down deeper, trying to bury the paranoia, not realizing that sometimes buried things get unearthed.

He heard a sound behind him, or maybe something closer to the *feeling* of a sound. Had Nathan been familiar with the history of these woods, he would have known this was a shared experience by many before him, although none were still alive to confirm it. Nathan stopped dead in his tracks, training his ear toward where he thought it came from, and fighting the urge to run. It sounded like a tree had groaned in the wind, or like branches cracking as they gave way too much. But when he looked, there was no wind; the trees had no hint of sway in their crooked limbs. Their very stillness set him on edge. The lack of movement was unnatural, almost more still than his photographs. It was like time itself had stopped.

Then, out of nowhere, movement caught his eye, just on the edge of his vision (or at least he thought it did). It happened in a flash, back in the trees. He wasn't sure what it was, but he thought it was *dark*. Yes, it was dark in these woods. But whatever he saw was somehow darker, more black than the night. As if it had eaten the light. The logical part of his mind told him it might be an animal; be careful. He thought about those bears he'd been so desperate to find. He wished it were a bear. The primitive lizard part of his mind screamed *evil*; *Run*. The darkness seemed to push right through him, to *know* him. Nathan felt his skin go cold, yet he was slick with perspiration. The night air chilled beads of sweat on his brow. The hair on his body had gone stiff. His mouth hung open, but he dared not breathe.

He kept his focus on the trees, and that dreadful unnatural darkness. He never saw it move per se, but it didn't quite stay still either. It shifted ever so slightly, like a distant star that disappeared when gazing at it head on. With each shift, the little light available scattered and fell short, as if knocked off its predetermined path. He teetered on the edge of losing focus, and he hated to stare at it, but he was terrified of losing track of where it was.

A wind swept through the trees, causing limbs to sway like a magician's hands over Nathan's head. The movement above broke the spell, moonlight scattered across the ground, and with it, the darkness. He checked over his shoulder, back into the trees, still wary. There was no more movement, but like those poor souls before him, he still felt he was being watched from a distance. He decided his safest viable choice was to reach the Manor. It wasn't far now. He resumed walking but maintained a watchful eye behind him.

Nathan emerged from the forest soon after, thankful for the open space. It felt like freedom. His breathing eased, and the terror he knew in the woods faded. Fields of grass were on either side, which he assumed to be pasture for the horses. Those animals were one of the few things Rachel ever spoke of fondly when discussing her childhood home. Nathan looked straight down the road. He would not permit his eyes to wander and risk catching sight of the barn. The horses may have been a fond memory for Rachel, but they would never be his.

Up ahead, Nathan could see the house, looking enormous even in the distance. It was three stories, with tall windows spanning the width and reflecting the moonlight like a mirror. Multiple chimneys stuck out from sharp roof angles like stray hairs, but none of them emitted any smoke. The grounds surrounding the house were sparse but well maintained. Small lamps atop iron posts were evenly spaced in the landscaping. They had a pale glow, but the light still seemed too little; like it was being smothered. Like the light was having difficulty cutting through the night.

Chapter Eight

The grandfather clock ticked the seconds away, the same as it had for years, its pendulum swaying back and forth like a hypnotist's charm. Charles Upham, the faithful servant known only by his last name around Thurman Manor, wiped the clock down and took care to set the hands to precise measurements. It was almost a quarter to 11, and he was nearing the end of his rounds. Thurman Manor had many clocks, though none as prominent as this one. It stood so tall that a ladder was required to make adjustments, which at the moment, Upham was doing, reaching over as far as he dared. Decorative hand-crafted bears adorned the top, and the work of skilled craftsmen was on display along each edge. For as long as Upham had been at Thurman Manor, which was longer than Edward himself, this magnificent piece of craftsmanship had stood as a centerpiece.

Above this was a large family portrait, seemingly larger than life, hung center on the tallest wall. Edward sat front and center, his demeanor serious. Elisabeth, his wife, stood just behind him, her hand resting on his shoulder. Supportive, loving, and beautiful. Rachel's siblings comprised the outskirts. Her twin brothers, Lucas and Tommy to the left,

Rachel and her sister Lily to the right. The brothers were in matching suits, an obvious play on their being twins. Although he would never say such a thing out loud, Upham thought both of them too old to be participating in such a thing. They tried to match the seriousness of their father but failed. Lily and Rachel both wore beautiful dresses, as well as smiles that seemed more sad than happy.

Upham had been the primary caretaker of both Thurman Manor and its occupants for going on sixty-three years. For all his responsibilities, Upham considered this to be his most important, and treated it with a degree of respect that bordered on religious. Having set the hands again, he closed the small window encasing the clock face with a tiny little click and climbed down the ladder, taking care on each precarious rung.

Upham had come to Thurman Manor as a young man, first serving Edward's father, Franklin. When he came, Edward had been only three, and Jonathan an infant. For the first few years, Upham spent his time overseeing the existing house staff, but being a hands-on kind of manager, he insisted on being intimately involved in every aspect.

When he first arrived, the strangeness of the house bothered him, and he often considered quitting. But he felt a pull toward the family; each day his sense of duty grew, especially toward the young boys. Eventually, loyalty won out, and Upham secured a firm place at Thurman Manor.

Upham spun around as three booming knocks echoed around the entry. The front doors were thick and heavy, as if made from a solid tree. Upham pulled them open, and on the other side was a disheveled man covered in dirt and blood.

"Mr. Stevens? Is that you?" Upham said. "Are you quite alright?"

"Hey, Mr. Upham," Nathan said, "Sorry if I woke you."

"No, no. You didn't wake me. I'm just finishing my nightly duties. Come in, come in..." Upham hurried Nathan inside and he secured the doors with a hefty thunk as they latched.

"I know I'm late," Nathan said. "I meant to be here much earlier. Had a bit of car trouble along the way."

"Here, give me your pack and sit down. Let me see your face." Upham took the pack from Nathan and guided him to a leather chair against the wall.

Nathan sat down with a sigh and massaged his legs. He craned his neck and looked up at the tall ceilings, and then to the chandelier overhead. "It's beautiful," Nathan said. "I know I saw it when I came before, but I never really looked at it."

Upham turned his attention upward and joined Nathan in his admiration. The chandelier was beautiful, just like every other physical aspect of the house. From the marble floor beneath their feet to the grand staircase behind them, every feature had received painstaking attention to detail.

"Here, tilt your head up this way and let me get a look at you." Upham positioned Nathan's head more toward the light, but it was difficult to see. Like the outside, the light inside the manor was dim, and somehow strange. It seemed to fall shorter than it should have, as if muted and diminished. Each section of the house was like entering a dark room after having been in a bright space, but it never allowed your eyes to readjust.

Upham frowned. "This lighting is making it so I can't see how severe your injuries are. Let's get you settled in a room. I'm certain the light will be better there." He stole a glance at the clock, knowing time was running thin. Each second pulled him closer to 10:57.

There's still time... If I hurry.

Upham stood and called for Nathan to follow him.

Long hallways ran to either side of the entry, and another ran straight back, leading deeper into the house. Esoteric paintings lined the walls, complemented by dark hardwood floors and expensive runners down the middle. There was a staircase leading to the second and third floors, but Upham led Nathan further into the house, to a small door hidden flush in the wall.

Upham saw a question on Nathan's face and explained, "A service corridor. We don't use them as much as we once did, but they still find some use from time to time. Originally, they served as direct routes for staff to move quickly between floors." Upham thought, *Tonight, it serves exactly the same purpose.* He expected it at any moment. Once the clock ticked over, things tended to become unpredictable in the house.

Upham gestured for Nathan to enter the corridor and closed the door behind them. The stairway was thin and plain. Dim lights lined the ceiling above. They climbed up the corridor to the second floor. For some time, age had been catching up with Upham, as evidenced by his current shortness of breath. Nathan turned back and saw him and stopped. He wore a look of concern.

"Upham, you ok?"

He tried to appear more relaxed than he was. "I've been a little under the weather, is all. I'm quite alright, just ready to retire for the evening." As if he had something to prove, more to himself than Nathan, he continued to climb and worked his way past Nathan, forcing himself to climb faster despite the discomfort in his knees. He did his best to hide his breathing.

"Ah. Here we are. You'll be on the second floor. If you'd follow me, please."

Upham gripped the door handle that would open them to the hall and froze. The handle was buzzing, as if each atom was vibrating itself into a frenzy. Upham felt the effects all the way up his arm, the effect similar to when he'd hit his funny bone as a child. There was no need to check, but he glanced at his watch anyway.

It was time.

The dim overhead lights began to glow brighter, and the buzzing in the handle seemed to spread all around them. Upham could hear it now, revving up like a storm, growing in intensity and pitch. The lights continued to glow brighter and brighter, until they became blinding and painful to look at, and there was a great POP as one burst. Glass clinked as it fell down the wood stairs. Then, just as quick as it came, the lights dimmed and the buzzing slowed, relaxing, relenting. Upham's heart raced, and he realized he hadn't released his grip on the door. Nathan was looking around, a bewildered expression on his face.

"What was that?"

The truth was, he didn't have the slightest clue how to answer that question, so he shrugged and feigned ignorance.

"Does that happen a lot?" Nathan asked.

Upham tried to seem reassuring. "It's an old house, Mr. Stevens. We will have someone out in the morning to investigate."

The expression on Nathan's face seemed odd, like he doubted his explanation. This added to his paranoia.

"Upham, you really don't seem well. You're drenched in sweat. Are you sure you're ok?"

"Quite sure, Mr. Stevens. This way, please."

Whether this satisfied Nathan, Upham wasn't sure. But he asked no more questions, and Upham offered no answers. The caretaker looked again at his watch, and it showed 11pm exactly. He allowed himself to exhale and opened the door.

Tall windows lined the second-floor hallway, allowing

for a full view of the grounds. Upham led Nathan down the long corridor, paying careful attention as he walked. In his early years, he often found himself lost, in part due to the Manor's size, but also because the hallways themselves had a strange quality to them, as if they led you where you did not intend to go.

They passed multiple doors, each closed, until they arrived at the end of the hall. Upham stopped at the very last door, dug a key from his pocket, and unlocked it. He stood with a degree of ceremony and allowed Nathan to enter.

Chapter Nine

Moments earlier, as Upham and Nathan had hidden in the service corridor, Lily Thurman was driving herself back toward the Manor, white knuckled and keenly aware of the time. Her headlights shot out in front of her, lighting up a new fourteen feet each second. Up ahead was pitch black darkness. To either side, tall trees stood at attention, as if welcoming her back home. In a fleeting moment of darkness, she considered what it would be like to wrap her car around one of the thick trunks, but dismissed it. She still had a chance to escape; if that weren't true, she might need to reconsider the date with the tree. Lily leaned into a curve and brought her car back to center and pushed down on the go-pedal, as if by increasing her speed she might escape her problems.

Earlier that day, Lily had been lying in a bed with one bare leg hanging outside cheap motel sheets. Bright mid-day light lined the drawn shades like a razor's edge. To call room 203 minimal would be generous. A small table was off to one side, and underneath on the worn carpet was a microwave.

God only knew if it worked. There was a television, but it was beyond ancient and might have worked as well as the microwave. Lily smirked at the chain securing it to the wall. *As if anyone would want that.* Years of hazy blue cigarette smoke had permeated the walls and carpet, making the room musty and sour.

She looked toward the bathroom and saw heavy steam floating out, making its contribution to the yellow stains above. For the last ten minutes, David had been running the water as hot as the boiler would allow. That, or the exhaust didn't work.

Hope he doesn't use it all up.

Lily sat up and yawned. Her mouth was dry, and like the hotel room she was in, tasted of stale cigarettes. She flung the sheets off to the side of the bed and padded over to the bathroom. The carpet felt thin and sticky on her feet.

"How's the water?" she asked.

"Starting to get cold," David replied.

"Would it have killed you to save me some?"

"Oh, come on. Don't be like that."

"Like what?"

"Upset about the hot water. I figured a fancy girl like you wouldn't even want to shower in a place like this."

"You could have asked. Maybe I wanted to shower with you. Or you could have stayed in bed with me. *Fancy girls still want to be wanted.*"

The shower dial squeaked as David turned it off. He opened the curtain with a swish and gave Lily an earnest look with his baby blue eyes. She wondered if he ever looked at his wife the same way.

"I do want you. Promise. Sorry about the shower. I should have asked first."

Lily crossed her arms across her chest and looked back at David. She made a show of clamping her mouth shut.

David sighed as he stepped out of the shower. He wrapped a towel around his waist and sat down on the toilet. His hair dripped onto the tile floor, adding to the dampness of the room. It made Lily's toes curl on the cold linoleum.

"What's really bothering you? It isn't just that I took a shower without asking, is it?"

"Did you tell her yet?"

David's head dropped as he shook it no.

"You said you were going to tell her. You keep saying it, but you're not actually doing it. So where does that leave me?" She held her hands out wide and spun in a full circle. "Here, in this trashy motel."

David opened his mouth to speak, but she stopped him.

"I've been patient. More than patient, actually. Wouldn't you agree?"

David's head fell, and he gave her a single, subtle nod.

"We both agreed it was time, didn't we?"

"Yes, but..."

"I can put up with this crappy motel. I can tolerate the sideways looks we get. And I admit, sneaking around was kind of hot - for a while. But I'm tired of sharing you. I'm tired of losing you over and over. I want a life with you. We need to get out of here, just you and me. Start something fresh."

David stood and wrapped his arms around her naked waist and whispered kisses on her neck.

"You're not losing me. And I promise, I'll tell her. But it's complicated. I'm waiting for the right time."

This had been David's standard excuse now for a few months, and Lily was wondering if he was ever going to get around to it. There was a lot that Lily could put up with: sneaking around in this dump of a room, being the "other" woman, David's clumsiness in bed. But if David wasn't ever going to end things with his wife, well... Lily would just have to find another man to get her away from the house for good.

"It seems to me like you don't want her to find out. I'm starting to think it's me that's being strung along."

David gave her a quick peck on the cheek. "I'm not playing with you. I promise." He walked out of the bathroom and stepped into his pants.

"Why do you shower every time we're together?"

David shrugged as he buttoned his shirt. "Uh... she thinks I'm at the gym. So, it sorta makes sense to come home showered."

"I think you're scared she'll smell me on you. And then I won't be your little secret anymore."

In a defensive tone, David said, "It's not forever. Just until the right time."

"When?"

David finished dressing and grabbed his duffel.

"Soon. I promise." He leaned down and kissed her. Then, as was their custom, left alone. He was always first to leave, and she always waited, careful to give enough time that a casual observer wouldn't connect the two. She dressed, ran her hand through her hair, and gave herself a once over in the mirror. Years of hairspray residue gave it a dull and fuzzy appearance.

A shrill ring broke the silence. Lily reached for her cell, but it remained dark and undisturbed. On the desk was the motel's room phone, discolored with age, wobbling with each ring.

Lily stared at it, suspicious of who might be on the other end. No one knew she was here, at least to her knowledge. Reasoning it to be the front desk, Lily picked the phone off the cradle and held the large earpiece up to her ear.

"Hello?"

There was light static, but no response on the other end.

"Hello?" she asked again, her annoyance coming through loud and clear.

There was just quiet on the other side, reminiscent of winter breezes and whispers. For a second, Lily thought she detected a voice. Thoughts of David's wife invaded her mind. For all her talk of wanting David to break things off, there was also comfort in the secret as well. Once word got out, there was no telling what nasty names people would call her.

Homewrecker.

Slut.

Whore.

All of which would be unfair, Lily told herself. She and David had just sort of happened, the same as any relationship happens. Life had become something dreadful, and they found escape in each other. Admittedly, their relationship focused on the physical aspects (albeit unsatisfying), but Lily was certain it would evolve into something more, if given a little more time. It could turn into something that could take her out of this town and away from The Manor.

Lily slammed the phone down. Her mouth was tight, her fingers still clenching the receiver. Then she snatched up her clothes and left.

Chapter Ten

Nathan crossed the threshold into his temporary accommodations. All at once, a musty odor caused his nose to wrinkle. The room had the aroma that only comes from long stretches of time and stillness. Nathan forced himself to breathe in the stale air. It carried faint hints of dirt and water. He couldn't help but think about the ditch.

Nathan looked at Upham, who almost certainly was avoiding his questions, but as to why, he wasn't sure. He told himself that it was unfounded paranoia, likely a symptom of his accident. For all he knew, he had a concussion, which was causing his imagination to act up. Like in the woods.

You didn't imagine the lights blowing up though...

Nathan tried to push the thought away, but it nagged at him. Something about it reminded him of Rachel's plate breaking.

"If you will forgive the room, Mr. Stevens. I don't have as much help as I once did, and the rooms on this side of the house just don't get cleaned as often as I'd like." Upham explained.

"No, this is fine. I'm sure I'll be very comfortable here,"

Nathan replied, although he made a mental note to open some windows. The night air would chill the room, but it would do the space some good. However, that would be for later. Right now, he craved a hot shower and sleep.

"Sit here on the bed. Let's see what the damage is."

He guided Nathan to sit and then peered down his long nose as he inspected Nathan's head. He squinted hard and puckered his mouth, as if in deep concentration. His glasses would slide down his nose, and he would push them back into place. Nathan grimaced as Upham parted his hair, combing for injuries.

"It's fortunate I hadn't gone to bed yet. You nearly had a cold night on the porch."

"I hope I didn't wake anyone," Nathan said through gritted teeth.

"No, they wouldn't have heard. Their rooms are much further back, and sound tends to travel up in this house. It was only chance that I happened to be there, and a good chance it was."

He parted another section of hair and peered, as if he were looking for lice. He picked a bit of glass from Nathan's scalp and held it out in his palm for Nathan to see. Upham stood and gave an approving nod, satisfied with his work.

"You've got a nasty bruise, but the cut isn't too deep. You should clean it though, to avoid infection. All things considered, it appears you were pretty lucky."

"Hm. I'll be lucky if I don't have a concussion," said Nathan.

Upham's eyes got a little wider, as if he hadn't considered that possibility. He made a move to resume inspection, but Nathan leaned his head away from further fussing.

"Upham, I'm fine. If I start acting weird, then go ahead and call an ambulance. But until then, it's not necessary. I'm fine, I promise."

Not yet convinced, Upham said, "How about a bottle of aspirin and some food, then?"

"That I would take. Thank you."

"Very well. You can shower and I'll bring it up to you. Are you ok to walk on your own?"

Nathan laughed. "I've walked this far. I think I can manage."

Upham pointed across the room. "You have your own bathroom and shower through that door. Every consideration was made when the house was built. I think you'll find everything you could ever need here at Thurman Manor." Upham stood a little taller when he informed Nathan of that part. He continued, "I'll leave you to get settled. If you'll give me a few moments, I'll go fetch you a sandwich and some aspirin."

"Thank you. I appreciate it," Nathan said.

Upham gave a curt little bow and left Nathan alone.

Nathan looked around the room at what would be his residence for the next several days. He was at the corner of the house. Two large windows, identical to all the others, lined each of the exterior walls. One side looked over the drive, the other provided him a clear view of the lake. Somehow, the room wasn't quite where he'd expected it to be. The bedroom sat further back from the main entry than he would have judged. From the front, a casual observer would have said the house was square in its construction, but Nathan decided square-*ish* was a better description. From his window, he could see the opposite corner of the house, as if the front curved into itself like a crescent moon. He hadn't noticed it before; everything appeared straight. But he knew it must curve, ever so slightly, to achieve such a vantage point from his room.

In addition to his bed, the room had a small desk with a lamp on top, and a large closet left bare. A reading chair was in one corner, and a full-length mirror was placed in the other. White crown molding accented cream-colored walls.

Nathan placed his pack near the desk and looked out the lakeside window. It was pitch black outside, making the water look oily and thick. He reached into his backpack and dug out his computer. He turned it in multiple directions, inspecting for damage. By some miracle, it survived. Nathan flipped open the screen and hit the power button and after a moment, he heard the familiar chime, and the screen lit up.

Finally, something went right.

The screensaver kicked on and hypnotic swirls danced across the screen in abstract shapes. Nathan massaged his neck as he allowed the lines and random movement to calm him. He wondered if this was the modern-day version of watching a campfire. He swiveled his head to the left and right, trying to loosen things up, but had no luck.

The shower helped to relieve the muscle tension. Nathan let the water sluice off his chin and watched dirt and blood swirl down the drain. He toweled off, careful to not rub his head too hard and re-open his wounds. With only the towel to cover himself, he stepped out from the bathroom and walked to one of the large windows overlooking the drive. Below him was a roundabout, connecting to the long drive that led beyond to the outside. Through the glass, Nathan saw beams of light approaching. The car came to a quick stop in the roundabout, and he watched as Lily stepped out. Her dark hair was shimmery in the moonlight. She walked away from the house and toward the lake. There was something about her that drew Nathan to watch, something more than her exceedingly rare and desirable figure. There was something in the way she walked that reminded Nathan of Rachel, and he cherished the reminder of his wife. He watched her from the privacy of his room, only wanting for his bride.

Nathan was still mid-dream when he noticed Lily looking up at his window. He had the distinct feeling they had made eye contact, but if she'd spotted him looking, she made no move to hide herself. Instead, she twirled her hair, twisting it around in spirals. He spun away as his face flushed with embarrassment at what she must have perceived as voyeurism.

There was a gentle knock on his door. Thankful for the interruption, Nathan opened it to find Upham holding a silver tray, complete with sandwich, tea, and the promised aspirin.

"This should do until morning, Mr. Stevens."

"It's great. Thank you, Upham."

"I've also taken the liberty of gathering a few clean clothes for you. These are fresh from Tommy's wash. He's roughly your size. I'm sure in the morning arrangements can be made to replace some of your things. But in the meantime, these should do."

Upham placed a bundle of crisp folded jeans, a hoodie and two t-shirts on the bed, and then turned to leave. When he got to the door, he turned and said, "Mr. Stevens, a word of caution. It would be best if you were to remain in your room for the evening. It's a large house. One can get lost in the halls. You would do well to not wander alone."

With that, he left Nathan alone in the room.

Just Outside Nathan's door, Upham was thinking hard. Wrestling with himself.

Leave it alone. He will be left alone. No need to involve him.

His hand was shaking. It was outstretched, and his fingers gripped a brass key. The tip of the key was just an inch from the lock. It would be easy, just a second's worth of time. Just a quick turn, and it would be done. Yes, probably Nathan would hear, but he'd be confused at first. He might even be in the bathroom. Maybe he wouldn't hear the rattle of the lock as the key turned in the old tumbler. There would be time. But Nathan would know. He'd have to be let out eventually. And when released, he'd emerge fuming. And worse than that, he'd have questions. Questions Upham didn't want to answer.

Somewhere in his head, a voice spoke to him. *Do it. Turn the lock. Keep him in there.*

He imagined inserting the key. It would be loose, a little too much slack from years of wear. But when it caught, he'd feel the brass head of the key bump up against the tumblers, and one by one they'd give. The mechanism would turn to the right, and he'd feel the lock secure. There would be a quiet but comforting little click. And that would be it.

The key vibrated like a hummingbird's wings, very near the lock, but not yet inserted. He shook the thoughts from his head like a boxer that had taken a hit. Upham stuffed the key back into his pocket and retreated down the hall.

Nathan collapsed on the bed, only to be visited by vivid dreams. He was in the bedroom, outside his own skin, looking at himself sleeping. He felt, rather than heard, whatever lurked in the hall. A dark ribbon was gliding outside the door, its diamond shaped head emerging from the shadows, slithering its way toward him. It worked its legless body down the corridor, and pausing outside his door, held itself rigid in the air, searching with a forked tongue. The snake dipped its head down, licking under the door. The serpent grew in size until its body was thick and fat and hungry. He tried to yell to his sleeping self and provide a warning, but nothing would come out. In the dream, there was only silence and slow movement. He saw silvery eyes in the dark, searching for his body that resided in the real world, unaware of imminent danger. Its pointed tongue flicked back and forth, tasting, sensing for prey. It's black form invisible in the dark, desperate to find someone to devour.

Chapter Eleven

Morning light crept in through the windows. As usual, Nathan's sleep had been tortured and restless, but he had no memory of what his mind had conjured in order to betray him.

Light evaporated his nightmares like it did the mist over the lake. Wearing only Tommy's loaned jeans, Nathan assessed his wounds in the full-length mirror. He turned his head and saw his injuries with clarity. The seatbelt had left a nasty bruise across his chest, and a knot decorated the left side of his head. It stuck out oddly at the point of impact. Nathan touched it and risked a little pressure. It still hurt, but the pain was a little less sharp than last night had been. He made an attempt to cover the lump with his hair but gave up when his bangs refused to cooperate. The bruise would be displayed like a badge of honor, the mark of a survivor. Then, all at once, the mood reversed, and Nathan caught himself wishing the crash had taken his life. But he pushed it back down where thoughts such as those belonged.

He finished dressing and then walked out of the room and to whatever the day had in store. In the hall, everything was quiet, not one sign that anyone else was awake. If they were, being breakfast time, Nathan reasoned the most likely spot would be near the kitchen, or a dining room of some kind. Nathan figured he should retrace his steps and go back the way Upham had led him the night before. He found the service door and pulled, but found it locked tight. He shrugged and headed off toward the other end of the hall, where he knew the main staircase to be.

The hall was long and tunnel-like, and it gave him an offsetting feeling, as if it twisted just enough to put a person off balance.

I must have smacked my head even harder than I thought.

He could imagine how he might frame a photograph here, with the seemingly unending sightlines and focal points. He kept walking past many doors, all of which were shut tight, until he came upon one that was ajar. Nathan peeked inside, and without having meant to, found himself inside Rachel's old bedroom.

Very little about the room had changed since she'd moved out and it had kept its adolescent atmosphere. A pink bedspread lay atop her mattress. Band posters decorated the walls, their edges curled up and yellowed with age. Both children's and young adult titles populated the bookshelves, and the in-between spaces housed toys she hadn't yet brought herself to part with. Stuffed animals, a red ball, dolls in frilly dresses... Basic things most kids would have played with. The toys weren't quite out of reach but were far enough removed to provide plausible deniability to a judgmental friend with an urge to tease.

No one had bothered to change a thing when Rachel moved out, having left it untouched, like a monument or a time capsule. The only remnants from her most recent life was the empty suitcase, lying on a chair, and its former contents, sorted and inventoried on the pink bedspread.

Nathan assumed Elisabeth had organized her belongings. The police would have searched through everything after her suicide, looking for a note. Nathan didn't think the police would concern themselves with tidiness during a search. To everyone's frustration, they had found nothing. Not in her room, nor in the barn where she'd hung herself. This complete lack of explanation seemed particularly cruel and only added to Nathan's confusion.

He looked at all her items spread out on the bed. Rachel had packed light, just enough for a few days' stay. Her toiletries were packed in individual plastic bags: toothbrush, comb, a hairdryer. Makeup and lip gloss. Enough clothing options to prevent wearing the same shirt two days in a row. All neat and tidy and organized, and yet it seemed to Nathan something was missing, something misplaced, although he couldn't decide what that might be. It was like having left home only to forget if you'd locked the door, or the nagging fear a burner had been left on unattended. Nathan pushed it aside; it would come to him later.

"Doesn't seem real, does it?"

Nathan's heart skipped a beat, and he jumped. He twisted around to see Lily in the doorway, a prankster's grin plastered on her face. Nathan felt his face flush red.

"I didn't mean to scare you," Lily said. "I wasn't trying to be sneaky."

Nathan laughed nervously. "Didn't realize I was so focused here. Jumpy, I guess. Nerves are all shot." Nathan massaged his forehead in a vain attempt to cure a headache.

Lily stepped into the room and sat on the bed. Her white skirt hiked up her thigh, and she pushed it back down in a smoothing motion. Soft black hair spilled over her shoulders, highlighting her beautiful blue eyes. But there was a danger there as well, as if a single glance could draw you in and make you happy to be eaten alive.

"I know what you mean. Nothing feels normal anymore. I can't believe she's gone."

"No, it doesn't seem real at all." Nathan looked down at Rachel's suitcase. There was a red sweater on top. He touched the soft sleeve and tried to think of the last time she'd worn it. He couldn't quite recall.

"I remember that sweater. Rachel always looked great in that," Lily said.

"I can't say I remember seeing her in it. I know she did. But I just can't seem to picture it."

Lily shrugged. "It'll come back. I bet I have a photo of her in it somewhere. Would you want it?"

"Yeah, I'd love it." Nathan remembered the video he was creating and said, "How many pictures do you have of Rachel?"

Lily scrunched her mouth up, and again Nathan was reminded of Rachel. "I dunno. A lot, I think. Why do you ask?"

"I'm making a video for her funeral. Still shots, all edited together. I'm just looking for any photos that might fit it well."

"Tell you what. I'll find whatever I can, and I'll get them to you."

"Thanks, I appreciate it."

"How's the other guy?" Lily said.

"Sorry?" Nathan looked at her, confused at what she was talking about.

Lily pointed to his face. "Your head looks like it took a beating. You get into it with the locals?"

Nathan smirked grimly. "No, nothing like that. I had an accident on the way here."

"That sucks. How's your car? I didn't see it parked here when I got home."

Nathan shook his head. "My car isn't doing so hot. Last I saw, it was sideways in a ditch. Unless someone towed it out, it's still there."

"So, you walked here? How far?"

"Not sure. Far enough, though. I got here pretty late. Everyone had already gone to bed. Except Upham. He got me setup in a room."

"That's good. Where?"

"Second floor. I've got a room toward the lake."

Lily twisted her thick hair around a finger and held eye contact for longer than necessary. "Beautiful view on that side of the house, isn't it?"

He remembered Lily by the lake last night, at the time reminding him so much of Rachel, and how he'd watched from his window, and how she'd looked up at him, and the distinct sense she'd caught him staring. Despite the fact he'd been fantasizing about Rachel, Nathan still felt like a child caught doing something forbidden. But what good would it do to defend himself? Any denial would only make him look guilty. He wasn't sure if Lily was waiting for a confession; she gave no impression she was angry. In fact, if anything, she appeared amused. Everything about Lily seemed to have an air of playful confidence, the sort that comes from being a popular distraction.

Certain she'd spotted him, though unsure of her intent, Nathan replied, "Yeah, it's a great view. The lake is beautiful."

Lily's grin widened and she said, "I agree. I think the lake view is probably the best in the house." She rose from the bed and leaned her head toward the door, beckoning for Nathan to follow.

"Come on. Breakfast is ready."

. . .

She led him downstairs to the dining room, which was furnished for far more people than currently occupied it. In the center was a large table, polished to a mirror finish. It was more rectangle than square, with an ornate runner down the middle. Off to the side was a skinny, matching table, upon which sat a coffee carafe and mugs, as well as a selection of various teas.

"Look who I ran into," Lily said. Two faces turned up at Nathan: the ever-inseparable twins, Tommy and Lucas. The third, Elisabeth, ignored him by pretending to absorb herself in her magazine.

Lily stepped to one side as if to present Nathan to the room. If he was waiting for applause, none came.

As usual, Tommy was the first to open his mouth. "You look terrible."

In fairness, Tommy was right. The bruising on Nathan's head had turned a darker shade of purple, and it had spread out across his face. His muscles were stiff from the whiplash and made his steps labored. On top of that, the borrowed clothing didn't quite fit right. The shirt was a little too big, and the pants were too short, giving him an awkward appearance.

Nathan smirked and replied, "Only 'cause these are your clothes."

Tommy laughed at the retort. "You only wish you could pull off my style. It takes years of practice to make it seem as effortless as I do." He pointed over to the skinny table. "Help yourself to a cup of coffee. Upham just filled it."

Nathan nodded in thanks and filled a cup before sitting down at the main table, across from the twins. They shared similarities but were easy enough to tell apart.

Across from him was Tommy, the elder twin, slouched

in his chair. He wore a slim fitting button down, untucked, and glasses that gave him a studious air. In contrast, his mere minutes younger brother, Lucas, wore his standard hoodie, which he'd pulled up over his head. Beneath the hood, his skin looked pale and oily. He gave a half-hearted grunt to Nathan as he chewed his breakfast with an open mouth. Flecks of mashed food fell back onto his plate, which he promptly scooped up with his spoon.

Lily was busy making herself a cup of tea, stirring in a spoon of honey. She let go of the spoon and it clanked harshly on the mug. She took two steps to her right, picked up an empty serving tray, and exclaimed, "Again? You do this all the time, Lucas. Leave some for the rest of us!" She held out the empty platter as if it were proof enough and wore an accusatory look on her face. Nathan thought he saw a slight little smirk on Lucas, but it vanished as soon as he'd spotted it.

"I don't know what you're talking about," Lucas said, and then turned his attention back to his plate.

"Oh really? I find that hard to believe."

Without looking up, Elisabeth scolded them. "Children, act your age. This isn't becoming of your heritage. And besides Lily, you could afford to skip a meal." Elisabeth glanced over the top of her magazine, her judgmental eyes looking down at Lily's waistline. Lily seemed to grow smaller and fell quiet, then grabbed her tea and sat down by Nathan. She resumed stirring her tea, making slow clockwise circles, but she didn't drink it. Eventually, her tea would run cold and be tossed down the drain.

Nathan kept his eyes down at his own placemat, feeling like an intruder. For some odd reason, he was terribly self-conscious of his hands. Needing to occupy them, he wrapped them around the hot mug in front of him and sipped at the coffee. By all accounts, it was delicious. But

Nathan found himself wishing to be back in the torn leather booth at Chuck's with Lewis, drinking cheap drip coffee and chatting with his friend. That booth felt like safety, a place where he could share his thoughts and fears. Terrible as it was, discussing Rachel's funeral felt simpler with Lewis. Now, he found himself struggling to find a way to address the obvious.

Elisabeth broke the awkward silence and said, "Nathan, I trust your delay yesterday won't prove too much of a hinderance to our funeral discussions."

"Why, what happened?" Tommy sat up straight in his chair, his attention rapt at the possibility of someone else's drama. Nathan wondered if Tommy was happy for a distraction from the elephant in the room.

Elisabeth answered for him. "He crashed his car on the way here."

"How did that happen? You fall asleep or something?" Tommy asked. "You seem pretty tired."

Nathan tried to hide his annoyance. "No, I didn't fall asleep. Not much to tell, really. It all happened pretty fast."

Memories of a ghostly phone call popped into Nathan's head. He remembered silence on the other end, and the desperation for an answer.

"A tire blew out, actually. The car spun and landed sideways in a ditch."

For the third time, Nathan explained the crash, answering the same questions about his car, his walk, and where Upham placed him. He left out his stroll through the woods. His conversations were starting to feel like déjà vu.

"Why didn't you just call?" asked Tommy. "We would have come and picked you up."

"Believe me, I would have. Things would have been a lot easier. But my phone got broken in the crash. It shattered, wouldn't work at all."

Tommy gave a little groan and nodded, understanding the impact that not having a phone would cause.

Lucas chimed in, "Tommy and I are headed to town today. You're welcome to tag along if you want. We could drop you off to replace some of your things." There was a clank from Elisabeth's end of the table as she set her cup down too hard.

Nathan swallowed the coffee in his mouth and said, "I'd appreciate it, thanks. What time are you leaving?"

"We'll head out right after breakfast, if that works for you?"

Wary of offending his mother-in-law, Nathan wasn't sure how to proceed. Elisabeth had invited him, not her children, and he wanted to find out what plans she had in mind before committing to anything. However, a fresh set of clothing would go a long way toward making him a bit more comfortable before diving into something as difficult as his wife's funeral.

"Maybe, as long as it works for everyone. Elisabeth, what were you thinking for today? When were you wanting to talk though memorial plans?"

Elisabeth took a sip of her tea before answering. "The schedule is already off, so what's a few more hours? Do what you want to do." She gave him a thin smile, but Nathan saw the stress behind the veil. On the surface, Elisabeth was a beautiful woman, with high cheekbones and the same enchanting blue eyes she'd given Lily. But it was a mask, hiding pain and grief and devastation.

Wanting to be accommodating, Nathan said, "If there's a schedule to keep, I can figure out how to get my things replaced later. It's not a big deal. I don't want to cause a problem."

Elisabeth relented, if only on the surface. "No, no. Go with the boys. Edward is in a meeting with Jonathan, anyway. They'll most likely be talking for hours, so you may as well make the most of the time."

Trying to make conversation, Nathan said, "Sounds like an important meeting." It was the sort of small talk comment one makes when nervous, equivalent to "what's the weather looking like this weekend", or "how's the job going", questions intended as filler to occupy empty space. But having no other starting point, Nathan was making whatever attempt he could at building a bridge.

For the first time since her mother's comment regarding her weight, Lily spoke. "Ugh, it's so boring. They just talk business for hours on end."

Nathan turned to her. "So, like forecasting and trend analysis? Things like that?"

Tommy's ears perked up, and he leaned toward Nathan. "Are you familiar? Some of this stuff gets pretty complicated. I'm in the middle of getting my MBA, so this is kind of a hot topic for me."

Elisabeth chuckled and shook her head. "No, Tommy. Nathan is a photographer. Remember? He didn't go to business school. He wouldn't have any interest in hearing about finance."

Nathan gave a half-hearted smile, unsure how to respond. It was true he hadn't gone to business school. In fact, if he hadn't found photography, chances were he would have dropped out of high school. He still remembered when Mr. Gibbons, who was in charge of the school yearbook, had reached out and asked if he wanted to be involved. At first, Nathan had no interest, but after he discovered Michelle Rodgers was on the yearbook committee, he was sold. Within a month, photography had overtaken the interest he had in Michelle. Over the years, Nathan watched friends and acquaintances flounder between one career path and another, struggling to find a balance between work and passion. He counted himself one of the lucky few to have found his calling in his teenage years.

"Uh, yeah. I never went to business school. Instead, I took some community college classes for photography, and then just kind of went for it." Nathan laughed nervously.

All their eyes were on him, none of them comprehending a phrase like *community* college. Nathan doubted the phrase had ever even been said within the walls of the house. Aside from Lily's constant stirring, awkward silence filled the room.

Elisabeth broke the tension. "Well, not everyone is meant for graduate degrees. It's a difficult path and requires a lot of discipline. Isn't that right, Tommy?"

Tommy nodded in agreement. "Yeah, Mom. It can be tough."

Elisabeth continued, "Tommy is studying so he can take over the family business one day. It's a big responsibility. So, we've ensured he's getting every advantage in his education, just to provide the tools available to run a company such as ours."

Unsure of what to say, Nathan simply agreed and said, "That sounds like a great plan."

"If you boys are going to run errands, you should get to it. Nathan, when you get back, please come find me. Obviously, there's a lot for all of us to talk about." Without waiting for a reply, she rose from her seat and left the dining room.

Lucas nudged Tommy. "You ready?"

Tommy sighed, "Yeah, let's go."

Chapter Twelve

By this point the morning had turned to early afternoon. Tommy was driving the three of them in his Land Rover, a congratulations gift for having started his MBA program. But started was about all that could be claimed in regards to his education. The truth was Tommy had studied the car more than his books. Lucas took the back, citing more legroom, which put Nathan shotgun. The drive would take a little less than an hour, a feature of living in a remote area.

Lucas fidgeted in the back and kept glancing over his shoulder until The Manor was lost in the rear window. As soon as they were out of eyesight, Lucas dug into his pocket and pulled out a joint. He fired it up and took a puff, and smoke overwhelmed the vehicle.

Tommy clicked a switch on his door and there was a whirring sound as the window rolled down.

"Can you not do that right now?"

"Do what right now?" Lucas asked, his voice strained as he held back a cough.

"You know what. Smoke in my car. It'll make the seats stink."

In response, Lucas took a massive drag and coughed out

a cloud of pungent blue smoke. He must have believed this to be a great joke because he cackled and fell over on his side. Not sharing his brother's comedic sensibilities, Tommy rolled another window down to vent the car. But he said nothing more about it.

As a matter of personal policy, Tommy had been saying nothing of his brother's habits for quite some time. After all, what Lucas did was Lucas's business, and so long as no one got hurt, what was the harm? There had been concerns in the past with Lucas's behavior, (skipping school, not coming home on time, acting out in public) but all in all, it seemed fine to Tommy. Sure, he smoked some pot, but who didn't? Tommy himself was known to partake from time to time, although not in his own car. No, Mom wouldn't like it if she found out (*she probably knew anyway, actually*), but that wasn't his problem.

Rachel had seemed to think differently. At one point, she came to him, concerned about Lucas. It had been after school one day. Rachel caught him in the drive when he got home. Apparently, the school had called and reported that Lucas never showed for class.

"I'm getting worried. He's not acting right."

Tommy rolled his eyes. "Oh, so what? He skipped class. Who cares?"

"It's not only that. He doesn't look healthy. His eyes are always bloodshot. And he tries to hide it, but I can smell alcohol on his breath."

"Rach, I don't see what the big deal is. Everybody drinks. Who doesn't party and get bloodshot eyes? It's all normal - just part of growing up."

Rachel paused, considering Tommy's statement. "No, this is something different. I think he's got a real problem."

"Fine. If you think it's so important, go say something."

Rachel shook her head. "He doesn't listen to me. But he would listen to you."

Deep down, Tommy knew all of this to be true, his proof being that his own relationship with Lucas had seemed different as of late. Instead of a tight bond shared since birth, Lucas had grown cold and distant, something that Tommy couldn't make sense of.

"Fine, I'll talk to him."

But Tommy never did.

Still chuckling to himself, Lucas leaned forward between the two front seats and offered the joint up toward Nathan.

Nathan held a hand up. "No, thanks. I'm good."

Lucas looked confused. "You religious or something? Don't tell me it's allergies." Lucas started into another fit of laughter.

"No, it's just not my thing," Nathan explained.

"Well, I guess I'll have to smoke your share," Lucas said before taking another long drag.

He passed it up to Tommy, who took it, but took only one shallow little hit before handing it back. In his mirror, Tommy saw Lucas reach into his jacket and pull out a crumpled packet, held tight with a red rubber band. He unrolled it, revealing bright neon letters that spelled out "Fun Dip" on the package. A wild cartoon drawing of a kid, tongue out and crazy eyed, decorated the front. Lucas wet a finger in his mouth, raked it through the powder, and sucked the candy clean. A few minutes later, he was passed out in the back.

With Lucas's antics at a temporary standstill, they drove in silence for a while. No conversation, no chatter. It made Tommy uncomfortable; he hated being alone with his thoughts. Quiet moments tended to allow uncomfortable subjects to surface. Before Rachel died, something as small as his overdue term paper seemed overwhelming. But grades hardly seemed worth worrying over in the present situation. He glanced over at Nathan, who seemed to be more than content to observe the landscape as they sped along. After a couple minutes, Tommy noticed a strange habit Nathan had, a constant patting of his jacket pocket, like a subconscious tick.

Unable to stand the silence a moment longer, Tommy said, "What do you keep checking?"

Nathan shook his head as if coming out of a dream. "I'm sorry?"

"You keep patting your jacket pocket. Did you forget something?"

Nathan gave a polite laugh. "Force of habit. I keep reaching for my phone. I keep forgetting it's destroyed." With a twinge of regret, he added, "Just like my car."

"Ah, that makes sense. Sorry man, that sucks." He added, "What else did you lose in the crash?"

"Pretty much everything. Except my computer, which is fortunate. My clothes might have survived, I'm not sure. They were all in the trunk. I couldn't get to them, so I'll have to find out about those once my car gets towed out."

"When we get into town, you'll be able to get set up. Not much selection in terms of shopping, but there's a Walmart. Nothing fancy, but they have pretty much everything. You can get your clothing replaced, plus I think they have one of those little cell phone booths. You know the kind; they have a little bit of everything, but never anything good... But you can probably get a replacement while you're there."

"Thanks. I appreciate the ride."

"No worries. While you shop, I have to run Lucas on an

errand. Will you be good for a while? We shouldn't be too long."

"I'll be fine. I'm sure I can find something to do."

"You'll be the first if you do. There's not much fun to be had in town. Small town like this, it's a miracle we have even a Walmart within driving distance."

They drove the rest of the way with scattered small talk, but nothing of consequence. Tommy kept meaning to bring up Rachel's death, to ask Nathan how he was doing, but each possible opening felt uncomfortable, so he said nothing. Instead, Tommy filled the space with weather, how he liked his car, generalities about school, and anything else that wouldn't risk pain. Although he put on his easy-going facade, Rachel's death had hit him hard. Growing up in Thurman Manor had always meant having a level of fear and uncertainty (never to be discussed, of course), but Rachel's death made it all more real, more *alive*. Before her death, they had just been stories, but now...

Trees turned to fields of grass, followed by increasing signs of civilization. Run-down houses popped up on the outskirts and transitioned to run-down houses of marginally better condition. Soon, it transitioned into storefronts and shops, the heart of downtown Silas Ridge. The Walmart came into view up ahead.

Tommy pulled into the parking lot, which was larger than Nathan had expected. Based on what he saw driving in, he wouldn't have guessed a little plaza like this would exist in Silas Ridge. It was like a slice of everything he found familiar plopped down in the middle of a foreign country. Tommy had made Silas Ridge sound out of touch and helpless, as if it were inhabited by a mere twenty-one people, two-thirds of which were rednecks. What Nathan saw instead was a bustling, respectable suburb.

Lucas was still snoozing in the back when Tommy pulled the Range Rover up to the entrance. Tommy hit the brakes harder than necessary at the passenger drop off, jerking the vehicle forward. Lucas ceased snoring temporarily, but instead of sitting up, repositioned himself in the back seat. Tommy shot Nathan a smirk. Nathan hopped out and worked his way past the hood. Tommy's window rolled down. "You'll probably get done before us. Get your stuff, and then go kill some time at the coffee shop across the lot. I'll pick you up there."

"Will do. Thanks again."

Tommy pulled away, leaving Nathan alone and smelling of weed. He swatted at his clothing like he was trying to brush the guilt away. An elderly man greeted him as he walked in. He was hobbled over, but everything about him seemed cheerful. His blue vest was too large for him, but that only added to his charm. Nathan returned the nod without breaking his determined pace. There was a massive stack of carts nearby, and Nathan scoped them out, trying to pick the one with four good wheels. He got three. The fourth spun around like an energetic, confused puppy.

He went to the men's section and grabbed a pack of underwear and socks, a pair of jeans, and a couple of simple button-down shirts, favoring muted colors as they were a better representation of his current state.

He noticed a small rack toward the back. A bright sign was on top: CLEARANCE, UP TO 70% OFF SUIT PANTS AND COATS!

For the first time, Nathan realized he didn't even own a suit. What was he expecting to wear to Rachel's memorial? He didn't oppose dressing up, but the need had never come up. Even on his wedding day, he'd only worn his nicest button down. He kicked himself for not having thought of this sooner. He imagined he'd be going to a proper shop for a proper fit, but reality caught up and reminded him that such an option would be outside his financial abilities. Form fitting black suits that came in garment bags were not luxuries he could afford. He looked again at the sign. The 70% discount called to him, a reminder that this was likely the best he may ever do. So, he combed through the rack and found a coat and pants that were a reasonable match. He tried them on and gave them a once over in the dressing room mirror. After that, he snagged a plain black tie and black shoes and a belt to complete the ensemble.

He tossed all the clothing into his shopping cart and wheeled it toward the back of the store. The front right wheel squeaked with each revolution, like a metronome. Nathan found the electronics section, filled with large televisions and loud signage advertising "LOWEST PRICE, GUARANTEED". There were long aisles filled with movies, and at one end a disorganized bin of bargain films, ransacked by children and deal hunters alike. In the center of all this, in between the aisles, was a booth of cellphones.

Various phones were out on display, highlighting the newest and most advanced models to date, all with more screen, more pixels, and more speed. Nathan was no luddite, but he found little use for many of these advanced features, especially regarding the camera, which always seemed to get the most hype. He just needed his old model back.

A kid was behind the counter playing some sort of game on his own device. He wore a polo shirt that made him stand out from the rest of the store staff. Maybe the cell companies leased space within the larger store. This kid might not even be a Walmart employee. Maybe he worked for the cell company and was assigned to this booth. Not that any of this mattered to Nathan. As long as he could get him back up and running, it didn't matter who signed his paychecks.

The kid's neck crooked forward at an odd angle, giving the impression that he rarely looked up from his screen. Nathan wondered what future generations would look like, and what sorts of back problems would be common to the population. In his mind, he saw the evolution of man advancing through the ages from left to right. At the far-right side was the new model of homo sapiens, with a long-crooked neck and hunched over a glowing square. And right behind him, peeking over his shoulder, was the outdated model, left in the dust.

Nathan waited just long enough for it to be awkward before realizing the kid wouldn't look up anytime soon.

Nathan cleared his throat to get his attention. "Hey, do you work here?"

The kid adjusted his crooked neck as if realizing Nathan had been waiting there for a time. "Oh, sorry. Can I help you?" His voice was nasal and unsure.

"I hope so. I need a new phone."

"New number? Or you want to upgrade the one you've got?"

"I want to keep my number. My phone got lost, so I just need to replace it. Nothing fancy."

"So, like, you want to upgrade the old one?"

The kid squinted at Nathan like his eyes hadn't yet adjusted from his video game, which made Nathan more annoyed.

Nathan tried to be as clear as he could. "No, I don't want an upgrade. That implies something better than what I had. I want the exact same thing as before."

The kid nodded like he understood. "I only do new sales here at the counter. If you want to just replace your old phone, it would need to go through insurance. Did you have insurance on your phone?"

"I'm not sure. Can you check?"

The kid traded the small cell phone screen for a larger computer monitor. He tapped several buttons, asked for Nathan's phone number and driver's license, and then looked at the screen some more.

"Good news. It looks like you have insurance on both your phones." The kid reached under the counter and came back up with a pamphlet. "All you have to do is call this number and they'll handle everything for you over the phone."

Nathan took the pamphlet in hand. "Is there any way I can do this here with you? I'm really stuck. I don't have anything, and I really need a phone today."

The kid tapped a few more buttons and stared at his screen, blinking at long intervals. "You're not due to upgrade for a few more months. You could buy one outright, though."

Nathan sighed in frustration. "And how much is that?"

The kid shrugged like the answer could be any number in existence. "Depends on the phone," he said. "On average they're around $1000."

Nathan looked at the pamphlet again. On the front cover he read "*$99, Overnight Guaranteed*" and decided he could wait a day.

"I'll go the insurance route. You have a phone I can use?"

The kid showed him the phone on the far-left display and went back to his game. Nathan picked the display phone up and found the dialer app. He punched in the number listed on the front of the pamphlet and an automated woman's voice provided navigation prompts. She sounded as fresh and chipper as the first time her message played. *"For new claims, press three"*, and he pressed three on the touchscreen. Nathan was told to hold for a moment, and after a short wait, another woman, a real woman, came on the phone and asked how she could be of assistance. Nathan explained his situation all over again. But the woman on the phone was quick, and it didn't take long for him to confirm his account and payment method. She explained that his claim would be processed, and a replacement would be overnighted to his home address. Nathan asked if an alternative address could be used. The woman explained that for security reasons, they could only ship the phone to the address on file.

"Do you still want to proceed with the claim?"

Nathan thought for a moment, and with a frustrated sigh, agreed.

What's a few more days?

He'd just get it when he got home. There's no one that he had to get in contact with, anyway. He could just email Lewis. Everything could wait for a bit longer. He finished the last details on the phone and let the woman recite a claim number back to him. He didn't bother to write it down.

Chapter Thirteen

After Nathan paid for his new clothes, he walked outside, giving a different greeter dressed in the same blue vest a little wave on his way out. He squinted in the bright sunlight, looking for the coffee shop Tommy had mentioned. He spotted his destination across the parking lot, set in a small strip between a dry cleaner and a hot dog shop. Nathan set off in a light jog across the blacktop, mindful of cars speeding through.

The coffee shop had a quaint, small-town atmosphere. An A-Frame stood to the left of the door, complete with curvy script displaying daily specials in colorful chalk. Most of the advertised choices were some variant of cinnamon apple spice, caramel apple, pumpkin vanilla lattes, or hot cider. Hand drawn renderings of each drink decorated the board, steam lines and all. A friendly chime greeted him as he walked through the door. The cafe was small, but clean, and offered the aroma of coffee beans and syrup. A pretty girl with a pony tail worked behind the counter. She had a petite frame and seemed to have a peppiness about her, like she was always bouncing.

"Be with you in a sec," she called as she rotated a mug

under a hissing machine. When it was done, she topped the latte with a generous portion of whip cream. She handed it to the customer in front of Nathan with a smile.

She turned her attention to Nathan as he stepped forward. Her smile matched the bright pink band in her hair. She had a name tag on that read Suzy.

"What can I get for you?"

"I'll have a coffee. Thanks."

"Cream and sugar?"

"Black, please."

She grabbed a mug and placed it under a large carafe, allowing it to fill up to the brim before passing it over to him. He handed a five to her and told her to keep the change.

Suzy nodded in thanks as she deposited the cash. "Are you new or are you passing through?" Nathan gave her a quizzical look. She shrugged and said, "Small towns. It's easy to recognize new faces."

"It doesn't seem that small to me."

Suzy leaned over the counter and looked at Nathan's shopping bags. "If you've been to the Walmart, you've seen it all." She grinned to herself and then added, "How long are you staying?"

"Only for a few days."

"Oh? Something fun, I hope. Perhaps a second trip to the Walmart?" She snorted as she laughed at her own joke.

Nathan afforded her a fake chuckle, but then hesitated, wanting to say more but questioning if he should. He preferred to maintain a healthy degree of privacy, especially with strangers, but Rachel's death weighed heavy on his mind. He needed to talk to someone, and Suzy seemed harmless, and for reasons unknown to him, genuinely interested.

"No, actually. I'm here for a funeral. Well, planning one anyway. Still figuring out the details."

Suzy's hand came up to her chest and covered her heart. "Oh no. I'm so sorry." She popped her cash register open and dug the five out and pushed it back toward Nathan. "Here, it's on the house."

"That's very kind," Nathan said, "but I'll pay for my coffee. You've got a business to run."

She shook her head. "Please, it's just a cup of coffee. It's not much, but I hope it can be a bright spot in your day."

Nathan shoved his money back in his pocket. "Thank you very much. Means a lot to me."

Suzy gave him a meek smile as Nathan took his drink. It might have been closer to pity. He looked around and found several chairs setup in a quiet corner. He sat down with his back against the wall and watched a few more customers come in. The first two ordered fancy drinks with lots of cream and spice; each drink required several minutes for Suzy to prepare. The third was a kid who, at a passing glance, looked to be edging out of his teenage years. He was bouncing back and forth on his feet like he was late for something. Nathan sensed a change in Suzy when he entered. A nervous energy. Rapid stolen glances in his direction. He watched her finish with the first two customers, and once they were out the door, the kid walked up to the counter. Even with his back turned to him, it was obvious the guy liked Suzy. Nathan watched her give a sweet-natured smile, patiently waiting for him to finish his shot, and then she agreed, her smile still in place. While Nathan was no lip reader, the shape her mouth made when giving her answer was an easy read. The guy stood a little taller, and walked out with a new bravado. Suzy took a deep breath and walked over to Nathan with a coffee pot in hand.

"Care for a refill?"

"That sounds great. Thank you."

Suzy poured until his mug was back up to the brim again.

"Thank you. Appreciate it very much." Nathan pointed toward the door with his mug. "That guy seemed sweet on you. He your boyfriend?"

Suzy's cheeks turned pink. "Oh, Ben? Yeah, I guess so. I mean, no. Not yet anyway. I said yes to a date with him. I'll see how it goes."

"And what's your gut feeling about how it's going to go?"

"Honestly? I'm not sure. Ben's nice enough, I guess. But he makes me feel weird sometimes. I can't explain it. I'm probably imagining it."

"Well, you gotta go with your gut. You can't force love."

"Yeah, I know. But sometimes I wonder - maybe I'm overthinking. It's not like there's a lot of choice to pick from around here. Ben might not be a perfect fit, but a girls gotta work with what she's given, you know? I don't want to end up alone."

Nathan sipped his coffee. "Well, the world's a big place, if you want to explore."

Suzy scoffed. "Easier said than done. People tend to stick around here. Once in Silas Ridge, always in Silas Ridge. Sometimes it seems like the only way to escape is to die." As soon as the last word had passed across her lips, she realized what she'd said and a mortified look came over her.

"I'm so sorry. That was a stupid thing to say."

Nathan gave her a forgiving smile. "Don't worry about it. No offense taken."

Suzy lingered a moment, hesitating to ask a question. When she worked up to it, it seemed like she had to blurt it out. "If you don't mind me asking, who did you lose?"

This was the first time he'd been asked the question. Until now, everyone already knew who Rachel was to him. Loving spouse, best friend. More privately, a fierce lover and a person who challenged him to be better.

Nathan's voice dropped. "My wife, Rachel."

Suzy covered her heart with her hand and her cheerful face fell. "I'm so sorry to hear that. It must be awful. I can't even imagine."

"Yeah... It's not been easy." He lifted his coffee up. "So, I extra appreciate the coffee."

Suzy said, "Where are you staying while you're here?"

Nathan finished his sip. "Not too far. But I guess that's relative. Her parents have a house up on the lake."

Suzy's eye opened wide. Her face turned several shades more pale. "You're talking about the Thurman place. Was your wife Rachel Thurman?"

"Stevens now, but yes. Thurman was her maiden name." Nathan's head tilted to one side. "Did you know her?"

Suzy shook her head in disbelief. "I knew *of* her," she said. "We didn't exactly hang out in the same social circles." Suzy's eyes darted around the room like she was looking for an explanation. "Everything seemed fine... I had no idea..."

"What do you mean by everything seemed fine?"

Suzy didn't seem to hear the question. She was looking at an empty seat. More to herself than Nathan, she said, "She was just here."

His ears perked, tuned up like a tight piano string. "What do you mean, she was just here?"

Suzy looked back. "Rachel was here, getting a coffee the other night."

Nathan was beyond intrigued. It was the start of an obsession. This was the first he'd heard anything about

Rachel doing anything other than being at her parent's house.

"When was this?"

"A couple of nights ago. I'm not exactly sure. Maybe early in the week? Sunday night maybe?"

Nathan did the math in his head, running dates and numbers and possibilities. Rachel would have been here right before she'd taken her own life. Either the day before, or perhaps mere hours before her death. If true, it was possible that Suzy was the last person who had seen Rachel alive.

Nathan leaned forward in his seat. "How did she seem? Was she upset?"

Suzy took a step back and eyed him, taking a more guarded tone. "I don't know. She was just here getting coffee. I didn't pay a lot of attention."

Nathan held his hands open at his sides and pleaded with her. "Suzy, please. Rachel..." He took a deep breath. "Rachel committed suicide."

He'd not said it out loud yet. It hit him hard; his own voice was foreign in that moment, uttering words he didn't quite comprehend. Like a virgin language; rough, clumsy, unfamiliar.

He continued, "There was no note, no explanation. I thought everything was fine. I didn't see it coming."

Suzy was clutching at her chest, like some sort of subconscious protection. "I'm so sorry. I didn't know."

"Please. Can you tell me about that night? I'm lost here. I... I just want some answers. You might have them."

Suzy made a quick glance at the door. "Ok. I'll sit down with you, and we can talk, although I don't know what all I can share that will help. And if any customers come in, I'll need to help them."

Nathan nodded that he understood. Suzy took a seat beside him, still holding the coffee pot.

"Thanks for doing this. Sorry if I get you in any trouble with your boss. You can tell him it's my fault."

Suzy sat up a little straighter and said, "There is no 'him'. I am the boss. I own the place."

Nathan's face flushed and he looked down, feeling stupid. "Sorry. I shouldn't have assumed."

With a little grin, she said, "That's nowhere near as bad as what I said to you. And anyway, I look younger than I am. I guess that's a good problem to have. I'll cash in on that someday, I'm sure."

"Suppose so. Still, I shouldn't have assumed anything. I didn't mean any offense."

She shrugged. "Well, like you said. No offense taken, right? And I still am young. Young enough that I shouldn't have been able to afford this place on my own, anyway." She looked thoughtful, as if she were recalling a memory. She said, "Oddly enough, in a sense, that actually has to do with the Thurmans."

Nathan looked surprised. "How so?"

"My grandfather worked construction. He was a roofer all his life. One job ended up with him working on the Thurman's house. Rumor has it there was a house fire and a section of the roof needed replaced, but that's neither here nor there. He had an accident one day. He fell while working and died on the job site."

Nathan pictured him slipping (*no, something inside said he was pushed*) from the roof, sliding down the shingles, trying to claw onto anything he could grip onto. Nathan saw him scream soundlessly as he tipped over the edge. In his mind, he didn't see the impact, but he heard the thud. And worst of all, the silence that came after.

"I'm very sorry to hear that."

"Thank you. But to be honest, we weren't ever close. I was a baby and never had a close relationship with him. If I miss anything, I guess it's missing what I never got to know, if that makes any sense."

Nathan thought about how grief and mourning weren't only about the past; it's for a future that will never be. He thought about Suzy not knowing her grandfather. He thought about the children Rachel wanted. The ones he'd never have with her. Suzy's comment made all the sense in the world.

She continued, "There was a large insurance payout. Grandpa left me some money, and lawyers put it in a trust. When I turned twenty-one, they turned it over to me. My family assumed I'd use it for school, but I was never very interested in college. Always wanted to make my own way, I guess. I decided to invest in this place. My parents almost had a stroke."

Nathan held up his mug. "The coffee is excellent. I bet you do well with it."

She made a face like she wasn't sure. "I do ok. It's hard in a small town sometimes. I've thought about expanding or moving into a larger city. But like I said, once in Silas Ridge, always in Silas Ridge. I've got deep roots here, I guess. It's hard to change unless something makes you." She tossed her hands up in a 'what are you going to do,' kind of way.

Nathan took another drink, trying to figure out how to start the conversation about Rachel. He had a million questions, and at the same time, couldn't think of a single thing to ask.

Suzy saw him struggling and gave him a head start by saying, "I'm very sorry for your loss. Rachel was a beautiful person."

Tears welled up in Nathan's eyes, but he bit down on his lip to keep from bursting out.

She continued, "I only knew of her from around town, but that's true of most everyone born and raised here. The Thurmans are a hard family to ignore in a small place like this. If you drop that name around town, you'll see what I mean. That name gets a reaction."

"What does that mean? What sort of reaction?"

Suzy rolled her eyes. "Small town rumors. Rich family. Big, obnoxious mansion. Leads to some hot gossip among old church ladies. Not that I'm above it," she said with a grin.

Nathan prodded. "What gossip would that be?"

"Promise not to laugh?"

"Promise."

Suzy paused a beat and lowered her voice as if conspiring. "If I'm being honest, it can be more than the old Baptist hens gossiping on Sunday afternoons. When I was growing up, there were rumors the house was haunted. Mostly it was kids being silly at school, but there's a certain section of residents here who take it seriously. Too seriously, in my opinion. Of course, I heard it more than most since my grandpa died on the property. But accidents happen, you know? Doesn't mean it's ghosts. People see what they want to see."

All at once, Nathan thought back to his phone call. The darkness in the forest. He recalled the oddness of the hallways and the strange way light carried around the Manor. He didn't find the idea of ghosts that far-fetched a concept. At the very least, he could see how the rumors would carry weight in the community.

"What else do people say? What other rumors are there?"

"For real? You want to hear more about this stuff?"

Nathan shrugged. "Yeah. My wife kept a lot of this to herself. I just want to know more about how she grew up."

"Hey, if you want to talk local folklore, I'm your girl. I

love this stuff!" Suzy gleamed as she began. "A long while back, even before the Thurmans got here, there were rumors the area was haunted. Local's thought the land was cursed. There were legends of a witch lurking about, so they steered clear of the woods. They didn't go out on the lake. Farmers couldn't grow crops, so the land was deemed no good. Hunters said the woods were empty; that animals wouldn't get near this area. It all changed when the Thurmans came along. They started clearing the trees, building their company, and ultimately founding Silas Ridge. Eventually, they started looking to build their estate, obviously that now being where Thurman Manor stands. At the time, the rumors actually helped them, because they got the land for a steal. Purchased it at a fraction of what surrounding areas were being sold for."

Suzy continued in a less excited tone. "Anyway, my grandfather wasn't the first one to have had an accident working on the house. There were several. That helped fuel supernatural gossip, but that's all for fun, in a sick, twisted way. The rational explanation is back then they had a combination of loose safety standards and some reluctance to investigate."

"Why wouldn't things be investigated?"

"You familiar with the phrase *don't bite the hand that feeds you*? That applies here. Virtually the whole town was on old man Thurman's payroll, so no one wanted to rock the boat and risk their jobs. There was a small group that didn't see it that way, though. It mainly consisted of all the people that really believed the rumors of ghosts and witches and hauntings. The way it was told to me is they filed a petition for the Thurman place to be demolished. The petition sort of died out, but that stemmed even more rumors that Mr. Thurman had paid people off. None of that is proven, though. Like I said. Rumors. This town is full of 'em."

Suzy made an awkward attempt at a transition. "How long were you married?"

Nathan pushed thoughts of ghosts from his mind and took a deep breath. "Not long. Just over a year." He shook his head. "I didn't see this coming."

Nathan found it difficult to ask his most pressing questions. Those were the ones he needed answers to; they were the ones he most wanted to avoid. But avoidance wasn't the path he would take. His voice was broken and soft.

"How did she seem?"

He waited while Suzy considered the question. He could see her thinking back to that night. She scrunched her nose up, and for some reason it reminded Nathan of Rachel, if only slightly.

"She was quiet, I guess. I don't remember what she ordered, but I do remember that she sat down for a few minutes alone, but changed her mind and asked for a to-go cup."

"How long was she here?"

"Not long. Probably ten to fifteen minutes."

"All by herself? Was anyone with her?"

"No, she was alone. She sat over there in that booth." Suzy pointed to where Rachel had sat. "She was on her phone for a while. It looked like she was texting someone. But I guess she could have been doing something else too. People come in here and play games sometimes. Like the one where you line up all the candies and stuff. Or work... People come in and work. I guess she could have been doing that, but it seemed like she was talking to someone."

"Rachel was never big on computer games. Did she take any phone calls? Did you overhear anything she said?"

Suzy thought back. "I don't remember. It's possible she took a phone call. There were some other customers to take my attention away, and I try to give people their space. I want them to like being here, and if I'm hovering, they wouldn't want to be here anymore. There's a lot of people that don't trust Big Brother and all that."

Instinct told Nathan there was something here, but it was like trying to solve a jigsaw puzzle without the box. There was a solution, but he couldn't see what the end result was supposed to look like. He hadn't received messages from Rachel that night. No phone calls. The question in Nathan's mind was "*who did*"?

"And then she just left?"

"Pretty much. Like I said, she sat there for a bit and then just asked for a to-go cup and left. That's basically all that happened."

In a grunt of frustration, Nathan said, "I wish I knew who she was talking to. That would at least be *something*."

Suzy shuffled in her seat, opening her mouth like she was going to say something, but nothing came out. She tried again; this time able to find the words.

"It's not really my place to say anything, and I hope you don't take this the wrong way, but why don't you just look at her phone? It would have everything there, right?"

Nathan pictured Rachel's room. The red sweater. Rachel's suitcase, open like it was laughing at him. Feeling things were out of place. About feeling like he'd left the house without something. About subconscious pocket checking. He remembered what he forgot. A puzzle piece snapped into place.

"I can't. Her phone is missing."

Chapter Fourteen

The other side of Silas Ridge was home to failed businesses and crumbling buildings, long abandoned by their previous owners. This section of town was grey and old; only a memory of times past, now a ghost of what used to be.

On the main drag sat an empty Ben Franklin, its windows dark and crusted with years of grime. Next door was another shop, its branding unknown, also in a similar situation. A two-pump gas station sat by its lonesome on the corner, the pumps having ceased long ago to function. Not a car was in sight.

Actually, that wasn't strictly true. Behind the Ben Franklin was a field, overgrown and neglected, but home to the former Silas Ridge schoolhouse. It was a simple one-room style that only the oldest residents retained any personal memory of. Its roof had collapsed on one side, revealing the heavy beam construction that had stood the test of time. It was here, beside the schoolhouse, that Lucas and Tommy found themselves.

Lucas checked out the window and glanced down at his watch as he clicked his tongue.

"Relax, man. He'll be here," said Tommy.

Lucas didn't look at his brother. "Don't defend him. It's unprofessional."

"I'm not defending anything. And if you want professional, Ben Carroll isn't the person to be dealing with."

Lucas licked his lips and felt the familiar urge to indulge in his fun-dip. He could feel it in his jacket pocket, somehow as loud and as obnoxious as its packaging suggested it should be. Lucas resisted this particular impulse, opting instead for a cigarette. He had to flick the wheel on his lighter a few times to get a flame, but it caught, and he was in business. A light blue haze filled the car, hovering around their heads like a thin cloud. Tommy said nothing, but rolled his window down an inch. Lucas smoked fast, using the end of his first cigarette to light the second. Once number two was going, he flicked the finished butt out his car window and into the grass.

"You know," Tommy said, "if you're trying to be discreet with this whole thing, starting a field fire probably isn't the brightest idea."

Lucas looked over at his brother as if to assess him. After a brief pause, he said, "You calling me stupid?"

"No, all I'm saying is a burning cigarette could catch in that tall grass. We'd have a real problem."

"If you're such a conservationist, go out and pick it up yourself."

"Why? I'm not your maid. You can clean up your own messes."

Lucas's mouth spread into a thin-lipped grin, making the cigarette dangle at a crooked angle. "Well, it doesn't sound like that big a deal then, does it?" Lucas blew a thin stream of smoke into his brother's face as a means of completing his thoughts.

Tommy waved the smoke away with his hand. "You're an idiot, you know that?"

Lucas flashed that same thin smile. Of course, his brother was correct. A wildfire was the last thing he needed right now. All the effort to find a secluded place, away from the ever-present gawking public; it would be for nothing if that field lit up like a smoke signal. No, it wasn't attention he needed, but a fix. And unfortunately, Ben Carroll was the man who could provide.

Before Ben, Lucas had to make his restock runs in bigger cities, where he was anonymous; where he could disappear. But that was time consuming, not to mention more dangerous. Anonymity in the big city was a double-edged sword. He was free to do as he wished (to an extent), but there would be no leniency with the cops. If anything, ever went bad, he'd likely spend at least a night in jail, which wasn't to be feared as much as his mother's reaction. He could hear her screaming at him now.

Do you have the slightest clue what this will do when it gets in the paper? Do you have any idea how much this sort of thing can damage our family name?

So, when he'd met Ben Carroll, Lucas saw a real opportunity. To be sure, Ben was as much a redneck as the rest of the yokels in Silas Ridge, but he could still get his hands on whatever Lucas had a hunger for, and that was good enough for him. Plus, there was an added benefit:

Ben was the Sheriff's son.

In Lucas's mind, that was insurance. No way would he be getting in trouble if he was ever caught. No sir, not without a scandal. And in his experience, scandal was to be avoided at all costs.

. . .

Lucas checked his watch again. *Where are you, you little...?*

"Do you think he'll figure it out?"

Lucas made a sideways glance at his brother. Tommy was looking at a distant point outside his window, his forehead resting against the glass and causing fog all around his head.

"What are you talking about?"

"You know what I'm talking about."

Lucas felt a headache coming on, a real skull-splitter by the feel of it. He closed his eyes tight as if he could push it back.

"No, he won't figure anything out. We've got our story from Mom, and as long as everyone sticks to it, it'll be fine. He's only here a few days, anyway. No one could make sense of this that quick. I've lived with it my whole life and don't understand it."

Tommy fidgeted. "I've been thinking maybe we should tell him. He kind of has a right to know."

Lucas leaned up in his seat and glared at Tommy with bloodshot eyes. "I think you might be the idiot. Do you hear yourself?"

Tommy stammered. "Y-Yeah, I know... It's just that..."

"What? It's just what?"

"He's not an outsider, though. Not really. He's Rachel's husband. That makes him family. Right?"

Lucas thought to himself for a moment. "You are going to keep your mouth shut. You got it? Mom already told you what to do. That's all we need to worry about." He took another puff and let a stream of smoke roll over his lips as he reclined again. "It never goes well when outsiders get involved."

Tommy looked like he was going to object, but backed down. It was then that Lucas spotted a car approaching.

"Heads up. Car's coming."

"Is it Ben?" Tommy asked.

Lucas squinted, but the car was too far to make out. "I'm not sure yet. Stay put. I'm going to see if I can get a better look."

Lucas opened up his side and took one last puff of his cigarette. He made sure Tommy was watching, flicked the butt out into the grass, and slammed the door in response to his twin's eyeroll. He laughed to himself as he walked away.

Off to the side of the schoolhouse was a swing set and a broken merry-go-round, now red with rust and flaking paint. The playground sat up on a hill and provided a clear view of the road while still allowing them to remain out of sight. Lucas walked up to the top and squinted again. It was brown, and a beater if there ever was one. The failed muffler thundered, and the sound grew louder as it approached. The car slowed, and Lucas watched as it pulled into the school's lot. Ben had arrived.

A lanky kid stepped out, and Lucas raised his hand, signaling him to come up to the playground. Ben returned a thumbs up and popped his trunk open, removing a bright blue backpack. He slung it over one shoulder and walked up to Lucas.

"You're late. Ever hear of a courtesy call?"

Ben held out his hands in a helplessly. "Sorry, man. I got here as quick as I could. Had another engagement. But I got your stuff, just like you asked."

"Well, let's see it."

Ben dropped his pack on the ground and unzipped it. Inside were a dozen or more zip-lock bags, each containing substances guaranteed to take you to the moon and back. Ben flipped through them as if looking through an accordion file and stopped mid-way through.

"Ah, got it. Here's what you asked for. This stuff is prime. You're going to love it."

Lucas took the bag from him, opened it up, and smelled the sweetness inside. It made his mouth water.

"Ok, well, that's it then. Thank you very much." Lucas started back toward his car.

Ben called after him. "Hey man, aren't you forgetting something? I didn't go to all the trouble of getting all that for you for free."

Lucas turned back and rubbed his chin. "Well, let's talk about that for a minute, hmm? About how much is this bag here worth? Just ballpark."

Ben crossed his arms. "I don't have to ballpark it. It's $100. So, let's have it."

Lucas took another step toward him. "Ok, $100. Got it. And about how much would you say I'm worth per hour? You can ballpark that too, if you like."

Ben looked confused, unsure of where this was heading. He shook his head. "I honestly don't know how much you make. A lot, I guess."

"A lot, you guess? Is that your official answer?"

Again, Ben looked unsure, but he shrugged and nodded yes.

Lucas spread his arms out and mimed as if he were addressing a crowd.

"Well, what do you know? He's right! That's the correct answer!" He took another step toward Ben, making a point of getting up in his space, nose to nose. "Now, think carefully about this one, Ben. Very carefully. How late were you?"

"About forty-five minutes."

Lucas nodded slowly. "That's right. Forty-nine, to be precise. I know because I was watching. Because my time is valuable, you see? So, the way I figure it, seeing as how I make – what did we say?" He shot a finger gun at Ben, signaling it was his turn.

Ben looked down at his shoes. "A lot."

Lucas snapped his fingers. "That's right. A lot. More than your product is worth, for sure. I think that makes me entitled to a discount. Consider it compensation for wasting my precious time."

"That's not how it works, man. Quit messing around."

"I'm not messing around at all." Lucas's voice hissed, sounding remarkably similar to his mother, had anyone heard. "You wasted my time, and I can't get that back. So, I'm taking this as a small measure of compensation. I'll expect you to repay in full, you understand?"

"You can't do that. You can't just take it from me. Come on. $100 is nothing for you. You've probably got that much in spare change under the seats of that fancy car you drive. So, I was a little late. Is it really that big a deal?"

Lucas was solemn in his reply. "It is a big deal, Ben. It's a very big deal. My time, that's something money can't buy me more of. It's ticking away, second by second, vanishing before my eyes." He jabbed a sharp finger into Ben's chest, knocking him off balance. "And I'm not wasting my most precious resource on a little insect like you." Lucas gave Ben one final push and started off toward his car again.

Lucas was just a few steps away when Ben said, "It would be a shame if my father found out what was going on. I mean, a family with a big name like yours, suddenly the focus of a drug investigation. Seems like it might be bad for business, if you know what I mean."

Lucas stopped in his tracks, a hot rage bubbling under his skin.

"Are you serious? You're going to threaten me? That's how you want to play this?"

Ben didn't move, further infuriating Lucas. Being late was an insult, and the lack of a phone call or text message was a slap to his face. To think that this lowlife, this redneck, someone with a social ranking on par with a spider would threaten him, and think he could do so successfully, only proved how stupid he really was.

"You should rethink your plan, genius. Look at you... Even your own father wouldn't believe your story."

"You're wrong there," Ben replied. He stood there, arms crossed, as if daring Lucas to call his bluff.

"Ok, fine. What do you think happens to you? You think you get off scot-free?" Lucas eyed him from head to toe, shaking his head at the sad sight before him. "No, you're not the type of guy to go down with the ship. You're a scrounger. A scrappy little bug, ready to run and hide at the slightest hint of light, just trying to save his own hide from being squished. You won't say a thing."

A little grin curled up at the edge of Ben's mouth, like he had a delicious secret that he couldn't wait to reveal.

"Wrong again. See, my dad, he can talk a tough game when he puts on his badge. But with me, he's just Dad. Maybe it's cause I'm an only child, I dunno... But it wouldn't be the first time he covered for me. I'm surprised you don't know how that works. Seems like your family has a long history of buried secrets and coverups."

The fire inside was too strong, and his fist had made contact before he'd thought it through. Ben's left eye absorbed the blow and he toppled backward, tripping over the rusted swing behind him. He scurried on the ground, trying to untangle, reminding Lucas of the creature he was, the worthless insect that needed to learn his place. Before the bug could get up, Lucas was on him like a rabid dog, pummeling his face, each hit smacking like a mallet tenderizing a slab of meat. His prey went limp. Even then, Lucas wasn't satisfied.

The swing had broken and lay twisted under Ben's body. Lucas rolled his victim over with his foot and grabbed at the disconnected chain. Brown rust stained his hands as he gripped the cold steel links. In a swift move, he wrapped the chain around his dealer's neck, placed his boot square between his shoulder blades, and pulled back. Small, wet, whimpering sounds came from Ben. His hands clawed uselessly at the noose. Lucas kept the pressure, even when the chain bit into his hands and drew blood. He was waiting for Ben's hands to fall; he wanted to see his arms lay lifeless before he released his grip.

"Lucas! What are you doing?" Tommy was standing beside him, looking mortified. "Let him go, man."

Lucas gave the chain one last tug, just to make sure he drove his point home. Tommy bent down and worked the chain free from Ben's neck. He coughed and sputtered and lay on his back, sucking air, his face already showing the first signs of the severe bruising that would come.

Tommy started back toward the car. "Let's go, Lucas. We gotta get out of here."

Lucas nodded his head and started to follow after. He stopped for a second, making sure he locked eyes with Ben Carroll. And in that moment, he saw an understanding, a submission. This feeling was as good as the high he would get later.

Almost.

Lucas grabbed Ben's backpack and slung it over his shoulder.

"This can be a deposit, huh? Same time next week? What do you say, Ben?"

Small lines of tears rolled down Ben's cheek, erasing dirt and blood as they did. He went to move his mouth, but no sound came out.

Lucas smiled. "No comment? I'll take that as a yes. See you then, Ben. Don't be late."

Chapter Fifteen

Nathan saw Tommy roll up and stop in a no-parking zone in front of the coffee shop. Rather than coming in, Tommy buzzed his window down and signaled for Nathan to come out.

"Looks like my ride is here," Nathan said to Suzy.

"Yeah, looks like it."

"Thanks again. I hope you didn't stick your neck out too much for me."

"I'll be fine. You keep an eye out, though. People can get weird around here. They get wind you're with the Thurmans you're gonna have trouble."

Nathan nodded. "I'll be careful. If you think of anything else, please let me know?"

"How should I contact you?"

Nathan grabbed a pen from the counter and wrote out his email address on a napkin. "I don't have a phone yet, but I've still got email. Write me here anytime."

Suzy took the napkin and looked it over before folding it and pocketing it inside her apron. Nathan wondered if he would ever hear any more from Suzy. Something inside told him no.

There was an impatient honk from outside.

"I gotta go. Thanks again." He grabbed his things and waved as he walked out.

The car door closed with a hefty thunk. Thick, sickly-sweet smoke filled his nostrils.

Lucas lay sprawled out on the back seat, puffing on a joint, his eyes bloodshot and glazed.

"How'd your errand go?" Nathan asked.

Lucas gave him a stupid grin and took a swipe of his fun dip. Tommy shrugged but said nothing.

With some effort, Lucas leaned forward and passed the blunt up to him. "Nathan, you gotta try it. It's the best man, the absolute best there is."

Nathan ignored the fact that he'd declined on their way to town just a few hours earlier. "No, thanks. I don't smoke."

Lucas looked at Nathan like he was an exotic animal. "What do you mean, you don't smoke?"

"I just don't care for it. I tried it before and it's just not for me."

Lucas pushed harder. "Come on, this stuff is the best. And with everything that's happened, you can indulge in a little something, right? We should treat ourselves." Lucas's face was right in between the seats. He looked at Tommy. "Tommy's going to have some, aren't you?"

Tommy shrugged, "Yeah, sure."

He looked back at Nathan and said, "See, Tommy knows what's up."

Tommy reached back to take it, but Lucas snatched it away at the last second. "But you gotta wait 'til we're home. No driving under the influence." Lucas cackled in triumph and leaned back, satisfied with a good day's work.

Nathan couldn't help but notice the wounds on Lucas's knuckles. He couldn't remember if the damage was there before or not, but he thought not. Regardless,

Nathan decided not to bring it up - it seemed like a bad idea.

Tommy rolled his eyes in response to Lucas's childishness. He pulled away from the curb and headed back toward the Manor. They drove the exact opposite route that brought them there, and Nathan observed the scenery unfold in reverse. The storefronts evolved into small suburbs, and then to open fields and space.

Once Tommy settled into a steady speed, he said, "You find everything you were looking for?"

Nathan, his mind still reeling from his conversation with Suzy, gave him a curious look. Questions buzzed in his head like a hive.

"What?"

Tommy pointed to the bags at Nathan's feet. "Your shopping trip. You get everything you need?"

"Oh, uh, yeah. I think I'm set. Thanks."

But the question made Nathan's mind race. He'd gone out for a routine shopping trip, a mundane requirement of existence, and in the process, by accident or fate, discovered he hadn't found what he was looking for at all. In fact, he hadn't even known he was looking for anything at all, at least not consciously. Suddenly, all his nervous ticks and that feeling of forgetfulness seemed to take on brand new meaning. All this time, feeling he was missing his own phone, when the reality was he was missing hers.

Aside from Lucas's backseat snores, they drove in silence for a few miles before Nathan spoke again. "Hey, you wouldn't happen to know where Rachel's phone is, would you?"

"Her phone?" Tommy's eyes squeezed shut like he was trying to remember. He shook his head. "No, I can't say I do. Maybe it's with her things back at the house?"

"I looked there this morning, but I don't remember

seeing it. I'll check again though. It's possible I overlooked it."

"I wouldn't worry about it too much. It'll turn up at some point. Lost things tend to get found when you least expect it."

When they arrived back at the Manor, Tommy and Lucas disappeared behind the house to enjoy their new purchase. For good measure, they extended Nathan one more invitation, but it was more a formality than anything. No one expected that he would say yes.

Nathan stood alone in the drive, contemplating his next steps. Wind swept over the lake, carrying cool air on its back and chilling Nathan down to his bones. He looked up toward the peaks of the house above him. Black spires towered overhead, making him feel dizzy and lightheaded. Their points seemed to stab the sky above. He imagined Suzy's grandfather up on those dangerous, steep angles. He didn't have a specific area of the roof to focus on; a number of spots looked precarious. A fall from even the lowest ledges looked to be fatal. He imagined a body slipping, sliding down the shingles, scraping and clawing for a grip, and then, failing to gain purchase, fall over the edge. There was no sound, just tumbling and helplessness against gravity. Nathan shook his head, forcing the intrusive thought away just before impact.

Nathan pulled his coat a little tighter and started his way around the side of the house. His thoughts had been held captive since the coffee shop, a single obsession taking form; what happened to Rachel's phone? On the drive, he ran dozens of scenarios, replaying Suzy's account over and over in his mind. With each iteration, he searched for clues he may have missed. By the end, he'd reached no better conclusion than the one Suzy had presented; that his wife visited a coffee shop, texted with an unknown individual, and then promptly returned home and hung herself.

Without so much as a note...

His recent obsession wasn't entirely fruitless, however. New considerations came to mind. For one, it was possible that what Suzy perceived as *texting* was a misinterpretation. Perhaps *typing* would have been more precise? While they had found no physical suicide note in the barn, was it possible she wrote one on her phone? Was it a possibility? Certainly, yes. Would finding such a digital note bring Nathan closure? Time would tell.

The second revelation had come to him midway through the drive back. Nathan had only been half-listening to Tommy as they drove, his thoughts focused only on what possibilities existed for a missing phone's whereabouts. So far, he'd come up with precisely zero ideas - until Tommy started up about his accident.

"Man, that sucks about your car. You think there's any chance it can be fixed?"

Nathan shook his head. "No, I think it's done for. It was probably time to look for something new, anyway."

"I wrecked a car when I was a teen. That sucked too. Took like a month for my new car to come in. Man, I was going stir-crazy. I had to get outta the house, or I was gonna lose my mind."

"Mm-hmm," Nathan mumbled.

Tommy laughed to himself. "Rachel was so sick of listening to me back then. Eventually she must have gotten tired of it because she threw her keys at me. I mean, literally threw them at my face!" He made a whooshing sound and dipped his head like a boxer dodging a jab to illustrate his point.

"She threw her keys at you?"

"Yeah, man," Tommy said with a grin. "She told me to stop whining and complaining, and told me to take her car if it would shut me up. So, I did. I drove hers until my new ride showed up."

Nathan rounded the corner of the house. He wasn't sure why it hadn't occurred to him before, but Tommy's story reminded him Rachel's car was still parked at the Manor. She had driven to town for coffee, and logic dictated she would have driven back. It was possible she had just left her phone in her car when she returned. He'd never known her to forget things inside her car, but he'd also never known her to be in the state she was in the night she took her life. He was beginning to wonder how well he knew her at all.

Hidden behind that front corner of the house was a cement slab with room enough for ten cars, provided the ones in back didn't need to get back out. Stone block lined three sides, creating a waist-high fence around the vehicles. This was the visitors' space, suitable for everyday use. Edward's more prized machines were kept in garages and offsite storage, where they would remain pristine and safe from the elements.

Rachel's car was parked in the corner. Nathan reached for his keys and again remembered he didn't have them; one more thing he hadn't retrieved from his crash. Hoping for a lucky break, he tugged at the driver's side door, but as always, Rachel had it locked up tight. It struck him as silly to have it all locked up out here in the middle of nowhere. Who would steal it? Locked doors this far from strangers would be a force of habit more than anything.

He cupped his hand over his eyes and moved in close to the window to peer in. His nose bumped up against the cold glass. His breath made the window fog as he looked for her phone, though there wasn't much to see. Rachel kept a clean car, and what Nathan saw was consistent with her history. There was a set of sunglasses on the passenger seat. He saw the to-go cup from Suzy in the cup holder, her lipstick smeared on the edge. An empty back seat. And no phone in sight.

He peered through each window and tugged on each door just to be sure none had been left unlocked. But no matter the angle he looked through and no matter the door he tried, there was no indication Rachel's phone would be found inside. Maybe it had slipped underneath one of the seats, but he had no way to confirm. He made a mental note that if he didn't find her phone elsewhere, that he should come back when he had his keys.

As Nathan started toward the house, he could see the last slit of the sun descending behind the trees. The world was a bath of red and orange and purple. Nathan took a deep breath of cool air, trying to cleanse his mind of all that had happened. But he knew it would be futile; cleansing breaths would do nothing to free himself from the trap he found himself in.

His eyes were drawn toward the woods. The trees appeared still, too still, almost like one of his photographs. They seemed inviting, and something about that disturbed him. The memory of what he'd seen, or rather, what he hadn't seen, was still fresh. A chill crept up his spine as he thought about walking through those trees, the feeling of unseen eyes watching his every step. The feeling he was being followed. Being hunted...

Suzy's voice rang in his mind, and he recalled her mentioning animals didn't like this area. Nathan focused his memory, trying to recall if he'd spotted or heard any animals last night. Birds, or a squirrel jumping a gap between branches. Maybe a small rodent burrowing down into the leaves. He couldn't recall any.

Out of the corner of his eye, he spotted movement. He turned his head and saw a flock of birds headed his way. Relief came first, followed by a sense of foolishness. He'd been stupid for believing Suzy's story, stupid for allowing himself to feel frightened by nothing. For jumping at shadows. For allowing the stress of the situation to get the better of him.

He laughed at himself as he watched the birds draw closer. The fading light was beautiful, and Nathan wished for his camera; it was a picturesque moment. They flew in perfect formation; an amazing thing birds did. Something about wind resistance and conserving energy.

He continued to watch their approach. They'd be overhead in just a minute. But when they got to the border of the woods, their formation broke, and the birds scattered in all directions.

Like they'd hit a wall.

Chapter Sixteen

Nathan walked back to Rachel's room. Aged floorboards creaked with each step, and the last remnants of light snuck through the tall windows of the Manor. Particles of dust floated in colorless beams of light, making the house feel gray and cold and odd. Nathan had always imagined sunlight to be yellow; this was different and somehow dirty, empty of any warmth or happiness or comfort.

He found Rachel's room untouched. Her suitcase lay open, her clothing stacked neatly on the bedspread. The cord on her hair dryer spiraled around the handle, and her toothbrush was sealed inside a clear plastic ziplock. Nathan wasn't sure if this was how Rachel had left things, or if someone had come in later, after she'd been found, and packed it up for whatever destination it was bound for.

He started through the stack of clothing, running his hands in between each section, probing for Rachel's phone. It was unlikely to be here, but still possible, and Nathan clung to any sliver of hope available. He moved on to her suitcase, unzipping each compartment, looking in every pocket. He got down on his hands and knees and peered under her bed, but all he found was a thick coat of dust. Nathan stood up and wiped his hands on his jeans.

Next to Rachel's bed was a nightstand, and Nathan spotted her charger, still plugged into the wall. He wondered how he'd missed it earlier. It was like learning the secret to a magic trick, and as a result, becoming blind to the illusion. And now that this illusion had dissolved, he recognized what had been nagging at him earlier. He just couldn't believe he'd been so oblivious. Nathan pulled the nightstand's drawer open but found nothing except a crumpled cough drop wrapper.

A knock from the door interrupted him. Nathan closed the drawer like a kid caught with a dirty magazine. Elisabeth stood in the frame, dressed in black slacks and a shimmery top. She was slender, with sad eyes that looked like they couldn't shed another tear, even if she'd wanted to. Nathan got the impression sleep had eluded her. She looked exhausted; the kind of wear brought on by the deepest of despairs. It was easy for Nathan to recognize it since it was the same exhaustion inside himself.

"What are you looking for?" Elisabeth asked.

Nathan hesitated, and hoped his answer would sound normal. "I was looking for Rachel's phone. You wouldn't happen to know where that is, do you?"

Elisabeth looked at him blankly and shook her head with a concerned frown. "No. I can't say that I do." She looked thoughtful for a moment, and then asked, "Where all have you looked?"

"I looked through her suitcase, and her clothes. It's not here. I even checked her car, but I didn't see it there either."

"Well, I'm sure it'll turn up."

"Yeah, that's what Tommy said."

"Oh? Was Tommy looking for it too?"

Nathan looked around the room, hoping the cell would

surprise him and reveal itself. "No, I just started looking for it, and I asked him if he'd seen it. But he hadn't either. I hoped it would be here, but no such luck." A thought popped in his head. "Do you think maybe the police took it?"

"I really couldn't say. But I'll tell you what. If I see it, I'll be sure to let you know. How's that?"

Nathan nodded, accepting that for the moment he would get no further. "Thanks. Maybe tomorrow I'll call the police though. I'll see if they took it, as evidence or something."

"Well, do whatever you think is best. I hope you find what you're looking for. But that will have to wait for later. Edward is waiting, and we have a lot to discuss."

Elizabeth led Nathan down several hallways, deeper toward the center of the house. Each hall had a near identical appearance, and after several turns, Nathan questioned whether he'd be able to navigate out of the maze on his own. If he paid very close attention, he could detect the slight curvature of the halls, but it was only when he passed by a window that he could orient himself. Each time, he found himself to be slightly off from where he would expect himself to be. Elizabeth however, navigated the house with expert ease. She walked at a swift pace, her heels clacking with each brisk step.

They approached a door with artificial looking blue light sneaking out a razor thin crack. Nathan could hear muffled voices from the other side. Elisabeth tapped on the door before stepping inside, poking her head through the entrance first as if she were deciding if it was safe to proceed. She turned back toward Nathan and nodded for him to enter.

The room was sparse except for a bed and several large machines that emitted occasional high-pitched beeps. Computer monitors sat atop machine towers, each one eager to tell a grim story. Tubes and wires ran from various pumps into Edward's arms. He was gaunt and his skin had a deathlike pallor. Thin grey hair was combed over to one side of his head, looking greasy and in need of a shampoo. But even in his current state, something about him spoke to many successful years of making shrewd and lucrative business decisions.

In contrast, Jonathan towered over his brother, a neckless juggernaut with impossibly thick arms and emerald-green eyes that winked with subdued cruelty. Both men tracked Nathan as he entered. Elisabeth took a chair, crossed one leg over the other, and stole amused glances as she pretended to examine her nails.

Aside from the chirping medical equipment, the room was silent, which made Nathan incredibly uncomfortable. No one spoke as he approached, and he sensed he was expected to speak first.

"Good evening, Mr. Thurman. It's good to see you." He held out his hand and approached Edward's bedside with a sort of reverence.

A reverence reserved for the dying.

Chapter Seventeen

"Good evening?" Edward scoffed. "Bull. There's nothing good. Everything I have is being stripped from me. My health. My daughter..."

He coughed violently into his fist. The skin on his hands was almost translucent, revealing tendon and bone. He reached over for his bed control. His fingers trembled as he fumbled with the buttons, but soon the bed made a light whirring noise and morphed into an upright position. Gravity made his face sag, which somehow made his weight loss even more apparent.

His voice was wheezy. "I need water."

Elisabeth stood. "It's time for your medicine, anyway." She walked to a cabinet and grabbed a bottle of water, as well as a colorful assortment of pills. She placed everything on a small silver tray and brought it over to Edward. He looked at them with disgust, but took them anyway, swallowing each one by one until the tray was emptied.

After the last painful gulp, he said, "Worthless, all of them. It's ridiculous that I take these. They don't do anything. What good is medicine for a dying man? What good does it do? Nothing, not one thing. It's a racket, is what it is. You know what happens when you get sick? They milk you for all your worth. I swear, it's like the doctors don't want you to get better." He curled his boney finger, calling Nathan a little closer. "You want to know what's really ridiculous. I've seen the bills for this stuff. It's outrageous! God forbid you break your leg or something. You'd end up funding a new wing for the hospital. Not that you'd have it named after you or anything." He shook his head in disgust. "These hospitals, doctors, drug manufacturers... all of them no better than organized crime. Vultures. They prey on the sick and weak."

Nathan was quiet for a moment, and then asked, "So, why do you take them then?"

Edward chuckled to himself. "Because I'm a fool, that's why. Deep down, I want to believe the lie. Deep down, I want to believe they will help take away my pain. But they're placebos all of 'em."

"That's not true," said Elisabeth. "They help you to rest."

"I have no rest," Edward snapped back. "Not until I'm dead."

"You're being dramatic." Elisabeth went back to her nails, done with the conversation for the time being.

"The vultures are circling," said Edward. "Buzzards lined up, just waiting for me to die so they can take over. People think that because I'm dying, I can't run the business." He raised his wrinkled boney finger and rapped it against his skull. "My body is broken, but my mind is sharp. I'll outsmart 'em, you can count on that."

Jonathan spoke, his voice deep and cavernous. "It wouldn't kill you to let me handle more of the business. I can take on more."

Edward smiled to himself. "It's not the business that's killing me, dear brother."

"I'm just saying -"

Edward interrupted Jonathan. "We've had this conversation. More times than I've cared for. My answer stands. You'll have your shot. But I won't be forced out of my own company before my time is up."

Echoing Jonathan's sentiment, Elisabeth said, "It might be good for you to share some of the responsibilities. You should consider your health."

"Let me worry about that." Edward leaned his head back on his pillow, longing for the days when people saw him as intimidating. A terror in the boardroom. A time when people didn't question his decisions, and God help the poor soul who did. Now, given his appearance, one might assume he was close to death. This, in fact, was closer to the truth than Edward would ever admit. Death, ever at his side, wished to make his acquaintance. Edward, for his part, had yet to respond to such an invitation.

Still, even in his frail condition, he commanded the room. It was a gift he had, and the reason his father had entrusted the family business to him over his brother Jonathan. Simply put, Edward possessed the capacity to make the hard decisions that no one else wanted to make. But the choice to retain control over his company, his *legacy*, was never a difficult decision.

Edward turned his head toward Nathan. "We have business to discuss. Or, more directly to the point, we need to discuss my daughter's funeral. Do you already have plans arranged?"

"I've done some. Mainly I've worked on a photo remembrance. I've been looking at funeral homes to handle some of the other arrangements."

"And have you decided on one yet?"

Nathan shook his head no.

"I'd like to make a proposition. It may sound odd at first, but try to keep an open mind. Once you've heard all the facts, I trust you'll find what I'm about to propose beneficial."

"Mr. Thurman, I loved your daughter very much. I just want to give her something beautiful. I'm sure that's what we all want."

Edward's eyes lit up. "Ah! That's precisely it. I agree - she deserves a beautiful funeral. Very well put. But have you stopped to consider what that means? Not for Rachel as your wife, but for Rachel as a Thurman?"

"I don't follow. She's the same woman. Why should there be a difference?"

A knowing look came over Edward. "There's all the difference in the world, boy. There's history here. For my family. For this town..." Another coughing fit forced Edward to pause. When it ended, he wiped his hand off on his bedsheet, leaving a smear of blood. He took a moment to catch his breath, and then said, "Were you aware my ancestors founded this town? Built it from the ground up. Before any Thurmans arrived here, it was nothing. My family made this town what it is."

"Rachel never went into details. I can't say I know much about your lineage, Mr. Thurman."

Edward nodded. "I'm not surprised. You're an outsider. Unless you grew up here, you can't understand."

"Understand what, Mr. Thurman?"

Jonathan squirmed in his chair. Elisabeth grew tense. Edward made eye contact with them, but for only a second, a silent communication to relax. As always, he had the situation under control.

"There's people - bitter people - that want to see my family suffer. They've always been here. They will cause trouble any chance they get. And Rachel's death provides them an opportunity."

"What sort of trouble?"

Jonathan's voice rumbled, "The kind you don't want."

"Let me tell you a story," Edward said. "I grew up in this house, as did my father. This home was built by generations before me. It took time. Many years. There were setbacks. But Thurmans are persistent."

"And stubborn," quipped Elisabeth.

Edward shot a glance at her but declined to engage. "My family spent a great deal of time, not to mention money, to ensure every detail was carefully considered. My father was one of those men."

"The house is very beautiful, Mr. Thurman. He did a great job," Nathan said.

Edward nodded, as if recalling past memories. "Yes. Yes, he did. My father spent the last good bit of his life making sure this house, and everything surrounding it, was perfect. He did very little otherwise, as I recall." He chuckled to himself. "Even after all these years, you know what I remember so clearly? The smell of his paper drawings. I remember he'd lay them out flat on his desk so he could see them all at once. They had a distinct aroma. I can't describe it. Never experienced anything quite like it again, but that memory is crystal clear."

"It sounds like a very happy memory."

Edward was quiet, and he looked down. There was the slightest hint of tears in his eyes when he looked back.

"I'm not sure it's a happy memory. What we didn't understand at the time was there was more going on in his head than his architecture. My mom might have known... Sometimes I wonder if she suspected, but if she did, she never said. So, his obsession grew. He wasn't sleeping normally; he was losing weight. But for me, what stands out the most was his constant muttering. He'd talk to himself, Nathan. As a child, I didn't understand. I thought he was talking to me. I would walk into his office thinking he wanted to chat. But instead, he'd look at me blankly. Like he forgot who I was. But then he'd remember and say, 'Daddy's working, Eddie, go play' and send me off. I learned to stop checking to see what he was saying. Eventually, whatever plagued his mind got the best of him, and he took his life."

No one spoke. Monitors continued their rhythmic beeps, and another machine hissed out a quick puff of air. An IV bag dripped its contents into a plastic tube.

"I'm so sorry, Mr. Thurman. That must have been awful."

"I don't tell you that for pity. I tell you because as much as my father obsessed over his papers, he had his reasons. Do you want to know what was so important to him?"

Nathan waited for the answer.

"He was building a mausoleum."

"A mausoleum?"

"It's a building for the dead, Nathan," Elisabeth said with a slight smirk.

"I know what it is," Nathan said. "I just don't understand why he built one."

Edward answered, "He wanted a safe place for all Thurmans to go for their final rest. He's there now. I'll be joining him soon. And, as I'm sure you will agree, it should be Rachel's final resting place as well."

"A safe place? Why wouldn't it be safe for Rachel to be buried in a cemetery?"

"The trouble-makers," said Jonathan.

Nathan waited for the explanation.

Edward continued, "They buried my grandfather in a

cemetery, as I'm sure you were planning to do for Rachel. But there's some people that refuse to let things go, even after death. They came at night, the day after his funeral. The dirt covering his casket hadn't even settled when they dug it up. They took his body, Nathan. They stole my grandfather, and we never found him again."

Nathan looked equal parts horrified and confused. "Why would they steal him? What would that accomplish?"

It was Elisabeth who answered. "Who knows why these people do what they do. They are convinced we've somehow cursed the town, which couldn't be further from the truth. But I suppose they need someone to blame for their misery. Somewhere along the line they decided it's their moral obligation to punish us. None of what they do is rational."

Edward watched as Nathan took it in. He could see equal parts shock and confusion, which was all to be expected. This was the important part; allowing Nathan to connect the dots, to realize the truth on his own. It was only a moment before Edward saw it happen in Nathan's eyes. The puzzle pieces had fallen into place.

"And you think they would come for Rachel?"

"I *know* they will, Nathan. Insanity aside, my father had good reason for building the mausoleum. These aren't just random acts of vandalism. They target us. They have targeted my family for generations, even before my grandfather. Protests at every new venture! Harassing us in stores! Digging up our dead! It's a type of religious fanaticism."

Nathan rubbed his face. "I don't know. It's so different than what I had expected."

Elisabeth stood and approached the bed. "Nathan, we can make it beautiful. We'll have the service in our parlor. It will be everything Rachel should have. That's what you said you wanted, right? To give her a beautiful funeral?"

"Yes, of course. But this is a lot. It's..." He stopped, searching for the words.

Edward finished his thought for him. "It's the only way for her to be safe."

Chapter Eighteen

After the meeting, Elisabeth retreated to her room. She pulled the door closed, as to not disturb the soundless house. Of all the strangeness Thurman Manor possessed, Elisabeth found the silence most unnerving of all. At times, she even wondered if the house was actually *listening*.

She walked across to the other side of her bedroom and sat down in a high-backed chair. Arranged on the desk before her was a wide assortment of makeups and brushes, each with their specific purpose and function. Across the desk was her mirror, and looking back at her was her true reflection, the one that only revealed itself behind closed doors. Here, and here alone, could she drop the controlled expressions and see them as the masks they were.

Elisabeth gritted her teeth together, her jaw going firm and rigid. Things were tense, that much was clear. But worse than that, the situation seemed unpredictable. There were too many variables now. Variables like Nathan.

Heavy footsteps shook from the hall, followed by light taps on her door. She stole a quick glance at the clock and breathed a sigh of relief. There was still time left. Had the clock read that dreaded number 10:57, those steps may have meant something entirely different. Something she didn't care to dwell on. She took a quick peek in the mirror and reapplied her mask.

Nevertheless, she opened the door only a crack, a sliver she could peek through and confirm the identity of her visitor. Jonathan's gigantic frame filled her field of vision.

"What are you doing here?" Elisabeth asked.

"Don't worry. I made sure no one saw me."

"That's unlikely," she remarked, and opened the door. After a quick glance left and right down the hall, she pulled him into the room and closed the door shut behind her.

The door had no sooner latched when Jonathan scooped her up in his arms. This place, where she was engulfed in him, was her favorite. She felt like a fragile porcelain ballerina, a treasure valued and cared for. And she was a prize, of that, she was sure.

Jonathan nuzzled his face into her neck. "I couldn't stay away. If you were all mine, I'd never let you out of my sight."

Elisabeth smiled but pushed him back all the same. "It was stupid of you to come here. Someone could have seen you."

Jonathan gave her a sly look. "I told you, no one saw me. You worry too much."

"Maybe you don't worry enough. Do I need to remind you about what would happen if Edward found out?"

"Let him. I'd love to see his face when he realizes he lost something for the first time in his life." His face turned to a scowl, revealing in it years of bitterness and resentment.

She put her hand up to his cheek. Her fingers appeared small and dainty against his stubble.

"You aren't thinking it through. Sure, you'd get your little moment of petty satisfaction, but what about after that?"

Jonathan looked away without reply, but Elisabeth didn't need one to know he understood the answer. This was merely the latest variation of the same conversation, one they often had.

"What would happen if Edward divorced me? He'd leave me with nothing. Is that what you want? I thought you cared about me?"

"I do care about you."

"Then I need you to suck it up a little longer. Edward is close, Jonathan. He's so close to death. It could be only days. Hours even. All we have to do is wait. That's it."

"You say that like I can have you right after he's rolled into the mausoleum. But it won't be like that, will it? Even then, I have to wait." He ground his teeth together. "He even gets to control me when he's dead."

"Ok, fine. It won't be right after. But it will happen. And at least at that point, we won't be at risk of losing *everything*. I've put in too much time. I've earned what I have, and I deserve to keep it."

Jonathan sighed. "You're right. I'm just so sick of Edward getting everything he wants." He took Elisabeth by the waist and pulled her close. "I'm sorry I get so frustrated. I promise, I'll make sure everything stays secret."

"I accept your apology, but you have to make it up to me."

Jonathan looked at her with coy eyes. "Oh? What exactly did you have in mind?"

"Not that, you animal." She pushed him off. "I need you to take Nathan to the mausoleum."

"What? Why?"

"Because even though Rachel and I had our differences, she should have a proper funeral. Nathan can't give her that. If he doesn't agree to Edward's proposal, Rachel will be remembered like a pauper. You need to help him say yes." Jonathan started to protest, but Elisabeth interrupted him. "Don't think of it like you're helping Edward. You're helping me, ok?"

Jonathan considered her a moment and then relented. "What time is it?" he asked.

"If you go now, you'll be back before. So, hurry. And make sure Nathan's on board."

Jonathan checked the hallway and crept out as to honor his agreement with Elisabeth. She listened as his footsteps grew quieter and quieter, until they disappeared. She was alone with her thoughts again, but there was only one thing on her mind.

Nathan's looking for her phone.

She opened her closet and walked inside. On one side were rows of shoes, laid out on wooden slat risers. Opposite those were jackets, skirts, and dresses, each hung in perfect rows and organized by color. But her eye was drawn to the back, to the boxes meant to be forgotten. Most of the containers were empty vessels branded with designer labels, but some contained jewelry that had gone out of style. Several boxes remained unopened with never-before worn shoes still inside. And in the second row, squarely in the middle, was the box that Elisabeth was looking for.

She slid it out as if the contents inside were volatile and dangerous. For a moment, she feared her secret was already out; that the contents of the box had been revealed, and she was discovered. But when she removed the top, she found it there, exactly as she'd left it, undisturbed and nestled in white cotton. Elisabeth pulled it from its nest, slipped on a jacket and smuggled it deep inside a pocket.

She didn't see a soul on her way to the lake. At one point, in the hall, she imagined a figure had walked in front of her, but it disappeared like a flash. She told herself it was nerves and pressed on.

The water was still and black and reflected the moonlight. Elisabeth reached into her pocket and retrieved her object, as smooth and dark as the lake's mirror surface. In one motion, she threw Rachel's phone, along with her secrets, as far as she could, into the depths of the lake. She watched the splash, small and uneventful, and saw concentric ripples work their way back to shore.

She walked back, unaware of Tommy in the shadowed manor window, watching his mother. But that would be of no consequence. He wouldn't do a thing.

Chapter Nineteen

Jonathan found Nathan hunched over his computer and clicking through photographs.

"Knock, knock. Mind if I come in?"

Nathan turned in his chair toward him. "Oh, hey. Yeah, sure. What's up?"

Jonathan ducked his head as he entered. Nathan looked small from his vantage point, but that wasn't a new phenomenon for Jonathan. Looking down, he could see Nathan's eyes becoming bloodshot from long hours at a screen.

"What are you working on?"

Nathan glanced back at his computer. "This? It's photos of Rachel. It will ultimately be a slideshow." He lingered, appearing lost in thought. "Uh, for her funeral. And whatever that's going to look like."

"Maybe I can help with that. You have time for a break?"

Nathan clicked a few buttons to save his work. "What did you have in mind?"

"Grab your coat. We're going for a walk."

Several minutes later, they were walking across crunchy

grass that bordered the back side of the house. Further out lay a line of trees, their naked branches motionless and looking like barbs of wire against the haloed moon.

"Where are we headed?" Nathan asked.

Rather than answering him directly, Jonathan said, "You must have a million thoughts running through your head. I know I would if I were in your shoes."

"Is it true?"

"Which part?"

"All of it, I guess. I mean, are people really going to disturb Rachel's grave? It all seems kinda..."

Jonathan chuckled. "Crazy. The word you want to use is crazy. And you'd be right. The whole thing is certifiable. For the record, my brother's a dirty cheat. He wouldn't think twice about lying to you if he thought it might get him a dime. But in regards to your question, unfortunately for us all, in this instance he's telling the truth."

"And you think it's all necessary? You don't think they might leave us alone this time?"

"In my experience, no. These people are fanatics, Nathan. If they get word of this, I can almost guarantee they will cause problems."

Nathan considered this a minute and then said, "So, you think I should agree? Do it Edward's way, have the funeral here, put her in that mausoleum?" Nathan sighed in resignation. "It all sounds so odd to me. I can't even imagine what a place like that would be like."

"Well, you're about to get a glimpse." Jonathan pointed further ahead. "You see that cut out in the trees? That's a path. My father had that put in when he had the mausoleum built. The whole thing is quite beautiful. You'll see."

They stopped just shy of the opening in the woods. It looked like a door constructed out of nothingness, empty space occupying this section of the woods. A square wooden post stood to the right of the threshold. Jonathan reached down, flipped open a weather cover, and flicked the switch hidden underneath. Small foot lamps illuminated the nothingness, spaced in even intervals down a stone walkway.

"This way," Jonathan called.

They walked single file down the lit path. The first row of trees to either side was visible, although dim, and behind them may as well have been eternity. There was no sound except for their footsteps and brushing fabric from their coats.

Soon, the path eased into a wider area. The lamps spread out left and right, creating a border around the open space. The path continued forward, and then split as well, forming a circle around the central structure, the mausoleum.

The edifice itself was constructed with dark grey stone. Pillars lined the front, supporting an overhang and sharply angled roof. Recessed into the stone was a heavy door, above which the Thurman name was etched into granite. Discreet, decorative lighting added atmosphere, a clear indicator of the care and forethought put into its planning.

Nathan looked around as he tried to take it in. "I have to admit, this is impressive."

"I should hope so, for all the time my dad spent designing it. It did a number on him when those ghouls dug up my grandpa. After that, it was very important to him we have a safe space to lay our dead. So, he made this." He gestured toward the mausoleum.

Jonathan dug into his pocket and pulled out a long, iron key. He put it into the door, and there was a metallic clunk as he turned it.

"Let me show you inside."

The door swung open, and they stepped in. Jonathan

flipped the lights on, revealing its beautiful interior. Small couches lined the edges of the room. Generations of family portraits hung from the walls, appearing to progress in chronological order. At the far end of this lineup was the current generation of Thurmans, looking out at the two visitors. Across from the entry was a set of descending stairs. A large clock hung above as a centerpiece, ticking away the seconds. Jonathan monitored the hands, inching closer to eleven.

"It's warmer in here," Nathan remarked.

Jonathan broke his gaze with the time. "Climate controlled year-round. Dad went all out."

"I can understand why Edward would want to use this. It is beautiful."

Jonathan turned to Nathan. "Can I ask you a question?"

Nathan nodded.

"Did Rachel ever show any signs of depression? Anything at all that would even hint she would do something like this?"

Nathan shook his head as he considered the question. "I'm asking myself the same thing. Wondering if I was stupid for missing the signs. I keep replaying our life over and over, looking for any slight clue. But there was nothing. I honestly thought she - that *we* - were happy."

"I guess it bothers me that we'll never know what it was. It just seems like there should be *something*. She really never talked to you about what was bothering her?"

"Nothing out of the normal. Certainly nothing that would cause me to think suicide." Nathan looked over at Rachel's family photo. "You must think I'm a fool."

Jonathan shook his head. "No, I don't. Being here, the whole thing, just makes me remember my dad, you know? Like maybe there's some sort of genetic thing that got passed down? That's a thing, isn't it?"

Nathan shrugged. "I don't know. Could be."

Jonathan stared hard at the family portrait, focusing all his attention on his brother, until all the others faded from view. The steady beeps from Edward's machines still reverberated in his head. He hated that sound, the constant reminder that his brother was still present, still breathing, still casting his shadow over him. How frail little Edward managed to keep control over a man of his monstrous size escaped him. It didn't seem natural. It didn't seem right. But, as is so often the case, he who controlled the cash controlled it all.

Not much longer... He's almost out of the way, and then you get your shot.

One step at a time. For now, he just needed to focus on the task at hand.

"Nathan, listen. I realize this isn't what you had planned. In any possible way. But this is where you're at all the same. The reality is Rachel came from us, and that makes your situation fundamentally different. You've only got two options."

"Which are?"

"One, you could proceed like your original plan. Scrape together whatever money you can, buy the cheapest pine box available, and then stand guard over her grave until the day you join her." Jonathan rubbed his boot on a random spot on the floor as he thought. "These fanatics are no joke, Nathan. They don't forget, and they don't move on. One day they'll come, and they'll desecrate her grave."

"And I suppose my other option is to put her here?"

"Is that really so bad? Look at this place. It's the best anyone could ever hope for. And, if I might be practical, it solves your cash flow issue."

"What about visiting her? How would that work?"

Jonathan made a display of stretching his arms out

wide. "Look around you, Nathan. This place was designed for visits year-round. There's no freezing in the winter. No standing in mud up to your ankles in spring. No sweat running down your back over the summer."

"I mean, without Rachel, I turn into just some guy. Would I be welcome to come anytime I wanted?"

Jonathan gave him a look that he hoped looked earnest. "Nathan, you were married." He knew this wasn't an answer, but hoped he'd put enough sincerity into his voice to satisfy Nathan's question. In reality, Jonathan had no idea how this might impact the widower. Over the years, he'd seen more than one of Edward's business deals go through *adjustments*, just so long as it turned out in Edward's favor. It wouldn't surprise him if this funeral arrangement ended with a few *adjustments* as well.

Nathan nodded his head though, apparently willing to accept this as an answer.

"At the end of the day, I just want to give her something nice. She deserves more than I'm able to provide at the moment, so maybe I should just see this as a stroke of good luck."

Jonathan smiled and extended his massive paw of a hand. "I prefer to think of this as family."

Elisabeth was standing in the parlor, watching as Jonathan and Nathan walked back through the grass. Upturned chairs sat upon tables, waiting like patient servants, their inverted legs casting thin shadows on the floor. If all had gone according to plan, she would soon transform this room to host those who wished to remember her daughter.

She examined the two walking, trying to read their body language. Was their little excursion successful? Nothing about their demeanor indicated one way or the other, but judging by their course, she would soon find out. They appeared to be heading straight toward her.

She stole a quick look at her watch. Less than an hour left now. Under normal circumstances, (whatever that meant in a place like this), she would have already tucked herself away in her bedroom with the door locked, and been the better of three drinks in. But she was curious about their meeting, and more importantly, there was the problem of what to do with Nathan tonight. If these next few minutes worked out the way she planned, she would solve both issues.

She heard them open the door and felt Jonathan's heavy frame vibrate the floor as he entered.

"Where did you two come from?" she asked, hoping it didn't sound overly intrusive.

Jonathan played right along, just as she knew he would.

"I took Nathan out to see the mausoleum. I figured it would help to see what Edward was talking about in person."

"Oh? And what are your thoughts, Nathan?"

"The whole thing is stunning. After seeing it, it's hard to argue. I think we should do her funeral here."

Elisabeth nodded. "You're doing the right thing, Nathan. Rachel would be thrilled."

"I hope so."

She continued, "It's been a long day for everyone. How about I go grab us a few drinks?"

"You want me to call Upham?" Jonathan asked.

"No, no. Let Upham be. I'm perfectly capable of doing it myself. Have a seat. I'll just be a minute."

Elisabeth left them and ducked behind the wet bar. Rows of glasses were stacked behind cupboard doors. They clinked like wind chimes made for drunkards as she removed a trio and set them on a tray. She examined various labels adorning the bottles, ensuring to select one of sufficient potency. Dark, amber liquid flowed from the bottle and settled heavy in the glasses.

"Need any help in there?" Nathan called.

"I'm almost done."

Elisabeth pulled a small, metal cylinder from her pants, and using her slender fingers, twisted the cap. She poured the vial into the drink nearest her and watched as the contents dissolved in a near instant. This was all strictly necessary, of course. The simple truth was there were certain events that occurred around Thurman Manor that Nathan should remain unaware of. In fact, she'd self-prescribed this particular formula many times herself, and could vouch that it guaranteed a quick and long night of sleep. The morning after, however, was usually rough.

She went to pick the tray up, but then reconsidered. Taking Nathan's glass, she held it close to her mouth, and spit a long string of thick saliva. A quick stir with a straw was all it took to dissolve the bubbles floating on top.

Jonathan and Nathan were sitting at a small table in the middle of the parlor. They stood as she approached, and she handed them their drinks with a pleasant smile.

"We should all try to get a good night of sleep," Elisabeth said. "Starting tomorrow, there's a lot of work to do."

Chapter Twenty

While Nathan entered his drugged slumber, on the other side of the lake, Ben Carroll inched his car back through the woods. His buddies liked to refer to it as a beater, but he preferred to think of it as a classic. And it got the job done. Every time.

He turned, and his high beams lit the pines up in front of them. The area gave him absolute privacy, but he still felt like he needed to act secretive. It helped the mood; set the tone. He killed the headlights and darkness surrounded the car like an avalanche.

"Come on, don't do that. It's freaky out here." Suzy reached over from the passenger seat and latched onto his arm.

A wide grin spread across Ben's face, invisible in the dark. This was *perfect*. Alone, out in the woods with Suzy Marshall. His "mad hot" dream girl. He couldn't believe it, especially since she'd declined his prior invitations three times, always using her coffee shop as an excuse. He'd started to think maybe she was untouchable, but the fourth time turned out to be the charm. He wasn't quite sure why she had changed her mind, but he was glad she had. She'd be his crown achievement if he could pull it off. And so far, things were playing out exactly as planned.

He'd used this trick (he liked to think of it as strategy) before, to varying degrees of success. Most of the girls he brought out here responded the way he wanted. A little fear was useful, some sort of psychology buried deep in human minds. Ben didn't need to understand why; how was enough to achieve his purposes. The seclusion, coupled with the dark, not to mention Thurman Manor off in the distance across the lake. Was it any surprise the girls wanted a protector?

The night started off fun enough, with burgers and shakes at Caspers'. Small town life had its drawbacks, but Caspers' was a real gem, small town or not. After their meal, he'd made casual mention of a "starlit" boat ride. Boat was a generous term, but he liked the way it sounded. *Dingy* just didn't have that same sort of ring to it.

Ben had been out looking for a good fishing spot one day, and he stumbled on it by dumb luck. It was just stashed away, hidden under a pile of branches. That first day he left it alone, but it kept catching his attention, just wanting to be used. Ben didn't catch a thing that day but, convinced there were big ones out in deeper water, he made it a point to come back. The next time, the boat was still there, still untouched. After several beers, he'd worked up the courage to just take it out. Borrowing really. A victimless crime. There had been no negative repercussions. No one saw, no one knew. Whoever owned the boat had probably died, or moved, and never came back for it. And what was the worst that could happen? Nothing.

It was possible Daddy Sheriff might give him a stern talking to, but that would be the extent of it. Nothing to be concerned with. He used the boat as his own the whole summer. And even though he never caught a single fish, Ben never let go of the idea that there were some monsters way down deep. He just needed to find them.

Ben parked the car, and they were greeted by a refreshing pine scent hovering in the night air. Just ahead was the lake, the surface reflecting dazzling sparkles off the black mirror surface. And as always, the boat, still hidden from view under loose camouflage. Ben tossed the branches aside and dragged their ship to port.

"Are you sure about this?" Suzy asked. "Is it safe to go out there at night? In the cold?"

"It's totally safe," Ben replied. "I've gone out at night plenty of times. Just wait until you see the stars from out there on the water. It's unreal." He grinned at her and said, "And if you get cold, I'll help keep you warm." He launched it into the lake, leaving just enough dry ground for Suzy to step in.

"Hop in and I'll push us out. Just make sure you don't get your foot in the water. It's cold."

Suzy held the sides and placed a toe into the boat while Ben kept it steady from the end. Once she was seated, Ben launched into the water and stepped in himself. He dug an oar into the soft lakebed below and pushed out to deeper territory. They cut through the water, making ripples roll out until they bounced back against the shoreline and returned. Ben relaxed his arms and allowed them to come to a stop. Apart from their bodies balancing and creating a gentle sway, the water was undisturbed.

The stars were brilliant. Ben watched as Suzy took it all in. She was mesmerized by the night sky, and he was mesmerized by her. He moved closer to her, low and gripping the sides of the boat, and she turned to him as he sat down. Ben leaned forward, but Suzy held back a second, making him wait. But only a second; she leaned forward, and their lips touched. They savored each other, embraced far from shore, floating and drifting while black waves lapped the sides of their stolen ship.

Suzy leaned out of the kiss and gave him an embarrassed grin. "That was really nice."

"We don't have to be done," Ben said. "We could do more." He moved in again, hoping to resume where they left off. Hoping they would move things forward.

Suzy did pull away this time. "I'm actually getting cold out here. It is beautiful though, and I've had a nice time. But I want to take things slow. You understand, right?"

Ben made a pleasant enough face and shrugged his shoulders, as if to say he understood. No big deal. But it was a big deal. He didn't go to all this trouble for nothing. His mind started running his various plans. Maybe once they got back to the car, he could try again. Forcing anything out here was risky. He preferred the girl to be willing; made things much more simple for the most part. But unwilling was fun too; just not out here, away from solid ground. If she struggled in the car, he didn't have to risk tipping the boat into a frigid deathtrap.

"Sure, we can head back. Whatever you'd like. I just want to show you a nice evening."

He stayed low and crawled to the rower's bench. He got into position, and for the first time saw they had drifted further than he realized. They were nearing the other side. Where the Manor was.

He looked up at the Thurman place looming over them. He'd never gotten this close before. It seemed larger from this vantage point. Taller. Like it was over top of him. Like most kids, he'd grown up hearing the rumors about the

Manor. He'd heard all the ghost stories that originated from the Thurman place. Stories about ghosts wandering the halls, driving the inhabitants crazy. Without realizing it his hand nursed the tenderness around his neck.

Would serve them right. Hope Lucas gets his...

Not one to back away from a challenge, he'd even accepted dares from his buddies to sneak up near the house. But on those occasions, he hadn't been able to get closer than he was now. Ben always made sure to get out of view, and then he'd wait a while, long enough to let them assume he'd gotten closer than he really had. Of course, he told them he'd touched the house, and for good measure he threw in a few extra details about hearing spooky moaning or something. But that had never been the case; he'd always just sat and hid by himself, too scared to get close enough to touch it. But he was close now. Close enough to see in the windows. Ben didn't like the feeling; it felt like the house was watching him. Drawing him closer.

"It's beautiful, isn't it?"

Ben jumped in his seat when he heard Suzy speak. She was looking up at the house, her eyes fixed on it. Admiring it. Her face looked expressionless, even with the slight upturn of her lips.

She kept talking. "I've never really gotten to see it before. The house is magnificent. I wonder what it's like inside?"

Ben rolled his eyes. "It's probably just rich people stuff. Fancy pictures on the walls, weird random items for decorations."

"Can you get closer? Maybe I could get a peek through one of the windows. I'd love to see."

Ben was getting impatient. He wasn't interested in any detours. "I don't know. I think we should head back. Like you said, it's getting cold out here. Heading back would be best."

He put the oars into the black water and started to row them back toward the other side. He watched the Thurman mansion diminish in size with each stroke back. The only sound was the gentle swish of oars cutting through the water. Suzy hadn't said a word to him. She didn't turn around. She didn't make any conversation at all.

Is she mad at me? Is she not talking to me now? She's acting like a child. No, a spoiled brat. And after what I did for her! She played hard to get, but I played along like she wanted. I got her dinner. I took her out here to see the stars. Maybe she should learn to be grateful.

He gritted his teeth together, his anger seething and growing by the second. But he kept his voice calm when he spoke.

"Hey, I know you're curious about the house, but there's nothing to it, really. It's boring. There's other stuff we can do that's more fun. Promise."

He smiled to himself, only thinking about how fun it would be once they got to the car. She'd see. She'd learn a lesson tonight. Ben felt his face get hot as she ignored him. *Typical of a girl*, he thought. *They don't get one thing they want and it's the silent treatment.* The wood oars thumped against the metal boat bottom, and he turned toward her, committed to telling her off. The look on her face made his stomach drop.

Suzy's eyes were open wide, unblinking, not focused on anything in particular. Her body was rigid, almost statuesque. Ben waved his hand in front of her, trying to break the trance, but she gave no reaction.

"Suzy, you ok?"

The only response he received was a continual stare into the darkness behind them. He got closer until he was face to face with her. She made no sign she perceived him. Their noses were nearly touching, and the way her hair smelled was intoxicating. He swept away a strand of hair from her cheek and pushed his lips against hers. He held the kiss, forced it on her, until it no longer satisfied him. Suzy sat still, unflinching. Unmoved.

No more waiting. He didn't care if she was a head case, or that they were on the water. He was going to get what he came out here for. Maybe it'd be better this way even. No fight; maybe not even a memory. It would be a secret they both could keep. Ben's hand moved to the top button of her blouse. His fingers had no more touched the white plastic disc when Suzy spoke again.

"Do you like my boat?"

He jerked back and fell off his seat. Cold water soaked the seat of his pants and he scrambled back onto the bench. Suzy was quiet again, staring, fixated on Thurman Manor. Ben felt his blood run cold. His hands shook. Something in her eyes, lost and far away.

It was in this moment that the rumors he'd ignored since childhood became more than gossip and hearsay, more than campfire ghost stories and tactics parents used to keep their children in line. Behind Suzy's dead stare was something, *someone,* invisible yet terribly present, someone that Ben had no desire to meet in this life or the next.

Screw this, he thought. *This girl is going to be more trouble than she's worth.* He reached down for the oars...

Where's the other one?

He heard the crack on his skull before he felt it. When the pain came, it was sharp and disorienting. The nausea that followed was overwhelming, and he puked into the water. The world started to spin.

Oh, is that Suzy?

He felt a warm trickle run down his face.

She's mad hot. It's so nice she brought me on a boat ride.

He couldn't quite keep his head straight up. It seemed to want to roll over to one side. The skin around the top of his skull seemed tight enough to burst.

Why is she standing up? It's dangerous to stand up on the water. The boat could tip.

The pain wasn't so bad now; just a heavy, dull, throbbing sensation, in sync with the beating of his heart.

Is that Suzy? What's she doing way out here?

Cold water shocked him back to his senses. He felt himself dropping, being pulled further into the dark deep of the lake. At the end, he could see Suzy above the surface, sitting in the boat, oar in hand, watching him sink. All he could think was *she's mad hot...*

She's mad hot...

She's mad.

The time was 11:01.

Chapter Twenty-One

Nathan woke the next morning with a throbbing headache at the top of his head, making him feel nauseous. He pressed the palms of his hands against his eyes, debating if he should get up at all. But one thought remained clear in his mess of a head.

Where was Rachel's phone?

Before he could talk himself into closing his eyes again, he shot up in bed and ripped the covers off. He picked up his wristwatch from the nightstand and fastened the band. As he did so, he noticed it was past noon. The day was already getting away from him, and if he wanted to ask the Sheriff's office any questions, he'd need to get a move on.

He threw on yesterday's clothing and ran his fingers through his hair before heading downstairs. In the time it took him to descend that single flight, he had reminded himself that he had no car, and no phone. If he wanted to speak with the police, he was going to need some small favors.

There were no signs of life that morning. The only sound to be heard was the faithful ticking of the grandfather clock. Nathan decided the dining room was as good a spot as any to find someone, and as luck would have it, he was right.

Lily was sitting with her legs curled up beneath her, looking lost in her thoughts. She turned toward him as he walked in.

"Hey. I was wondering if you were ever going to get up. Upham's already put breakfast away, but I'm sure I can scrounge something up if you're hungry."

"I'm fine right now, thanks. But I was wondering if you'd seen Tommy. I had a question for him."

"Wouldn't bother. I haven't seen Tommy yet either, which means he's slept longer than you have." She grinned and said, "And that's saying something. What did you need?"

Nathan ignored her teasing. "I'm actually looking for Rachel's phone. You haven't seen it, have you?"

She shook her head. "Can't say that I have. Did you check her room?"

"Yeah, I searched all over. I can't find it anywhere."

"So you're checking with Tommy?" Her eyebrows shot up in surprise and she giggled. "Tommy can barely find his own shoes. I can tell you right now you're looking to the wrong person."

Nathan sighed. "I was hoping he could take me into town. I keep wondering where it could possibly be, and I realized I should check with the police. Kinda obvious, I know."

"Why go all the way to town? You could just call."

Nathan held out his empty hands to demonstrate his current phone challenges.

"All you gotta do is ask a girl," she said. Lily grabbed her phone and did a search for the Silas Ridge Sheriff's office. The result came back in a snap, and she dialed the number and put her phone on speaker so they could both hear.

There was a very brief silence as the call connected. But instead of an answer, a recording came on, requesting their name and number, and in return offered the promise of a callback as soon as possible. All emergencies were directed to call 9-1-1.

Nathan frowned and rubbed his forehead, trying to decide on his next steps.

Lily stood up and said, "Come on. Let's go."

And before Nathan could respond, she was leaving the table, headed for her car.

The drive to Silas Ridge was gray skies all the way. Lily wore dark, oversized sunglasses that made her look like a movie star. She never took them off, as if she expected the sun to pop out from behind the clouds and blind her. At one point, spots of drizzle hit the windshield, but Lily never even had to turn on the wipers. The droplets just evaporated in the wind.

Rachel was Nathan's constant thought, and he remembered her as they drove. She was ever present at all times, ingrained in everything he experienced. Even the act of driving itself brought back memories. He caught himself reminiscing about drives he and Rachel had, very similar in scene to the current one. He didn't remember where they were going; some place inconsequential. But he remembered how he felt. With Rachel, he'd felt safe and secure, and everything seemed right in the world. But right now, life was anything but right. And he felt suspicious of the girl next to him. Lily was friendly, but in a playful, flirty way that made him uncomfortable.

Like yesterday, the route was the same, but unlike Tommy, Lily seemed to relish speed, taking turns fast and tight. When a long straight-away came, she would press the accelerator, and her thigh would tighten under her tight black jeans.

They made the drive faster than Tommy had. Nathan saw the Walmart and Suzy's coffee shop pass by. Lily sped through one light that was arguably orange, and a few blocks later pulled the car to a stop on the curb. The Sheriff's Office wasn't much to see, just a simple square building like so many others. If not for the shield on the glass door, it might have passed for a small business, maybe an insurance agent, or a financial planner's office. The exterior consisted of simple white brick, and there were sparkling windows all around. The walk leading up to the entrance was spotless, as if it had just been power washed, and the landscaping favored rocks over mulch.

"I really appreciate you driving me, Lily. I know you hadn't been planning on this today."

She pushed her sunglasses back into place and smiled. "No problem. I didn't have anything going on, anyway. Besides, I go crazy just sitting around in that house all day long. I'll do anything to get outta there."

"I'm not sure how long this will take. Did you want to come in?"

Lily leaned forward and peered over her frames toward the front doors. "No, I think I'll just hang out here. I don't mind waiting. Do your thing. I'll be here whenever you're ready."

Inside the Sheriff's office was clean, with wood slat benches against the wall and a table displaying pamphlets of various sorts. On the other side of the table was a cork board with multiple public service announcements, some advocating against drunk driving, and a few with phrases like "Click It Or Ticket", or "This Could Be Your Last Text". Given his drive into town, Nathan felt these were appropriate. At the very top of this board was a photo of the current Sheriff dressed in his uniform and smiling a big politician's grin. Below, embossed in a gold painted strip, was his name: Sheriff Jack Carroll. A long counter spanned the front, acting as both a service desk and a barrier to the back offices. A woman in a crisp blue uniform was at a computer typing away. She was blonde, her hair pulled back tight into a ponytail. She had brown eyes and looked older than her actual age. Worn and thin, as if life had taken a recent toll.

"Can I help you?" she asked.

"I hope so. My name is Nathan Stevens. I was hoping to speak with someone about an investigation that happened last week."

She forced a polite smile. "Hon, you're going to have to be more specific."

Nathan hesitated. Not because he didn't know what to say, but rather because he wanted to be as un-specific as possible. Repetition did nothing to ease the retelling of Rachel's passing. Each time he heard himself say the words, it only became more real. Given the choice, he might opt to let the details become so murky that it was impossible to recall any specifics at all. But, as much as he hated to say it out loud again, to allow the tragedy to take shape, he knew it was the only way to get answers.

"It's regarding my wife, Rachel Stevens. Maiden name, Thurman. Her body was found last week. I just need to ask a few questions."

The officer looked at him with skepticism. No hint of shock or sympathy. If it weren't for the uniform and badge, Nathan might have been speaking to a bank teller or renewing his driver's license. She was cold, like she'd turned off emotion long ago.

"Thurman? You a reporter or something?"

Nathan shook his head. "No, I just told you, I'm -"

"I heard you the first time. But your story doesn't make any sense."

Nathan thought back, replaying the few words he'd spoken in the preceding minutes. Nothing he'd said seemed to be confusing, or cause for concern. He put on as friendly a smile as he could manage.

"I'm sorry, I'm not following. I'm trying to find out some details regarding my wife."

"See, that's the issue right there. If you'd done your homework, you'd know Rachel Thurman wasn't married. Your story doesn't make any sense. Try again, sir." She turned her attention back to whatever was on her computer screen.

It took Nathan a moment to process what she'd said.

"Not married? I can assure you we were. Now, if I could just have a few minutes of time with whoever investigated things, I'm sure I can clear this up."

"Sir, you can stop whatever game this is. I'm looking at it right here." There was a folded over newspaper lying beside her keyboard. It rustled as she picked it up and handed it across the desk to him. "First page, top spot." She jabbed her finger toward the page.

Written at the top of the page, in thick black ink, was *Obituaries*. Below that was a photo of Rachel, complete with a write up.

But not the one Nathan had been working on.

Nathan's eyes darted back and forth over the page in a frantic search for answers. All the details were right: her birth and death, family lineage, place of birth. But any mention of her life with Nathan was as vacant as their marriage bed.

"There's been some mistake. I don't understand this, but I *promise* you, I'm telling the truth. Look me up. Take my prints if you want. Just let me speak with someone. Please."

"Unfortunately, we only work by appointment." The officer removed her hands from her keyboard and gave him eyes that said she was through with the conversation.

Nathan broke. Under different circumstances, had he been of sound mind, he would have approached the situation differently. But he was anything but sound. Exhaustion and grief and frustration clouded his judgement, and he thought nothing of consequences. He was only thinking of his wife. About her frame of mind when she committed suicide. He was thinking about the crime scene, and what was, or possibly wasn't found there. And he was thinking about where on earth her phone had ended up, and what it might contain that would give him some clarity as to what happened.

Nathan slammed his fist down on the counter. The whole desk shook. The officer's eyes opened wide in shock as she moved to a standing position. Her hand was out in a *stop right there* position.

Nathan's voice was a low growl. "Listen to me. I've just lost my wife, and I need some answers! There's no one here. You clearly don't have *customers* to serve, so why don't you save your solitaire game and get me someone useful!" He wrenched his jaw shut and glared, almost daring her to use her cuffs.

Behind the counter, curious heads poked around door frames. Nathan could feel the stares as they wondered what sort of disturbance was happening at the front desk. Several deputies emerged, taking up strategic positions. Another man vacated his office and walked to the desk and placed a gentle hand on the woman's shoulder.

"Hey. Sarah, I got this. Why don't you go take a breather?" Her eyes darted back and forth between this man and Nathan. He gave her a reassuring pat on the shoulder and nodded in affirmation.

Sarah's face was set hard. She scowled at Nathan, and then marched through the station and out the back door, letting it slam behind her. Once the onlookers saw the situation had quieted, they retreated their way back to their offices. But Nathan caught the deputy's keeping a watchful eye. Based on their looks, he could imagine a few of them secretly hoped he'd cause a scene again.

Nathan's heart was beating fast as he waited for his temper to fade. Adrenaline had spiked his blood stream, and if his hands hadn't been clenched, he would have felt a trembling in his fingers as the rush wore off. Every sense seemed to be firing on high.

The newcomer on the other side of the desk looked him up and down in a quick examination. Then he said, "I'm Sheriff Carroll. I understand you'd like to have a chat."

Carroll's office was small. A wooden desk was home to a computer whose primary job appeared to be covering up a line of old cigarette burns. There was a small window behind the desk with its blinds drawn closed to keep the sun's glare off the screen. Outdated carpet lined the floor and seemed to hold years of stale smoke within its worn fibers.

Carroll himself was fairly plain; medium height and grey hair that may have once been brown. His shirt was stretched a little too tight for his aging midsection. He sat down at his desk and indicated Nathan take the seat across from him.

"Can I get you something to drink? Coffee? Water?"

"No, I'm fine, thank you," Nathan said.

Carroll grabbed a stack of papers that were strewn on his desk. He tapped them against the wood in an attempt to consolidate, but he just ended up mashing the edges. After looking for a better place and not finding one, he opted to put them on the floor by his feet. Carroll pulled a cigarette from his jacket pocket and placed it between his lips. He offered the pack to Nathan, but Nathan shook his head.

Carroll made a 'whatever' face and said, "You'll have to forgive my co-worker. Sarah's going through some stuff. Divorce can be a nasty business."

Nathan had nothing to say. At the moment, he couldn't bring himself to care about someone's relationship problems. All he could think was, *at least she's got a marriage to fix.*

Carroll waited a beat for Nathan to respond, but in the end, gave up. "What's all the ruckus about, Mr. Stevens? What can I help you with?"

Nathan's heart was still thudding thickly inside his chest. He took a deep breath to take the edge off, and said, "As I was explaining to the girl up front - Sarah, I mean - my wife died last week. I have a few questions."

"And your wife was Rachel Thurman?"

"Stevens now, but yes."

Carroll's face was grim. "Well, I'll answer what I can. What do you want to know?"

Nathan tilted his head in surprise. "Just like that? After what just happened at the front desk, I didn't expect you'd work with me."

Carroll thought for a second and then grabbed a photo frame from his desk.

"You see this here? This is my family. My wife, and my son, Ben." He shifted in his seat and pointed out his wife. "Me and my wife, see, we've been married for over thirty years. Got married in the chapel not too far from here. Seems like it was yesterday." Carroll took a drag on his cigarette and studied the photo for a moment while Nathan waited.

"I couldn't afford much back then. I was downright poor, if you want to know the truth. But I was in love." Carroll smiled and his eyes turned warm as they do when recalling fond memories.

"Congratulations," Nathan said.

Carroll continued. "When we picked out my wife's ring, there wasn't much of a choice. I'm fairly certain even the cheapest band was outside my budget."

"I don't mean to sound rude, but I'm not following where you're going with this."

Carroll held his hand up, signaling to bear with him a moment longer. "I was the first to respond when the call came in about Rachel. When a family like the Thurmans report an issue, it's best to respond quick, if you know what I mean." Carroll's chair creaked as he leaned back. "You know what stood out to me?"

Possibilities assaulted Nathan's mind, each more fearful than the next. What could stand out in a scene like that? Nathan wasn't sure he was ready to hear the answer, and his body went rigid and breathless as he waited for what might come next.

"Rachel was wearing a wedding ring. It looked remarkably similar to what I got my wife all those years back." He leaned forward again. "Now, a ring by itself isn't really surprising. But in this case? For a Thurman? No... You'd expect something more grand. This was a simple thing. Pretty, don't get me wrong. But not exactly what you'd expect from a rich family. Wealthy girl like her wouldn't be wearing something like that unless it meant something to her."

Nathan remained quiet.

"Yeah, I read the obit. Can't explain why a husband wasn't mentioned. Maybe just an oversight. But I remember that ring - it just seemed out of place. And you don't look like much of a reporter to me. So, what do you want to ask me?"

Nathan's voice was quiet when he spoke. "What else did you find when you got there?"

"To be honest, not much. The barn was fairly empty, other than the stuff you'd expect to find in a place like that. Tools. Hay. Horses, obviously. Is there something specific you had in mind?"

"I'm looking for her phone. It's missing from her things. I've tried retracing her steps, but so far I've got nothing. I was hoping you'd found it."

Carroll took a sip from his mug and tapped his keyboard. He clicked a few times, scanned the screen with his eyes, and then said, "Hmm, no phone."

"What about the surrounding area? Was anything found outside? Along the path maybe?"

"An officer walked the path from the house to the stables, but he also came up empty. Our primary focus was inside the barn. But again, no phone."

"You didn't search the property? Isn't that standard or something?"

Carroll took a deep breath. "Nathan, look around you. What do you see? This is a small department. We've got ten people employed here. Several of those are office support only. On a good day, there's maybe five officers on duty. And those five are the ones responsible for everything that happens around here." Carroll spread his hands out and made an all-encompassing circle. "That's everything from drunken redneck bar fights to underage teenage drinking. We don't have the manpower to launch a full-scale property search. And even if there were, we'd need either a warrant, or the property owner's permission."

"You had the owner's permission. They called you, right? Once they found Rachel, they called and had you come out? Isn't that permission?"

Carroll rocked his hand from side to side. "Yes and no. We had authority to look in and around the barn. There was no issue there. But the house wasn't technically the scene of the crime. That's a whole different thing. Every scrap of info was inside that barn, none of which suggested we inspect the house. So, that's where the search ended."

Nathan shook his head. "That doesn't make sense to me. Why wouldn't you search the house?"

Carroll sighed and held his hands out as if trying to calm the situation. "Nathan, listen. We did our job. I personally oversaw the entire investigation. You can believe me when I tell you it was all done right - all by the book. When you deal with people that have money like the Thurmans, you cover your butt, that's for sure. I don't mean to be crass, but this was as straightforward as these things get. There were no signs of a struggle. No indication of foul play. Without evidence to make me think this was a homicide, my option was to close the case. Anything beyond that, and I'm liable to get sued for harassment."

Homicide. Nathan hadn't considered Rachel being murdered. The thought made his skin crawl.

"How can you tell?" Nathan asked.

"Tell what?"

"That it was suicide. How do you know?"

"How much detail do you want? It can be grim."

Nathan took a deep breath. "Tell me straight. I need to know, even if it's hard."

Carroll nodded. "Ok. But if this gets to be too much, you gotta tell me. Deal?"

"Yeah, deal."

Carroll accepted their agreement and began. "First, no sign of a struggle. At least with another suspect. She had some rope bits under her fingernails, but that's to be expected. People tend to grab at the rope. Survival instinct or something. But in a homicide, you'd expect to see other injuries. Signs of a fight. Bruised knuckles, or other wounds from being hit. Nothing like that, though. And the toxicology reports all came back clean. That rules out poison or drugs. We looked all over the barn for anything out of place. Weapons, tracks - any appearance of a cover up. Any sign that someone else was there. Now, admittedly, it's a barn. Lots of work going on, people coming in and out constantly. There were horse prints in the dirt, making it difficult to see things like boot prints. But we looked all over, and there wasn't anything to suggest Rachel was dragged or forced there against her will. Doing ok so far?"

Nathan nodded, but he was doing his best to keep this as clinical as possible. He didn't want to associate this with his wife. If his thoughts carried him any further, he was going to lose it.

Carroll continued. "It mainly came down to the rope pattern. Ropes leave a mark; they bruise the flesh. Rachel's bruising was all consistent with suicide."

"How so?"

Carroll stood up. Held his hands like he was holding an imaginary rope. "Try to imagine how the rope would work. Picture a person in front of me. If I placed a rope around their neck, I have to pull backward, right?" Carroll yanked at an invisible rope. "The bruising pattern is specific. Everything happens at the front of the neck. When looking at a hanging, all the bruising is different. It's at the front too, but also up under the jaw." Carroll rubbed both his hands alongside his neck, just under his jawline. "Gravity pulls the body down, the rope resists, and in turn, the bruising pattern is up higher. And then there's the internal examination, the way the neck bones break..."

Nathan's face was getting pale and sweat beaded on his forehead. His hands were wet. He'd thought he wanted it straight, but he was rapidly changing his mind.

Carroll stopped and his hands dropped to his sides. "I'm sorry. This was a mistake. I shouldn't have gone into detail with you."

Nathan shook his head. "I asked for it. Thought I wanted to know."

The Sheriff adopted a soft tone and said, "Here's what you should know. We did our job. No one dropped the ball. What happened is tragic and devastating." He paused, waited for Nathan to make eye contact. "Can I offer you some advice? Have the funeral. Go through the grieving process. Don't let all these little details get in your way. In my experience, those left to deal with tragedy try to find distractions. They want something to focus on that's not the main thing. Because the main thing, the death... That's hard to deal with. It seems impossible. But that's exactly what needs to be done. It needs to be dealt with. Sooner or later, it'll force you to deal with it. A thing like a death doesn't just go away. It makes itself known. It grabs you by the face and forces you to pay attention to it. Don't pretend you can avoid it. Don't find little distractions to take you away from the real issue."

Nathan nodded half-heartedly. Carrol was right about one thing, though. It seemed impossible. How could he deal with something he could scarcely comprehend? Where does someone start with a thing like this?

"So, you're telling me to quit the search for her phone?"

Carroll's chair squeaked as he leaned back again. "Her phone will turn up, eventually. You might have seen it already and not realized it. I've thought I lost my phone before, looked for ten minutes before I realized I was talking on it. You'll find it, probably when you stop looking. Lost things have a way of turning up."

Chapter Twenty-Two

Muffled shouts from outside brought their conversation to a halt. At first, Nathan thought it might be from the street, a couple hotheads arguing over right-of-way. But it was getting louder.

"What's that?" Carroll swiveled his chair and peered through the slats of his blinds. They gave a plastic snap as he pulled a section down with his index finger, and he groaned.

"What?" Nathan asked.

"Come see for yourself."

A fresh wave of stale smoke hit Nathan as he came around the desk. A crowd had gathered in front of the Sheriff's office, looking angry and primed for a fight. Picket signs made of two-by-fours and poster board, sporting slogans like, "No Room For Sinners", and "Erase the Evil", bounced up and down like pistons. Lily was nowhere to be seen.

"Looks like word got around," Carroll said.

"I heard about these people," Nathan said, "But it's different seeing them in real life. I didn't know what to expect."

"Yeah, they're a real bunch of charmers. I suppose every town has their whack-jobs. These are ours."

"How'd they even find out?"

Carroll rubbed his chin as he considered the question. "Probably the obit. But I'm surprised at how fast they coordinated. Where else have you been in the last few days? You been talking to anyone about Rachel?"

Nathan shook his head. "Just the Manor. Other than when I got clothes and - "

It hit him like a flashbulb pop, bright and instant. "I talked to a girl at the coffee shop. Do you think she had anything to do with it?"

"Suzy? No, she's a sweet girl. But I wouldn't put it past some of her patrons. That place can be a real hot spot for gossip."

"Can you get rid of them?"

Carroll chuckled. "Son, these fanatics have been here nearly longer than the town itself. There's no getting rid of these people."

"I mean, can't you make them leave?"

"They aren't doing anything illegal. They're on public property, exercising their right to free speech." And on second thought, added, "But all the same, you better sneak out the back. Let's not give them anything more to get riled up about."

Sheriff Carroll led Nathan to the back of the station. After a quick check through the peephole, he opened the door and stepped out to the back lot.

It was exceptionally plain behind the station. A chain link security fence enclosed the area. A single tall parking lot light stood above, pointless in the daylight. Several idle squad cars sat off to one side. Only two people were seen in that private space. Sarah, who still looked a little red after her encounter with Nathan. And parked in a corner, waiting patiently, Lily.

"Is that your ride?" Carroll asked.

"That's my ride." Nathan put his hand out toward Carroll. "Thanks for talking to me. I appreciate what you did."

Carroll's grip was firm and confident. "You keep an eye out. Those folks out front are unpredictable."

Nathan nodded that he understood.

Carroll turned to Sarah and said, "We've got this whole thing sorted. You wouldn't mind seeing these two safely out of town, would you? Just in case one of these good ol' boys decides to follow."

Sarah's eyes were hard, but she forced a smile, anyway. "I'd be happy to, boss."

———

Lily was slouched down in her seat, still sporting her movie-star sunglasses.

"What took so long?" she whispered.

Nathan buckled his seatbelt. "I'll tell you on the way. Let's get outta here."

Lily shifted the car into drive and pulled out of the back lot as inconspicuously as she could. After a minute, the deputy followed and kept pace about a block behind them.

"Why is that cop following us?"

"The Sheriff asked her to make sure we weren't followed by the crazies up front." He added, "If I had to guess, she's not thrilled about it."

"Why do you say that?"

"I kinda went off on her. Actually, it was more like a full meltdown."

"Well, while you were in there making friends, I nearly

got surrounded by a mob. I was lucky, though. I saw them coming and hid out in the back."

"This town is crazy. Is it always like this?"

Lily shrugged. "Sometimes. As weird as it is to say, you get used to it. Sorta." She bit her lip as she mulled it over. Then she changed the subject with, "Were you able to find what you were looking for?"

Nathan watched the buildings passing by on his right. "No, I didn't."

They cleared the boundary line of Silas Ridge without further incident. Once they were out, Nathan leaned back in his seat and breathed out in relief. Lily enjoyed no such release. She glanced at her rearview, taking careful note of the cruiser still following. A cold twinge of paranoia crept up her spine.

It's fine it's fine it's fine it's fine it's fine it's fine it's fine...

Nathan shifted beside her. "I saw something weird at the station."

"Oh, yeah? What was that?" Lily was only half-listening. She glanced in her mirror again, trying to decide if the cop was closer than before. As a precaution, she checked her speed; the itch to floor it was a constant battle. But she fought her urges and maintained the posted limit of seventy to a digit.

"That deputy I got into it with - she showed me an obit for Rachel. I didn't know we had released one. I realize I'm all over the place right now, but I *don't* remember us ever talking about that. Did you know one was going out?"

"An obit? No. I had no idea. Are you sure?" Lily turned her head to check this time; the deputy had gotten closer yet. Her heart raced, and oddly enough, her feet began to tingle as if they'd fallen asleep.

"Yeah, I'm sure. It was the weirdest thing." Nathan bounced his fist up and down on his knee. "I'll ask your mom when we - "

"Why is that cop still there?" It poured out, abrupt and loud and surprised even her.

Nathan turned back and made a face like he wasn't sure. "I dunno. Maybe she just wants to make sure we get back safe?"

The only thought Lily had was how *safe* was a very relative term. Sure, they might be *safe* from the fanatics (for how long?), or she might feel *safe* when in bed with David (also, for how long?), but sooner or later, all roads led her back home, where *safe* was as elusive as love. Life seemed to be a series of narrow escapes from one set of jaws to another. One day, the teeth would snap shut and...

It's fine it's fine it's fine it's fine it's fine it's fine it's fine...

Lily shook her head. "That doesn't make any sense. There's no reason for her to still be here. I mean, how far does her jurisdiction even go?"

Nathan shrugged. "I'm not sure. I wouldn't sweat it. Everybody gets a little paranoid when a cop is behind them."

Not everyone is being followed by this cop, though, she thought.

Without question, the deputy was closer now, close enough to make out the details of her face. Thoughts were swirling through Lily's mind, foremost of which was why she hadn't been pulled over yet. Part of her wished to just get it over with, the other part wanted to floor it and put all of this life behind her. To escape her life, her family, The Manor... even David, who, as much as she wished for it, would never really be hers.

She turned to Nathan. "What would you say if I asked you to run away with me?" She hadn't expected to say it. The words came like an impulse, raw and unfiltered.

"What?"

"You and me. Let's just go. We've got a full tank of gas; I can take us anywhere in the world. Think of it as a fresh start. We could both use a fresh start, don't you agree?"

"Wait, you're serious? Lily, I don't know where this is coming from, but... We barely even know each other. And Rachel..."

"Rachel isn't here, Nathan. She left us both. I don't know about you, but I think we deserve some happiness." She reached over and squeezed his thigh. "I could make you happy. If you gave me a chance."

Before Nathan could answer, a shrill *whoop whoop* sounded behind them and brilliant red and blue lights danced in the mirrors. Lily cursed under her breath.

"You should stop."

Lily slowed and pulled over, not bothering to clarify what Nathan was referring to.

There was a thump behind them as the deputy closed the door to her squad car. Gravel crunched under her boots as she approached. On the exterior, Lily appeared perfectly still, but underneath she was a storm. A disquiet unease fell on her.

We're alone. She waited until we were far from town, and we're alone.

It's fine it's fine it's fine it's fine it's fine it's fine it's fine...

A sharp tap came on her window. Deputy Sarah stood outside with the sun glaring off her aviators. The window made a soft humming sound as Lily rolled it down. A sobering wash of cool air hit her face.

"Do you know why I pulled you over?"

Lily shook her head, looking straight ahead and avoiding Sarah's eyes. The road ahead looked narrow and distant, the end an impossible distance she would never be able to reach.

Sarah leaned in a little closer. "You have a taillight out."

"A taillight? I don't think - "

She stopped short when the deputy turned and walked to the back of the car. With a violent strike, Sarah smashed the left side out of the car. There was a crushing, shattering sound, and Lily stifled a scream. The car rocked as Sarah kicked at the back, denting the bumper and trunk, as if for good measure.

"What the...?" Nathan muttered.

Lily kept quiet as a single tear rolled down her perfect face.

Sarah came back up to the window, her voice a breathless hiss. "Listen to me, you whore. You stay away from my man. David's mine, understand?"

Almost imperceptibly, Lily bowed her head. Nathan was quiet as he watched the scene unfold.

Sarah patted the hood of the car, and as she walked away called back, "Get that taillight fixed!"

The squad car's door slammed shut and stones kicked up as Sarah sped back toward Silas Ridge. Lily and Nathan sat parked until the deputy was out of sight. Without a word, Lily pulled back onto the road and headed back to Thurman Manor.

Neither spoke for the rest of the drive.

When they arrived back at the Manor, Lily pulled the car around the loop and parked off to the side, facing the way they had come in. She looked down the drive, wishing with everything inside her to just take off and not look back. Forget Sarah, forget David, and most of all, forget this godforsaken house. But she knew she was going back in there. It was a foregone conclusion, as if fate had a plan for her.

"I'd appreciate your discretion," she said to Nathan. Her voice was quiet and dejected.

"Sure. Of course."

His hand rested on the door handle, and his seatbelt was already off, as if ready to run from her presence at his earliest opportunity. She laughed to herself at the idea of the two of them; her desperate to flee her life, and Nathan desperate to flee from her. Something told her she'd made more of a mess in this situation than she had with David, and that was saying something. Without a word, she opened her door and stepped out.

They walked the steps leading to Thurman Manor's front door, and before it had swung shut, Elisabeth was barreling around the corner, her heels clacking on the hard floor. She stopped under the chandelier in the entry and put a hand on her hip.

"Where have you been?"

Lily and Nathan looked at one another, unsure which of them Elisabeth was addressing. Lily's head dropped like she was waiting for a beating, reflecting a fear that had built up year after year.

"It was my fault," Nathan said. "I asked her to take me into town."

Elisabeth's eyes shot toward Nathan.

"Do you understand what needs to happen around here? Do you have any idea how much work needs to be done to be ready for this funeral? We only have two days! Two! How are things supposed to be ready unless everyone is helping?"

"What do you mean, two days?"

Elisabeth's arms folded across her chest. "I made some calls, just getting things started. When I called about catering, there was only one place available. Unless, of course, we're willing to wait a few weeks, but that's out of the question. So, I booked it. The food will be here in two days, which means everything else will be too."

"You should have talked to me first. We're supposed to be doing this together."

Elisabeth's voice was accusatory. "You weren't here, were you? I made a decision. If you want your opinion heard, I suggest more participation and less joy riding with my daughter."

Lily jumped in. "We weren't joy riding, Mom. Nathan needed to talk to the police."

"The police? Did something come up?"

"Not exactly," Nathan said. "I wanted to check and see if they had Rachel's phone. But they said they didn't find it."

Elisabeth went quiet for a beat. She came back with, "I'm sorry to hear that. Did they have any ideas about where you might look next?"

Nathan shook his head. "Our conversation got cut short."

Elisabeth looked back and forth between them; her eyes full of questions.

"Mom, they found out. Those people from town. A group showed up at the police station, like, protestors or something. We had to leave out the back."

"What?" Elisabeth rushed to her daughter's side and took her hands. "Are you ok? Were you hurt?"

Lily shook her head. "No, we're fine, Mom. But the car - they damaged the car. I think they threw a rock, maybe. Or a few rocks - it just happened so fast."

Lily shot Nathan a sideways glance, almost imperceptibly. For the time being, his mouth remained closed. But his eyes questioned her.

Elisabeth stormed over to the window and looked out at the car. Her fists shook down by her sides as she assessed the damage.

"That's just what we need right now. As if we didn't have enough to deal with already." Elisabeth was talking to no one in particular, dangerously close to a rant. "We should find out who they are. We'll sue them for everything they have. I'll make sure they're sorry they ever heard the name Thurman."

"Mom, it's not worth it. Just let it go. I'll get the car fixed, and we can just forget all about this, ok?"

Elisabeth turned away from the window and toward her daughter. "It's not your fault, dear. It was those nasty people. They have miserable little lives, and they decided you were a good target to vent their frustrations on." Elisabeth closed her eyes and let out a cleansing breath. She moved her hands out in front of her chest like she was practicing yoga, or tai chi. "We're going to focus on the funeral. We can't get distracted by things like this. I won't let lesser people bring us down." Elisabeth looked back out at the car while Nathan and Lily stood behind her in silence.

Lily was the first to speak again. "I'm going to go freshen up, Mom. It's been a day."

Elisabeth remained silent in the window, wrapped in gray light.

———

"Elisabeth, we need to talk."

The entry was quiet except for the constant ticks of the grandfather clock. If he concentrated hard, Nathan guessed he could hear the beeps of Edward's machinery pumping away further back in the house. But it also could have been his imagination.

The day was dramatically different from what he could have imagined, but one event stood out among the rest. He hadn't expected it in the slightest, but he'd read Rachel's obituary. And it wasn't his. One might argue it was the smallest event to have occurred, but that was a mere technicality. Those words, and the critically missing ones, loomed in his mind, like a cloud ready to release a torrent.

Elisabeth turned to him with a polite smile. She raised her pencil thin eyebrows in curiosity. She afforded him not a single word, instead opting to address him with a stare and wait for him to start.

Nathan felt embarrassed and alone. What he envisioned to be a simple conversation now seemed more like a confrontation, one in which he would make baseless accusations. His tongue felt dry and stiff, and the words were hard to come by.

As lightly as he could manage, he said, "I saw a paper today."

Elisabeth smiled. "Yes, Rachel's obituary would have been in there. It was very nice, don't you think?"

And just like that, it was out, without so much as a shred of denial, leaving him surprised and confused. Was he wrong about the whole thing? Were his feelings unfounded? If an offense had been committed, Elisabeth's face didn't reflect it. Nathan looked again, searching for a shred of guilt in her expression, but he found none.

"Uh - I'm confused. I had an obituary already written. Why didn't you at least speak with me before releasing one?"

"Well, it's like I said. We have very little time, Nathan. I had to make some executive decisions to make sure everything comes together properly."

"Elisabeth, this is my wife's funeral. I feel like I should have some say here."

Her face hardened. "And it's my daughter's. I'm just doing what I consider is best for her. I thought you'd be happy! You seem so overwhelmed by all of this. I figured I was taking some responsibility off your plate."

"Why would I be happy about being cut out of the plans? You should have talked to me about this, Elisabeth. I'm not even mentioned in the obit! I poured everything I had into..." He stopped short, too frustrated to finish. "Why didn't you talk to me first?"

Elisabeth took a step away from him, now looking to be near tears. She wrapped her arms around herself, as if cold, or as if shielding herself from harm. "I don't want to fight about this. Right now, we're all hurting. I get that you lost your wife, but you should remember I lost my daughter."

While hurt and upset over what had happened, it hadn't been his wish to take it out on Elisabeth. Maybe the truth was this was all a simple misunderstanding, and although terrible, something he needed to forgive and forget? After all, his own state of mind had been more than fragile since Rachel's death. Why wouldn't Elisabeth be as well? Maybe, in the midst of all the stress and insanity, she'd made an honest mistake?

Nathan tried to be gentle. "I understand all of that. I do. And I'm not trying to make a bad situation worse here. I'm just confused by why it happened, that's all."

"I didn't do anything wrong. All I did was make sure everything was moving along the way it's supposed to." She wiped at her eyes. "How do you expect this funeral to happen if I don't? These things don't just plan themselves."

"No, they don't plan themselves. All I'm asking is that I get to be included in the decisions. Can I at least be a part of this?"

Elisabeth released another one of her yoga sighs. "Yes,

of course. I was only trying to get the ball rolling. I assumed you'd appreciate what I did for you."

Although he couldn't explain it in that moment, Nathan felt put back on his heels. Somehow, in a strange reversal, he'd become the offender, and Elisabeth the victim. Yet, in his heart, he knew this to be untrue, even if he couldn't give it definition.

"I'm not ungrateful for all you've done. I just don't like surprises, that's all."

"Well, I'm willing to put this behind us if you are," Elisabeth said. She seemed to Nathan somehow taller in that moment, and the tears had all but vanished.

"Uh, yeah. It's forgotten. Let's just move on with the rest of the plans. When would you want to talk it through?"

"The biggest concerns have already been addressed, have they not? The burial plan is decided, as well as where the service will be held. I've handled the catering already. What else is there?"

Nathan searched for an answer. His face grew hot. Terrible middle school feelings rushed back, the gut sick sensation of being called on in class when you hadn't done your homework. The surprise of it left him speechless and numb in the mouth.

"What about flowers?" It was all he could think to say.

Elisabeth gave him a knowing smile, one dripping with victory. "All handled, dear."

Nathan looked around the room, as if the clock or wood floor or large portraits would give him an answer. But none came.

Back home, before all this, it had been up to him alone to plan Rachel's funeral. And while bills were a hurdle, this was a fundamentally different problem to navigate. Having all responsibility taken wasn't a blessing; it made him feel pointless and unnecessary. If he couldn't contribute to his wife's memorial, what good was he?

Unable to think of anything else, he said, "Well, I guess I'll just keep working on the video then. What point in the service did you want that to happen?"

"The beginning would be best. Before we walk her down to the mausoleum."

"That would be nice. I'm pretty close to being finished with it. Were there any special pictures you wanted to have included? Baby pictures? Or maybe special holidays?"

"I'll look through some and have Upham bring them to your room."

"There were a couple good ones in Rachel's bedroom. I can grab those. I was headed there anyway, to run through her things one more time. I just can't figure out where her phone went, but it has to be around here somewhere. It's driving me nuts."

Elisabeth looked concerned. "Oh, dear. That's going to be a problem. I'm afraid I've packed up all her things."

Visions of Rachel's belongings, packed and placed by a door as if ready for a trip, popped into his mind. Something about Elisabeth's tone caused him to doubt the accuracy of his imagination.

"What do you mean?"

She jerked her hands back and forth as if swatting at flies. "It was all too much to deal with. I had Upham pack everything away and place it in the basement. The sight of it was just getting to be too much."

Nathan almost said something, but worried it may come across as combative again, so he stopped.

"Well, maybe I can just look anyway. Maybe it got missed, you never know."

"I think it's best if we leave that for another time. The

basement's a disaster - old relics and storage. I wouldn't even consider it safe."

"I'll be ok. It'll just take a few minutes, I promise."

Elisabeth reached out and placed her hand on his shoulder. "Nathan, it's best if we leave that alone for the time being."

"Why? I just want to know where it is. What if she had a note or something on it? I've got questions, and I'm sure you do too. What if the answers are on that phone?"

She shook her head, as if pitying him. "You're reaching for something that isn't there. Maybe you're deflecting? Maybe you don't want to accept the fact that she's gone, and this is just a way to avoid the things you don't want to deal with. Like the funeral?"

"No, that's not it at all. I just - "

She stopped him short. "We need to put this to rest. At least until we have the funeral taken care of. Now, I'll speak with Upham and have him bring you some photos. Why don't you head up to your room and focus on the memorial?"

A single, definitive nod signaled the conversation had ended, and Elisabeth turned and walked away, her heels clicking in sync with the grandfather clock. Soon, she was gone, leaving Nathan alone and questioning what had just happened.

Chapter Twenty-Three

As Nathan was left standing bewildered in the entry, Lily was trying to forget the day's events. Yesterday, she'd wanted nothing more than for David to confess everything to his wife, thinking that somehow that would make things easier. But now, after her encounter with Sarah, all those prior ideas seemed stupid and childish.

Lily stripped down and piled her clothing on the floor. After a quick turn of the handle, the shower head gave an unsure spit of water, and then allowed a heavy downpour to flow open and free.

In contrast to the rest of the house, her bathroom was clinically bright. White tile glowed under the bright fluorescents that bordered the mirror over the sink. The shower was inside a glass enclosure, with a door that swung out wide for entry. She stood naked in front of the glass, waiting for the water to reach temperature. As soon as it began to steam over, she stepped into the warm water.

She positioned her head into the stream, allowing it to wash the day from her hair. A quick twist of the shower dial brought the heat up again, followed by a wonderful stinging sensation. Lily rotated her neck around, wishing the heat and steam would erase her past.

The glass had fogged over, obscuring the outside. Droplets of water sparkled like diamond vapor. Mist hovered in the shower like a cloud. Lily breathed in the moist air and felt her lungs open. Soap bubbled at her feet, white and sudsy, before being sucked down the drain. Lily increased the heat again and sat down on the tile floor. Water raced down her cheeks and dripped off her nose and chin. She sat there under the stream, allowing her skin to turn red. She closed her eyes and meditated on the water, on the heat; anything other than Sarah and David and Rachel and her life.

A peculiar itch scratched at the back of her neck. Like a point, causing pressure and demanding attention. Lily looked up and tried to focus through the glass, sensing she wasn't alone.

"Hello? Anyone there?" No reply.

Beyond the glass, a dark shape came into focus, lurking just beyond the fog. Lily felt her gut drop. The figure stood motionless, so still that she couldn't quite decide if there was a shape at all. Maybe her mind was playing tricks? Lily tried to decide what she was seeing, but she couldn't bring her hand to open the shower door and look.

The absolute stillness was unnerving. Lily stood rigid as it watched her, afraid to move, trapped. She considered how fast she could get out of the shower and out the door. If she was fast, and if surprise was on her side, there was a chance she could escape. But what if she didn't? Would she have to fight? And what if she succeeded? Would she just run out soaking wet and naked and screaming for help? Who would come to help way out here, anyway? Who would want to?

The shadow moved without moving and appeared closer. To Lily's eye it was like a picture fade, a seamless transition from one image into another. It was possible the figure drew Lily closer to it, instead of bringing itself closer to her.

She was close enough to touch the apparition, if not for the thin barrier separating them. Just outside the shower, through the steamed over glass, a hand appeared, reaching for her, with a ghastly long finger. The fog around the hand faded, like a window to elsewhere, and in the mist, it scribed one word:

Whore...

Though the water ran hot, the air became chilled and sharp and hurt her lungs. This sudden difference confused her body and mind, and her nerves screamed that the water was boiling. She scrambled to get out of the trap, and the figure dissolved into the fog. Water scalded her arm as she reached for the door, causing a gasp as she yanked it back from the stream. Lily backed against the far wall, as helpless and defenseless as a caged animal, trapped by a waterfall of deadly heat. She was certain she would cook in this shower. There was no escape.

And then, as quick as it came, the air returned to normal. The water she thought was boiling had turned cold; she'd drained the tank. The handle gave a meek little creak as she turned the shower off. She stood in quiet shock, dripping in the shower, listening for any sign other than the blood rushing in her ears. There was nothing except the chattering of her teeth.

She screamed at the top of her lungs. "IT'S NOT EVEN TIME!"

Chapter Twenty-Four

Nathan sniffed at the air and frowned. The stench in his room had become a little less earthy and taken on something closer to decomposition, reeking of rot and wet. He fumbled with a window latch and heard paint crack as he forced it open.

When was the last time these were used?

Soon he was wondering who the last person was that slept in this room. Maybe no one ever had. In a house this size, there were bound to be a few unused rooms here and there; this may have been one of them.

Nathan repeated the process on the other side of the room and a cross breeze cleansed the foul air. He would need an extra blanket tonight, but that was preferable to the smell, and a fair trade in his estimation. More fair than the hand life had been dealing him as of late.

There was a light tapping on his door. Nathan opened it to find Upham standing there, holding a shoebox filled to the brim with photographs, most of which showed their age with curled edges.

"Mrs. Thurman instructed me to bring these to you." Upham said, as he handed the box over to Nathan.

Nathan held the box in his hands and realized he didn't have the first idea about how to get these onto his computer. Had he been home, it wouldn't have been a question. There, he had his pick of scanners. Once he had to make do with a camera, snapping shots of the photographs, which he admitted was sort of "meta", but effective all the same. But his current situation left him without even his cell.

He turned to Upham and gave a sheepish shrug. "You wouldn't happen to know where I could get a scanner, would you? I didn't exactly think this through all the way when I talked to Elisabeth."

Upham considered this for a moment. "I could check, Mr. Stevens. I'm sure we have something tucked away. I'll ask Mrs. Thurman if she knows where one might be."

A twinge of panic rose up in Nathan's gut. "If you don't mind, can we keep it between us for now? I'm kind of embarrassed. I wouldn't want to give the impression I'm being careless."

Upham, always polite and accommodating, smiled. "Of course, sir. Whatever you are most comfortable with. I'll see what I can find on my own. Is there anything else you might need before I attend to the rest of my duties?" He looked toward the open window. "An extra blanket, perhaps?"

Nathan shook his head. "No, I think I'm set. Thank you."

"Very well. Again, it would be best if you didn't wander the halls. It's very easy to get turned around." Then he gave his signature bow and left Nathan to sort through the box of pictures.

He pulled them out in stacks and set them on the bed. Granted, he couldn't scan anything yet, but he could get them prepared. Photo selection was the lengthiest part of his process. Once he knew which he would use, the rest would come together on its own.

Nathan picked a pile at random and started flipping through one by one. There didn't seem to be any specific order, chronological or otherwise. Photos of Rachel as a child were mixed in with images of her as a teen. There were photos of her with her horses, and others on holidays. Scattered throughout were family portraits, some of which didn't even feature Rachel. He developed a rhythm of sorts, where he flipped through the pictures, making snap decisions on whether they qualified for consideration. Those he placed in a stack together, and the others, the throwaways, he put back into the box.

After several dozen, he came across one that caught his eye. Nathan held it at waist level, studying the image. It captured Rachel as a young girl. She wore a flowery dress and had a ribbon tied up in her hair. Her eyes seemed to look right through him, seeing him, even as he stood there so many years later. But the girl in the photo was unknown to Nathan; yes, it was Rachel, but long before he'd come into her life. It was not his wife, only a version of her, and one he didn't know at all. He tapped the photo against his palm as he dwelled on that and decided it belonged in the shoebox.

Soon, he'd sorted through all the pictures. The pile of potentials was notably short; he'd filled the box back up with photos that were either blurry, or damaged, or pointless, as they didn't even feature his wife.

His computer sat closed, and for the time being, would continue to sit that way. Lacking the ability to digitize these few photos left him stuck; one more frustration in an increasingly long line of setbacks. Nathan lay back on the bed, tracing imaginary paths through the swirl patterns in the ceiling. Chilled air drafted across his nose, still carrying remnants of foul odor. He stayed there, motionless, replaying the day's events over in his head. After a few minutes, he got up, determined for at least one thing to go right. Determined, but mistaken all the same.

It was 10:45pm.

Nathan worked his way toward the basement, taking the service corridor, keeping as quiet as he could. Elisabeth had already communicated to leave this whole phone issue alone until after the funeral. But as he'd reclined on his bed, it came right back to him, and stronger than ever. If answers existed, he had to know; that was non-negotiable. And what Elisabeth didn't know wouldn't hurt her.

The halls were empty at the base of the service corridor. Tall windows that ran the length of the hall looked like dark mirrors. The stranger that had been reflecting back at him in his coffee cup just a few days ago was looking at him again; not much had changed for the better.

The basement door might have been mistaken for a pantry, but when opened it led to a narrow staircase. Nathan flicked a switch, and a hanging bulb illuminated the shaft with dim yellow light, revealing simple wooden stairs and unfinished gray block walls. It was as if the builders had carved a tunnel out of the foundation. Boards creaked under his boots as he descended into the basement.

Underneath the house was dark and damp. The floor was stone, and little utility lights hung from the ceiling, but weren't bright enough for their intended purpose. Somewhere, Nathan could hear the faint, slow clink of water dripping. The sound echoed around and made it impossible to discern its direction. Further back, Nathan could make out what appeared to be a wine rack. In spite of the dank conditions, the consistent air temperature year-round made this an adequate wine cellar.

Nathan moved back toward the storage, looking around

for clues to where Rachel's belongings might have ended up. There were stacks of cardboard boxes, crumbling with decay. Trunks containing unknown contents gathered years of dust. Rachel's things were nowhere to be seen. Soon, Nathan found himself in front of the wine racks. Bottles rested in little cubbies and extended well up over his head. He estimated at least a hundred bottles or more to be stored on these shelves.

Nathan had never been a wine *connoisseur*, as he'd always been more of a beer man himself. He knew there were reds and whites, but down here, each bottle looked the same to him. All he could see were racks of thick green glass, each as meaningless as the next. He grabbed one at random and looked at the label, but it meant nothing to him. As he studied the wine, his wristwatch advanced, and he arrived at 10:57.

There was a sudden impact as the basement door above slammed shut. Overhead, the utility bulbs flickered, and even though the air was still, they swayed, as if caught in a pre-storm breeze. The bulb furthest from him popped and went black. One by one, in order, they winked out, leaving Nathan in the dark.

Nathan called out, "Hey, is anyone up there? Upham! Elisabeth! I'm down here, the lights are out. Can you bring a flashlight?" But the only response he got was the drip of a leaky pipe.

He stood still, alone in the darkness. The chilled basement air seemed to penetrate him right down to his bones. The space felt smaller. Constricted. Nathan was certain the ceiling was right on top of his head, ready to crush him. Instinctively, he ducked his head down to avoid a blow. He gripped the wine bottle a little harder. *It's a straight shot*, he told himself.

One step in front of the other. You'll touch the wall on

the other side, and then it's just a turn to your left, and it's up the stairs. Easy. Just one step in front of the other.

With the wine clutched in his right hand, Nathan put his left arm out in front of him like a blind man. And blind he was. The darkness was complete, his hand invisible in front of him. He could still hear the water dripping: *clink... clink... clink...* He took a small shuffle forward, waving his hand around in the nothing. Guessing his path forward to be clear, he took another step. He repeated the slow, constant process, with each inch trying to guess how far he'd come. Halfway? Less? It was impossible to tell. Nathan waved his hand out front, felt nothing, shuffled forward again. Rinse and repeat.

Up ahead, masked behind a corner, he saw a faint, blue flicker of light. It came and went, growing brighter as he approached, flashing like a bulb and lighting the room up like lightning. His breath was quick and shallow. Nathan wanted to run, but where? Behind him, it was only pitch black, and to his knowledge, there was only one way out of the basement. And that lay further ahead, past the blue flicker. He got down on all fours and crept closer to the strobe. When he reached the edge, he peered around and into the unfathomable.

Through the course of his life, Nathan would never be able to purge his memory, although he would often wish to. Against the wall was a fuse box, the cover removed and its wires exposed. Angry sparks spit against the wall in bright flashes. A thick black wire hung down like a snake writhing from the wall. And impossible as it was, beneath the fuse box, a man biting the thick wire, his face blackened and burned. Blue arcs spanned across the man's teeth. All the hair had been burned from the top of his head, leaving the scalp blistered and charred. Nathan retched as the smell hit him.

Something musty and decomposed.

He tasted bile in his mouth. Overcome with horror and terror, his only thought in that moment was to escape this basement, to never see this, or anything like it, ever again. He ran but slipped and fell face first, his hands flying out to brace his fall. The wine bottle smashed, and dark liquid ran across the cold floor. Nathan winced and clutched his hand, feeling the sting of a cut and the warmth of fresh blood. But in the dark, it was impossible to know how deep it was. He scrambled again to his feet, but felt his foot caught on something. Or more accurately, something had caught his foot. Despite the darkness, he saw them, the unnaturally long fingers, cold with death. He saw long cracked nails, gripping, clawing, scratching excitedly at his foot.

A scream was stuck in his throat. He was suffocating. The room was growing smaller. The time to act was now, or the decision to give himself over to unknown depths of insanity would be made for him. He lashed out with wild, frantic kicks to free himself from whatever gripped him.

And then, without reason, it was gone. He gasped for breath, panting on the cold, wine-soaked ground. His clothes were wet again, this time not drenched in ditch water but expensive alcohol. And although irrational, he wondered how much money he'd just shattered across the floor.

Nathan charged across the gap, pumping his legs like pistons, giving no caution to his steps. He hadn't gauged how quickly he would cross the distance and he slammed into the wall on the other side. The force knocked him back and he lost his wind, but he regained his balance and bolted up the stairs. He feared he would find the door locked at the top, that he would be trapped down here with the fingers and the corpse and the dark. But the door opened with ease.

He stumbled out and fell into the light. He twisted

himself around and kicked the door shut. As it slammed, just on the edge of his vision, he caught (or thought he caught) a glimpse of a hideous charred skull with silvery white eyes and a vicious grin.

Nathan lay on the ground, heaving in deep breaths, his heart thumping in his chest. His eyes stayed locked on the basement door. Scary movies had taught him this was the point at which the dread would swell, that evil was lurking just beyond his view, that it was right behind the door, ready to pounce, desiring nothing more than his blood and his flesh. The knob would rattle and turn, and the door would open. And then there would be nothing there, just an empty door. But that would be false relief, a ruse, because as the image lingered a little too long, building tension, a hidden face or a hand would shoot out from behind and grab the person distracted by the anticipation. He prayed it wouldn't open on its own.

It never came. The door stayed shut.

There was a rattle and clink behind him, and he spun, expecting something villainous. He saw Upham, dressed to the nines, carrying the scanner he'd gone off in search of and bearing a look of grave concern. He examined Nathan, still sprawled on the floor, and covered in wine.

"I told you not to wander the house alone."

"What was that Upham? Tell me what that was."

Nathan paced his bedroom, his mind searching for an acceptable explanation for what he just experienced. He couldn't think of one. Upham watched him pace. He stood with astonishing ease, more calm than Nathan thought he should be. In fact, Upham showed no sign of surprise at all after hearing Nathan's account of the basement.

Nathan stopped and crossed his arms. "Say something. What's going on?" He waited.

Upham regarded Nathan for a moment. Then he looked over his shoulder at the open door. He hurried across the room, peered down either end of the hall, and closed it behind him with a conspiratorial click.

His voice was a whisper. "There's a madness in this house. It's always been here. Sometimes it's less, sometimes it's more. What you saw in the basement was - more."

Nathan almost laughed. "I don't even know what I saw in the basement. How did I see that? I keep asking myself, and the best I can come up with is that I'm losing my mind."

Upham's face turned deadly serious. "Don't make light of such things. This house decides when you lose your mind, and if it decides to take it, you'll know."

"The house decides? What is that supposed to mean?"

Upham sighed and his shoulders slumped. "I came to work for Edward's father when I was a young man. At first, things were everything I expected. He was driven, and difficult to please at times, but I would have been unhappy working for a lesser man. Mr. Thurman was a pioneer, a visionary. It was an honor that he'd entrusted his family to my care, and I've done my very best with them, each and every day. It's been the great privilege of my life to have cared for two generations of Thurman children." Upham's eyes wandered as if he were reliving a distant memory.

Through clenched teeth, he said, "Eventually, it all changed. At first, it was too subtle to notice. A flickering light here, a random noise there - but nothing more than a normal house would make. It was easy to overlook things. That might be a part of it too. Overlooking things, I mean. Sometimes I wonder if the house wants to be subtle, just to draw you in. At a certain point though, it snaps. Like it did with Edward's father." Upham's eyes met Nathan's. "Like it did with Rachel."

Nathan sat down on the bed, his mind darting back and forth. His thoughts were slippery, and he was unable to focus on any single one before it was gone and another danced in front of his attention. He shook his head like he was trying to rid himself of his thoughts.

"No. I won't believe a ghost killed my wife. That's not possible."

Upham's tone stayed level. "It took me years to accept it, and even now, I won't claim to understand it. I don't know if it's ghosts, or if it's tricks on the mind. I suppose it could be both, I'm not sure. But if you decide to be honest with yourself, you'll find it all to be true. Think about what you've already seen. There's more to this house than just what you saw in the basement."

Nathan thought about strange darkness in the woods. Lights that didn't appear bright enough. Hallways that seemed to take you further than you meant to go. He thought about what Suzy told him in the coffee shop.

"There was a girl in town, at a coffee shop. She said the house was haunted too."

Something like a grunt came from Upham's throat. "There have been rumors for as long as I can remember. They aren't mistaken, but it's not spoken of in the house. I would advise you to avoid such conversations. The family does not appreciate the speculation around town."

"You mean the fanatics?"

Upham's head bobbed. "Them and others. It's not only the most radical of the community that can damage reputations."

Nathan's hand brushed against the box of photos. The stack tipped, and whether by fate or chance, the photo of Rachel appeared, the one discarded not an hour before. Her eyes still seemed to look right through him. This time, he allowed himself to linger in her gaze for a moment. He thought of her life before they'd met, and all the hesitancy to speak of her past.

He looked back at Upham. "Is this what Rachel grew up with? Is this why she didn't like to talk about her childhood?"

Upham shook his head. "That I can't answer for sure, but it's a good guess. No one here enjoys discussing such things. The topic is avoided, if at all possible." Then he added, "And I'd appreciate it if we kept this conversation between us. I shouldn't be talking about it, but after what you saw, it seemed unavoidable." Upham turned to leave. "I'll remind you once again. You'd be wise to not wander the house alone."

When he got to the door, Nathan called after him. "Upham? What happened to Edward's dad?"

Upham hesitated. Then, almost with reverence, he said, "He electrocuted himself. In the basement, at precisely 10:57."

Chapter Twenty-Five

Doors stayed closed as the family hid in their rooms, until all sound, save for the occasional groan of the house, ceased. At one point, Upham had knocked on his door to see if Nathan wanted tea, but the delivery went ignored. Soon, Nathan could hear Upham shuffle back down the hall. He left a tray with cups and boiling water just outside the door. Nathan left it to grow cold.

Neon swirls fluttered across his laptop screen. Nathan studied them, trying to guess which shape they would take next, leaving his eyes half focused like he was trying to see a picture hidden in the code. He accepted that this was a distraction, something to take his mind off the stress and hallucinations and ghosts, or whatever was going on.

With each passing minute, Nathan found himself wishing for this all to be over, to be home, to mourn as he saw fit and in his own time. Maybe when he got back, he'd find a counselor, like Lewis had suggested. Or maybe instead of a counselor, a shrink.

Lewis. I completely forgot.

He punched a key, and the screensaver died away. With another click, he was in his email. He composed a new message to Lewis and began punching at the keys, starting at the beginning, and detailed the events of the last few days. After several minutes, he looked back over his message, and then deleted what he'd written. It sounded insane, or at a bare minimum, something to be discussed in person. Instead, he sent just the date and location for Rachel's service. The computer made a little whooshing sound as the email hurried on its way.

Nathan looked at his watch. It was close to one in the morning, and sleep seemed an impossibility. The mere idea of closing his eyes for an extended period of time... Nathan dreaded what he might see if he did.

A gust blew through the room, and Nathan rubbed his stiff, cold hands together. The windows had done their job well, but that meant a dramatic drop in temperature. However, after the basement, that smell simply could not stay.

Better frigid than that stench.

He wanted nothing to do with that basement again. Ever. He sniffed the air for hints but detected nothing. Now that the room seemed clear, Nathan decided to close the windows. But he told himself that if the slightest whiff returned, the windows were going right back up, even if it dropped to fourteen degrees outside.

Nathan closed one window. It stuck at the top, but he used his body weight and it gave all at once and slammed shut. At the second window, the one closest to the lake, he anticipated the same. Nathan hooked his fingers along the edge of the sill and prepared to pull, but stopped short.

Two stories below, he heard singing. It was faint, near imperceptible. If the window hadn't been open, he would have missed it. The girl, light and cheerful, singing and humming to herself. He looked down below and caught sight of her moving in between the trees. It looked like Lily.

He watched her, curious as to what she was doing. She had no coat, and no shoes, yet she moved through the woods as if she didn't notice the freezing air. Frolicking is the word Nathan would have used. Yes, frolicking through the woods at night, barefoot with no coat in the cold. Curious... Was she drunk?

Madness...

She hadn't been drunk earlier.

Madness...

As he watched, it became clear she was headed toward the water. Nathan told himself that she wanted a quiet moment to herself on the dock. After all, the afternoon's events were upsetting, and he himself was having trouble sleeping. But Upham's voice was loud in his mind.

There's a madness in this house...

Lily stopped at the water's edge, her feet halfway off the dock, and stared out upon the lake. She matched the stillness of the water; only the hem of her dress swayed in the night breeze. Despite the freezing cold temperatures, she didn't shiver at all.

When he remembered to breathe again, his breath was a cloud. She appeared as a statue, or a sentry, motionless, and Nathan couldn't look away. Nathan squinted his eyes, afraid to blink in case she would vanish.

Lily turned a slow pirouette, her gaze no longer on the water, but directed toward Nathan. They locked eyes. Even in the dark, he knew it, just as he'd known it on his first night. She had made sure she had his attention. He felt it. She gave him a mournful smile, and then she stepped into the water.

She's killing herself. God, please no, please God, no.

He flew down the stairs, three, four at a time, coming

wildly close to losing his balance and tumbling down as he did so. Narrowly avoiding a fall, he rushed toward the front door, pulled the great frame open, and dashed toward the water. His legs pumped. His heart pounded. His feet had trouble keeping balance at this breakneck speed. He was on the edge of chaos, breathless, trying to keep it together.

Madness.

He ducked his head as invisible branches slapped at his face, but it was impossible to avoid all of them. One lashed out and slashed him across the cheek. Roots in the ground reached up like boney fingers trying to grab him. One gripped his foot, and he fell headlong onto the ground. His skull ignited and brilliant white light flooded his vision. He got on his knees and shook his head clear. Ignoring the pain, he picked himself up and scrambled toward the lake.

When he reached the water's edge, it was clear as glass. Nathan gasped for breath as he searched the lake, looking for any sign of where she might be. The air was silent. No splashing, no cry for help, no reassuring sound of help on the way. Nothing but still water, silent and reflecting moonlight and stars.

Just as he was on the verge of losing hope, he saw her, floating, a disruptive form against the mirror surface. Nathan dove in without regard. Frigid water smacked him as he went under, and the air was sucked from his lungs. Automatic response took over, sending him into near panic from the shock. His breathing became shallow and rapid. With great concentration, he forced his breathing to submit to his will. He took long slow inhales, and let short staccato bursts out, mimicking Lamaze techniques the best he knew how. Within a few minutes, his body calmed, and he swam out toward Lily as fast as his limbs would propel him. He focused on each stroke and put as much force into his kicks as possible.

The dark water was impossible to navigate, and he could only hope he was swimming the right direction. Adrenaline would only carry him so far; he hoped it would be enough to find Lily and get them both back to shore. He didn't linger on what would happen should he run out of energy. Each stroke pulled him further, each kick propelled him away from safety. He felt the depth of the lake deep below him. Dark water surrounded him on all sides, and a primitive part of his brain feared what lurked below. Underneath was vast darkness without a bottom, and it desired to consume him.

A yelp escaped his lips when his leg bumped into something large in the water. Nathan spun his body away, his mind giving way to monsters and sharp teeth and black eyes in the depths. He looked all around him, searching for the hungry creature that had investigated his leg. He saw a faint figure in white under the surface, illuminated by the moonlight.

Lily.

Nathan dove down. He could see her suspended in the water, unconscious, and sinking fast. If he didn't reach her now, she would be lost forever to the freezing depths. He kicked hard, away from the surface. His hands reached for her, desperate for a hold. He was just inches from a grip. Their fingertips touched, but again she slipped away.

It was then that Lily's eyes popped open. She was blurred, dark and muted in the water. But somehow, Nathan could see her clearly, even if only in his mind. Her lips parted into a nasty grin, revealing needle-like teeth, ivory and vicious.

Madness.

She grabbed him. She locked her grip around his wrist and yanked him down. Nathan pulled back, trying to break free. She was forcing him into the deep. They thrashed, each fighting to go in opposite directions, each determined to get the other to their side like a deadly game of tug-of-war. Nathan pulled back as forcefully as he could, but each time she pulled back, and he fell deeper. She fought him like an animal, scratching and pulling. He was losing. The pale light above was growing dimmer, and he knew he was getting deeper. His lungs ached and he gulped for air in vain. If this insanity that had overtaken Lily didn't end, they would both be lost. Any second now, he would lose consciousness.

Time was up. Nathan's vision was growing as black as the lake. In one last attempt, he balled his free hand into a fist, and in one motion yanked Lily as he threw the haymaker, hoping to God it would make contact. His fist smashed into the side of her head and Lily went limp. Her grip relaxed.

He grabbed under her armpits and kicked with everything he had left toward the surface. He was desperate for air. His lungs forced him to inhale, and water flooded his lungs. Everything was pitch black, impossible to know up from down. Just when he thought it was the end, his head broke the surface. He coughed and sputtered and vomited up water. Nathan bobbed just on the surface, getting his breath. And with one arm looped around her, he started the journey back to shore.

Moving his arm was difficult, and he was losing his sense of where the shore was located. Soon, he'd lost all sense of direction. His face was level with the water's surface, and there wasn't a single landmark in his view to orient himself with. There was only dark above him, and dark below. Where was the shore? Which direction was he supposed to go? He panicked, worried he was swimming further out and away from where he needed to be. Everything had failed. After all this, he and the girl would sink to the bottom of the lake. In a few weeks, a thick slab of ice would form over the lake's surface, sealing them in their tomb like a stone.

Then, by some miracle, he heard a voice. It was faint, but he heard it all the same. With the little remaining energy he possessed, he swam toward the sound. Nathan only hoped he had the strength to make it. Hands grabbed at him, and he could feel himself being pulled onto land.

Obscure shapes dominated his vision and his teeth chattered against each other. He lay on his side, and through distorted vision, saw a figure around him. The shape approached, anonymous and mysterious. It grew closer, growing in size as it came nearer, until it took over his entire field of vision. Nathan felt himself falling, and then everything went black.

Chapter Twenty-Six

"It almost had you there," he said.

Nathan found himself in a bed, wrapped in thick, heavy blankets made from tightly wound wool. A comforting fire glowed nearby.

"The lake," the voice repeated. "It almost got you. Couple minutes more and you'd have been at the bottom. But you made it. You'll be happy to know she made it too. Miracle if I ever saw one. If you hadn't dove in all foolheaded, the lake would have taken Lily tonight too. And that - well, that'd be too much for this family to bear."

An older man, a stranger to Nathan, sat before him. He had gray hair and a thick mustache that drew the eye from hard facial features forged by years of hard work. But there was also an uncommon kindness in that face, possibly a result of those same years. He sat in a rocking chair near the fire, tending to it and Nathan.

"I saw her go into the water. I ran in, but I don't know what happened after that," Nathan said.

He screwed his eyes shut and tried to remember. Bits came back, but he wasn't sure. It was like trying to recall the details of a dream after waking. The memories were slippery, right at the edge of his consciousness. Or like gazing at a distant star, barely there until you looked directly at it, and then it vanished.

"What happened was you got some hypothermia. But you managed to save Lily. God only knows what she was doing, but it was a good thing you were there."

"I saw her from my window, and she just went into the lake. I thought she was taking a walk. Or that maybe she'd been drinking. When she went into the water, I freaked out."

Nathan sat up, but kept the blanket wrapped around his shoulders. The room he was in had wood walls, like a cabin, and a stone fireplace glowing hot. The fire snapped and sap boiled and spit from a log. There were lamps around the room, set low and casting warm light. Nathan saw now he was on a cot, not a bed, as he'd first imagined. It had been set up in the middle of the room, as if it was supposed to be close to the heat.

"Where am I? How did I get here?" Nathan asked.

The old man didn't answer right away. Instead, he handed Nathan a large cup.

"Here, drink this. It's my secret recipe."

"What is it?" Nathan asked.

"Chicken broth. Drink up. It'll help your body recover."

"Thank you," replied Nathan. The broth was salty and hot and it stung the back of his throat, but as Nathan drank, he felt his stomach warm, and it comforted his body.

"I sorta remember getting back to shore, but it's fuzzy. I can't... I remember hands... Was it you? Did you pull me back?"

"You'd made it almost all the way, but you were moving real slow at the end. It'd have been a real shame if you'd made it all that way only to drown in waist deep water."

"I guess I owe you a pretty big thanks. You saved my life."

The old man shrugged it off. "Not so much. You did most of it. I just kind of helped you along at the very end."

"I don't know your name," Nathan said.

The old man reached his hand out for a handshake. His grip was firm and his skin rough with callouses. "Everyone calls me Hancock. Pleased to meet you."

"Nice to meet you too. And thank you, Hancock."

"My pleasure. Just glad I was there."

Nathan sipped his broth and an odd thought occurred to him. "We were in the middle of nowhere. How were you in the exact right spot at the exact right time?"

Hancock fussed at the fire with a poker. He said, "I think the term is *serendipity*. But luck suits my tastes better and does just as well, in my opinion. Truth is, you came to me more than the other way around. My cabin is right here on the lake, not far from the Manor. I was getting ready for bed and heard splashing. I walked out and saw you struggling, so I called out. Once you got close enough, I just had to pull you to shore. I saw Lily, and I called up to the house right away. They took her back. Wanted her in her own bed and all. I figured they'd have their hands full up there, so I asked if I could keep an eye on you here. Just to be safe."

"You live here? I didn't think anyone except the Thurmans lived on the lake?"

"Been here quite a while. I tend to the horses. It's a time-consuming job. Being close to work is a nice advantage." He smiled to himself. "The Thurmans have always kept their staff close at hand. Always ready to go at a moment's notice."

The horses. He works with the horses.

A question burned in Nathan's thoughts, one he knew

the answer to, but was still afraid to ask. He considered his next words and gathered courage for what would come.

"You care for the horses?"

Hancock hesitated, like he wasn't sure he wanted to answer the question. Or maybe that he wasn't sure he should. When he did, the words came out slow and reluctant.

"Yes, I've had that job for quite some time."

Nathan's voice, close to a whisper, choked. "Did you find my wife?"

He was keenly aware of the silence that followed. The air felt thick. Nathan knew the answer. But he needed to hear it out loud.

Again, Hancock was slow to respond. For a few moments, all Nathan heard was the hiss and pop from the fire.

Finally, he said, "That morning felt so normal to me. That's a funny word, isn't it? Normal. What does that even mean? I know what everyone *thinks* it means, but normal is different for everyone, isn't it? I thought I was going to have a normal day. Get some breakfast, head down to the stables, do my chores." Hancock stabbed his poker at a log and sent sparks erupting all over. "Things didn't go that way, did they?"

His eyes were dry as a bone, but his sniffling nose gave his emotions away. "I've heard people use the phrase *new normal*, which is really just a marketer's term for saying things have changed, but we'll get used to it and forget the way things were." He shook his head as if the idea revolted him. "There ain't no gettin' used to this stuff, though." The pair sat for a long while, watching the flames dance and embers pulse.

"I'm so very sorry for your loss," Hancock said. "I knew

Rachel ever since she was a little girl. Never guessed this was how things would end up."

"Yeah, me neither." Nathan quipped. "Like you said, things turn out different than you expect."

"Life's always different than you expect; that's my experience at any rate."

Nathan scoffed. "Glad I have so much to look forward to. You know, there's a part of me that wishes you would have left me." His blanket slipped from his shoulders, but Nathan made no move to put it back.

Hancock moved the logs around to get better airflow. The fire got brighter with the increased oxygen and cast an orange glow on their faces. He considered his next words.

"It's ok to feel that way. For a while anyway. But don't stay there forever; people will need you. Like Lily needed you." Hancock placed another log on the fire. It spit sparks, and then settled down. "Don't let ghosts haunt you forever. Ghosts get stuck, they can't move on. People can, and that's what gives us hope in this life."

"You sound like Upham with all the ghost talk."

Hancock chuckled, more to himself than Nathan. "I suppose that's true." He looked at Nathan and asked, "You up for a walk?"

Brisk, early morning air greeted them as they stepped outside. Warm light coated the world, melting overnight frost. The areas the sun hadn't touched yet made pleasant crunching sounds under their feet. It was peaceful, something Nathan had been lacking for what seemed like a long time.

He looked out on the water. He couldn't quite picture what happened last night. In the early light, everything seemed tranquil. But the trenches in the bank where

Hancock had dragged them out reminded him that terror was just below the surface.

"This way," Hancock called.

Nathan turned back away from the water. Hancock was already several paces ahead, waiting for him to follow. He started walking down a thin path lined by pines on either side. Nathan followed, curious about where this may lead.

"Where are we going?"

Hancock didn't directly answer. "I've been working here for longer than I can remember. Came on as a young man. I'll leave not so young. I always liked animals, you know? Thought it would be fun to work with horses." He smirked, adding, "But again, life turns out different. I used to walk this path a lot. Helped me think. I drive the truck more often now. Old age is a taker, that's for sure. But when I was younger, walking was my time to reflect. Like meditation. By the time my walk was finished, I'd have some clarity."

"Yeah, I know what you mean," Nathan replied.

Hancock stopped on the path and put his hands on his hips, taking deep breaths. "What you did for Lily was very brave. Miracle that you were there."

Nathan shrugged. "It was just chance, really. I heard something outside my window and happened to look outside and saw her. After that I just reacted. Same as anyone would do in that situation."

Hancock shook his head. "I disagree. Not everyone would do that. You jumped into action when it counted. Some people freeze up and don't move at all. Maybe there's others that would call for help but sit back and wait for someone else to do what's necessary. And maybe some people would ignore the whole thing, roll back over in bed and let it happen. Pretend later they didn't see. That could have been you. No one would have known otherwise; you could have done nothing. Never told anyone you heard her, and this ends up just another a tragic story."

"Didn't seem like a choice to me. It's just how it happened," Nathan said.

"There's always a choice, conscious or not. Sometimes, people make their choices long before they realize it. Maybe that's fate, predestination, whatever. Point is, the choices we make determine the next set we get to choose from. Like it or not, there's going to be some hard decisions that come your way. Ain't no avoiding it."

They walked on, and Nathan shrugged out of his jacket. His blood was moving, and the symptoms of his hypothermia had all but vanished. His head was clear, his limbs were loosening up. The pines started to thin out, and it opened into a wider area with fences surrounding a large grassy area. Up ahead and beyond the grass, Nathan caught sight of a large barn, painted white. He stopped dead in his tracks and a cold shiver shot up his spine. All his warmth dissipated, and he wanted to put his coat back on. He understood where Hancock was leading him.

Hancock turned back to Nathan. "Here's the next choice for you. Up ahead is the barn where I found Rachel. Just beyond that, not far, is the house. You could go back up there, maybe get in your warm bed, that little man Upham can bring you some tea, and you can try to forget about your problems. But you already know you can't forget your problems. They won't let you."

"Or?"

"You make the hard choice. You come with me into that barn, face your problems head on. And you can try to start finding some closure."

Nathan stared at the barn, terrified to go inside. And despite a sense that the choice had already been made, it surprised him when he heard himself say, "Show me."

. . .

The barn itself wasn't anything fancy. In fact, it was in need of some repair. Wood rot was visible on the doors and trim work. Everything needed a fresh coat of paint. But the bones were good; no flaws significant enough to make it unusable. To anyone else, this would appear to be a very normal barn, but Nathan knew better than to see this on a surface level. He knew what he was walking into. Nothing about this was normal.

Hancock spoke first. "I got here early that morning. It was cold, nasty weather. I heard the horses. That's what stands out the most to me now. Horses are smart animals. They knew. Thinking back, it's obvious, but I didn't put it together at the time. How could I? I thought maybe they got spooked by a snake or something. That's not uncommon. It's taken days for them to calm down, but even now they're on edge. Rachel loved these horses ever since she was a child, and I'm pretty sure they loved her back."

The hinges creaked as Hancock pulled the barn door back. Nathan gazed inside. His eyes were still accustomed to the bright light outside; he couldn't make out many details. Everything seemed dark and foreboding. After pausing a moment to gather his will, he forced himself to step forward. His feet dragged like his boots were made of lead, each step labored and forced. Hancock followed behind. Nathan heard the creak of the barn door being closed.

He spun back around. "Don't close that. Leave it open. Please."

Hancock paused mid close and saw Nathan's pleading face. He let go, and the door swayed back and forth until it settled and stopped. Nathan released his breath, realizing he'd been holding it in. His body trembled. His left eye twitched, which he pretended was allergies.

When he felt he had control, Nathan turned back toward the center of the barn and took a few more steps in. Behind him, he could hear Hancock rattling a latch on a stable door, muttering about how he needed to get it fixed. A horse put his head over the gate, flaring its nostrils and shooting out great puffs of air. Hancock stroked the horse's neck and made soothing sounds. Nathan hadn't been around horses often, and their size in real life shocked him.

Stale beams of light shot through the cracks in the barn, highlighting the drifting dust and hay that floated in the air. A large, thick wooden beam spanned the entire width of the structure. There was nothing there anymore, but he didn't need to ask Hancock if this was where he found her. He could see it all in his mind. Rachel was there, plain as day before his eyes. Nathan walked to where he knew her heart took its final beats and stood quiet and still. No tears came. Hancock waited silently off to the side and allowed Nathan to take the time he needed.

"This is it, isn't it? This is where you found her."

"Yes."

"What else did you find?"

"Nothing. Just her."

"The police never found a note. You didn't see one here either?"

Hancock shook his head.

"What about her phone? That's turned up missing. Did you find that anywhere?"

"Just Rachel. That's it."

Nathan kicked at the hay with his toes, moving it around, sifting through.

"Is this the same hay as before? How often does it get replaced?"

"I change it about once a week," Hancock explained.

Nathan got on his hands and knees for a better look as he combed his fingers through the bedding.

"Has this been changed since Rachel passed away?"

"Yes. It was on my list to do that same day. As soon as the police gave the all clear, it got changed out."

"And you're sure you didn't find anything? Nothing out of place?"

"I'm positive. But it wasn't me who cleaned this out. There was help that morning. While I was being questioned by the police, the crew we hired cleaned up the barn and stables. I wasn't even here. Nathan, if there was the slightest possibility the police missed something, it's long gone."

Nathan stood back up. He poked the toe of his boots through the hay, but he knew it was pointless. A crew had cleaned it. He could picture it all. Multiple guys, each hauling full shovels as rapidly as possible. Each trying to get the work done quick so they could get off to the bar or the ladies or both. No one was looking for anything. It easily could have been scooped up and hauled off with the trash. More than easily. It was likely. Nathan was staring down a dead end.

Hancock looked at him and said, "Son, it might be time to move on from this. I know it's tough. The toughest thing anyone ever has to do. Even harder than your own death. But you're living, and you need to keep on living. It'll be hard at first. Hardest thing in the world. But it gets easier somehow, even though it's impossible to believe that right now. You're not in a spot to see through the pain you're in. I'd even venture to guess the pain might get worse, if such a thing were possible. But one day you'll wake up and the tide will have turned. Things will feel a little easier."

Tears formed in Nathan's eyes. "I don't think that's true. I don't think this is going to get easier."

"It will. I've seen it, right here in this family." Hancock paused as he gathered his next words. "Earlier, back at the cabin, you asked me if I believed in ghosts."

"Do you?"

"No. I do not believe in ghosts. But I see why Upham does. I've seen enough bad things happen around here that I've second guessed it myself a few times. Examined my own philosophy, you know what I mean?"

Nathan started thinking about the dark woods. About birds that wouldn't fly overhead. But he didn't want to think about the basement. Or, for that matter, the lake.

Hancock continued, "I've been here a long time. Almost as long as Upham. Rachel isn't the first, you know. There have been others."

"Like Edward's father."

Hancock nodded. "He started acting strangely. Talking to himself, wandering around at night. Similar to what Lily was doing last night, I suppose. And then one day, he wandered himself right down into the basement. Took a bite right into a power line."

Hancock shook his head as he recalled the memory. Nathan tried to fight back the bile rising in his throat.

Hancock kept talking. "Edward, he had to grow up quick after that. No more time to be a little boy. He struggled. Fought hard. Which, I might add, earned him several nasty yet well-deserved titles. But he learned how to win. He made this family money hand over fist, and he got things turned around for himself. Built that business up more than his father ever did. Bought up most of the town. And then he met Elisabeth, and everything seemed good again. But it didn't last too long." He paused before saying, "Did you know Rachel wasn't their first pregnancy?"

Nathan could only shake his head.

"It's tough to lose a kid. Ain't right that a child would go before the parents. It's not the way it's meant to be. But that's what happened all the same. Elisabeth was beside herself. Edward - he threw himself into work to try and cope. Buried himself in the business, but he was buried just the same. And Elisabeth, I didn't think she'd ever recover. But then they had Rachel, and some hope came back. A few years later, Lily was here. And then the twins. I'm sure they still think about that baby that was lost, but things seemed to be better for a while."

Hancock lowered his head and his voice broke. "But now... Now all this with Rachel? It feels like it did before. And whatever this is, it almost took Lily too."

Nathan said, "So if you don't believe in ghosts, how do you explain all this? How do you explain multiple suicides? Or Lily walking into a freezing lake? How do you explain the fact there are no animals anywhere?"

Hancock pointed back to the horses. "What do you call those?"

Nathan scoffed. "The horses were brought here. Nothing's here that has a choice about it."

"The Thurmans aren't haunted, Nathan. They're damned. Always have been... For all their fortune, bad things seem to follow. Like it's in their blood. I suppose some people, like Upham, say they're cursed. Easier to explain it that way, maybe. But I don't see it that way." He looked Nathan in the eye. "I'm sorry you're mixed up in this."

Hancock shoved his hands down inside his pockets. "Time to move on, son. Forget this business with the phone. What you're looking for... It's not there. And even if you did find it, which you won't, more than likely all you'll find is new pain. It's better to let the past stay where it is. Where it belongs. I've seen this too many times. It's best to move on from the hurt. You can't carry this forever. This sort of weight kills a man. Some faster than others, but it kills them all the same. The Thurmans know more about that than most."

Nathan could see in the old man's eyes he was telling the truth, or at least the truth as he understood it. They left the barn the same way they came in. The big doors creaked shut and Nathan stood in the sun, processing what he'd heard, though nothing he had learned put his mind at ease. Rachel's phone was most likely rotting in a dump somewhere. For all the fear he had going into this place, it turned out to be just a barn, plain and simple. Nothing suspicious, everything as you'd expect. Anyone on the outside looking in wouldn't have the faintest clue a woman had died here only days ago. But the dead woman was all the two men standing outside the barn could think about.

Chapter Twenty-Seven

As Nathan was standing outside the barn contemplating what Hancock had said, Edward was busy trying to process what Lily had just told him. He looked to his wife to confirm he'd heard correctly, and seeing Elisabeth's mouth hanging open in disbelief was answer enough. Lily's eyes scanned between the two of them, anticipating their reaction.

When neither spoke, Lily repeated herself. "I can't stay here. I have to leave."

"I heard you the first time," Edward replied. "But I'm having a hard time understanding what on earth you're thinking."

Leaving was simply not the way things were done. No matter what might be said about his family, they were not counted among quitters or cowards.

Lily appeared hurt by her father's tone, but she held her ground. "Dad, I nearly died. There's something terrible and wrong about this house. Whatever it is, it tried to kill me, just like it did Rachel."

Elisabeth scoffed. "This is nothing like what happened to Rachel."

"And what exactly is the difference, Mom? What would need to happen for you to take this seriously? Do I need to die too?"

Elisabeth's eyes filled with tears and anger. "Don't you dare. Don't you dare turn this around and make me the bad guy."

"I'm not the one making you the bad guy. You seem to be doing a fine job of that by yourself." Lily sat back and crossed her arms tight against her chest. Chirps from Edward's machines pierced the air.

Elisabeth brought her hand to her face as if she'd been slapped. "How can you say that?"

"Having a near death experience changes your priorities pretty quick. I'm seeing my life a lot more clearly this morning." Lily shook her head and chuckled to herself, sounding more remorseful than funny. "Do you realize you weren't even there last night? Lucas and Tommy brought me home from Hancock's. Upham wrapped me up and brought me soup. Where were you all that time?" Elisabeth was shooting daggers while Lily continued. "If Nathan hadn't been there, you'd be planning two funerals."

"I see what's going on here," Elisabeth said. "It's Nathan, isn't it? What sort of lies has he been feeding you?"

Edward interrupted with a violent cough. When the fit ended, he gulped a breath of air, and in a strained voice said, "Lies? What are you talking about?"

Elisabeth looked smug. "It's obvious. Nathan's been spending a lot of time with Lily. It's clear he's trying to steal her away. The same as he did with Rachel."

Lily's mouth hung wide open. "Are you serious? That's what you think? If anything, you should be thanking Nathan for saving me."

Elisabeth jabbed a sharp finger at Lily. "Have you stopped to wonder how he got there so fast? Did it ever cross through your pretty little head that he might have been watching you?"

Lily shot right back. "Did you ever stop to wonder what I was doing out there in the first place?"

Edward's voice was weak. "Stop..." Lily and Elisabeth argued back and forth, their voices raising with each volley. Summoning his strength, he called again. "Stop..." But they drowned his voice out.

"SHUT UP! RIGHT NOW!" All at once, the fight came to a halt, and they looked at the patriarch. It had taken nearly all his energy, but it had worked. And while he couldn't manage the volume that he'd been able to command in his prime, the rush he felt was every bit as potent.

When he spoke again, his voice was hoarse. "Lily, you can't leave. It's not how things are done."

"Rachel did."

"And look what that got her."

She looked at her dad, her huge eyes full of sorrow and regret. "Daddy, you can't stop me. I'm leaving. Today."

"And go where? This is your home, Lily. You belong here, with us."

She shook her head. "No, I don't think I do. Not anymore, at least."

Elisabeth had retreated to a corner and was wiping a tear from her eye. "And what about your sister's funeral? You're just going to walk out now? Before we've buried her?"

Lily avoided eye contact as she said, "Rachel would understand, Mom." Elisabeth could only shake her head and return to her corner.

Edward looked hard at his daughter, examining her, and in doing so, saw a reflection of himself. In many ways, she mirrored his own ambitions and desires. When Edward had set his sights on a target, he was bound and determined to hit his mark, whether that be quarterly revenue, EBITA margin, or increased dividends. Lily was similar in that she chased what she wanted almost single-mindedly, but she lacked one crucial component; the key that guaranteed his success. Without it, failure was all but certain. The fact that this universal truth eluded so many people had always amazed Edward, because to him it had been apparent all his life. And the truth was this: Life was a zero-sum game. In order for him to win, someone else had to lose. Was it cruel? Sometimes. But Edward hadn't lost sleep over his choices. Survival of the fittest, just as life had intended since the dawn of time. He'd made a life for himself, built a legacy that would last long after he was gone, and that's what mattered most.

He examined her again, trying to get a glimpse of what she was made of. While there was something fierce there, it hadn't developed into maturity yet. She still lacked the killer instinct that he possessed. Given enough time, and pain, it might grow into something she could work with. But not yet.

"All your life you've lived under my roof, under my care. Everything you have is because of what I worked for. It's because of the things I've done. What makes you think you can make it on your own?"

"I have to try, don't I? If I stay... I won't get lucky twice. Next time it'll get me, I know it."

"Oh, you've gotten lucky more than once, dear," Elisabeth quipped. Her voice was only a murmur, and Edward missed what she'd said. The cut wasn't missed on Lily, however. Her face turned a shade of red and she hung her head again, but she didn't take her mother's bait.

Edward repositioned one of the opaque tubes

connected to his arm. "If you leave, you understand what that means, don't you?"

Lily's head remained down.

"Lily, look at me. I need to know you understand what you're choosing." Lily raised her eyes to meet his.

"If you leave, you'll no longer have my support. If you choose to go against the family, you won't get one red cent. Not for rent, not for food. You will be on your own, completely. And if you're thinking you can just hedge your bets until I die, guess again. I'll redistribute your inheritance. God help me, I'll find a way to take it with me before you see a dime. Do you understand?"

Lily's eyes filled with tears. She stood and gave Edward a kiss on the forehead, then left without a word.

Nathan took his time walking back to the Manor, grateful for the solitude. Last week he was a happily married man whose biggest problems were career and money. And now? It was safe to say last week's problems had fallen by the wayside.

Hancock was right - it was a fool's errand chasing after this phone. What could he hope to learn if he found it? The possibilities raced through his mind. A suicide note? There wasn't an explanation on earth that would satisfy him. What if the texts had been to another man? If that had been the case, he might actually snap. And worst of all - what if he had been the cause of her death? What if he'd said or done something (intent being a moot point) that was the final straw, driving her to suicide? Would he ever forgive himself? Maybe some knowledge was best left unknown.

He shook his head in an effort to rid his mind of these thoughts before he spiraled. It would do no good to trade one obsession for another. No, for the time being, he would make his focus the funeral. Once that was through, he would go home. And maybe have a chance to mourn.

The Manor lay in front of him, vast and sprawling. He cut across the grass, making a straight shot for the front doors. To his left, the sun was glimmering off the surface of the lake and he paused. It was so different from what he'd experienced last night. Today, it sparkled. Last night, it was dark as ink, almost as if created for the sole purpose of getting one lost and disoriented. Still, it was beautiful, despite being deadly if not enjoyed properly.

He heard crunching gravel behind him as footsteps approached. He turned to see Lily coming his way. She wore a white hoodie with dark jeans, and a red and white knit stocking covered her head. A backpack was slung over one shoulder, and the other arm held a duffle bag. A tuft of hair was pulled forward in an attempt to cover the bruise Nathan's fist had left. But there was something else there, something harder to define. There was less confidence. For the first time in her life, Lily Thurman looked unsure of herself.

She stopped a few feet from him, dropped her bags, and pulled her hands into her sleeves. The distance between them was filled with unspoken words.

"I saw you from the window." She looked back toward the house. "I guess we've switched roles today." A question must have passed across Nathan's face because she jumped to clarify. "I just mean you're out here, and I was at the window instead. Only I didn't have to fish you out of the lake." She tried to smile, but it came out all wrong and just made her embarrassed. She pushed a lock of her hair from her eye.

"Don't worry about it. It's nothing."

Lily stepped forward. "No, it's not. What you did means everything. Thank you."

"Well, you're welcome. I'm glad to see you back up. Feeling better?"

"Yeah, I think so. Warm again, at least. There's gaps about last night." Her eyes squinted as she tried to recall the night's events. "I keep trying to remember, but I can't. My best guess is I was sleepwalking. It happens to people, right? They go to sleep and wake up in a strange place, unaware of how they got there?"

Nathan shrugged. "I'm not sure. I've heard that it happens. But I've never met someone that actually does it. You'd be the first."

They stood side by side, neither speaking, looking at the water from a distance. Neither wanted to get closer than they were; even one step would feel like they were getting too close to danger. Although, Nathan felt that to go back toward the house was just as dangerous. Unlike Lily, Nathan's recollection was becoming more clear. He remembered the lake. He remembered the basement, and why he'd shattered that bottle of wine.

Lily gave him a small, sad smile. "I also wanted to say goodbye."

"You're leaving?"

"Yes, I think I have to. Listen, I know how it looks, skipping my own sister's memorial. But of all people, Rachel would understand. She wanted out of here more than any of us. And you were the way out, Nathan."

"Are you sure you won't have regrets?"

She nodded. "I've had a lot of regrets, but this won't be one of them. This is overdue - Rachel would agree. In a way, I feel like this is the best way I can honor her. I'll find my own way, make a new life. Rachel would want me to start fresh, so that's what I'm going to do.

"Where will you go?"

"I have some friends out east. I'll head that way, just until I can get settled. Look me up if you're ever out that way." She got up on her tiptoes and gave him a light kiss on the cheek.

Nathan watched her toss her bags into the backseat of her car and drive off until he couldn't see the busted taillight anymore. He wondered how long it would take her to remember what happened last night. He hoped she wouldn't.

Chapter Twenty-Eight

Nathan had almost reached the front door when he heard a car approaching. He spun around, his initial thought being that Lily had changed her mind and decided to return after all. Maybe she would stay for the funeral, or maybe it was something more simple, like she'd forgotten something? But the car approaching was different. It was wider than her vehicle, and black, both in color and mood. Nathan squinted his eyes and could make out two heads behind the windshield. They moved slowly, almost with reverence, but there was nothing about their arrival that Nathan found encouraging, although he didn't yet know why.

Soon, the vehicle pulled up parallel to the front of the house. Two men dressed in black suits exited and walked toward the rear of the car. At first, Nathan thought the car to be a little odd, a strange cross between a sedan and a station wagon. But a split second later, when his mind allowed him to process the truth, he saw it for what it really was.

The back door of the hearse opened wide, and the first man pulled a collapsible cart out from seemingly nowhere.

It appeared to be made of brass crosshatches that snapped into place and little black roller wheels for easy transport.

The second guy had his hands on his hips, examining the stairs, his face contorted as if he were solving an equation. He looked back at the cart, returned his attention to the stairs, and then threw his hands up in resignation.

The first man saw the problem all at once and called out to Nathan. "Hey, buddy! Anybody around that could help us move this where it needs to go?"

Nathan's eyes zeroed in on the car's back door, both dreading and anticipating who he knew to be inside. The question shook him out of his thoughts. "Uh - what do you need?"

"A few guys? At least two per side, and one on either end. Is that doable?"

"Let me see who I can find." He left the two men standing in the drive and headed into the Manor.

It wasn't long before he found the family in the parlor. Funeral setup was in full swing. Elisabeth was giving orders to the twins, waving her hands wide as if she might push the flower arrangements with telepathy alone. She waved Lucas and Tommy to one side and then made scooting little motions to pull them back in the other direction. On the other end of her gestures, Lucas and Tommy pushed the arrangements back and forth, trying to get them in the correct position.

"No, no... That's too far - the other way. I said the other way!" Elisabeth was shouting at them, struggling to be heard over the din of tables and chairs being moved. Soon, the screeching of metal and wood became too much for her and she slapped her hands down on her thighs in frustration. "Do you think you could make a little more noise?"

Jonathan put the chair he'd been moving down. "I thought this is what you wanted me doing?"

"What I wanted was for you to help get the seating ready. I didn't know it would require earplugs."

"I'm doing the best I can here. Should I do this after you've gotten the flowers where you want?"

Elisabeth abandoned Lucas and Tommy and turned her attention to Jonathan. "No, that won't work at all. There's no time."

Upham came out from behind the bar, rag in hand and looking disheveled and out of breath. "Mrs. Thurman, everything should be ready in the bar area. We are fully stocked, and..."

Elisabeth held up a finger and the room stopped, waiting on her to complete her yoga breath. Tommy and Lucas looked at each other, uncertain if they should continue to hold the flowers or place them down. Upham had stopped mid-stride and didn't dare continue his update. Elisabeth let out one last long exhale and opened her eyes. That's when she noticed Nathan.

"Nathan, we're in the middle of getting everything ready. Is there something you need?"

Under different circumstances, Nathan might have felt slighted, if not outright offended. But the fact that Rachel's body was waiting outside overshadowed Elisabeth's comments.

"There's two men here. I think they have..." He couldn't find the words to complete his thought. "Um - they need some help outside."

Jonathan walked to the window, saw the hearse, and then gave Elisabeth a subtle nod. That was all the communication required for her to understand.

Elisabeth appeared to shrink, like a weight had pressed

on her from above. "Ok... boys, go on out. Jonathan, if you would help?"

All three responded by moving toward the front door.

"I'll help too," Upham said, and he followed behind.

They were put into position behind the hearse, Lucas and Tommy on the left, Nathan and Jonathan on the right. Upham stayed by to man the front door, ready to swing it open on their approach. The two suits from the funeral home took position on either end of the casket.

They moved in a sort of awkward unison, a mess of shortened steps and shuffled feet. Nathan kept a tight grip around the wood handle, not wanting to let go. One of the suits was giving instructions as they navigated the casket up the steps and through the door, but Nathan heard very little. Rachel may have been inches away, but in all his life, he'd never felt so far from her.

Upham guided them to the parlor, where Elisabeth was waiting. She directed them toward one end of the room, where flowers and a large portrait of Rachel created a focal point. A hush fell over the room once the casket was in position. Nathan watched as Elisabeth wiped tears from her eyes. Tommy's head hung low, and Lucas stared somewhere beyond his deceased sister.

They stood in a semi-circle, a distance back from Rachel's final bed, as if hesitant to approach. There were no words, and the parlor seemed to be filled with the occasional sniffle and stifling of tears.

Nathan broke the silence. "I'd like a few minutes alone with her." He moved toward the casket and placed his hand on the wood. It seemed impossibly smooth and cold and final. "I need to see her. One last time."

"I don't think that's a good idea," Tommy said.

Lucas agreed with his brother. "It's a closed casket for a reason, Nathan. You don't want that opened."

Elisabeth shook her head. "The boys are right, Nathan. Rachel's injuries were... Not something that could be covered up."

"It can't possibly be worse than what I saw at the morgue. I'm not telling anyone else how they should say goodbye. But I need to do this." Nathan looked back to where his wife lay. He didn't know what awaited him under the lid, but he knew that if he missed this opportunity, he would regret it forever. His heart raced in anticipation, but he steeled himself and moved to open the casket. It didn't budge; it was locked up tight.

Nathan turned back to his wife's family. "Who has a key?" No one moved. An equal mix of desperation and indignation boiled under the surface, but he kept his tone level. "Please, this is something I have to do."

Elisabeth took a step forward toward him. "I understand. Really, I do. But right now, there simply isn't time. Perhaps later, after the memorial, we can make some sort of arrangement?"

"Why isn't there time now? We have a whole day before the funeral. I'm just asking for a few moments alone to say goodbye to my wife. That's not unreasonable."

An odd expression came over Elisabeth, and she looked at him with curiosity. "Nathan, the funeral is *today*."

The days swirled around in Nathan's mind, a jumbled mess of timelines and starts and stops. How long was he out at Hancock's? Longer than a day? No... he was certain it had only been one. Had he misheard Elisabeth when she told him when the funeral was scheduled? He could almost hear her verbatim - *the funeral is in two days* - but it was possible he was mistaken. Nathan ran the timeline back in his mind, trying to find out where he'd gotten mixed up.

Not that it mattered - either way, the end result was the same. Ready or not, this funeral was happening.

Elisabeth continued, "What were you thinking when the hearse showed up? Why else would they come today?"

Nathan looked around for support. He found none. "I wasn't thinking about that. It seemed like it was all part of the setup or something."

Elisabeth looked back at the twins. "Boys, why don't you go help your father get ready. People will start arriving before long." She turned back to Nathan. "Is the video ready to go?"

Nathan was reeling, trying to put the pieces back together and figure out how he'd lost an entire day. But he managed to respond. "Pretty much. I have to get it exported, so it's ready to play."

"How long will that take?"

"I'm not sure. I thought I had more time."

"Well, then you'd better get started. The clock's ticking."

Chapter Twenty-Nine

"What about this one, Dad?"

Tommy pulled a blue suit from the closet and showed it to his father. For the first time in as long as he could recall, Edward was out of his bed. Granted, he was in a wheelchair, complete with oxygen tanks and an IV drip, but he was as upright as he was ever likely to be. A thick wool blanket covered his lap. Tommy hated thinking about how thin his father's legs had become. He'd caught a glimpse as he and Lucas helped Edward to the chair. Tommy averted his eyes almost at once, but even the brief view had revealed not much more than skeleton and skin. Moving him wasn't any effort at all.

Edward was slumped to one side, and his voice showed signs of strain. "No, I said black. Who wears blue to a funeral?"

Tommy placed the blue one back and combed through a few more. Silver, grey, another blue... He pulled a black one from the far corner. "How's this?"

Edward nodded, his breathing labored and wheezy. "That's the one."

Tommy examined his father. He looked pale and worn,

and Tommy couldn't help but think they'd have another funeral soon. "You doing ok, Dad?"

"Fine. Just tired, is all. Let's get this over with."

Light as his father was, getting him dressed was a two-man job. One needed to hold him steady while the other worked his limbs through the garments. Usually, Edward's hands or feet would get tangled up in the fabric, causing a delay, and more often than not, a berating comment or two.

Tommy called Lucas over. "Hey, we're ready."

"Just a sec. Be right there," Lucas replied from around the corner.

Tommy waited a beat but saw his father becoming agitated and impatient. He called again, "Lucas! Let's go, man. We're on the clock here." Lucas appeared into view, breathing hard like he'd just run down the hall.

"What are you doing?"

"Just grabbing Dad's medicine. That ok with you?"

Lucas handed several pills to Edward, who gulped them down with a glass of water before leaning back and closing his eyes. Tommy started to wonder how his father would make it through the funeral. Even something as simple as sitting up seemed to exhaust him.

Tommy shook his head in annoyance. "Let's get him dressed. It's your turn to hold him up." Tommy caught the tail end of his twin's eye roll but ignored it and started getting the clothes laid out on the bed. The black suit stood out sharply against the white bedsheets, like a stain.

"Where do you wanna start? Top or bottom?" Lucas asked.

Tommy looked down at the wool blanket covering over his dad's legs. It struck him as utterly pointless to struggle with the pants. That blanket wasn't going to come off the entire day, and anything beneath it would stay hidden. He could just do the dress shoes and socks, and no one would ever be the wiser. But knowing his father, he'd never go for it.

"Let's start at the top," Tommy said.

Lucas leaned forward and made a loop under Edward's arms. He locked his fingers together, and then lifted. Edward made a little grunt but held still as Tommy slipped one arm through the dress shirt, and then the other. After the shirt was done, Lucas lowered his father back in his seat and arched his back while Tommy readied the coat.

"Back all better now? Think you can handle round two?"

"Shut up. Let's just get this done." Lucas hoisted Edward up again, and Tommy maneuvered his father's arms through. Something got stopped up in the first sleeve. Tommy was fooling with it, trying to pull it over his dad's hand, but failing to make any progress.

"What are you doing? Hurry up," Lucas grunted.

"I'm trying. I just - " and it released all at once. But what popped out the sleeve wasn't a hand.

Some ancient instinct kicked in, and Lucas began to squirm. "What is that? Tommy, I feel something on me. What's on me?"

He looked at his twin but couldn't respond. A swarm, thousands of unknown somethings, were flowing out the suit and onto Lucas's arm, moving up his shoulder and neck. Legions of frantic legs skittered and crawled, one over the other, as they advanced. Lucas cried out as one bit him, and then another. He let go of Edward and swatted at himself as if he'd caught flame. Edward fell with a grunt as he hit the floor, and then he went limp.

"They're in the coat! Get it out of here!" Lucas yelled. He looked crazed as he flailed around, trying to separate the insects from his skin. Bugs fell off in clumps, landing on

Edward's back and head before scampering off into shadowed nooks and crannies.

Tommy didn't move. He stood back, watching the scene unfold, mouth open in horror.

"Don't just stand there! Do something!"

This seemed to wake Tommy. He grabbed the coat and bunched it together in an attempt to contain the infestation. It worked in part, but not before a few escaped and crawled up his arm. They looked like centipedes, near weightless translucent slivers connected to a hundred scrambling legs. He felt a sharp sting on his wrist and slapped at it, splattering one into a mess of legs and guts. The others scattered in chaotic unison.

"Kill 'em!" Lucas screamed. At this point, he was stomping at them, dangerously close to Edward's head. His kicks were wild and uncontrolled, and he missed more than he killed. Even after the last of them had escaped, he continued to lunge at dark spots on the floor, whether they be previous kills or innocent marks in the wood.

Tommy opened the window and threw the entire coat outside. It fell in a lump, and he thought he could see squirming under the cloth. He slammed the window shut again, half expecting to see the centipedes jump and sacrifice themselves against the glass in a suicide attack, but the coat merely deflated on the ground. A burning red welt was throbbing on Tommy's wrist. He saw several identical looking marks on his brother's neck. The twins both stood there, panting and searching for any remaining potential attackers.

Edward let out a low groan from the ground. They grabbed him and got him back into his seat. A bruise was already turning black on his forehead.

His voice was raspy and labored. "What did you do to my suit?"

"The suit's no good, Dad. It was infested. We had to get rid of it."

Edward sighed and leaned his head back. "That was my favorite. You wrecked my favorite suit."

Tommy went back to the closet and grabbed the blue one, and they started the dressing process from the beginning.

Chapter Thirty

Lucas tried to hold his lighter steady, but it danced around in front of his face, as if dodging his attempts. For the third time in as many minutes, he looked at the clock, but found no comfort that it wasn't near that dreaded time. After another try, he was able to steady his hand just long enough for his cigarette to catch. He inhaled and let the nicotine run its course, allowing it to round the edge off his nerves.

Under normal circumstances, Lucas would have been blitzed by now, able to avoid the festivities by way of unconsciousness. Sure, there was the inevitable hangover and corresponding splitting headache, but both were preferable to whatever the house would throw his way. He learned that long ago, and his nightmares were a consistent reminder. Over time, Lucas discovered a way to avoid it all, nightmares included. It only required minimal chemical assistance.

He was only a boy when it all became real for him. Back then, Thurman Manor had been bustling. There were groundskeepers, house staff, even a live-in nanny for Lucas and Tommy. He often wondered what kept old Upham around; it was amazing he didn't pack his stuff and leave a long time ago. But then Lucas would remember that he was still here too, and the thought didn't seem so odd after all.

There are certain defining moments in life. For Lucas Thurman, that moment came early, and hit like a hammer. It was the sort of thing that he couldn't have imagined on his own, but once seen, couldn't be forgotten. The image lingered, replaying over and over, never losing its potency and robbing him of sleep. When his dreams came, there was nothing exaggerated or false. His mind punished him in this way, forcing him to re-live that night over and over.

It was always dark in his dreams, and although he never saw a clock, there was no need. The electric feel in the air was enough to know what the clock would show. He walked from his bedroom, looking back only once and wanting to call out for Tommy to wake, but stopped himself. The next thing he knew, he was walking down the hall from his bedroom, his bare feet soundless on the cold floor. Not just cold though - wet. He would look down and see his pajama pants soaked to his ankles. Lucas moved further, toward the open door, toward his nanny's room. Her name was on his lips, nearly able to be spoken, but then it slipped from his memory as though into nothingness.

He could hear her faucet running, and the plops of water as they fell from her sink. Each night was the same. She stood in her nightgown over the sink, looking into the pooled water. He would say something, but it was voiceless and unknown. But it was enough. She would turn toward him, and he'd see the sadness in her eyes. And something else, something he didn't care to think about. And then she plunged her head into the sink. And continued to do so, virtually every night of his life. After a minute, her body would shake, splashing water over the brim. It was almost as if she'd been pushed into that water and made to stay down, but there was never anyone else. Eventually, she'd go quiet. The water would keep running, and Lucas would be alone in the door with pajamas soaked to the knee.

His father found him that way, a curious child staring at a lifeless body. He didn't remember his father shaking him, but he did recall the single slap that brought him out of his trance. The sting spread across his cheek and turned hot and red. Lucas looked up at his father and started to cry.

"Stop that right now, Lucas. This isn't how we're going to handle this."

Lucas screwed his mouth shut. His little chest heaved in and out as he tried to bury the sobs. Edward walked over to the sink and turned the faucet off. Small and vacant drips continued, but soon tapered off into silence.

Edward knelt next to Lucas and looked him in the eye. "This might not be fair, but it's our lot. Look at me." He grabbed Lucas's face and pulled it toward him. "You'll deal with this like a Thurman, you understand? We're strong. I've done it. Uncle Jonathan's done it. It's your turn now."

And that was the end of what Edward had to say on the matter. With time, Lucas found a perfect little way to deal with the nightmares.

He took another puff and realized he was going to need something stronger. He buried his head in his hands and looked at the sands of bliss scattered across his desk.

Just a taste. Just a little taste. That'll get me right. God, I need to get my head right.

White granules were sitting there piled into a small mountain, practically begging him to partake. He'd spent the better part of the last hour carefully twisting the gelatin capsules apart and emptying their contents onto his desk. The empty halves were all piled up off to the left side. Soon, he'd refill them with sugar, and they would find their way back to where they came from.

For a moment, Lucas felt a twinge of guilt. It wasn't like he didn't realize what he was doing. Or, for that matter, who he was doing it to. He understood the cost at which this came. After all, his father was under the same roof, literally only rooms away, struggling through the pain. And that made his actions worse; that he knew what he was doing, but chose to do so anyway. It added to the guilt; made it more damnable. He couldn't plead ignorance. This wasn't some harmless *nobody is getting hurt, why shouldn't I do it* thing. His relief came at the expense of someone else's pain; his salvation was only at the loss of another's. Every time he stole the pills meant to help his father's pain, he was paying for it with a bit of his soul.

Lucas pushed the guilt down deep where it might drown. Even though it never died, the pills kept it quiet.

What good do these do for Dad, anyway? All he ever does is whine and moan about what a rip off his meds are. What if my pain is actually worse than his? Who knows? Maybe I'm the one who needs it more?

His father was close to death, and pretty soon there wouldn't be any more pain for him. But Lucas would still be here, fighting and struggling. Trying to stave off his demons. And the only thing that worked lay before him like fresh winter powder. He felt like a kid waking up to a virgin snow.

His conscience wouldn't stay silent for long, so he made his work quick. He wet his finger in his mouth and ran a swipe through the powder. He stuffed his powdered digit back into his mouth and savored the bitter, gritty, and wondrous qualities. Sure enough, he relaxed now that the deed was done.

There was a pile left. *Waste not want not*, like Dad always said. Lucas dug into his desk drawer and retrieved an empty package of "fun dip", all bright and neon and cartoonish. He'd loved this candy as a kid - pure sugar and pure bliss. The package still contained his bliss, but a different variety now. He scooped up the remainder of the white powder and got it into the package, careful not to spill any. He rolled the top down and secured it with a rubber band. Back into the desk it went. And Lucas felt fine.

Chapter Thirty-One

Nathan tugged at his tie, trying to get the stiff fabric to cooperate and form a proper knot. As it looked now, that might not happen. A loose thread dangled from the bottom, and Nathan tucked it back inside the seam that had already begun to fray. Nathan looked at himself in the mirror, noting the pants that fit a little long, and the coat that fit a little tight in the shoulder. If Rachel could only see him... she'd have found the situation humorous. The teasing would have been merciless, but then, still with that ornery grin plastered on her face, she would have slipped her arms inside the jacket and given him a hug, and everything would have been right in the world.

The tie was a lost cause. Nathan buttoned his suit coat and stuffed the tail end inside. Outside, he could hear vehicles starting to arrive. A lineup of cars was forming down the driveway, each waiting their turn for their chance to park. Tommy was further down, trying to give directions. Nathan could see him stooped over, trapping his loose tie against his belly and leaning his head into rolled down windows. Each interaction was the same; a quick exchange, followed by a quick nod, and then he'd move his hand in a chopping motion toward the Manor. Down at the receiving end, Jonathan flagged them down with his massive arms, signaling them into spots on either side of the drive. A narrow path cut down the center, not more than a car's width. Nathan combed the parade of BMWs, Mercedes', and Land Rovers', his eyes peeled for a Chevy, the one vehicle carrying the single person coming on his behalf. But he didn't spot Lewis's truck.

The video render was a good news bad news situation. Nathan was relieved when the export finished, but it left him with no time to review the completed version. The original plan had included a buffer, which would have allowed time for any last-minute edits he deemed necessary, but that margin had evaporated. Whatever this current version was would be the final product. Still, he had reason to feel confident. He'd put in the time and effort, and he knew it would have been very minor adjustments, if any at all. Nathan took one last look in the mirror before grabbing his laptop and heading down to face the crowd.

Lucas was standing at the parlor doors, running his tongue along his gums and completing the final fold on his ever-present Fun Dip pack before securing it with a thick rubber band. He spotted Nathan and walked to his side.

"You ready for this?" Lucas asked. They stood with their backs against the wall, watching and nodding to the new arrivals. Someone reached their hand out to Lucas, offering condolences and sympathy.

"Not really. But the video is done. I think that will be a nice touch." Nathan fidgeted with his collar; it was already heating up in the room and he felt an uncomfortable itch creeping up around his neck. He did another quick scan for Lewis, which only required a passing glance at head height.

The only person in the room bigger than Lewis would be Jonathan, and that would be true of any room in the world. Finding Lewis in a group like this would have been an easy task. If he were there. But, for as much as Nathan wished for his presence, Lewis hadn't shown.

Lucas reached into his suit jacket and retrieved a silver flask. The cap came off, and with it, a strong, dangerous smell. Lucas took a quick slug, wiped the nozzle with his tie, and handed it over to Nathan with a Cheshire grin.

"Better get one in now. You'll need it before the day is out."

Nathan looked at what Lucas was offering. Faint vapors dissipated like aimless spirits around the mouth of the bottle, and he knew whatever concoction was in there would burn going down. But even if it literally set his insides on fire, there was also a chance it would numb some of his pain; or at least give him fresh pain to focus on.

Nathan took the flask and drank. The liquid went down fast and did about what he'd expected. It stung his throat, spreading up through his sinuses and down into his stomach. He let out a wheezy cough, and Lucas clapped him on the back. A few curious eyes raised in their direction.

"That's good, right? Take another. The more you drink, the better it gets."

Nathan shook his head as he handed it back to Lucas. "No, one was enough for me. How do you drink this stuff?"

Lucas tucked it safely away in his pocket. He shrugged and said, "I dunno, never seemed to bother me. Maybe it's a Thurman thing?" He pointed to the laptop tucked under Nathan's arm. "Is that what we're using to play the video?"

"Yeah. I just need to get it hooked up." Nathan started searching the room for the TV.

"Here, I'll take care of that. I know how it all works. You should make your rounds. Come find me if you change your mind about that drink." Lucas took the laptop and went off to get it all set for the viewing.

Nathan stayed put at first, taking in the space and the people. The parlor looked meticulous. Small round tables were spaced evenly through the room, each covered with a white tablecloth and a floral arrangement at the center. Guests mingled throughout, some standing by the bar waiting their turns, others took their seats at the tables. Nathan caught a few sideways glances, but no one said anything. He straightened his coat out again, feeling self-conscious in this den of strangers.

At the focal point of the room was Rachel's casket. A monochrome line of people had formed, waiting for their turns to pay respects to both the dead and the living. Elisabeth stood to one side, taking hands and receiving condolences. Her black dress sparkled, contrasting her tired and grim face. Edward was beside her, slumped low in his wheelchair. A bandage had been put on his head. His blanket had bunched up underneath his chair, revealing a bare and sickly leg, but either no one noticed, or they didn't care to cover it. Some gave his withered hands a timid squeeze. Others seemed to keep their distance, like they could smell death on him and didn't want the stench on their clothes.

On the other side was a large black and white portrait of Rachel. Nathan looked at it a long time, thinking about how it was just a representation, dots on canvas that gave the impression of life and vibrance without being the real thing. He wondered if it would be relocated to the mausoleum after the service.

The chatter fell to a hush as Elisabeth stepped forward to address her attendees. Every eye was on her as she spoke.

"On behalf of my family, I wanted to extend thanks for you being here today. Rachel would be thrilled. I'm sure she is looking down on all of us, thankful that you're all here." There were affirming murmurs from each table.

Nathan surveyed the room one last time, resigned to the idea that Lewis wouldn't make it. Then he spotted him slipping through the parlor door, head ducked and trying to make himself small and unnoticed. Their eyes met, and they exchanged a single nod. Lewis took a seat at the back, his presence a welcome relief to Nathan. His shoulders relaxed a little bit, and he turned his attention back to Elisabeth.

"Edward and I have invited you all here to celebrate the life of our daughter, Rachel. Life was too short for her... She was deeply loved." Elisabeth stopped and wiped the tears from her eyes. "Today, we share our memories of her. Today, we'll walk her to her final place of rest. And today, we say our goodbyes."

There were more sounds of agreement from around the room. Tommy and Lucas were up front, arms around each other's shoulders. Jonathan stood behind Edward's chair; his head hung low. The room fell silent again. All except for the muffled shouts coming from outside.

A few heads turned, first out of intrigue but evolving into concern. Chairs screeched as people jumped up and rushed to the window. Someone asked, "What's going on?" Another voice answered, "There's people outside. What are they doing?" Another exclaimed, "They're surrounding the cars!" The questions continued and the volume rose until their voices became a wall of white noise.

Jonathan's voice boomed. "People, please take your seats. I'm sure there's nothing to be concerned about." His words were not received with reassurance.

Nathan looked back for Lewis. He was standing now, his head up and scanning the room for threats. Nathan worked his way forward, pushing himself up to the window.

A crowd had gathered on the drive, pointing and shouting indistinct threats toward the Manor. Others were moving through the parked cars, keying doors and chucking eggs. He recognized a few of the faces from the other day at the Sheriff's office.

Jonathan raised his voice louder. "Everyone, move away from the windows, right now!"

The guests returned to their seats, looking unsure and wary of the mob outside. Jonathan went to the wall and pulled a string, drawing thick, heavy curtains across the windows, blocking the outside from view. The room buzzed with nervous energy.

Elisabeth tried to bring order. "Quiet! Quiet, please! There is nothing to be concerned with. We are getting this handled. Sit tight, enjoy your drinks. This is only a minor disruption."

Nathan met her at the front. Tommy and Lucas were looking side to side, as if expecting a window to break at any moment. Jonathan secured the last curtain and then joined them.

He looked at Elisabeth. "It's them."

"I can't believe this is happening. They have no shame. Why will they not let us mourn in peace?" Elisabeth hissed.

Nathan asked, "Are we in danger here? Do we need to move everyone to a safe place?"

Elisabeth's reply was sharp. "We aren't moving anyone anywhere. As soon as we do that, it's going to be mass panic. We're better off staying put."

Tommy turned to Elisabeth. "Mom, I think we should reschedule. It doesn't seem like the right time to do this."

She looked incredulous that he should suggest such a thing. "We are not going to reschedule. I will not allow these psychopaths to ruin this day. We are going to proceed exactly as planned."

"We need to wait to move Rachel down to the mausoleum, at least until they're gone," Jonathan said. "I saw a few of them scattering around the property. Some down by the path. A couple took off toward the lake."

Elisabeth's voice was getting louder and drawing some attention. "Well, get the Sheriff down here. They're trespassing. I want them arrested."

"Calling right now." Jonathan stepped away as he dialed.

Elisabeth turned back to Nathan. "Is that video ready to go?"

"It should be. I was able to complete the export earlier today."

"Should be? Or it's ready? Which is it?"

Nathan wanted to lash out, to snap back and set her in her place. But he saw the eyes on him and restrained his tone. "The video is ready. Lucas, any issues with the TV hook up?"

Lucas shook his head. "It's good to go. I just need to roll the TV out so people can see."

Jonathan came back to them. "Talked to the Sheriff's office. A few deputies are heading out right now."

"Good.... Good..." Elisabeth closed her eyes and took a long, slow breath. She looked almost meditative. Then she addressed the small circle again. "Here's what we're doing. Lucas, you go get that TV out here and ready. We're going to run that video. Make sure the volume is up loud. I want to drown out any sounds from outside."

Nathan pushed back. "Elisabeth, I get what you're saying. I really do. But I don't want Rachel's funeral to go like this. Her video is supposed to be a tribute, not some... tool. It's not just a distraction from what's going on outside."

Elisabeth glared at him. "And what do you think we

should do instead, hmm? Do you have a better idea? Do you think this is how I wanted this to go? For *my daughter*?"

The subtle emphasis wasn't lost on Nathan. With those two simple words, she'd made a weapon and cut at him, daring him to challenge her. Elisabeth's whole body was rigid and primed; she looked like she might actually bite. Nathan could imagine fangs behind her clenched mouth, like a cobra. He could feel hot stares on the back of his neck. More than one tension was rising in the room, but this was the only one Nathan had an ounce of control over. He raised his hands in a truce.

Elisabeth's body still looked half ready to strike, and her voice was low and threatening. "You all need to act normal. Everyone here is looking at us, and they will do as we do. If we're under control, then they will be too. Got it?"

Each acknowledged that they understood and the circle broke. Lucas went for the television while Tommy took his seat by Edward. Jonathan walked back over to the windows to stand guard. Elisabeth put on a campaign smile and spoke to her guests.

"Thanks for your patience. The authorities are on their way, and these vandals will be gone shortly. As I said before, there's no cause for concern. This is a minor disruption, I assure you." People looked around, still uncertain. Elisabeth called them back to her. "My family and I spoke. We all agreed the best way to honor Rachel is to keep going forward. We're all here to honor her, aren't we?" There was a low rumble of agreement. Elisabeth said it louder, rousing her guests. "Aren't we?" Their response was more certain now.

Nathan could feel the crowd relaxing. He even heard a few nervous chuckles from around the room. The mob outside had seemed to quiet. He wondered if that meant the deputies had arrived, or if the heavy curtains were blocking the noise. A familiar hand rested on his shoulder. Nathan turned and embraced Lewis.

"You ok?" Lewis asked. "I'm sure this isn't how you imagined this going."

"No. It's not. Nothing has gone the way it was supposed to."

By this time, Lucas had rolled a flat screen TV up near Rachel's casket. The wheels squeaked as he got it into position. He pointed a remote and brought it to life. The room fell silent.

Elisabeth addressed them again. "We have a video prepared. Let's watch and remember Rachel together." She stepped aside, and Lucas pressed play.

It started with a black screen. Rachel's name faded in, light music began, and then the screen lit up to a photo he'd taken of Rachel right after their wedding. She looked radiant and full of life and hope. The photo dissolved, and another took its place. She was on a swing. Youthful. Laughing. Nathan had snapped the shot at the height of the swing; she looked light as a feather and ready to soar into the blue sky. Music swelled and moved along with the photos as they traveled through Rachel's life. Nathan had taken great care to time the photos along with the music, and it achieved the desired effect. The crowd seemed captivated. Women wiped tears from their eyes, as well as several of the men. The video continued, each picture highlighting a beautiful creature, although her eyes seemed far away sometimes. Nathan buried his face in his hands. Hot tears filled his palms as he wept. The music carried on; the video was getting close to the end. Nathan kept his face in his hands as the video continued.

A gasp came from somewhere behind him, immediately followed by hushed voices. Nathan wiped his eyes and looked up. With horror, he saw the cause of the disturbance.

The video continued, but it was no longer what Nathan had created. Something else, something vile, had taken its place. A sick feeling settled in Nathan's stomach, and his body went cold and numb. He was looking at a photo of the barn, looming larger than ever, as if it had always been the intention to have it be the dark and forbidden centerpiece of Thurman Manor. The screen flickered, and they were transported inside. The stables were there, but the horses were missing. Far back, just out of focus, a shape hovered in the frame, impossible to ignore.

No. Oh, no. This can't be happening.

Another flick of the screen, and a new image, this one removing any shred of tact. The blurry shape came into terrible focus. She was hanging in the barn, her face bloated and lifeless. Except for the occasional gasp, the room was silent and thick and heavy enough to keep everyone in their seat until every last horrifying image was permanently burned into their minds. The image changed again, this time hurting Nathan's eyes like a flash bulb. As his vision returned, her casket came into view, but it lay open, almost like it was inviting them in. This time there was no flash, no fade. Rather, the video gave the audience a first-person perspective as it approached the casket and hovered above. It stopped Nathan's heart. Rachel's eyes were vacant and bulging, and signs of vibrance long gone. Rope marks wrapped around her neck like snakes. And worst of all, she was smiling.

Jonathan walked to the wall and unplugged the TV, finally having the presence of mind to end it. The entire room was on the edge of their seats, unable to look away from the black screen, expecting it to roar back to life. When the shock waned, Nathan could hear uncomfortable shuffling behind him as people weighed whether they should leave now or wait for a dismissal. Someone whispered, "let's go."

Nathan had no words, no explanation for what had just occurred. He looked at Lewis as if he might have an answer for him, but of course there was none. He saw the twins still looking at the TV, mouths open in confusion and disgust. Edward's face had gone beet red and his whole body seemed to shake. And Elisabeth was standing, fists clenched, sending needles of hate toward him with everything she had.

She uttered only two words. "Get. Out."

"Elisabeth... This wasn't... I didn't..." Nathan looked around for support. With the exception of Lewis, everyone seemed to have taken a step back, distancing themselves from him.

"I don't know what just happened. If I could look at the computer, I'm sure - "

Her hand shot up to stop him. Her voice was louder now. "You couldn't leave it alone, could you? Ever since you came into my life, you've done everything you could to work against me. It wasn't enough that you stole Rachel away from me. You had to ruin her funeral, too."

"What? I didn't do this. How could you think I'd want Rachel's memorial to go like this?"

Elisabeth hadn't seemed to hear him. "You wanted that casket opened. All of us said to keep it closed. The wounds were too severe. But you wouldn't listen, would you? As usual, you just had to have it your way."

"Elisabeth, please..."

"I said get out. Get your things and leave. NOW!"

Elisabeth was shaking. The crowd was hushed. Nathan turned and found himself the object of their disdain. Old men shook their judgmental heads, more than one sneered in his direction. Several men put their arms around their wives' shoulders, pulling them close like they needed to be protected from him.

Nathan felt Lewis put his arm around his shoulder. "Come on, let's give this some space."

The crowd parted, and a gauntlet was made. Increasing measures of shame and embarrassment seemed to come with each step toward the exit. Lewis opened the door for him, and they left without looking back.

Chapter Thirty-Two

The sun had dipped below the tree line, and an icy breeze made their eyes water as they walked down the center of the drive toward Lewis's truck. Neither had the words to speak, so they didn't. They walked side by side, and that was a comfort enough to Nathan for now.

The mob was gone, scattered to who knew where. Except for the five guys sitting on the lone Chevy. The years hadn't been kind to them. They were guys who enjoyed big beers and never realized they had small dreams. They were all laughing and jostling each other as Lewis and Nathan approached. One in the middle had greasy red hair and a malicious look.

"Hey, Mikey. Look what we got here."

The one called Mikey looked up, having previously engrossed himself with something under his fingernails. He angled his thumb in his mouth and bit at the end before spitting out whatever he'd chewed up.

The first guy with the red hair slid off the hood of Lewis's truck. The others followed suit, two on either side. They grouped up like they'd done this many times before. There was an untested confidence about them, like their numbers had always been enough to do the job for them. Lewis wondered if any of them had actually taken a serious hit before; the kind that humbles you.

A skinny one said, "This is a nice truck. This yours?"

Lewis kept his eyes focused on their hands. In his periphery, he could see cars on either side, not impossible to get around, but still a barrier if lateral movement was necessary. It was like the cars had formed a tunnel, a satisfactory tactical advantage, just so long as he was the one aiming toward the mouth. But being inside one was a different story. It made him feel on edge, which was bad news for anyone on the receiving end of what was coming.

Lewis kept his voice level. "My names on all the paperwork, so yeah, it's mine." His sarcasm seemed to go over their heads.

Big Red walked forward until he was face to face with Lewis. He seemed to be sizing his opponents up - and unfortunately arrived at the incorrect conclusion. Maybe he interpreted Nathan's dejected face as weakness, or maybe he thought five on two were odds to bet on.

"You think I care what some paper says?"

Lewis shrugged. "No. I don't think you can read at all."

Red appeared confused at first, and then his cheeks started to match the color of his hair. He scanned side to side, like he was making sure his boys were still with him. A tall one confirmed his loyalty with a crisp little snap as he flicked a knife open. He made a show of making sure Lewis and Nathan saw the blade. This gave Red a boost of confidence because he got right up in Lewis's space and pushed a finger toward Lewis's chest. "You listen here..." The first jab never even landed.

Lewis caught the finger and twisted it sideways in a clean break. He spun Red around and shoved him into the tall guy with the knife. They fell over each other onto the ground. Lewis saw Nathan move right, positioning himself for a massive blow to one of the three standing. The punch landed like Nathan had channeled all his emotions into that single blow. The guy was out before he hit the ground.

Red and the tall guy were trying to pick themselves up. Lewis closed the gap on them in two quick strides. On the third, he kicked his boot forward, connecting with the tall guy's jaw like he was hitting a field goal. That made two down for good.

Nathan and Lewis converged again at the center, advancing like lions on the final three.

Red looked back and forth between his remaining crew. He yelled at them, "Come on, go get those guys!" But they stepped backward instead, leaving Red out on his own.

"Looks like your buddies are the only ones with some sense. Just you and me now, Red. You should walk away."

"I'm not walking away! You're with them! You got bad stuff coming your way. I'm gonna make sure you get yours."

Red rushed forward, only to be rewarded with a blunt strike from Lewis's forehead. Blood dripped out from Red's nose onto the ground, and he fell down to his knees as he wailed.

Lewis walked past and got into his truck without a second thought. Nathan stopped as he walked past, squatting down so he was eye level.

"I'm not a Thurman." Then he joined Lewis in the truck.

———

Later that night, across the lake and three streets west of the center of town, a cell phone would ring and wake Sheriff Carroll from sleep. His wife would hear only one side of the conversation, just grunts and basic acknowledgements that her husband was listening to the caller. He would hang up, sigh, and shake his head.

She'd ask, "What was that about?"

And he would tell her, "Sounded like one of our locals, up at the Thurman place with that fanatic group. They found another body."

Chapter Thirty-Three

They were quiet for a long time. After they cleared Silas Ridge, Lewis spoke.

"Do you want to talk about it?"

"No."

Lewis only asked once. Experience had taught him that sometimes there were no words, and the best thing was to just be there with someone. Hurting alongside with them, without offering well-meaning but ultimately unhelpful advice. They stopped only once for gas and a bad to-go cup of coffee.

It was close to midnight when they arrived back at Nathan's house. White streetlights reflected off the damp pavement. The tops of the trees were hidden from view, but it appeared the last of the leaves had fallen and riddled Nathan's lawn. Across the street his neighbor's yard was pristine - not a single browning leaf to be found. Nathan felt like he'd been away a long time. Lewis followed him up the walk to his front porch. The storm door opened with a rattling snap and a small brown package tumbled out on Nathan's toes.

My insurance replacement. I'd forgotten all about that.

He snatched the package up off the ground, fumbled with his keys in the lock, and got inside. His keys clanked on the table as he tossed them aside. Nathan turned the box over in his hands and felt the weight shift as the contents skidded from one side to the other. It landed in a thud as he tossed it with less care than his keys. There were only two people he cared to speak with anyway, and one was in the room with him. The other never would be.

Nathan's voice was tired and raw. "I appreciate you being there today. And thanks for the ride back. You should head home, though. I'm sure Rita is missing you." Nathan collapsed into an armchair and sank down low.

Lewis shrugged and said, "She didn't expect me until tomorrow. She took the kids to her mom's. If it's all the same, I'll stick here with you tonight."

Nathan looked around his house, taking a quick assessment. All was as he'd left it, although it smelled a little stale from the stillness that comes from absence. He caught a quick glance at where he had flung Rachel's plate. He stared at the wall, examining the indentations for a moment, remembering his fury.

"You don't have to, you know," Nathan said.

"Don't have to what?"

"Babysit me. Worry about me."

Lewis placed a hand, heavy and comforting, on Nathan's shoulder. "I'm not babysitting. I'm only being a friend. Just being here." He sat down in a chair nearby and rubbed his eyes. "But I am worried. You're right about that."

"Well, don't. I'll be fine."

"That's a lie if I ever heard one. You, my friend, are conclusively *not* fine." He sat down by Nathan and studied him. "Maybe I'm out of line for what I'm about to say, but I care too much about you to stay silent. Don't bottle this all up, man. This isn't like what happened with that explosion. This is a different kind of trauma. If you don't deal with this, I'm afraid it's going to ruin you."

They looked at each other, years of things left unspoken dangling in the air, primed to be said now. For years, Nathan had tried (unsuccessfully) to forget, but it never really left. Memories followed him around like a shadow. He was too tired to fight it, both physically, but more so emotionally.

Nathan sank deeper into his chair. "Can we not talk about that right now?"

"When will we talk about it? We barely ever talk about it." Lewis turned his head to one side to highlight the scarring on his cheek. "I see these every morning. I shave around them each day. Little kids stare, and their mothers pull them away before they can say something that would embarrass them. But I don't mind them. You know why?" Nathan had no response, he only stared ahead into the blank space. Lewis leaned in close. "I don't mind because these scars are a reminder of what you did for me. It reminds me I'm one of the lucky ones."

"It was nothing."

Lewis shook his head. "That's not true. You saved my life, and it had a cost. You saw some stuff that's stuck with you. It stuck with me. I wonder everyday why I got out, and they didn't. It haunts me. I think it might haunt you too."

Nathan's mind flew back to that day. When the bomb went off, he didn't have time to be scared. It all happened in the blink of an eye. He had crawled away from the truck, coughing and suffocating in the surrounding fumes. His head hurt. He couldn't hear anything other than a high-pitched ringing in his ears. He looked back and could see the truck's underbelly, like it had rolled over in surrender from the blast. Glass was all over the road. Black smoke filled the air, and he could see flames. He could see bodies.

Lewis was crumpled like a crash test dummy, not moving. If he didn't act, death would come for him too. There was no consideration of heroics or honor. It was a simple decision. He didn't think, he just did it. He tugged at Lewis's uniform and dragged him out from the broken window. There was a giant whoosh as the flames erupted and swallowed the truck whole. Then Nathan couldn't see the bodies inside anymore.

"You remember the first time we met?"

Nathan grinned. "I remember."

"I hated your guts. Back then, I was perfectly happy commanding my squad, but some genius up the food chain got the bright idea to send in a photographer. All the typical stuff. Document the troops. It'll be good for recruiting, good for PR, all that. We need to update the civilians back home. I kept wondering why we didn't use one of our own guys. But somebody up top wanted something different. When I heard a war correspondent was getting assigned to my unit, I about messed myself."

A breath that resembled a laugh came out of Nathan's mouth. "Yeah, I remember not getting the warmest of receptions."

Lewis laughed. "No, you certainly did not. If I'd have had my way, you wouldn't have been there." Lewis paused. "But if I'd gotten my way, I wouldn't be here, either."

Nathan let out a puff of air. "I don't know what to say."

Lewis shrugged. "Say whatever you want. It helps to talk. It lifts the weight a bit, helps to let go of the weight you can't carry. At some point, it's gotta go."

Nathan wiped a small tear away and fell quiet for a

moment. "We aren't talking about the war anymore, are we?"

"You tell me." Lewis waited.

Nathan shook his head. "It's all going to sound crazy. I don't even know where to start."

"How about the beginning?"

And so Nathan recounted the last few days, starting with the phone call from Rachel and the accident that followed. He tried to describe the uneasy feeling he got in the woods, and how odd the house felt. He told him about meeting Suzy and finding out about Rachel's last messages, and how he couldn't find the phone. In obvious frustration, he outlined how all his attempts to locate it led to nothing. As he described what happened in the basement, Lewis's face darkened, and when Nathan described the lake, it grew darker still. The barn. And when he decided to give it up.

"And you pretty much know the rest. You saw how the funeral went." Lewis stared at him for a long time until Nathan couldn't stand it a moment longer.

"Come on, say something. I realize how it all sounds, but I swear I'm not crazy."

"I didn't say you were."

"But you don't believe me."

"I didn't say that either."

"Then what?"

Lewis's hands folded into a steeple; the point pressed against his mouth. His tone was even and measured. "What I think is that you've been under a lot of stress -"

Nathan scoffed. "Stress? You think this is all - "

Lewis held up a *let me finish* finger and stopped him. " - a lot of stress, and it's taking a toll."

"This isn't stress. I know what I saw."

Lewis shuffled in his chair. "Nathan, I've seen what

extreme situations can do to a person. The mind can play terrible tricks."

"It's not all in my mind. Other people have seen stuff too; you included. If it's all made up, how do you explain what happened at the funeral?"

"Maybe it was on purpose."

Nathan's mouth dropped. "You seriously think I did this?"

"Of course not. I know you better than that. But based on the mob I saw outside, it seems to me there's quite a few suspects that wanted things to go wrong. I'm saying someone sabotaged it. Someone who wanted the family to suffer."

Nathan went quiet as he considered this. In all the chaos, he hadn't considered that someone intended for this to happen. The horror had blinded him to any practical considerations. And the longer he thought, the more he realized Lewis was right.

They leaned toward each other, their heads now less than a foot apart, looking like spies conspiring in hushed voices. Even though it was only the two of them in the house, Lewis kept his voice low. "I was thinking about what happened the whole way back. For three hours, I tossed it around in my head, replaying it all in my mind, over and over. And I kept coming back to this thought... Where did those photos of Rachel in the barn come from? I mean, someone had to have taken them, right? I know there's all sorts of fancy Hollywood tricks and stuff, but I sincerely doubt anyone there would have that sort of skill. So, I'm left wondering, how did those photos turn up? Where did they come from?"

"I'm not sure. There was something unnatural about them. They all seemed a bit *off*. I don't think I could have gotten those pictures without any editing. If I were trying to recreate images like that, I'd need time to make them on a computer. So, I guess someone made them, using Photoshop or something."

"Fair enough. But there's still a photo that's being worked from, right? They weren't like a drawing or something. So even if they were edited, who got the original pictures? Who took photos of Rachel in the barn?"

Nathan shook his head as he looked off at nothing in particular. "I don't know. Someone who wanted to ruin the funeral. And they got exactly what they wanted."

Nathan spun a coaster around on a side table as he considered what to do next. He was torn. On one hand, he could just move forward. Forget about everything, let it go, and try to get on the best he could with his life. What did he stand to gain by pursuing any of this anymore? He could be done with it. Done with the family, done with the tricks. On the other hand, didn't he owe something to Rachel? To her memory? Would he be able to move on when this injustice stood un-reckoned? Someone had wrecked Rachel's memorial, and didn't he owe it to her memory to expose that? To make it right?

"What are you thinking?"

Nathan looked back at Lewis, his face hardened and resolved. "I'm going to find out who sabotaged Rachel's memorial. I'm going to find out why. And I'm going to make them pay for what they did."

The plan was still forming in Nathan's mind, half-baked at best. But for his plan to work at all, he'd need to get connected again.

Nathan tore the tape off the box, revealing his insurance replacement. A little black rectangle was secured on a small white tray, covered in shrink wrap. No fresh box, just the phone and a charging cable. Buried at the bottom was a piece of paper, folded in half, that listed the setup instructions. There weren't many steps, and each carried the promise of ease and simplicity.

He plugged the phone in to make sure it had some juice, and after a minute, the screen came to life. The instructions indicated he could power the phone up and it would automatically program itself, so he went ahead and advanced the phone screen. There was a loading prompt, followed by a spinning wheel, and then a simple message.

Activation failure. For 24-hour assistance, please call us at...

Nathan cursed under his breath. He wanted to throw his phone. Throw it right between the two biggest indentations the plate had left.

If I could call for assistance, my phone would already be working.

Was the expectation that he call from a home phone? Nathan seemed to recall a land phone at his house growing up, but cell phones had dominated for so long he could barely remember. Memory seemed to tell him it was a sort of dirty white color, like it sat in a window that got a lot of sun. He remembered a large earpiece covering the majority of his face when he talked to his grandmother on holidays. But who had a landline phone anymore? No one he knew. The entire world seemed to revolve around cell phones. Your whole life reduced to a rectangle of glass and plastic and electricity, no bigger than the palm of your hand.

"Hey Lewis, can I borrow your cell? I need to call and have them get my phone activated."

"Sure." Lewis pulled his phone from his pocket and slid it like a frothy beer down a bar-top, minus all the slopping hoppy ale. Nathan snatched it right as it was about to topple over the edge.

Nathan looked back at the instruction flyer, found the 800 number listed, and dialed. A too friendly voice came on the line and assured him she was thankful for his business. Several pre-recorded prompts played, and when he heard "press three to speak with a representative", he pressed three and waited. A moment's pause, and then the woman said, "one moment while I connect you." Another brief pause. Silence. And another woman came on the line, this one real. She was cheerful and thanked him for his business, stated her name was Michelle, and that she'd be happy to help him today.

Nathan shifted the phone from one ear to the other. "Hi, I'm trying to get my replacement phone activated."

Michelle was chipper, and Nathan believed her. He could tell when someone was faking, and this wasn't it. "Ok, I'd be happy to help with that. Can I get your mobile number?"

Nathan recited his number and heard keyboard clicks on the other side of the line. There was another pause before Michelle had him confirm his password. Nathan confirmed everything, and Michelle said, "Ok, I can help you get this setup. The process is easy. Once I get it activated, all you'll have to do is follow the prompts on the phone to do a restore from the cloud."

Something sparked in Nathan's mind. Like a dream that you almost remember after waking up or having a word on the tip of your tongue. It was so close, but not there. Yet.

"I'm sorry? Can you repeat that?"

"Cloud storage? It's really great. It's just online backups. Everything you had on your phone before will download itself from the last time it saved. Once I have the phone activated, you will get prompts to restore your phone to from the latest backup. It's a very simple process."

Nathan's mind raced. He was on the edge of an idea,

but it wasn't quite there. And then all at once he had it. He stood up in his chair. His heart was racing in anticipation. The words poured out like a burst dam.

"Can you change which number I activate my phone on?"

Nathan paced the room like a caged animal. Lewis was about to ask a question, but Nathan held up his hand, a silent *give me a minute* sign. Lewis sat back down as Nathan continued his pacing.

The phone representative continued, "Of course. I can activate on whichever number you'd prefer."

Nathan gave the rep Rachel's number, and after a few clicks on the other end of the phone, the rep said, "Your phone should be all set."

Nathan stared at the screen, mouth half open and unable to blink. Lit up in front of him was a prompt: *Restore from cloud?* Then he burst, pumping his fist, whooping and hollering and jumping around the room as Lewis looked on in wonder. He stopped, breathing hard, and looked at it again in disbelief, daring himself to believe it to be true. After all the questions, all the searching, he'd finally found Rachel's phone. At least, in a manner of speaking; a clone of sorts. Her information, her number, only on a different piece of hardware. But for all practical purposes, it was Rachel's phone. He wasn't sure what he'd find, if anything, but here it was in his hands, and just a click away.

Lewis was still in the dark. He had a puzzled look on his face. "I'm not sure I like that look in your eyes. What's going on? What happened?"

Panting and buzzing with excitement, Nathan said, "It's Rachel's phone. It was missing. Just gone, without a trace. No one could find it, not even the cops. But I did. I found a way to get Rachel's phone. I had given up, but it came right to me!"

Lewis grinned from ear to ear and shot up out of his seat. "What are you waiting for? Let's do this!"

Nathan's thumb hovered over a simple button that said *restore*. He hesitated; excitement now replaced with doubt. He turned to Lewis. "What if I don't find anything? Or what if I find something I don't want to know?"

"There's only one way. If it were me, I'd always wonder what would have happened."

Nathan pressed the button. Before long, the phone opened up to the main screen and apps and info started to download. He gave it a few minutes to make sure everything had come through, but impatience soon got the best of him. He flicked through a few screens. Everything seemed to be in order and transferred. It was now or never. He opened up the texting app.

There were dozens of threads in the history. He saw his own name second from the top, that thread a mirror image of what would be on his own device. At the top of the message list was just one name. Mom.

Nathan frowned. "It looks like the last person she texted was her mom. Elisabeth never mentioned it."

"What did she say?" Lewis asked.

Nathan clicked the thread. He didn't have to scroll far; what he needed was right there waiting for him, plain as day. It was from the day before Rachel's body had been found, and it wasn't what he'd expected at all. In a single instant, a new layer of complexity was added, changing the entire situation.

Nathan didn't move. He read it again to make sure he hadn't made a mistake. Lewis waited in anticipation.

"What is it?" Lewis asked again.

In lieu of answering, Nathan turned the phone over to

Lewis. Down at the bottom of the thread, time-stamped a day before Rachel took her life, was a photo of Elisabeth, nude, and coupled with a less than subtle message clearly not intended for Rachel.

After that, the following exchange occurred:

Husband is knocked out from his meds.
Have about an hour.

The timestamps showed roughly a minute passed...

PLEASE DELETE.

??????

Rachel, please delete the message.

WHAT THE HELL MOM???!!

I can explain. Please delete that.

Are you serious right now?
Does Dad know?

Can you call me? Can we talk?

Rachel? Please call me.

Rachel?

That was it. The messages stopped. There wasn't anything after that.

They looked at the phone and digested the information

they were now privy to. It appeared Elisabeth was having an affair, and Rachel had inadvertently found out. But why would that be enough to kill herself? People had affairs all the time. Only a select few concluded in death, and those were usually candidates for a Dateline episode.

"We gotta go back to the house," Nathan said.

Lewis opened his eyes wide. "What? Now? After what happened at the wake? That seems like a seriously bad idea."

"Yeah, right now. This has something to do with Rachel's death. I know it. You saw it right here." Nathan pointed to the message. "Elisabeth wanted to talk." He opened up the phone app and scrolled to the log. "See, right here are multiple missed calls from Elisabeth. There were seven calls in about a ten-minute span where Elisabeth tried to reach Rachel. But she ignored them. Then just one outbound call, where Rachel finally called her mom back." He jabbed at the phone again, his finger making a dull knocking sound on the glass. "See, right there. That must have been when she left the coffee shop. She called her mom on the way home. I need to find out what they talked about."

"Think about this. What are you going to do? Just walk up to her mom and confront her?"

"Yes. That's exactly what I'm going to do. I'm getting some answers, Lewis. I'm owed that much."

Lewis shook his head. "Man, you better think this through. The family is already pissed about the video thing. They might not talk to you at all."

"I had nothing to do with the video. If anything, they should be apologizing to me."

"I know that. But they don't. You need a good plan, or you're going to get shut down. You've got some intel, but you don't have enough. Remember the truck? Remember what I got when I had bad intel? You sure you want to be asking these sorts of questions? Like they say, don't let it blow up in your face." Lewis highlighted the scars lining his cheek.

Nathan looked Lewis dead in the eye. "I'm done being in the dark and not getting answers. I have more information than ever about Rachel's death. And the info is telling me that before my wife decided to hang herself, she found out her mom was having an affair. That made an impact. And I'm going find out the truth, even if it's the last thing I do."

Lewis relented. "Fine. But at least sleep on it. If you feel the same in the morning, we'll go back."

They shook on it, sealing the deal.

Chapter Thirty-Four

Morning came. A gurgling coffee maker spat out the last reserves into a pot, and Lewis poured two cups before heading toward the kitchen table. He handed one to Nathan, who was already sitting down.

"Did you get any sleep?" Lewis asked.

Nathan sipped from the steaming mug. "Some. Not much."

"And how are you feeling about things?"

Nathan set the coffee down, remembering that first awkward breakfast at the Manor, how he'd wished to be back home, drinking his own coffee with Lewis. And now, here he was, but he couldn't stay. Not yet. On the outside, he may have appeared calm and composed, but it was inaccurate. Inside, his thoughts were all fire and brimstone, churning and bubbling like a witch's brew. He felt he could erupt, and God help the poor soul who stood in the way when he did.

The look on his face was answer enough for Lewis.

"Ok, we'll go back then. But we need to figure out a plan."

"My plan is to confront Elisabeth. She lied, Lewis. There was more to the story, and she kept it hidden."

"Of course she did. If you weren't aware, most people aren't forthcoming about cheating on their spouses. Just because she didn't volunteer that info doesn't mean she has answers for you."

Nathan shook his head. "Maybe she doesn't. But I'm done waiting to find out. I don't care about having a carefully thought-out plan. They already hate me. What do I have to lose?"

"It's your call, brother. I'm in it with you, no matter how it goes."

———

They retraced their route back to the Manor, stopping again just once for gas and coffee. Nathan showed Lewis where he'd crashed, and though his car was now gone, deep gouges and ruts in the bank made the severity apparent. For a fleeting moment, he wondered who had towed the car out, but then decided he didn't care. *Let it go, it's someone else's problem now.*

Light mist sprinkled the windshield as they approached the Manor, and the wipers squeaked in protest across the glass. The woods seemed as still as they ever had, and Nathan caught himself thinking about the birds that didn't fly overhead.

There are no animals out here...

The Manor came into view once they cleared the trees, the dim lamps lining the drive washed out by pulsing emergency lights. They found three police cars circled around the roundabout drive, and Lewis backed his foot off the gas.

"What's going on, Nathan?" Lewis asked.

The two peered through the windshield to get a better

look. When they got close, a deputy held up his hand and motioned for them to stop. Strobing red and blue lights bounced off his trench coat, which was slick with rain. The brakes squeaked as Lewis brought the car to a stop. He rolled his window down as the officer came around to his side.

"What brings you boys out all this way?" the deputy asked. There was an undertone in his voice, like he might be hoping for an excuse to whip out a baton.

Nathan leaned across the seat. "This is my in-laws' place. What's going on?"

The deputy ignored the question. "Your names?"

"Is there a problem? We're just wondering what's going on."

The deputy took a more aggressive tone. "I asked you a question. State your names and why you are here."

"Nathan Stevens."

The deputy shifted his attention to Lewis, letting his eyes ask the question for him.

"Lewis. Driver."

After considering them both, the deputy said, "Pull around up there. The Sheriff will have some questions."

He took a step back from the car and pointed to where he wanted them to go. Nathan and Lewis exchanged a private glance as Lewis pulled up to the spot as instructed.

Nathan whispered, "Driver? Are you messing with him on purpose?"

"He's being a dick. We didn't do anything wrong, and he's got no reason to be that way."

"I don't know what this is, but it can't be anything good."

They watched him outside, speaking something into his radio, but they couldn't hear through the glass and doors. The deputy rapped on Nathan's window with the butt of his flashlight and called for them to come out. Nathan and Lewis opened their doors and walked to the front of the vehicle where the deputy was waiting. He let them stand in the drizzle for a couple of minutes, daring them to challenge his authority.

There was a crackle of static, and then a voice sounded over his radio. "We're ready. Bring them in."

"Ok, you two follow me."

He led Nathan and Lewis up the stone steps toward the Manor's front door. When they stepped inside, the entry fell silent as multiple sets of eyes focused on them. The twins were separated off to either side, both in a seated position while several officers stood over them. Nathan recognized a few as the heads that popped out at him during his visit to the sheriff's office. It looked as if Lucas had been getting the worst of it. At the center of the room was Elisabeth, speaking with someone else Nathan recognized. Sheriff Carroll. She stopped mid-sentence when Nathan entered, her eyes full of disdain and contempt. But he was past caring. Let her glare; he knew the truth. Soon, she'd understand that too.

Carroll gave no greeting. He offered no friendly gesture. In fact, aside from a sideways glance, he gave little acknowledgement of any kind to their presence. Nathan studied him, trying to guess at what the Sheriff was doing at the Manor. He seemed to be working quick calculations in his head. As to what riddle he was working out, that was yet to be revealed. But whatever it was, it seemed to be taking a toll on him. Carroll's face looked worn and tired, as if he'd transitioned into old age overnight.

The deputy asked, "What do you want me to do with these two?" He jabbed a thumb toward Nathan and added, "This one here says he's related."

Carroll didn't look up from his notepad when he spoke.

"I know who he is. Set them down in the den. I'll be there once I'm finished here."

The trench coat deputy escorted Nathan and Lewis down to the makeshift holding pen and instructed them to wait. The room smelled of cigars and whiskey enjoyed long ago. A coffee table was positioned squarely in the middle, surrounded by a leather couch and chairs. Nathan and Lewis took their seats, and the deputy took a guard position outside the door. Nearly fifteen minutes passed before Carroll arrived. Dark circles underscored bloodshot eyes, and grey stubble had grown beyond a five o'clock shadow. He carried an air of danger about him, like a wounded animal backed into a corner.

Carroll looked them up and down before sitting across from them. He pointed at Nathan and said, "You I know," and then his finger slid to Lewis, "But you I don't."

Lewis remained silent, offering neither name nor information. From the mood Nathan was picking up on, this was a wise decision. Carroll seemed a different man than the one he'd met a few days ago. This version of the Sheriff seemed hardened and capable of cruelty. Had he not made prior introductions with Carroll, he would have opted to keep quiet as well.

Carroll kept his attention trained on Lewis, sizing him up. Without breaking eye contact, he called to the guard. "Hey Bates, go run their tags. I want to know everything about that car. Who it's registered to, where it came from, what year it was made. I want to know the last time the oil was changed, got it?" Something unspoken passed from Carroll to Lewis. Something that said, *you don't have to talk; I don't need you to.*

The Sheriff gave them a hard look and launched into his questions. "Heard you boys got out of here pretty quick. What was that about?"

"I needed to go home," Nathan said.

"Home? What for?"

"There was an incident. A misunderstanding. I needed some space."

Carroll glanced down toward Nathan's hand. "Wouldn't have anything to do with those busted up knuckles, would it? Seems to be more than one set of those around here tonight."

Nathan moved to cover his hand and immediately regretted it. He and Lewis may not have started that fight after the funeral, but the local Sheriff might not see things that way. He removed his hand, hoping it didn't look like he was trying to conceal something.

"No. I just realized I still had some things left to do."

"What sorts of things?"

"It's personal. I can promise you we didn't do anything wrong."

"No offense, but promises mean very little in my line of work."

"That's the best I can offer right now."

Carroll's face was impatient. "I could get a court order. Get you under oath. Make you talk and make it legal. On the books, so to speak."

Something told Nathan that Sheriff Carroll might be just as happy to get his info in private, where *on the books* and *legal* were only suggestions.

"Ok, I guess that's your decision. But I've got some rights and I don't have to share every personal detail about my life. In case you forgot, I'm dealing with some abnormal stress at the moment. Maybe I just need a bit of space."

"And maybe you're hiding something."

Lewis chimed in, unable to hold his tongue. "Somebody played a nasty trick on Nathan. Messed up the funeral, caused a big scene."

"A trick, huh? And would that have anything to do with your sister-in-law leaving?"

Nathan looked confused. "Lily? No, she left before the funeral."

Carroll wrote something down on his notepad. "I'd be interested in a statement from her. Any idea where she took off to in such a hurry?"

"No. I have no idea."

"She didn't say anything? No details? No forwarding address?"

"I'm just her brother-in-law. I don't get those details."

Carroll shifted over to Lewis. "What about you, friend? Where have you been the last forty-eight hours? Roughly speaking, that is."

"Been right at home. Friend..."

"I assume you can provide verification of that?"

Nathan held his hand up, interrupting before Lewis replied. "I'm very confused. What's with the third degree? Are we under some sort of investigation here? What happened?"

Carroll regarded them a moment before removing a photograph from a manilla folder. He slid it across the table to Nathan. The picture showed a young guy, maybe twenty or so to Nathan's eyes. Could have been a few years either way. Lopsided grin, wavy blond hair swept over to the side.

"You recognize him? Ever seen him before?" Carroll asked.

Something about him seemed familiar to Nathan, but he couldn't place it. And that's how Ben Carroll would remain in Nathan's mind - familiar but unrecognized as the boy that liked Suzy so much. He kept his mouth shut all the same. In the moment, it didn't seem wise to confirm anything one way or the other.

Carroll turned to Lewis.

Lewis scanned the photo. "Never seen him. Who is he?"

Tears welled up in the Sheriff's eyes and he wiped them away with the back of his hand. "This boy is Ben Carroll. He's my son."

Carroll took the photo back and looked at it as only a grieving father could. "I've seen a lotta messed up situations in my time. It's all part of the job, I guess. This is a small town. No one's a stranger. These are people I know, folks I grew up with. But I always tried to be professional about it. Impartial. I was even willing to let the little stuff go."

He closed his eyes and closed his fist tight. "I know my Ben wasn't perfect. I thought he just needed to get it out of his system. If it would have stayed little fights here and there, I could have dealt with it. Just boys being boys." He looked back at the photo. "But this time? This is different. This job has become very personal to me, and I promise you, I am making it my life's work to find out who killed my son. And I have more than a few suspicions about the people in this house."

There was a dangerous fire behind Carroll's eyes, revealing a man ready to snap if someone said or did the wrong thing.

The fact Nathan had nothing to do with this didn't make him feel any better. He didn't like the direction this was heading. He could see Carroll eyeing him, examining, trying to make guesses on suspects. And there was something about the Sheriff that wasn't there the other day; like one suspect might be just as good as another. In his first meeting, he'd seemed accommodating. Now Nathan wondered if that was a ruse. Maybe Carroll's demeanor was meant to lure him into sharing more than he should. Was this the real Carroll? Nathan told himself to play this as safe as possible. No lies, but not the whole truth either. He'd play his cards very carefully.

Carroll placed the photo back inside the folder, tapping the edges to ensure the papers were aligned. He stood and walked to the door, calling back over his shoulder.

"Stick around a bit. Fella takes off after something like this, doesn't look too good for him, you know what I mean?"

He turned his attention toward Bates, still positioned by the door in his trench coat. "Might want to spend your shift tonight at the end of the drive. We don't want anyone speeding out on those old country roads. Give me a ring if anything interesting comes up." Bates glanced back at Nathan and gave a single nod in response.

Then Carroll left, leaving Nathan and Lewis alone in the den to consider his warning.

Chapter Thirty-Five

"What's our next move?"

Having been put on unofficial house arrest, they were back in Nathan's assigned room. Lewis was pacing, but not in worry, as some are prone to do. This was when Lewis did his best thinking. Moving helped him focus. Over the years, Nathan had watched him wear ruts into the ground while ruminating.

Nathan hadn't moved yet. He was deep in thought, thinking about that picture. Thinking about the kid because that's what he'd been. Nathan wouldn't have pegged him for much more than twenty-one. What would drive someone to murder a kid? His whole life was in front of him. Career, love, family... All of it gone.

Nathan chewed his lips and said, "I'm not sure what to do next. But maybe there's a silver lining here?"

Lewis stopped mid-step; his expression skeptical. "How do you possibly figure that?"

"For one, I was worried the Thurmans would throw me out the second I got here. If that happened, I wouldn't ever get an opportunity to talk to Elisabeth. That problem is pretty well sorted out now. Cops said to stay. Not much they can do about that, is there?"

"I suppose not. So, what are you going to say to her?"

"Still working on that."

Lewis resumed pacing.

Nathan found Elisabeth in the parlor. It hadn't taken him long. In fact, it seemed to Nathan that his search should have taken him more time than it did. While his previous wanderings in the house had proven maze like, this journey felt more like a shortcut. The distances felt smaller, and the halls had less turns than before. Still, with the rest of the family having retreated to their individual rooms to worry about the orders given, the house retained its vacant, abandoned quality.

But Elisabeth hadn't gone to her room. She was sitting, still as stone, in the same seat she'd occupied during the wake. Blue moonlight snuck in through the windows and skylights, casting long, eerie shadows. Not long ago, this room had been bustling with people. Mourners for sure, but also kiss-ups and sycophants looking to gain position with the Thurmans. Now, the parlor was dark, and Elisabeth was alone. The chairs were still set up, but aside from Elisabeth, they were empty; lonely seats waiting in vain for someone to arrive.

Elisabeth held a glass of wine, and her face glowed red as she dragged on a cigarette. She was looking at Rachel's casket, unmoved and ominous. That box was the only thing in the room that didn't feel empty. Nathan walked past her without acknowledgement and stood before the coffin, placing his hand near the top where his wife's head lay underneath. The silence said more than they did for the first few moments.

Finally, Elisabeth spoke. "How did you find me?"

Without turning, he said, "It's a funny thing. I had the impression the house was difficult to navigate. But tonight I had no trouble at all. It was almost like I was meant to find you."

Aside from a scoff, she had no reply.

Nathan turned to her. "Elisabeth, I need to speak with you."

She didn't move. Her head stared straight ahead; her perfect face steadfast. Like so many aspects of her life, her voice was calm, controlled, and without hesitation. "Let me be clear. I have nothing to discuss with you." She swirled the wine around in her glass, letting it dance with breaching the rim. "And although seems that for the time being we are required to be together, make no mistake, as soon as this little legal issue is resolved, you'll be gone."

This was his point of no return. Once the words crossed his lips, there would be no re-do's, no take backs. But Nathan didn't mince words. He gave no lead up, no brace for impact. The words came out pedal to the metal, full force, full steam ahead, ready or not here it comes...

"I know about the affair."

Now, Elisabeth did turn. Her eyes were open wide. Two bright white spots in an otherwise dark room. They appeared illuminated, and Nathan thought he detected a hint of fear.

Elisabeth said, "I have no idea what you're talking about."

But there was less confidence, more caution in her voice, and Nathan knew he'd hit a nerve.

"Don't pretend. I saw the text messages, Elisabeth. The one you accidentally sent to Rachel."

Nathan couldn't see all the details, but he sensed Elisabeth stiffen. He knew her cheeks would be red with indignation. He could almost feel the heat coming off her face.

Elisabeth's voice was tight. "You went through my phone? Have you been spying on me?"

Nathan shook his head. "No, I didn't. I went through Rachel's."

Elisabeth huffed. "Impossible. Rachel's phone is missing."

Nathan moved to an adjacent row. Not beside her, but close. He hoped that by sitting, he might come across as less judgmental. Not that he cared. But he didn't want her clamming up if she felt condescended.

"Technically, it's not Rachel's phone. I just programmed her number on my new one. Everything came over as soon as I activated it. Pretty easy, actually."

"Looks like I can't deny it then."

She sipped her wine. Now that he was closer, he saw the muscles in her jaw tighten.

"Listen, I'm not looking to throw you under the bus. The affair means nothing to me. I'm only interested in finding out what really happened to my wife. And from where I sit, this had a part to play."

"And if I refuse to discuss this with you?"

Nathan sighed. "Let's just skip that part. I'm sure you want to keep this between us."

Elisabeth paused and examined Nathan. After a moment, Nathan saw her jaw muscles relax, resigned to her fate. No more secrets, no more hiding. She tilted the wine glass high and drained the remainder.

"Have you ever had a secret, Nathan?"

Nathan stayed still and let her talk.

"It's actually a relief. To not have to cover it up. It's like a weight gets lifted. It's exhausting to constantly be under pressure. Always worrying about being caught. Wondering what will happen when the truth comes out. So, when it finally does, in a way, it feels like freedom."

"So, what is the truth?" Nathan asked her.

"The truth is complicated."

"Simplify it for me. Explain what happened."

Elisabeth scoffed at him. "Explain what happened? As if things were ever so simple. I wish it were."

"My wife is dead, and I know it has something to do with your affair. I just want some sort of explanation. I'm owed that much. Just start at the beginning."

"The beginning is like every affair. I was unhappy in my marriage, so I found someone who valued me. Made me feel cherished and beautiful. I gave them what they wanted, and I got what I wanted in return. But I can assure you it had nothing to do with Rachel's death."

"You don't think Rachel finding out about this had anything to do with her suicide? You don't find it odd that she killed herself right after learning you cheated? You were the last person to talk to her! There has to be something."

Elisabeth conceded with a nod. "Yes, I agree that the timing is difficult. I can't say why she chose to end her life now, but it's what happened." Elisabeth paused, as if deciding whether or not she believed her own words.

"Tell me about the day Rachel died."

"Rachel left the house for town. She said she just wanted to get out and grab a coffee. Read a little on her own. She always liked having some space. She was more of an introvert, so private time was important to her. There wasn't anything odd about that. Rachel often went off by herself."

Nathan encouraged her to continue.

"We all went about our day as normal. Edward's nurse came, he fell asleep. And I was... lonely. I wasn't thinking. It was just a quick message; I didn't mean for it to go to her.

When I realized my mistake, I was mortified." Elisabeth took a deep breath. "And scared, if I'm being honest."

"Scared? What were you scared of?"

"What do you think? Of being found out! It's embarrassing. If word got out it would be scandalous. What would people say? What would they call me?" Her voice traveled off into a whisper, more to herself than Nathan. "And Edward... If he ever knew... he'd leave me nothing." Then she found her voice again, firm and confident. "It wasn't even a big deal. It meant nothing to me, not really. Besides, if Edward had really loved me, I wouldn't have had to find it someplace else."

"I'm not judging you."

Elisabeth continued like she hadn't heard him. "You don't know what it's like. Edward's been sick for years, and I've been alone, in this horrid house. Being tortured every night. I deserved an escape. And I found someone who prized me. I liked the feeling. I'm owed that, aren't I? The sex was... necessary, I suppose. But I at least was valued again. The way he looked at me... That's something Edward withheld. He always did enjoy keeping something back for himself. For all I have, that's something he never gave me."

"Ok, so you accidentally sent the text to Rachel. I saw the messages back and forth. What happened after that?"

"I called her. Multiple times. She wouldn't pick up. Eventually she did, but it was obvious she didn't want to speak to me. She was furious. She would barely talk to me. I asked her to come home so I could explain. Or at least try to. I practically had to beg her. The last thing she told me was that she was on her way. And that's it. I waited for her at the house. When she never showed up for our meeting, I just figured she changed her mind. I didn't even realize she'd come home. I didn't see her until... Until after." Elisabeth put her hand over her mouth, muffling her heaving sobs.

"I waited all night for her to show up. So, I started calling her again, but she wasn't picking up anymore. Her phone never even rang, it just went straight to voicemail. I assumed it had run out of battery. Or that she turned it off because she was done talking to me. I thought she'd never talk to me again, but not because of this."

He waited for her to gather herself before pressing her for more.

"What happened to her phone? I looked everywhere, but always came up empty handed. It was just dumb luck that I figured out that I should activate her device over my own."

"Hancock was upset when he called the house. He told me to come to the barn as quick as I could. I admit, I found her phone. I didn't know what to do. All I could think about was the police would find it, which meant they would search it, and then everyone would know my secret. So, I threw it in the lake. I know I shouldn't have done it. But I was terrified my secret would get out. Edward would have divorced me and left me with nothing. I'd be mocked and shamed. I was afraid I'd lose everything."

She sat up a little taller. "And I'm worth more than that. I've put in my time. I've earned what I have. I don't deserve to lose everything over this. If letting that phone sink to the bottom of the lake is what it costs, then so be it."

Nathan examined her face in the dark and saw her jaw muscles all tight and rigid again. None of this explained why Rachel would hang herself. Would she have been upset? Probably. Most children would be if they discovered a parent's infidelity. But Rachel was a grown woman. Something like this seemed unlikely to push her over the edge.

"There's more here. Something's missing that you aren't saying. What else is there?"

With tears in her eyes, she said, "You're right. But it's not the *what* that's missing... It's *when*."

As the hands of the grandfather clock inched toward 10:57, Nathan followed Elisabeth toward the barn. Their deal was conditional. If she was to show him what he was seeking, then he would have to swear to keep quiet about her affair. Under no circumstances could he speak of her infidelity. Ever. It would ruin her. He'd agreed, and Elisabeth grabbed a flashlight for the journey while he waited in the parlor.

The world was silent. In the last hour, the sky had gone dark. Not a single star penetrated the dense cloud cover above. It was the thickest version of black Nathan had ever seen. Being miles from the town, and hundreds from anything resembling a major city, light pollution was non-existent. There was nothing except the dim glow of lamps lining the walks around the house.

They walked a decent way before Elisabeth dared to turn on a flashlight. Nathan stumbled more than once. When she finally clicked it on, a bright white light shot out into the darkness before them - and then disappeared into nothingness. She aimed it down at a shallow angle, as if the flashlight were a lighthouse that would guide watchful eyes to their position.

"This way," she called. Nathan followed behind her. He took cautious steps, but his feet seemed determined to find every dip and rock and stray root along the way. Before long, they came to the same path Hancock had led him down. The ground smoothed out. Elisabeth risked casting the beam further, and walking became easier. Not far ahead, grunts and shuffling hooves in the barn disturbed the night.

"A little help, please?" Elisabeth asked as she stepped to one side of the doors.

Nathan moved forward and started on the chain securing the doors. It was cold and damp, and he could feel the grit of rust staining his hands. The chain clanked as Nathan removed it, and the gate creaked open. Elisabeth walked in first and lit a small lantern hanging next to the door, bathing the barn in shallow warm light.

"Would you mind closing the gate back up?" she asked. Nathan turned and moved the gate back into place. When he turned back, Elisabeth was already at the back of the barn. She held the lantern off to her side. The orange glow lit just one side of her face.

"Back here. It's almost time," she said as she curled her finger for him to follow. She pointed toward the ground, but Nathan couldn't make it out. He squinted and tried to spot what Elisabeth was calling attention to.

The rope came over his head when he took the next step. He felt a quick tug and the rough braids tighten around his neck, and then his feet left the ground. There was no path for air to get to his lungs. Tremendous pressure built up in his head, like a tank about to blow. His eyes felt like they might burst. Oddly enough, he caught himself wondering about how much it would take for an eye to pop out of socket. He guessed not a lot. Maybe the eye socket was a type of relief valve for this very type of thing. His hands flew up to his neck and clawed at what gripped him.

Elisabeth's face looked full of satisfaction. And despite Nathan's altitude, she still managed to look down on him. Nathan's legs kicked and flailed, but his attempts to break free were growing increasingly hopeless.

"I suppose you have a lot of questions," Elisabeth said. "I thought to start, you might want to meet my lover."

She took a few steps toward him. When she got within

touching distance, she pushed his shoulder with one finger and spun him around. Halfway through his rotation, he found himself face to face with a giant of a man. His hands were up above his head, gripping the rope that Nathan found himself hanging from. A wicked grin was upon his face. His arms didn't even shake as he held Nathan up off his feet.

"Hey there, champ," Jonathan said. "I hear you're quite the sleuth."

Nathan tried to speak but only managed spittle.

Elisabeth spun Nathan back around and said, "I'll make it quick, as you don't have a lot of time." She sneered, her perfect white teeth looking as venomous as fangs. "It's not like we necessarily intended to end up together, but hey, why not? We both got something out of it."

She came closer to Nathan. His world was reeling. He was close to blackout.

"Did you want to say something? Let me guess. It's probably something like, '*You'll never get away with it!*'" She cackled. "But in reality, of course I will. In fact, we've already gotten away with it once. Your wife found that out. When she came home, she was furious with me. All sorts of *how could yous'*, and *it's not right*, blah blah blah. She wanted to tell Edward. She wanted to tell her *daddy*. And we couldn't have that, could we?"

Elisabeth turned her hand over and took care to examine her nails. "I could tell you were the same. And like I said, Edward can't find out. He'd leave me with nothing. That part's true."

Jonathan's deep voice boomed from behind him. "My brother can't find out, Nathan. There's too much to lose. The family company should have been mine long ago. I can't risk Edward appointing someone else. It's my birthright. I'm sorry it all had to be this way."

Elisabeth looked at Jonathan. "Did you bring it like I asked?"

"Of course I did. But like I said earlier, I don't need it. I can handle this without a gun."

"Nathan isn't the only one we have to worry about this time. Where is it?"

Jonathan tilted his head, pointing with his eyes toward the weapon. Elisabeth walked around and pulled it from his waistband. Then she reached into Nathan's pocket and slipped his phone out.

"Finish up here. Same as last time. No signs left. I'll handle the phone and the friend."

"Are you sure that's a good idea?"

Elisabeth looked down at the revolver she held, weighing it in her hands.

"We don't know what all they talked about, so we have to assume Nathan told him everything. We can't risk it."

"And what will we say when they investigate?"

Elisabeth shrugged. "We'll tell them exactly what happened. Nathan was distressed, and he shot his friend. Then, in his mental anguish, he killed himself just like his late wife. I think a murder/suicide works quite nicely for a story." She turned and stormed out of the barn, leaving Jonathan and Nathan alone.

Nathan kicked his feet in vain until he had virtually nothing left. He was almost at the end. He knew then Elisabeth would get away with it. Sure, the police would come. But what would they find? A grieving husband, a mentally unstable spouse unable to cope with the grief. Like Romeo and Juliet, his own private tragedy. Only it wasn't suicide. It was manipulation and trickery. It was an execution.

Jonathan spun Nathan around, so they were face to

face. His big, toothy grin had stayed right in place. His arms were like tree trunks, rigid and thick. When the police found his body, it would look exactly like Nathan had hung himself. All Jonathan would have to do is tie the rope up on the beam after the fact. No one would question a thing.

Nathan was almost there. It was almost time. The pain was gone. Darkness was creeping up, something darker than the black night outside. But he wasn't scared; he welcomed what was coming. Maybe he could see Rachel again? Maybe they would reunite on the other side? She was there, almost within reach, her arm outstretched toward him. Calling him. Welcoming him. She smelled of melons...

The clock hands reached their destination. Outside of both of their vision, a stable gate rattled and something broke loose, allowing a giant of a different sort to emerge. Jonathan detected the movement and snapped his head to that side. Maybe he could have moved, but he didn't. The horse kicked as soon as he looked. Hooves smashed into Jonathan's ribs, pummeling him into the opposite wall. Wood splintered and cracked as he made impact.

Nathan lay crumpled on the barn floor, heaving air into his lungs. As the light returned, Rachel faded away. He grabbed at the noose and tore it from his neck and collapsed flat on the ground. His neck was raw, and his lungs felt like they were on fire.

Something blurry was moving in front of him. He pushed himself up, wobbled, and then got his balance. Jonathan was twisted up unnaturally on the ground. One leg was bent underneath his back, and his neck was bent at a sharp angle. The horse was over him, sniffing and snorting and stomping the earth with a force that rattled Nathan's chest. Mist exploded out of its nostrils. Its large head dipped up and down over Jonathan's belly. Nathan was still coming to - he could swear the horse was pulling taffy. Long strands stretched and snapped as the horse tugged at them. He could hear the taffy pop as it separated. The horse head went back to Jonathan's belly and Nathan could hear wet, sloppy, sucking sounds. When the coppery smell of blood filled the barn, Nathan realized the hideousness of what was happening, and terror flooded his bones.

Nathan jerked back, and the horse raised its head, tracking his movements with a large black eye. The horse snorted and Nathan jumped. A fine mist of blood hung in the air. The horse watched with hungry eyes as Nathan crept back toward the rear door. He bumped the back wall and felt for the handle. The horse took a step toward him. Another snort, another mist of red in the air. Nathan's hand found the handle. He lifted the lever and backed out, never taking his eyes off the beast. The beast never took its eyes off Nathan, even as the door was closing.

Chapter Thirty-Six

The house was full of long hallways that seemed destined for running. The straightaways of solid wood flooring were perfect for rolling balls, pushing toy trucks, even bike rides when they could sneak them in.

On this occasion, the halls facilitated the simple joy of running. Rachel rounded the corner of the hall at full speed, only to crash into her mother. Her face smacked into Elisabeth's thigh, and Rachel fell backward, her rear hitting the hardwood floor with a solid thump. Rachel looked up to see her mom's trademark frown of disapproval.

"What have I told you about running through the house?" Elizabeth scolded.

Rachel hung her head. "Sorry Mom, I forgot." Rachel was just seven. Her sundress had a cute pattern of flowers on it. She had pigtails tied with matching red ribbon.

"You always seem to forget. What do I need to do to get you to remember?"

Rachel's pulse kicked up a notch, and she felt her guts drop. Elizabeth shot a familiar glare, one that Rachel knew all too well, the one that meant she was on extremely thin ice. Rachel hated that look. She wished to be smaller at that moment. Small enough to avoid her mother's gaze, small enough to disappear. She wished to vanish into thin air, if it were possible.

Her voice was quiet. "I'm sorry, Mom. I'll play quietly. I promise."

Elizabeth stared at her a moment longer, and then relented. "Make sure you do. You don't want to disturb your father. You know how hard he works."

Rachel wasn't as concerned about her father. Sure, he might pop his head out of his office, yelling at her or her siblings to keep it down, but he rarely left the office. All the ruckus she and her siblings could muster wasn't enough to draw his attention from work. Her mother was the one to carry out punishments, and she made sure they were severe. Rachel still had the greenish-yellow marks from the last time her mother had issued such discipline. There was no room for error in her mother's house. No place for childishness. Rachel sensed she had dodged a beating. The rapid flutter in her chest started to slow.

After one more warning from her mom, Rachel went her way, eyes down and looking at her dress, swishing with each step. She turned a corner and then peeked her head back around the wall. Pretending she was a spy, Rachel watched her mother go down the stairs, until she disappeared below her sightline.

She made her way up to the third floor. She knew from experience that the sound didn't carry as much from up there, and she would have the freedom to play as she wished. At first she walked, but once she got halfway up the stairs, she charged ahead, ignoring her mother's warnings. She flew to the far end of the house, where she knew it would be quiet. Where she became small and invisible. Where she could vanish into thin air.

Rachel got to the midway point of the hall and stopped.

Right in front of her, just steps away, was a wall of inky darkness. The opposite side had become veiled. Of course, she knew the wall was there, but it made her uncomfortable to not see it. It reminded her of a black hole. She'd learned about those in school, and those made her uneasy too. Her teacher had said they used to be stars, but now they were collapsed and sucked everything inside, even light. She asked her teacher where the light went when the hole sucked it up. Apparently, no one was quite sure, but it was being studied. The thought of an invisible hole in space, impossible to escape once it had you, was overwhelming to her. It made her feel lonely.

She'd played up here dozens of times, but she didn't recall things being so dark before. Tea parties with her dolls, or the occasional puzzle, but those only as a last resort. If she was in a sporty mood, like now, she played a bit of ball.

Rachel pulled a small red rubber sphere from a stitched pocket. She held it in her small hands and looked down the hall, into the darkness. The wall was just beyond, but she couldn't make it out. She chucked the ball with as much might as her little arm would allow and listened to the smack as it made contact. The ball bounced once on its way back to her and she caught it. She smiled to herself, relieved that she heard the wall beyond. This was almost more fun since she couldn't anticipate where the ball would land on its way back. She threw again. *Smack, bounce, catch. Smack, bounce, catch.*

She thew again, but on this throw there was no *smack*. No *bounce*. Just empty silence. She waited, wondering what she had done wrong. She took a step forward, but stopped. Something told her not to go any further.

Childlike fear of the dark.

Black holes and eternal descent.

Rachel's body seemed trapped for an eternity. But then

her little red ball came rolling back, releasing her from the trance. Moments ago, this would have seemed perfectly normal. Expected even. But nothing about the delay had been normal. It was unexpected that the ball had disappeared into space and time, for God knows how long, only to return to her.

The ball rolled toward her feet and bumped off her toes. She leaned down and picked it up. Examined it. Wondered if a trick had somehow been played on her. Some sleight of hand by an invisible magician beyond her view. She looked deep into the dark end of the hall, eyeing it suspiciously. Rachel held her gaze a long time, examining as hard as she could. She scrunched her eyes tight to get a sense of what lay beyond the light.

Then, a crisp, fair voice spoke out to her. "Hi there! Do you want to play catch?"

The voice was light, lady-like. Almost friendly. Almost. Something about it seemed strange to Rachel. Familiar somehow, but she was unsure why. She thought the voice had come from a far corner of the hallway, but it might also have been behind her. Sound moved oddly in the narrow corridors of the house. Subtle echoes reverberated in multiple places, all at the same time.

Rachel squinted her eyes into narrow slits to see who spoke. She wouldn't swear to it, but she thought she caught a perceptible form, like a shadow. Her eyes might have been playing a trick on her. It was like spotting the glint of a star. She had to look beside it because looking straight at the thing would cause it to disappear.

"Who are you?" Rachel asked.

The voice came back. "I'm a friend. Do you want to be my friend?"

Rachel frowned. She thought about her father warning her against speaking to people she didn't know. He told her stories about people who wanted to snatch her up and take her away from him forever. He had painted a grim picture of what happened to little girls who got snatched up by bad people.

"I'm not supposed to talk to strangers."

"Oh, I'm not a stranger. I live here. I've known your family for a long time." The voice spoke with such simple honesty it could have fooled even discerning adult ears. Rachel was only seven, and a new seven at that. A mere child.

Rachel considered this revelation. This was her family's house, and so far, only her parents and siblings lived here. And Upham, he lived here too. There were always a lot of people around, coming and going. Other grown-ups visited and had grown-up talk with her dad. Usually, people wanting to talk business. Meeting the voice in the hall didn't necessarily seem strange because Rachel was always meeting new people.

Still, there was something uncomfortable about the voice. But that wasn't necessarily strange either, because sometimes her daddy's friends made her uncomfortable too. Something in their eyes made her very wary. Like these were the bad people her daddy had warned her to stay clear of; that they would be the ones to snatch her up if the opportunity presented itself.

This voice wasn't like that. It was strange, but there was also a familiar quality to it. Now that she had thought about it, the voice didn't seem so strange after all. Why would it be strange for a new person to be here? Why wouldn't there be more people in this big house that she hadn't seen before? In fact, she was quite certain the voice was a friend. It would be nice to have a new person to play with. Lily was still too small. Someone to play with would be a wonderful change from her usual lonely playtimes.

"I live here too," Rachel said. "But downstairs. I only come up here to play, so I don't bother Mommy and Daddy."

"I know you do. I hear you playing. I like to play too. Would you like to play catch with me?"

Rachel beamed with excitement and tossed her the ball. It crossed into the dark and disappeared again, but quickly came rolling back toward her. Rachel could have burst. A new friend to play with! She was tired of playing alone. She was tired of being alone. But Rachel didn't feel alone as they volleyed the ball on the third floor.

The voice spoke again. "It's so nice to have someone to play with. I get so lonely up here."

"Me too," Rachel said. "Maybe we can play again tomorrow? Then we won't have to be lonely."

"I'd like that very much." The ball rolled back toward Rachel again. As she leaned over to pick it up, she'd resolved to be up here more often, visiting her new friend. She made it official with a proper introduction.

She flashed a big, friendly smile toward the shifting shadow. "I'm Rachel," she said.

A gleeful squeal rose out of the darkness. Like a scream trying to be muffled, or an excited shriek.

"I love that! It's very beautiful." There was a pause, and then a question.

"Can you keep a secret?" the voice asked. It was a whisper, near inaudible.

Rachel shook her head yes and waited. She took a step toward the darkness, listening as if for a pin drop. All other sounds seemed to mute. She couldn't hear the wind outside, or the tick of the grandfather clock. No boards creaked, no pops as the house settled. All she heard was the beautiful, clear voice of her new friend.

"Rachel is my name, too!"

Chapter Thirty-Seven

Cool air helped Nathan regain his senses. He reached up and touched the skin around his throat. It stung like a ring of fire around his neck. Each breath burned and ached. His voice would be only a whisper, if he had even that. Panic and terror gripped him. How could he have been so blind? So stupid? How did he not see this before? But it was all clear to him now. Rachel was dead because of her mother's sins, not his.

What about the friend?
I'll worry about him.

Elisabeth's last words haunted him. She was going for Lewis. And Lewis didn't have a clue.

Nathan kept off the path for fear of being spotted. He darted through the trees, ducking under branches and scurrying over fallen logs as he worked his way toward the house. He hadn't seen Elisabeth yet. But she was there, and with her secret out, more dangerous than ever. Nathan's only advantage was that he might have surprise on his side. But it wouldn't last long. Jonathan would be expected back soon. When he didn't return, she'd grow suspicious. He wasn't sure how much time he had. Possibly mere minutes.

He arrived at the tree line and skidded to a stop. The house was just ahead, but every last inch between him and the house was open and exposed. And Elisabeth had a gun. He imagined her in a shadowy corner or tucked back behind an open window like a sniper, ready to pull the trigger. The hammer would fall, causing a chain reaction that would build up to a fiery flash exploding from the barrel. The entire process would happen in the blink of an eye, its end result deadly. He might not even have time to hear the gunshot crack through the air.

Nathan scanned the area, looking for the best option for entry. How could he get to Lewis? Hidden in the shadows, he spotted the window of his own room. It was still open. Maybe he could climb up? Wishing for a ladder, he looked for anything remotely scalable. There was a lattice, but it was at the wrong end of the house. There were no pipes, no ivy, not even a loose gutter spout to shimmy up. His only available route would be to enter at a lower level and sneak through the house. Once he got to Lewis, they would work together to get out.

Just leave. Get out while you can.

He swatted the intrusive thought away like a fly. Leave without Lewis? Not an option.

Nathan scanned the house, paying attention to the windows. Several times he thought he spotted a figure looming, but when he looked again, he found only empty space. The distance from the trees to the Manor wasn't far; he'd only be left exposed for seconds if he ran. While running would mean less time in the open, he knew the human eye was drawn to fast-moving objects over slow ones. Crawling would take more time, but in the darkness he might go unnoticed. Probably.

It was awful work, on his belly, getting scraped and scratched with each tug forward. He was certain crosshairs were trained on his spine. Every impulse in him screamed to get up and run, but he forced himself to go slowly. He would be no good to Lewis if caught, so he needed to be careful. He would only get lucky one time tonight, and he spent that chance in the barn. There wouldn't be a second.

He inched his way closer, pausing every so often to blend in. He kept his face buried in the dirt and listened, dreading the sound of a gunshot within the house. But all he ever heard was his own blood pumping through his ears. The process was slow and repetitive. Pull himself forward, stop and listen, repeat. Pull himself forward, stop and listen, repeat.

After what seemed to be miles, he reached the house and got up on his hands and knees and listened for activity. The house was quiet. Nothing moved. Not a single creak or groan. But Nathan sensed...*something*. It felt more alive now; almost as if the Manor were *breathing*.

He moved along the side, crouched and close to the wall, reducing visibility from the upper windows. Before him lay the parlor door, the same one he'd walked through just a short time ago with Elisabeth. That door represented a sort of baptism. He'd left one thing; now returned something else. Something dangerous in his own right.

"Damn this house!"

Had the clock hands advanced beyond 10:57, it might be said that Elisabeth grew more frustrated by the minute. As it was, every clock in the house stood still. The same couldn't be said of her. Elisabeth stormed the halls, blind to the imperceptible curves that led her in apparent circles.

I've walked these halls every day for years. Years! I know my own way... I know my own way...

She charged forward, certain that at each next corner she would get her bearings, but each time she found herself increasingly lost within her own home. The hall behind her looked long; longer than it should have. She'd gone too far, more than she'd intended. She scratched an invisible itch on her head with the barrel of her gun, her mind far from the finger resting on the trigger.

Her thoughts were on Lewis and the job she needed to finish. Her eyes narrowed and focused on the path forward.

―――

He reached out and touched the handle like it was fragile, as to not cause a sound, hoping to find it unlocked and empty on the other side. To his relief, the handle turned, and inside, he found only a room full of orphaned chairs waiting to be filled.

Nathan entered and let the door close with a soft click. The parlor was dark and empty; the smell of Elisabeth's cigarette still lingered in the air. He stopped at Rachel's casket, placed his hand upon it again, and whispered all that he'd wished he could have said at her funeral. How he was sorry for pushing her back home. That he wished that he would have said no to the job. That he loved her, and would continue to love her. He said that despite the pain he was in, he'd endure it all over again if it meant getting to see her one more time. And that now that he understood the truth, he would find her justice, even if it killed him.

Nathan wiped tears from his eyes and once again walked down the parlor aisle, glancing to his left and right, remembering the jeers and judgment.

He reached the main hall and risked a glance outside. There was nothing. The house felt vacant, but Nathan didn't allow a false sense of security to trick him. Elisabeth was here, and she had blood on her mind.

The obvious next step was to take the staircase and look for Lewis on the second floor, where he was likely getting ready for bed. (If sleep in this place were possible.) However, he'd almost certainly be spotted on his way up. He may as well shout out his arrival now. *Here I am! Come get me in the parlor!* Not ideal. No, the service corridor would be a better path. A hidden one.

As he stepped into the hall, the parlor door was ripped from his hands and slammed shut. The boom reverberated through the house, announcing his presence as if he'd knocked on the front door. If the silence that followed hadn't been so deafening, Nathan might have noticed the grandfather clock, with its great bears on top, had come to a full stop, its hands having come to rest at that most dreaded time.

Always 10:57.

A light shattered behind him, but it was the footsteps above that gave way to fear. He ducked as if he could shrink and hide simply by being closer to the ground. The steps moved fast; a sprinter's stride, headed for the main staircase as if it were a finish line. Terror of being discovered gripped him. Nathan scrambled to find a hiding place, and spotting a closet, dashed inside. He smashed himself in against the coats and bags and whatever else had been stuffed in there over the years. It was a tight fit, but he wedged himself in between two puffy coats and closed the door just as the footsteps hit the bottom floor.

It crept closer now, its pace steady, no longer running, but careful and deliberate, like a hunter stalking prey. There was no clack of a shoe, no heel striking hard wood. The steps were soft and padded, like bare feet, but Nathan didn't dare peek. He held his breath, afraid to move. Afraid to even blink. It inched closer, and when it got to the closet door, stopped. Nathan didn't budge. He held as still as he'd ever been in his life.

The air grew icy; not even the coats he was crammed between could temper it. It was as if the cold originated deep inside him, and no external warmth could fight it back. The hairs on his forearm shot straight up like soldiers. His stomach wretched, and he struggled to keep the vileness down. It went on like that for what seemed an eternity, but just as he felt he would explode, the steps moved on. They were slow, working their way down the hall, until he could hear them no more.

Nathan remained silent for a while longer, fearing a trick. When he ventured out, it was cautious and slow and with the expectation of being bludgeoned in the head as soon as he stepped from concealment. But it didn't happen. He emerged alone. No one in the hall. No steps rushing from above. Or from below, for that matter. He swallowed once and moved to the service corridor.

And still, the clock hands stayed in place.

He scaled up the service stairs and reached the second floor without incident. After checking to ensure the hallway was clear, Nathan crossed and slipped inside the room he'd occupied for the last few days.

The door had no sooner latched closed when Nathan's leg flew out from under him, sending him down toward the floor. His back hit hard and all the air inside his lungs expelled in a rush. Blinding stars filled his field of vision. They faded, and he saw Lewis standing over him, one hand pressing his shoulder, the other balled into a fist, ready to strike. Lewis's face relaxed when he saw it was Nathan.

"What in God's name are you doing? Do you have any idea what time it is?"

"Emergency." Nathan's throat felt like someone had scraped it with a brillo pad. Everything came out hoarse and labored.

Lewis spotted the red ring around Nathan's neck. He leaned his head forward and narrowed his eyes to inspect the damage.

"Tell me what happened." Lewis's tone and expression were familiar; one he took on when his training kicked in. He was the kind of guy who could go from easy going to a hardcore fighting machine in a split second. He was going through his warrior's playbook and calculating angles. It wasn't so much that Lewis was running threat assessments, it was that he'd already done them, and it was now time to execute. He saw Lewis eye the window, then the door as he counted exits for what wouldn't have been the first time since their arrival.

"Elisabeth."

Lewis's concern deepened. "Is she hurt? Does she need help?" Lewis stood up, ready to take action. Nathan grabbed his hand and pulled him back down.

Nathan shook his head, and with his hands, mimed being choked. As if to drive the point home, he tensed his arms violently when they got to his throat.

Lewis's eyes grew wide. "Elisabeth did this?"

Nathan confirmed it with a single, grave dip of his head.

"Why?"

Nathan's throat was on fire, but he managed a single word, "Rachel."

Years of friendship, forged through hardships and tragedy, bonded them deeper than they understood. The truth was, they shared something closer to telepathy than either of them realized. Lewis knew what that single word meant as soon as it left Nathan's lips. No more would ever need to be said. And neither would ever want to.

Lewis reworked the math in his head, factoring in the new variables. "We gotta get out of here. Screw the police orders. This family is insane. Let's just go now. Who's going to stop us?"

From Lewis's point of view, it was a valid argument, but Nathan wasn't so confident. Elisabeth's ruthlessness and cunning had trapped him once already; he didn't want to make the same mistake twice. Luck had been on his side earlier. If that stable gate had been working properly, that horse would have stayed put, and Jonathan would have been left to finish his murderous errand. Without that horse, he'd be hanging in the barn attracting flies.

Why it attacked was beyond him. He'd never known of a horse to attack so viciously. He'd never heard of a carnivorous horse before, either. Maybe there was some mental disease at play.

Madness...

Whatever the reason, he'd gotten lucky. He wasn't about to take that for granted and underestimate Elisabeth. If she were willing to kill her own daughter to keep her secrets, there was nothing she would stop at.

Nathan put a single finger to his lips and started toward the door. They stopped once when a board creaked under their careful steps but heard no alarm and resumed their progress. Nathan was the first to get to the door, and he peeked out. He turned his head one way, and then the other. The hall was empty. He signaled for Lewis to advance.

Lewis whispered to him, "Let me go first."

Nathan shook his head, but Lewis insisted. "Listen to me. You're hurt, and you're not as experienced as I am. I know how to clear a house. This is the reason I'm here. I can feel it. Now, let me do my job."

Lewis was firm, and there was no moving him once he'd made a decision. Nathan stepped back, conceding to his friend. Lewis peeked around the door, and seeing the hallway still clear, stepped out and waved Nathan forward.

The footsteps came faster this time. They were downstairs, but they smacked the floors like they were moving in a flat sprint. They were on the stairs. They were in the hall. Nathan was still in the bedroom, eyes opened wide, his heart beating fast. Nathan took one desperate step toward Lewis and could only mouth *"run"* before the bedroom door slammed shut. There was a deafening crack as it crashed against the frame. Nathan ran to open it, but it was hopelessly stuck. He rammed his shoulder into the door again and again, but it didn't budge. Not even a shudder. It was like trying to move a slab of stone. The only reward he received for his effort was a numb shoulder. Outside the door, Lewis yelled once, and then stillness fell like winter snow.

The silence scared Nathan to death.

Chapter Thirty-Eight

MOMENTS EARLIER, while Nathan was creeping up the service corridor, Lucas was in his father's room acting the good son. Edward was in a dreamless, semi-drugged slumber. Lucas hovered over his father, looking down on him, his eyes tracing the highways of plastic tubes that delivered chemical peace to his father's old, frail body. He imagined the tubes leading to his own arm; the chemicals dripping into his own veins instead.

Lucas scratched at a red lump on his neck. The sting from the insect bite was coming back. A shiver ran all the way up his spine as he recalled those endless legs all over his body. He could almost feel them inside his shirt. He closed his eyes and imagined the relief pills would bring. No more pain, no more anxiety. He'd have his own sweet rest. It wasn't fair for his father to receive such peace while he suffered the way he did. It was maddening.

You can end it, you know?

Lucas thumbed the pills he held in his hand. He'd swiped them only a moment ago from his father's supply. A handful of happiness, just waiting to go down the hatch. Red pill, blue pill, green pill, more... Lucas shuffled them in his palm, looked at the shape of each. Admired the colors. Wondered at the power contained in each tiny capsule. Where would this batch take him? Without fail, each trip he took proved to be better than his current reality.

Come on, take them now. The old man's on his way out - he doesn't need them. No one will know. It'll be your secret. It's easy to fill the prescription back up; no one questions a refill for the terminally ill. They'll just give the old man what he wants... Just like everyone always has. It's the merciful thing to do.

The merciful thing to do. What should mercy look like? Lucas opened his eyes and looked again at his father. He was grey and gaunt, a shell laying on a gurney, unrecognizable as the man he used to be. In fact, he was closer to a corpse than a man.

Are you any better? Do you really think you look much different? You're as much a shell as he is. Maybe a bit more plump, but you'll still pop like a balloon with a tiny little pin prick.

Lucas knew it to be true. Even with the pills, he barely held it together. He looked again at the assortment in his hand, hating them and loving them all at once. He was tired and worn. And he didn't want to fight it anymore.

All at once, he gobbled them up. They hurt going down, but that would be over soon enough. Moments from now, their effects would kick in and he would have some peace. The nagging thoughts in his mind slowed, satisfied now that chemical peace was on its way. Lucas sat down in the chair by the bay window and turned the crank. A blast of cool night air swept in.

Edward stirred. Lucas turned and met his father's beady, glaring gaze. Edward's mouth was cinched up tight, his brow furrowed into an arrow. An accusatory boney finger, shaking with nerves and hate, aimed right at Lucas.

Edward's voice was low and full of accusation. "I saw what you did, you thief. You think you can steal from me?"

Lucas froze in his chair. He sat there, letting the terrible realization that his father had seen what he did set in. He felt like a child again, caught in the proverbial cookie jar. But these weren't cookies.

"D-Dad, it's n-not what you think," he started to say. Lucas was blubbering.

Edward's voice was louder now. "Don't lie to me! I know what I saw! You took my medicine! It's mine, and you took it!"

"Dad, please..."

But Edward wasn't listening. Edward thrashed his limbs in his bed. He kicked the blankets off to one side, revealing his papery thin legs, covered top to bottom in black stringy veins. And maybe it was the drugs kicking in, but it seemed to Lucas that his father's veins weren't filled with blood, but rather tiny insects that ran through the black tunnels just below the surface. The skin looked thin enough that if it were to be cut, the critters would pour out in a swarm. Thinking about it made his skin crawl. Lucas could see them flowing from Edward's open mouth, black and hairy, thick and fat. They were coming for him.

No... Not again... I can't do this...

Lucas grabbed a pillow and stuffed it over the insect's hole. He pushed hard, trying to drive their assault back. Edward's fingers tried to grab at Lucas, but Lucas pushed down harder. Edward flailed at his son, but his punches landed with the force of a small child. Lucas increased the pressure; he couldn't allow these *things* to get free. Black legs spasmed on the edges of the pillow as they tried to squeeze out and escape. He'd shove them right back into place, force them back down in their hole, and block up their nest once and for all.

I'll kill 'em, he thought. *I'll kill 'em all.*

He pushed the pillow down harder and felt a sudden snap as a tooth broke free. It made a dull popping sound, followed by a muffled whimper from Edward.

It wasn't long. Edward stilled, and Lucas released the pillow. He watched as the last of the vile creatures crawled back down inside Edward's gaping mouth, back to their home where they would stay put. Lucas looked at the empty spot where Edward's front tooth had been. And rather than grief, relief washed over him. The insects were gone. But they'd return. Infestations always returned.

There was no more thrashing from his father, verbal or otherwise. He could feel the pills working their magic. The chemicals were working through his blood stream, delivering sweet, sweet release to every receptor they touched. Lucas was completely confident they would take him to a better place. His brain thanked him with dopamine blasts. Asked and delivered, thank you for doing business.

And at that, Lucas Thurman decided he wanted to take a walk as he waited for the drugs to work their final bliss.

Chapter Thirty-Nine

Nathan stood motionless, his ear to the barred door, listening for any clue as to what happened to Lewis. The only sounds were the small creaks coming from an old house. For a second, he'd imagined a shout and the shattering of glass, but it stopped as soon as he'd heard it. Then there was silence again, the kind that brings unease and loneliness. The quickness at which the sound stopped is what made him uncomfortable, like the sudden stop after a long fall.

In addition, the air in the bedroom had become particularly pungent. Suffocating, in fact. Decomposition and decay, wafting up from the basement. He could taste bile in the back of his throat, rancid bitterness rising up from a pit inside. Nathan pulled his shirt up over his nose in an attempt to filter the stench, but the assistance was minimal.

Nathan looked back to the door, and to his surprise, found it ajar. Confused and cautious, he nudged it open with the tip of his finger. Lewis was gone. The hallway runner was bunched up in waves down the hallway. It looked as though Lewis had been in a violent fight, ending with him being dragged all the way down the hall. Whatever had the ability to drag Lewis against his will was not the type of thing Nathan would want to encounter. He found himself wondering if Jonathan survived; maybe he'd imagined what happened in the barn. A part of him actually found this theory a relief. At least that could be understood. Alternative solutions weren't thoughts he cared to dwell on.

He followed the runner rolls down the hall, checking each door along the way, but finding each one locked. Nathan continued until he found himself by the staircase. Again, no one was here to be found. The house remained still as the grave, leaving no clue where Lewis may have gone. Nathan looked for any sign of him, first up the stairs, then down, but neither direction offered a clue which way he should go. Logic told him that down would be easiest. Pulling a struggling Lewis up to the third floor would have been problematic, even for a beast like Jonathan.

What if Lewis wasn't struggling? Nathan shuddered at the thought.

Nathan inched down the stairs. When he hit the entry, a sound from the dining room caught his attention. He tuned his ears and thought he heard crying, or someone in distress. He picked up the pace, worried it was Lewis. He tried to call out, but shouting was impossible. His throat was shot; not a chance he could speak now, let alone yell. He wouldn't be able to give Lewis any signal that he was coming.

Chapter Forty

Tommy decided to ignore the yelling from his father's room. It was faint, and it had only lasted a moment. It wasn't his concern, anyway. He'd learned long ago not to stick his nose in other people's affairs, and that went doubly so for his father's dealings.

Once, when he was a young boy, he'd been curious about what his father was working on. Everything his father did seemed so important, so terribly vital. Tommy daydreamed of being his father. Working business deals, making the important decisions, being respected. Even being feared. He'd snuck into the office to get a peek. It was innocent, the actions of a curious child, but his dad hadn't seen it that way. Edward's belt had come off with a swish when he found his son *nosing around*, as he had put it. Tommy didn't retain every memory from his childhood, but he remembered his father's belt, and he remembered the heavy brass buckle attached to the business end.

So, it was no surprise Tommy didn't go *nosing around* at every little noise. And how could he be sure? It was so brief, so faint. He listened for a few moments, but there was nothing. Just a quiet that set him on edge.

Despite its familiarity, the house still weighed on him, even after all the years he'd lived there. The silence kept him in a state of expectation, like the calm before a storm. He needed something, anything, to make the place feel more... he searched for the word. Solid. That was what he was looking for. The lack of sound reminded him of emptiness and void. Like being out at sea, endless depth below and above, alone, floating further and further from shore. Just waiting to be forgotten and abandoned into nothingness.

Tommy put his headphones on and cranked the music. He lay his head down on his pillow and let its softness absorb him. Deep bass notes pounded his eardrums, and he bobbed his head to the beat. A guitar riff came in on the next measure, mean and full of attitude. He leaned back on his bed, letting his head sink into his pillow as he allowed the music to carry him away. He reached over to his nightstand, removed a pack of cigarettes from the drawer, and lit one up. The nicotine hit, and he exhaled a thin stream of smoke from his lips. He was in his own little world, oblivious to the fact his twin brother was standing in the doorway.

Tommy rested for a few minutes like that, with his eyes closed, lost in music, trying to avoid being disturbed. He was feeling quite peaceful, and it came as a severe shock when the hands smashed down on his face.

He found himself looking up into his twin's eyes, glazed and filled with fear. In his panic, the only thing he understood was that he couldn't breathe. He was trying to push Lucas off, but he lacked the strength. Lucas just kept pressing down, muttering something over and over. Tommy couldn't make it out. The headphones were still on his head. A new song was blasting, something spirited and optimistic. The drums were upbeat, and the guitar played a peppy lick that highlighted the off beats. Lucas's mouth was moving, but the loud music made it impossible to hear his homicidal ravings.

Tommy struggled for air. Like his father before him, he swung his fists up at Lucas, managing a few blows to the side of his head. Lucas didn't budge; he didn't even seem to feel the punches. Tommy swung again and landed a fist on Lucas's ear, but Lucas wasn't fazed. He just kept pressing into his face, harder and harder. Spittle rested on the edges of Lucas's mouth as he continued his vile, murderous muttering.

The effort of striking at Lucas sped the whole process up. Tommy gasped for air that would never come. At the end, Tommy wondered what he'd done to make his brother hate him so much. He couldn't think of a single thing. Then, the peppy tune ended, and the next song queued. But Tommy never heard it.

Chapter Forty-One

Lucas felt heavy, as if the world itself pressed upon him. Unearthly tiredness bubbled up from deep inside, working its way from the tips of his toes to his head. It was pleasurable at first, in the way a heavy blanket weighs on you on a cold night. But then it changed, becoming overbearing. Lucas was sure he was about to vomit. He took deep, measured breaths to resist, holding, and exhaling in measured time, trying to think about anything other than losing his lunch. He tried to picture clear water flowing in a brisk stream. Ice cubes on his forehead. But nothing helped. His lungs wheezed when he inhaled, and his chest ached like a great weight was upon him. His heart couldn't beat fast enough, each pulse striking like a hammer. He swore he could actually hear it.

His twin, Tommy, was laying in the bed. He looked peaceful at last. When Lucas had walked in, the room had been a den of centipedes, like a hive had exploded, but Tommy hadn't even seemed bothered by it. As before, it had been up to him to rid the room of the creatures. He'd pushed them back successfully, same as he did for dear old dad. Now they were gone, thank God. But this house had an infestation. Something would need to be done about it. But for now, Lucas needed to rest. He lay down beside Tommy, who was oddly still.

As he lay there, out of the corner of his eye, he saw the faint orange glow of a cigarette only a few feet away. It wasn't his, and he realized Tommy must have dropped it just seconds ago. He stretched his hand out, trying to grab it, willing his fingers to travel a little further, straining until his joints hurt. His fingers brushed up against it, but a fraction too short. He tried to reach further, felt his shoulder stretch and the muscles in his arm overextend. But the fire stick was out of reach.

He shifted his body to get a better angle, but he found himself stuck. His body may as well have been a thousand pounds. The weight was unbearable, as if someone were standing on his chest, keeping him from being able to breathe.

What was in those pills?

He'd never had a trip like this. His arm hung limp at his side, unable to move. His fingers were numb. He was fully aware of his surroundings, but his body would not respond. It *could* not respond. Ironically, the drugs had numbed everything but his mind, the one thing he most desired silence from. He lay flat on his back, desperate to move, trying to breathe, but unable to do either.

That's when he smelled the smoke. Like most disasters, it started out small. Just a whiff. He told himself it was just the cigarette. The floor was hardwood. It would take more than one small ember to ignite. He'd dropped his share of cigarettes on the floor himself and stamped them all out without ever starting a fire. His room was covered in small burn marks, and none of them had amounted to anything more than a dark mark on the floor.

In a different setting, the crackle of the fire would have

been comforting, but the sound of the spreading fire only sent Lucas into panic. Smoke filled the top of the room, obscuring the white ceiling with a thick cloud of black poison. It rolled up and around the edge of the walls, and as it filled the space above, began creeping its way down toward his face.

He grunted for Tommy to wake up, but his twin rested still as death, and Lucas began to cry. Tears rolled down his face and pooled in his ears. He found it odd that the room was so dark, despite a fire growing beside and under his bed. What a strange thing to have so little light beside the fire. The heat was growing under the bed, working its way from the floor and up. The flames were spreading up the walls, into the vents. He didn't have long, and he wished for his twin, for Tommy to be here with him, comforting him. He wished that in his last moments, he wouldn't be alone.

To his great relief, he felt a hand grab his. Someone was here, someone to save him.

"Help me! Get me outta here!" Lucas squeaked out. Smoke filled his lungs, prompting a violent hack that brought with it black slime.

No response came. The grip relaxed, and the hand moved slowly, patiently, up his arm. It caressed his shoulder. It lingered a second on his neck, then to his chest. And then it pressed down with an unworldly force. Stars exploded in Lucas's eyes; the fire all but forgotten. The world was pressure, and he was under it. He felt his sternum crack. A rib snapped and punctured his lung.

Smoke and flame swallowed Lucas Thurman, and he was no more.

Chapter Forty-Two

Nathan tried to be stealthy, but the urge to charge forward was overwhelming. This was in part due to his concern for Lewis, but it was also because he wanted it over with. He hated the idea that a bullet might strike the back of his head at any moment. Elizabeth might be hiding in any number of dark nooks and crannies the house possessed. The possibilities were endless. And while he feared a deadly projectile to the skull, he feared the dark corners of the house more.

There were pockets of empty light everywhere. Shadows were cast in odd directions, looking like other worldly entities waiting to descend upon him. Once or twice, he swore he saw them move, but as he looked at them, they stilled. Something was always just out of his sight, evading his eyes a split second before he spotted it. But Nathan sensed the truth; he wasn't dodging its gaze. It was watching him. He was the pursued.

If you want to kill me, let's just get on with it.

He heard the whimpering again, this time from the dining room. Nathan looked in and found Upham slumped in a chair, weeping in despair. Upham pulled his hands from his face and repositioned his glasses. He wiped the snot from his nose with the sleeve of his suit coat, coating it with a stringy, clear ooze.

"It's all over. We can't do anything to stop it now."

Nathan knelt down by the old man and put his arms up on his slumped shoulders.

"What are you talking about?" Nathan said. His voice was a labored and hoarse.

In between sniffles, Upham said, "It's here. The end. It's time... It's finally here."

"No, Upham. It doesn't have to be the end." Nathan gave Upham a gentle shake, forced him to make eye contact. "Where is Lewis? I need to find him. And then we need to get out of here."

Upham's eyes filled with anguish. He was muttering, only making partial sense. Through his babbling, Nathan was able to make out a few phrases: *Dark... It saw me... Hide...* None of which brought Nathan any comfort.

Nathan stood back up. Upham's current state left him in no position to help. The old man looked more shriveled than he had just a day ago. He was hunched over, rocking himself like a child. Nathan promised himself he'd come back for him.

He turned to resume his search and felt a tug at his arm. Their eyes met and Nathan recognized the fear in the old man's eyes, but he was lucid, at least in this moment. He'd gathered himself long enough to say whatever it was he needed to say.

"Don't leave. It's not safe. Please, don't leave."

"Upham, that's why I have to find Lewis. I can't leave him."

"They're dead, Mr. Stevens."

Nathan dropped back down to be face to face. "Who?

Who's dead?" He couldn't bring himself to ask if this meant Lewis.

Upham shook his head. "It's Edward, Mr. Steven's. I found him. I was just doing my normal checkup. He was due for his meds. I found him..." Upham broke again into sobs. "He's gone, Nathan. The ghosts finally claimed their prize."

Elisabeth, Nathan thought. *She's killed him.*

Without a word of explanation, Nathan headed for Edward's room as quickly as he dared. Every nerve in his body buzzed, ready to pop at the slightest disturbance. Nathan had yet to understand just how thin a line he was walking; how thin the membrane was between sanity and whatever had infected Upham.

Edward's door was closed. Nathan put his ear to the thick wood and listened. There was nothing. No beeps, no air hiss from pumping machines, no rattle of the metal bed frame. But the door felt warm.

He realized his mistake too late. When reaching for the handle, the possibility of disaster on the other side never occurred to him. A fresh rush of oxygen fueled the fire and caused it to roar up in anger. In an instant, the room transformed from a smoky, dark smolder into a raging fury. The curtains ignited, and the flames jumped to the ceiling. Paint bubbled and turned black, blistering like a festering wound on the wall. Jets of fire poured out of air vents like rockets, and the terrible realization that the fire was using the ventilation system like a highway hit him square in the gut. He could picture the fire slithering through in all directions like a serpent made of flame. Its white-hot tongue flickered in search of what it would consume.

There was a sudden flash of brilliant light, and Nathan recoiled. It was like a fireball exploded, and a bright stream of light cut through the smoke. Edward's oxygen tank -

punctured at the top and lit like a roman candle. It hissed as gas escaped and caught fire like a blowtorch.

Nathan shielded his face with his forearm. Hot air came at him fast. Enough to take his breath away and sting his eyes. In the flames, he thought he saw a figure, but it vanished. Shadows, moving and hiding just out of sight of the living.

He slammed the door shut, trying to keep the inferno contained. Finding Lewis was of the utmost importance now. He needed to get them clear of this place before it went up like a pyre. He tried to shout, but his voice was still hoarse. Nathan wasn't sure where to start. Time was running out. He could see the smoke creeping out from under the door now. The fire wouldn't stay contained for long. It would find its way out, crawling through vents, working its way up to the next floor, destroying everything in its path. There was no hiding from the flame. The fire wanted to consume. To be fed. It would make the house and anyone inside its meal.

He ran, no longer concerned with remaining undetected.

Chapter Forty-Three

Hancock shot up in his bed, alarm bells ringing in his head, although he wasn't sure why. Something in the air...

He sniffed and detected smoke, but there was no pleasantness to it. Curious, he swung his feet over the side of the bed and walked to his front door, dressed only in his boxers. The sky was glowing orange, much brighter than it should have been in the dead of night. And growing brighter by the second. The smoke was stronger out here and had a noxious quality to it. Something in opposition to sweet-smelling hardwood burning over coals. This was foul, black smoke, rancid and poisoned, filled with the toxic fumes of plastics and synthetic materials. It was anything but a campfire.

He looked toward the manor and realized the source of the light.

"Oh, dear God..."

Chapter Forty-Four

Lewis came to on the grass outside the Manor. He winced as he lifted his head to look around. Shards of glass were scattered around him, and while he had multiple nicks, none appeared to be fatal. He tried to push himself up, but his right arm gave out as soon as he put any weight on it. Pain shot through his shoulder like an ice pick. He rolled onto his back and sat up with the assistance of his left arm, which, aside from several gashes, seemed to be operational.

He'd been dragged, that much he remembered. But by who (make that what), he wasn't sure. Resistance had been useless, a rare occurrence in his life. He'd been treated like a child's rag doll, a despised one, meant for the trash. He remembered the terror on Nathan's face right before the door slammed, separating them. Nathan had mouthed *run*, but it had been too late. Something wrestled Lewis to the ground and then pulled him down the hall and down the stairs. He couldn't see much, just a few brief glimpses, but he would swear he was being pulled by a shadow. It was formless, invisible when he tried to find it. Only when Lewis looked away did he get a sense of what was there.

Like the thing disappeared from view when you might recognize it for what it truly was.

A low groan escaped his lips as he felt the back of his head. His skull had smacked the stairs multiple times going down, and he could feel lumps from each impact. They'd get bigger before they got better. He figured there might be a mild concussion as well, if not a severe one. Whether that was from the initial slam or the stairs, he wasn't sure.

The broken glass made a trail from the gaping window all the way to where he sat. At some point, he must have lost consciousness because he didn't recall anything past the stairs. But judging from the debris, it had thrown him out the window.

What sort of thing had the strength to just toss me like I was nothing?

He managed to get his wobbly legs to cooperate and regained some sense of balance. The window was wide open now, like a ravenous mouth, daring him to jump back inside and into its gullet.

Come on, Lewis. Come on in. The water's fine.

Lewis shuddered, sensing a trap. He knew he had to get back to Nathan, but he wouldn't be good to either of them dead. He needed a plan, and quick.

Lewis stumbled around to the front, taking note of his surroundings. The Manor towered over him like a cliff. He heard a shattering of glass and snapped his head toward the sound, expecting to see a body being flung through a window. Instead, flames erupted from the gap. Forked tongues of red and orange flicked their way up the side of the house.

The house was going up in flames, and Nathan was still inside. Hopefully alive. Lewis ran up to the front door and tugged at it with his good arm. It didn't budge. He pounded it a few times with his fist, but there was no response. He cussed at the door, spit on it, and went to search the side for an entry point.

Before he'd rounded the corner, he heard the roar of an engine, soft at first, but getting louder in a hurry. An old truck, noisy, heavy, and made of pure American steel, was fast approaching. It sped toward the house and then skidded to a stop. Black streaks of rubber marked the perfect concrete behind like magic markers. An old cowboy jumped out and looked at the inferno before him, his mouth open wide in awe and horror.

Lewis shouted, "I need help! There's people in there. We gotta get them out!"

The cowboy shouted back, "How do we get through those flames?"

Lewis looked back. The fire was growing on both sides. It was on the verge of being uncontrollable. But there was time. He knew it. There had to be. He only needed a few minutes. Seconds, even. He'd beg, borrow, and steal them if he had to.

Lewis paced, thinking hard and quick. Every disadvantage worked against him. He was injured. He wasn't familiar with the layout of the house. And whatever was waiting inside was ready for him. He needed a way in, and he needed it to be unexpected. The element of surprise was a key battle tactic that should be generously applied. He just needed to figure that part out.

And then Lewis had his plan.

Chapter Forty-Five

INSIDE WAS AN INFERNO. Flame and embers were everywhere. Nathan heard glass pop and shatter in the heat. Every second it grew in intensity and rage as it threatened to consume the house. Nathan ran back to the dining room, hoping he'd have time to warn Upham. He found him right where he'd left him.

"You need to get outta here!"

"What about your friend?" Upham asked.

"I'll keep looking. You get out and call for help."

As if to highlight Nathan's point, a nearby beam broke and crashed to the ground, and sparks exploded in all directions. Nathan swatted at the embers, trying to keep from catching fire. He looked back at Upham to make sure he hadn't been injured. They had both narrowly avoided ignition. Another window burst, bringing a fresh supply of air to feed the flames.

"No offense, Upham, but we're short on time and you're slowing me down. Go get help! I'll try to find Lewis!"

Upham lumbered off for the nearest exit. He stopped as soon as he left the dining room and looked to Nathan with dismay. Just on the other side of the fallen beam was the door, their exit, now blocked by fire and debris.

"Come on, Upham. Move to the front. Fast!"

They retreated and made for the front door, but Upham was slow. Nathan put his arm around the old man's waist for support. They choked on the poisonous air. Each passing moment made it increasingly more likely they wouldn't escape alive, but their dire situation hadn't yet reached its lowest point.

From behind came an inhuman shriek. Nathan spun to see Elisabeth, wild-eyed and unhinged, raising her weapon toward his head. The barrel looked like an eye, hovering in thin air, eager to blink and send a message of death his way.

He realized with terrible clarity how he would die. He'd feel the hot sting of lead as it passed through his neck, or maybe it would hit his chest, shattering bone into his heart. Nathan closed his eyes and waited for the end.

The gun roared, but the hot sting of metal never came. Instead, Nathan felt a shove from one side, and he tumbled to the ground. He scrambled back to his feet, anticipating another shot, but Elisabeth was already running away down the hall. He looked to where he'd been standing, where he was certain he'd die, for the second time this evening. In his place stood Upham, his hands cupping the blood pouring from his stomach.

He rolled his head to Nathan and looked content. There was no more fear. And then all at once his knees gave out and he collapsed on the floor.

Nathan rushed to his side. "Hang on... Hang on... I'm going to get you outta here. Just hang on..."

Upham's breathing was labored and shallow. His face had become ghostly white. Nathan reached for him, but Upham intercepted his hand and shook his head. He held it like that for a moment, and then spoke, his voice fragile and fading.

"Find her... She'll show you. She'll show you."

At that, Upham's eyes went dark, and Nathan was alone.

Chapter Forty-Six

"You want to do what?" Hancock looked at Lewis like he was crazy.

"It'll work," Lewis said. "Trust me."

Hancock ran his fingers through his gray hair. "I don't even know you," he said.

"In case you haven't noticed, we're a little short on time to make friends." Lewis pointed to the Manor. The fire continued to grow. Both men understood only mere minutes remained for anyone inside.

Hancock leveled his eyes with Lewis. His head was down, making him peer over the rim of his glasses. "It's crazy. You know that, right? I'll for sure lose my job."

Lewis smirked like he had heard a funny joke. "What job would that be? What exactly do you think is going to be around tomorrow?"

Hancock frowned as Lewis scored a point.

Lewis held his hand out. "Fine. If you aren't going to cowboy up, I'll do it myself. Hand the keys over."

Hancock let out a long, slow breath. "Fine, let's do it. But it's my truck. I'm driving."

Chapter Forty-Seven

The fire forced Nathan to abandon Upham where he fell. Aside from vengeance, nothing more could be done for him. Nathan had turned back once, overwhelmed by guilt, but the blaze had already consumed Upham's body. There was nothing left to do but move forward.

Nathan got to the main doors only to find them stuck. He tried to work the deadbolt, rotating it one way and then the other, tugging on the door between the turns. But the door refused to budge as if barred on the other side. He searched for another exit. Fire was surrounding him on all sides, save for the one, the path he least wanted to take - the main stairs. Somehow, like the parted Red Sea, the stairs had a clear path in the midst of flame. It was as if the house wanted to steer him upward, but the thought was fleeting, and he rejected it almost immediately.

Not that it mattered. It was up or inferno.

Nathan tugged his shirt up over his mouth and started his ascent. Above, the ceiling hid behind a rolling black cloud of smoke. It swirled and twisted, thick and nasty and deadly. The fire hadn't overtaken the upper floors yet, but the smoke had. He coughed and choked on toxic fumes as he navigated with his hands like a blind man. The darkness was trying to suffocate him. The house fire was indiscriminate; anyone caught in its path would be swallowed up, either by suffocation or flame. It didn't care which.

He crawled on his hands and knees, trying to stay as close to the floor as possible. He gasped for air, but gagged on the retched vapors instead, vomiting soot onto the floor. But he didn't stop. He inched through the smoke, pushing doors open and searching best he could for Lewis. And with each inch he crawled, every room that opened, he wondered about where Elisabeth might be.

Without reason or logic, the black skies parted. The fire receded into the background, as if waiting for direction. Nathan rose and looked around. The dark cloud above had slowed, but still obscured the ceilings. Fire stopped in place, just small licks of flame, like it had eaten its fill, satisfied in its desire for unending consumption. Thick smoke was replaced by thicker tension, like the calm before the storm. He was no longer in the inferno. Rather, he was in the capability of one, waiting for something to happen, for fate to take its course. Elisabeth was near. He *felt* her waiting. The air wasn't filled with smoke alone; madness and mayhem were there, keeping him company.

Nathan reached the third floor and Lewis was nowhere to be found. Despair and panic set in. He realized he wasn't going to find him, and all at once Nathan understood he'd failed his friend. He shouldn't have brought him here in the first place. All those years lost in one stupid instant. One incorrect decision, one massive oversight on his part. He cursed himself for not having seen the truth earlier. He'd overlooked things. Saw what he wanted to. He let himself be fooled, just like everyone else. Their wealth and power blinded him. He was drawn to a big fancy house and, if he was being honest, what he could get from them - even if only a nice funeral for his wife. There was nothing different about him; he'd ignored all their nastiness and failed to see them as the vile creatures they were. And now, it was all going to end. Even his so-called heroism pulling Lewis from a burning truck was for nothing. He'd saved him from one fire, only to lead him to another.

Nathan felt the hairs on his neck stiffen, and a chilling voice from behind hissed.

"I'll kill you for this. My house, my life... RUINED!!!"

Nathan turned to face her. Elisabeth stood in the hallway before him, her gun dangling in her hand. Her features had changed, revealing her true nature. Her once beautiful face was now hideous with hatred. Soot covered her clenched hands. Her hair was frayed and wild. She was gaunt; her thin frame made her arms look abnormally long. She had the appearance of a creature dragged from hell. And the creature was stumbling toward him.

He took a cautious, retreating step. "You did this to yourself," Nathan said. "And for what? Nothing. You have nothing." He scowled at her. "You are nothing."

Elisabeth continued her advance, now screaming at him, shrill and hideous. Her white teeth gleamed like fangs.

"I am more than you could ever hope to be! I am a *god* compared to you! You would have had a quiet life if you'd have left it alone. But you didn't. You had to dig and pick. Couldn't mind your own business, could you? Neither did Rachel. She probably learned that from you. She used to be on my side. She used to be one of us. You pulled her away from me. Until you came along, she was going to be like me, perfect in every way."

Nathan scoffed. "Rachel was never one of you. She hated you. It was torture for her to come back here, but she did it anyway. Why? Because I told her to. Because I thought she'd have regrets. But if I'd seen you for what you really are, like Rachel saw you, I would've known better. You can't regret something as worthless as you."

Elisabeth shrieked as she lunged for Nathan. He raised his arms to shield himself just as the muzzle flashed. There was a deafening bang, and then his whole arm went numb. The pain wasn't sharp, as he'd expected. Rather, it sent everything from his elbow to the tips of his fingers into a dull ache. His arm fell limp to his chest.

Elisabeth fired again, this time aiming for his head. Nathan saw it coming; if she hit him, it'd be lights out. But he skipped sideways at the last second. He felt a nasty swish of air as the metal chunk narrowly missed his face. He took a step back, only to have his foot hover in empty space above the top step.

For a moment, he floated, and time seemed to stop. Flames danced on the walls. The huge family portrait of the Thurmans was bubbling and turning black from the inside out. Cracked black marks spread across the family photo like lightning streaks, erasing their memory.

He fell like that for a while, then hit the steps hard, head-first. He felt a sharp pop in his shoulder, followed by more pain and electric tingling down his arm. The wind was knocked from his lungs; he gasped for breath.

Elizabeth stood at the top of the stairs, looking down at him. Her eyes were wild with malevolent intent. Her breast heaved in and out as she prepared to finish what she started. Nathan tried to get up, but his smashed and broken arms did nothing for him. He pushed himself further down the stairs with only his legs for assistance.

The calm manner in which she spoke was unnerving. "No more games. I'm done now. It's time to end this."

Hate flashed across her face as she descended. Nathan was stuck between flights of stairs. He tried to push himself up, but his arm gave out and he fell again. Elisabeth continued her slow descent, filled with madness and rage. Her broken fingernails scraped against the blackened handrails like claws.

Suddenly, the smoke above started to swirl in a vortex, as if a tornado were forming. Fire danced and walled them in. And then out of the smoke, a figure appeared, terrible and beautiful, a specter out of flame. Nathan hardly dared to look, but he was captured. Captivated, unable to turn away. Everything inside him screamed run. This was the darkness, this was the terror, this was the forever torment of Thurman Manor. No longer hiding in shadows out of view, no longer glimpses in the corner of an eye, he saw the ghost for who she was, clearly and without masks. Rachel, but also not Rachel, made of flame and fury and vengeance.

Elisabeth's mouth gaped open in horror. Rachel seemed fixated; her fury concentrated on her mother. She brought her hand up, and Elisabeth seized up like a stone, as if frozen by Medusa's head. Rachel raised her hand higher, and Elisabeth lifted from the ground. She hovered there, frozen in space and time. Then Rachel turned her eyes down toward Nathan.

Nathan froze, his limbs paralyzed in fear and dread. He saw pure, unbridled fury in the form of his deceased wife, who was no longer his wife. She was something else, something unknowable. Unfathomable. To see her was to be intimate with madness, to understand torment upon torment. Nathan was coupled with pain, one with anger. It was like her eyes reflected the entirety of time. Nathan felt centuries pass in an instant. In that one moment, he understood the years, past and future, all wrapped up in one. Time became fluid as he stepped over the thin veil of his reality and into the eternal – where his wife had always been. A worker fell from the roof while Suzy killed that boy. Edward was dying as his father gnawed at a live wire in the basement. Insects buzzed, plates shattered, whispers were heard, shadows crept, people drowned, brothers couldn't be trusted, and mothers ceased to be mothers at all.

She'll show you. She'll show you.

Elisabeth floated in the air, alone and powerless, her mind broken, unable to fight Rachel.

"Please, please," she begged. Elisabeth's whispers turned to incomprehensible muttering, babbled pleas for release, be it mercy or death. The begging grew louder, more desperate. Elisabeth made high pitched animal whines, mixed with spit and panic.

A venomous, knowing grin grew across Rachel's face. It transformed into a snarl, and she threw her hands back, propelling Elisabeth through the air and out over the stairs. There was a tremendous crash as Elisabeth sailed through the chandelier hanging over the entry. Glass exploded like a geyser and showered down on Nathan.

Elisabeth regained her sanity mid-fall, realizing her fate as the hard floor rushed up at her like a hurricane. She screamed as she fell, but it stopped at once when the thump came.

Nathan studied her at the bottom of the stairs, crumpled and twisted in unnatural angles. Her legs twitched and jerked like frog legs in salt water. Nathan looked back up the stairs. The fire was no longer contained, it was spreading faster than ever. Nathan watched Rachel descend on her mother, crumpled on the floor like old laundry. A hideous scream filled the house, coming from all directions. Rachel's mouth opened impossibly wide as her jaw unhinged, like a snake ready to consume her prey. Her eyes seemed like black holes, her very essence fire. Rachel lunged forward, enveloping her mother's body as they erupted in white hot flame.

She's taking the house... She's burning it all to the ground... She's taking it all with her...

Nathan searched for an exit but found none. The bottoms of his shoes turned soft in the intense heat. The screams that had been so terrifying before were a roar. He couldn't tell if it was just the fire now, or if there was some other quality to it, something inhuman. He couldn't move. Nathan coughed and choked. It was like the oxygen itself was running low as the fire consumed it along with the house.

A low roar was growing, but not from inside. Before he figured out where it was coming from, the front doors smashed open, and two lights shot through like a battering ram, blasting debris into the entrance. Nathan could make out the front end of a truck. It spun its tires as it backed out, making a gaping hole through the front of the house. He spotted Lewis first, running into the hellfire, followed by Hancock. They searched through the flames like wild men and spotted Nathan on the stairs. They sprinted to him and heaved him up between them.

He heard Lewis say, "Quick now, this place is going down."

They half dragged Nathan through the new opening their steel dragon had made. The room erupted just as they cleared the gap.

Nathan looked back over his shoulder. The un-Rachel was still consuming what was left of Elisabeth. Lewis was moving fast, so he only caught a few seconds, but he thought he saw her flicker, her shape alternating between a fiery apparition and a small girl. There was another flicker, and now she was Rachel, as he remembered her. They made eye contact for only a second. They hoisted Nathan into the truck bed, and she was lost to view.

Lewis jumped in beside him while Hancock popped

into the driver's seat. Lewis smacked the top of the cab twice and Hancock floored the gas pedal. The truck sped backwards, away from the fire and the house. Once they were clear, Hancock smashed the brakes, shifted into drive, and pushed that old truck as hard as he ever had.

They sped away, watching the Manor grow smaller and smaller as they put distance between them. The inferno had reached the roof. Fire danced and flitted across every surface.

"I thought you were dead," Nathan said.

Lewis shook his head. "Me too, for a minute. That thing grabbed me, pulled me right down the stairs. Nothing I could do to stop it. It threw me through a window, I think." He rubbed at his arm, massaging a pain. "Must have knocked me out cold. When I came to, I tried to find a way inside to get you, but I was locked out. It was like everything was blocked up." He jerked a thumb to the cab. "Glad he showed when he did."

Hancock. Always there at the right time.

Even as they lost sight of the Manor, they could still see the night sky lit up red. Smoke piled high into the sky like a signal. A signal to everyone that the Manor was gone.

Chapter Forty-Eight

The Manor burnt down to the foundation. Still guarding the entrance, Deputy Bates saw the fire lit sky and called in for help. But the fire department hadn't been able to arrive until well after the blaze was unstoppable. By that point, the firemen could only try to contain it; there would be no stopping the blaze. When things started to spread out too far from the house, they would douse it with water and push it back. They watched to make sure floating embers didn't start a forest fire. But everything stayed within property boundaries. They watched it burn straight to the ground.

Sheriff Carroll, convinced the evidence he needed was contained within the Manor, watched in horror as his investigation literally crumbled. Unable to restrain himself, he charged into the flames in search of those responsible for his son's death. Rescue attempts were initiated, but unsuccessful. In the end, Ben Carroll was ruled an accidental death.

Of the bodies they found, little remained to identify them. Two sets of remains of approximately the same size were found, and they theorized these were the twins. They found them lying side by side, but as to who each twin was remained a mystery. One had a crushed sternum, and a few cracked ribs, guessed to have been the result of a falling beam. The other set of bones appeared to be intact, so the assumption for the cause of death was smoke inhalation.

Authorities had no issue identifying Edward. Although his skeleton was all but dust, a gold tooth survived the inferno, proof enough when coupled with his dental record.

What they found in the stable was a different matter. Jonathan's corpse made even the seasoned guys sick. His guts had been ripped out and mashed into a pulp. There wasn't much question as to what happened. They found the horse wandering, its snout covered in blood. They had no choice but to put it down. When they cut the horse's stomach open for autopsy, they found Jonathan's missing parts.

Regarding Elisabeth, no account was ever made. There was no trace of her left.

Demolition crews were brought in to clear the rubble. They plowed the entire lot, leveling it. The job took longer than expected. The contractor cited "staffing issues" due to the fact that his crew kept quitting. Nobody liked being out there. No one could explain it, but they didn't like the way it made them feel. Everyone felt on edge. They blamed it on the fire, but the townies knew better. Houses might burn, but ghosts remain.

Chapter Forty-Nine

Nathan was back home. Snow had fallen, coating the tall trees around his house in white, shimmery frosting for what would be the last time that season. Winter gusts would rattle the trees, shaking clumps of snow loose so they'd fall from their high positions and hit the ground with soft thumps.

Lewis sat with him at his table, overlooking the porch and the snow outside. He pointed toward the floor where Nathan's camera sat unpacked.

"Did it feel good to be back out in the field, shakin' off the rust?"

Nathan rocked his hand back and forth, hoping Lewis wouldn't pry. His camera bag sat on the floor near his door, packed up tight and ready for another outing. None of his trips had rewarded him with a bear spotting yet; not even so much as a rabbit. He'd almost convinced himself that's what he was out there for. Deep down, he knew better. Silas Ridge wasn't the only place to photograph bears, but he felt drawn there all the same. He'd head out into the deep woods and wait, and despite the conviction it wasn't good for him, he couldn't help but hope for a shifting shadow or icy breeze. He'd wait until eleven before packing it up and heading home.

"You doing ok?" Lewis asked.

Nathan nodded. "I'm getting there. You?"

Lewis nodded in return. "I've had worse. A few stitches and I'm all healed up." He held up his arm. A line of black thread ran along his forearm, spanning about 7cm. "All in all, it worked out pretty well. I got to save your skin this time." Lewis shot Nathan a grin. "Now we're even."

Even. It was anything but. While Nathan had pulled Lewis from a bit of rubble, Lewis had been attacked by an unseen force, tossed through a window, and still drove back into the fires of Hell for him. No, not even. Nathan was in his debt, he was sure of it.

"How's the therapy?" Lewis asked.

Nathan shrugged. "It's different than I expected. But also better. It's weird to say, but I'm learning to grieve. I never realized what a process this would be. Or how long it might take."

"There's no rush, you know. Grief takes as long as it takes."

"Yeah, I know. But this will take me a really long time. Maybe my whole life."

"Maybe. But you've started the journey. Let that be enough for now."

"Made a mistake, though. I told the truth. I was honest about what happened. Doc said it was stress induced hallucinations. Gave me a whole bottle of pills that are supposed to help me calm down." Nathan picked them up from the table and rattled them around. "Haven't taken any though."

He paused and looked over at Lewis. "I wasn't hallucinating, right?"

Lewis was somber. He shook his head as he considered

the question. "No, you weren't." Then he added, "But I can't say I understand it. I'm still not sure what we saw."

They sat in silence, watching the snow melt and looking forward to spring.

Somehow, it was her...
Always her...
Rachel.

A Note From the Author

I'm going to ask for a favor.

I say that up front because this feels strange to me. After all, who am I to ask you for a single thing? You owe me nothing. But if you read this far, maybe you think I don't suck. Who knows... Maybe you even liked it?

To all others, my apologies for any disappointment experienced. Consider yourself off the hook.

If you find yourself in that group that liked this story, find a friend you suspect likes this sort of thing. Find a few people, actually. Talk to them about it. Let them know a story like this exists. Take it to your social media platform of choice. Post, blog, tweet, do a dance... Anything to get the word out.

The bottom line is this story can't spread without your help.

Yes, reviews are good. If you have a moment, please leave a note for those that will come after you. But I have a hunch that for this book to reach its potential, it will take more than that. It'll take you and countless others, spreading it by word of mouth.

I hope I've worked hard enough to make this worthy of being a word of mouth story. Those are always the best kind.

Hiram

Acknowledgments

Writing a book is largely a solitary process, but that doesn't mean I did this alone. During the course of this book I had an incredible crew surrounding me, letting me use them as sounding boards and giving me insight and feedback.

To my wife, Brittany. Just thank you. This took countless hours, and you gave that to me. Every minute I spent writing, the hours my mind drifted out to who knows where, that was a gift.

To my brother, Alex. You liked my writing before anyone else did. You encouraged me to write more. I don't think I would have started this crazy adventure if you hadn't pushed me toward it.

To my editor and writing mentor, Steffon. Your insight brought new levels, and a much better flow. Let's do another one.

About the Author

Hiram Foster lives in Northwest Ohio with his wife and eight children. You can find out more and stay up to date on his latest work at www.hiramfoster.com.

Made in the USA
Monee, IL
11 May 2024